Panda Books
Stories from the Thirties I

Modern Chinese literature, which had its origins in the New Culture Movement of 1919, reached a high level of achievement in the thirties. During this period, many fine writers emerged and a large number of their works have won critical acclaim abroad. The thirty-eight stories published in the two volumes in this collection describe urban and rural life, and provide a vivid insight into Chinese society at different levels during a time when the country was threatened by foreign aggression and in the ferment of revolution. The different styles represent the various literary trends of the period.

Panda Books
First edition, 1982

ISBN 0-8351-1019-2

Published by CHINESE LITERATURE, Beijing (37), China

Distributed by China Publications Centre (GUOJI SHUDIAN)
P.O. Box 399, Beijing, China

Printed in the People's Republic of China

Stories from the Thirties

1

Panda Books

CONTENTS

Ye Shengtao

YE Shengtao (1894-   ) is a native of Suzhou in Jiangsu Province. He began his writing career in 1914 and in 1921 was, along with the celebrated author Mao Dun and others, a founder member of the Literature Research Society. He has worked as an editor and a middle school and university teacher. Since 1949 he has held leading positions in the publishing and educational fields and is now a member of the standing committee of the China Federation of Literary and Art Circles.

Ye Shengtao's work has been extremely influential in the history of modern Chinese literature. His richly textured writing covers a wide range of subjects in a natural and straightforward manner. His language is concise and elegant and he is known as a consummate stylist. *Ni Huanzhi* is considered his representative novel and "How Mr Pan Weathered the Storm" and "Night" are his best-known short stories.

A Year of Good Harvest

IN front of Wansheng Rice Shop was a wharf, and moored at all angles to this wharf were the open boats in which the villagers had come to sell their rice. These boats, loaded with new rice, were riding low in the water. The space between them was filled with cabbage leaves and refuse, round which swirled greasy bubbles of white scum.

From the wharf climbed narrow steps, up which no more than three men could walk abreast. The rice shop stood at the top of these steps. The morning sun, slanting down through gaps in the tiles of the roof, shed broad beams of light on the tattered felt hats bobbing up to the counter.

The owners of the felt hats had risen at dawn to row here. And once at the wharf, not waiting to catch their breath, they rushed up to this counter to see what fate had to offer.

"Polished rice, five dollars. Paddy, three," was the manager's laconic answer to their question.

"What!" The peasants in the old felt hats could hardly believe their ears. Their hopes were dashed to the ground. They were dumbfounded.

"In June you paid thirteen dollars, didn't you?"

"We paid as much as fifteen, let alone thirteen."

"How could the price drop so sharply?"

"What else do you expect in times like these? Rice

is flooding the market. A few more days and the price will fall even lower."

Coming here, the men had plied their oars as if rowing in the dragon-boat race, but now all the energy drained out of them. This year Heaven had been kind, rain had fallen in due season, there had been no plague of pests and each *mu* had yielded a few pecks more than usual. This time, they had thought they could have a breathing space. To end up even worse off than the previous year was the last thing they had expected.

"Let's not sell. Row it home and keep it!" cried one simple soul indignantly.

The manager uttered a sarcastic laugh. "Do you think folk are going to starve because you won't sell? The whole country's full of foreign rice and flour. Before the first lot's finished, foreign steamboats are shipping in a second.

Foreign rice, foreign flour and foreign steamboats were too remote to worry them. But not to sell the rice in their boats was unthinkable. That was simply angry talk. They had to sell. The landlord would be coming for his rent, and old debts must be cleared — they had run into debt to pay day-labourers and buy fertilizer and food.

"Why don't we try Fanmu?" It occurred to one of them that they might find a better price there.

But the manager snorted with laughter again and tweaked his sparse beard as he said: "Even if you go to the city, you'll find our rice guild has reached a common agreement. The price everywhere these days is five dollars for polished rice, three for paddy."

"It's no good going to Fanmu," put in one of the

peasants. "You have to pass two toll-houses, and there's no knowing how much they'd charge by way of tax. Who's got so much money to spare?"

"Won't you raise that price a little, sir?" another pleaded.

"That's easy to ask. We've sunk capital into this business, I'd have you know. To raise the price would mean giving you something for nothing. Do you take me for a fool?"

"But this price is too low, honestly it is. Who ever dreamed of such a thing? Last year we sold at seven dollars fifty. This summer rice went up to thirteen, no, fifteen, sir, as you said yourself just now. We were sure this year we'd get at least more than seven dollars fifty. Only five dollars – no!"

"Give us last year's price, sir! Seven fifty."

"Have a heart, sir. Be content with a smaller profit."

Another merchant, losing patience, hurled the stub of his cigarette into the street. "So you think the price too low!" He glared round at them. "You came of your own free will. You weren't asked to come. What's all this fuss about? We have silver dollars. If you don't sell, others will. Look, more boats have just stopped at the wharf."

Three or four more old felt hats were mounting the stone steps, the ruddy faces beneath them bright with hope. The sunlight slanted on the shoulders of their tattered cloth jackets as they joined the group.

"Wait till you hear this year's price!"

"It's even worse than last year – a paltry five dollars!" Utter despair was on the speaker's face.

"What!" Hope vanished like a pricked bubble.

But though hope vanished, they had no choice but

to sell the rice in their boats. And fate compelled them to sell to Wansheng Rice Shop. For the rice shop had silver dollars, and silver dollars were precisely what the empty pockets of those tattered cloth jackets lacked.

As they haggled over the grading of the rice and whether the measure was full enough or not, the rice boats were slowly emptied of their loads. They rode higher in the water, and the cabbage leaves and refuse between them disappeared. The peasants in the old felt hats carried the rice they had grown into Wansheng's godown in exchange for varying numbers of notes.

"Give me silver dollars, sir!" White rice should at least be exchanged for white silver dollars. If not, the bargain seemed an even worse one.

"Ignorant clods!" A hand holding a fountain-pen rested on the abacus, while scornful eyes looked at them from over spectacles. "A dollar note is as good as a silver dollar. You're not being cheated of a single cent. We don't have silver dollars here, only notes."

"Let me have notes of the Bank of China then." Judging by the design, the notes in this speaker's hand were from some other bank.

"Pah! These *are* from the Central Bank of China." The accountant levelled the forefinger of his left hand. "If you refuse them, we can take you to court."

Why should refusing banknotes be a crime? None of them understood that. After checking the figures on the notes and exchanging half-convinced, half-sceptical glances, they tucked the money into the empty pockets of their shabby jackets or the empty wallets at their belts.

Cursing under their breath, they left Wansheng Rice

Shop as another group mounted the steps from the wharf. More bubbles of hope were pricked, destroying all the joy the peasants had taken since early autumn in their heavy ears of paddy. They carried their precious white rice into Wansheng's godown in exchange not for white silver dollars but paper notes.

The streets began to hum.

The owners of the old felt hats had come to the market today intending to buy many different imported products. They had run out of soap and must take back another ten bars or so, as well as a few packages of matches. Paraffin bought from the pedlars who came to the villages cost ten coppers for a small ladle, if several households combined to buy a tin they would get much better value. Moreover it was said that the gay foreign prints displayed in the shop windows were only eighty-five cents a foot, and for months now the women-folk had been dreaming of buying some. That was why they had insisted on coming today when the rice was to be sold, having worked out exactly how many feet they needed for themselves, how many for Big Treasure and Small Treasure. Some of the women's plans included one of those oval foreign mirrors, a snowy white square towel or a pretty knitted cap for baby. Surely this year, when Heaven had been kind and each *mu* had yielded an extra three or four pecks, they were entitled to loosen the purse-strings usually held so tightly. For there ought to be something left over even after paying the rent, their debts and the guild. With this in mind, a few of them had even toyed with the idea of buying a thermos flask. Now that was an extraordinary thing! Without a fire, the hot water you'd poured in stayed just as hot hours later when you poured it out. The difference between heaven and earth could hardly be greater than between a thermos flask and the straw-lined box in which they kept the teapot warm.

Cursing beneath their breath, they left Wansheng Rice Shop like gamblers who have lost — lost yet again! The extent of their losses was still not clear to them. At all events, of the wad of notes in their pockets not half a note or ten cents was truly their own. In fact, they would have to raise a good many more notes somewhere to discharge their obligations — they had no idea how they were going to satisfy their creditors.

It was clear anyway that they had lost, and rowing straight home would not save the situation. If they strolled round the town and made a few purchases that would merely put them a little further in the red. Besides, there were some things they simply had to buy. So the streets began to hum.

In threes and fours, casting short shadows behind them, they walked the narrow streets. The men muttered over the price they had just been given and damned all black-hearted rice merchants. The women, a basket on one arm, a baby on the other, let their eyes dart from shop to shop on both sides of the street. As for the children, they were fascinated by the celluloid dolls, tigers and dogs from abroad, as well as the red and green tin drums and tin trumpets — also made abroad. It was almost impossible to drag them away.

"Look, sonny, at this fine foreign drum, this foreign trumpet! Want one?" Tempting voices were followed by a rub-a-dub-dub, a toot-toot-toot!

Dong-dong-dong! "Highest quality face-basins of foreign enamel! At forty cents apiece they're going dirt cheap. Buy a basin, friends!"

"Walk up, friends! Here's a splendid variety of foreign prints selling at cut prices. Eight-five cents a foot! Let me measure a few feet for you!"

The assistants in the chief shops were going all out, shouting to the villagers at the top of their voices, pulling at their cotton sleeves. For this was the only day in the year when the peasants' pockets were lined. This was a chance not to be missed.

After some deliberation spent in cutting down their budgets, the villagers handed one note and then another to the shop assistants. Soap, matches and the like were necessities, but they bought a little less than originally planned. The price of a tin of foreign paraffin was so shocking that they refrained from buying; they would have to go on purchasing a ladleful at a time from the pedlar. As for cloth, those who had decided to make two suits bought cloth for one; those who had planned new jackets for mother and son, bought enough for the son only. The oval foreign mirror, after being lovingly handled, was replaced on the counter. The knitted cap proved a perfect fit for baby; but his father's sharp veto made mother put it hastily down again. Those who had wanted a thermos flask dared not even ask the price. It might be as much as a dollar or a dollar fifty. If one threw caution to the winds and bought one, white-haired grandad and granny would be bound to scold: "Hard times like these — yet all you can think of is comfort! Throwing away a dollar fifty on a falderal like that! No wonder you've never amounted to anything. We've managed all these years without a thermos." No, life would not be worth living. Some mothers couldn't resist the longing in their children's eyes and bought the cheapest and smallest celluloid doll: you could move its arms and legs, make it sit down, stand up or raise its arms. Naturally, the children without one were green with envy, while even the grown-ups were much impressed.

Finally, having bought a little wine and some pork from the butchers, the villagers went back to their own boats moored by the Wansheng wharf. From the stern they brought out dishes of pickled vegetables and bean-curd; then the men sat down in the bow to drink while the women started cooking in the stern. Presently smoke was rising from most of the boats, and tears were flowing from the peasants' eyes. The children alone, tumbling and rolling in the empty holds or playing with grimy treasures rescued from the water, were happier than words can tell.

Wine loosened the peasants' tongues. Neighbours or strangers, the same fate had befallen them all, and they drank together on the river. Raising his wine bowl one would voice his views, while another, putting down his chopsticks, would chime in with approbation or an oath according to the sentiments expressed. They needed this outlet for their feelings.

"Five dollars a bushel, devil take it!"

"Last year a flood, a poor crop — we lost out. This time a good year, a big crop — but we lose out again."

"We are worse off this year than last. Last year we still got seven dollars fifty."

"We've had to sell the rice we need ourselves. Heaven! The men who grow the grain can't eat it!"

"Why did you have to sell it, you old devil? I'd have kept some for the wife and sonny. I wouldn't pay the rent, but let them have the law on me and lock me up."

"We can't pay the rent whether we want to or not. To pay the rent we'd have to run up fresh debts. If we borrow more money at forty or fifty per cent interest, what's to become of us? Next year we'd be crushed by debt."

"There's no living to be made on the land any more."

"Give up the land, I say, and take to the road. Tramps have a better time of it than we do."

"Famine refugees needn't pay their debts or guild money. A good idea. I'm for the road."

"Who'll be the leaders? Refugees always have a few leaders whom all the others — men and women, old and young — must obey."

"Seems to me it wouldn't be a bad idea to go to Shanghai to find work. Young Wang of our village went, didn't he? He works in a Shanghai factory and gets fifteen dollars a month. Fifteen dollars — that's worth three bushels of rice today."

"You're behind the times, you fool! In Shanghai the Japs are fighting. Most of the factories have closed down. Young Wang's a beggar now, didn't you know?"

Every road was closed. They were silent for a moment. Their bronzed faces flushed with sun and wine were ugly, as if dark blood were oozing through their skin.

"Who are we sweating for every year anyway?" asked one man hoarsely after a swig of wine.

"It's staring you in the face. We're sweating for them!" Someone pointed to the tarnished gilt signboard of Wansheng Rice Shop. "We nearly kill ourselves growing the rice and running into debt at wicked rates of interest. And without moving a muscle they say:

'Five dollars a bushel!' They might as well tear out our hearts and have done with it."

"If only we could fix the price ourselves! We'd be fair. I wouldn't ask more than eight dollars a bushel."

"Are you crazy? Didn't you hear? The rice merchants sink capital into the business — they can't let us have something for nothing."

"Well, we sink capital into the land. Why should we give them something for nothing? Why should we give the landlord something for nothing?"

"In the godown just now I was thinking: You're sitting pretty today with all this rice stored here. But if a time comes when we've nothing to eat, we'll be back to help ourselves." The speaker kept his voice down, his bloodshot eyes flickering towards the shore.

"If men are starving, it's no crime to take a little rice from those who have plenty." This was said in righteous tones.

"This spring, didn't they break into the Fengqiao rice shops?"

"The militia opened fire and two men were killed."

"There may be shooting here this year, for all we know."

Nothing came, naturally, of this wild talk. When the wine was drunk and the food eaten, they rowed back to their respective villages. The wharf was left silent and deserted, lapped by dark, dirty green water.

The next day another batch of boats rowed up to moor here and the same scene was re-enacted in the town. This scene was being enacted in towns all over the country. In fact, it was only too common.

"When grain is cheap the peasants suffer." This old saying made the headlines in the papers in town.

The landlords, finding it hard to collect their rent, held meetings and dispatched telegrams. The gist of these was: This year there was a bumper harvest. A glut in grain has caused a drop in prices and the peasants are destitute. Public assistance should be given.

The financiers, anxious to do business, drafted a plan for relief: 1. Funds should be raised by the large banks and money-changers for the purchase of rice from all parts of the country, and appropriate places appointed for its storage. The rice was to be sold the next spring when there was a shortage of food. This would keep the rice price stable. 2. The rice should be mortgaged as security for loans to prevent the rice merchants from buying up the whole crop and hoarding it. 3. The financiers should be responsible for collecting the fund to buy grain to be stored. The funds should be paid back after the sale of grain with interest calculated according to the profit made or losses incurred.

The industrialists said nothing. The drop in the price of rice was to their advantage since it freed them from the necessity of giving their workers a "rice subsidy".

The social scientists published their views in different journals. They marshalled statistics and theories to prove that it was ridiculous to talk of a glut in grain, and not necessarily true that "when grain is cheap the peasants suffer". Even if grain were not cheap, the peasants would suffer anyway under the double oppression of imperialism and feudalism.

Since all this happened in the towns, the villagers remained totally ignorant of it. Some of them sold rice they needed for themselves, or their gaunt, half-starved buffalo. Some borrowed money at forty to fifty per cent interest to pay the rent. Some stubbornly refused to pay and were arrested. In bitterness of spirit some paid a few cents today, a few more tomorrow, depriving themselves of food. Some took to gambling, hoping for a run of luck enabling them to win nine or ten dollars. Some begged friends to put in a good word for them to the landlord, so that they might stop renting his land, for they would be better off without. Some left home to seek their fortune, buying a fourth class ticket on the train to Shanghai.

Translated by Gladys Yang

How Mr Pan Weathered the Storm

THE station was crowded with people, each of them preoccupied with his own problems and looking not quite his usual self. The porters, hands thrust into the pockets of their numbered uniforms, stood motionless as if they had fallen asleep on their feet. They knew they still had a long wait ahead; it was not yet time for the tips they were hoping to get so there was no point in looking energetic at this moment. The oppressive atmosphere made breathing somewhat difficult. It looked like rain. The lights which had been turned on for some time were dimmer than usual and made everything appear as if in a fog.

A notice on the blackboard announced that the incoming express from the west was going to be four hours late. This notice had been read and reread several hours ago and now, like those old, torn theatre bills left to flutter in the wind, could no longer draw a single glance from anyone. Since such notices had been posted for practically every incoming train this week, they had become the thing to be expected.

This train which had been on the minds of so many people finally appeared. The sombre station became a hive of activity. We shall not go into the relief of the travellers who had reached their journey's end, the joy of those waiting for them, or the tips received by the porters. We are concerned only with a certain Mr

Pan who had come from a nearby small town, Rangli. Before the train chugged into the station, he had managed to arrange everything to his satisfaction: He was at the head of his small family, his right hand holding a black leather bag and his left leading his six-year-old son. The child's other hand held on to his eight-year-old brother who in turn held his mother's hand. Mr Pan said he would not be able to take care of them all unless they held together like this. For with hands linked, they could wriggle through like a snake wherever they wanted to go. He told his family again and again to lock their hands tightly; they were not to let go whatever happened. Lest the others should forget, he kept swinging his left hand as a reminder to be passed down the line.

It was good of course to form a line, yet not without disadvantages too. As the train slowed to a stop all the passengers with their luggage surged towards the door. In this exigency, the line formed by Mr Pan and his family suffered for its length. Using his black leather bag to clear the way, he had pushed on vigorously with his chest and stomach till he was only two windows away from the door. But his six-year-old son was still four windows away, wedged tightly in between other passengers and the wooden seats. Arms stretching out in two directions and pulled vigorously from both ends, the child felt that his limbs would soon be torn off. "Oh, my arms, my arms!" he wailed in desperation.

The other passengers were not aware that there was a child wedged in between their legs until his cries reached their ears. A closer look revealed that the family of four was linked in a long line with hands tightly locked.

"Let go at once," ordered one passenger. "Or else you'll be pulling the child apart."

"What's this! Why doesn't the man carry the child?" muttered another, his tone full of scorn, as he edged his own way towards the door.

"No," Mr Pan disagreed with them. There were good reasons for holding on together. He realized, however, on second thought that not everyone was intelligent enough to see these reasons and it was a waste of breath to argue with them. But the six-year-old was still yelling, "My arms, my arms!" Since Mr Pan could see no way either to advance or to turn back, he had to be the first to violate his own admonition and let go of the child's hand. "Keep your eyes on me, don't lose sight of me," he ordered, flustered and worried.

The train stopped with a clang and a jerk. A number of people shot out of the carriage door and Mr Pan felt the pressure from in front suddenly relax but the pushing from behind gained in momentum so that his legs carried him forward without any effort on his part. He meant to turn to rally his small forces but finding that impossible merely shouted at the backs of the heads before him, "Follow close behind me! Follow me!"

Somehow or other he too shot out of the door. Turning round quickly, he saw that his wife and sons were not behind him; they were still squeezed in somewhere in the train. Waiting by the door seemed to him the best possible solution. Another hundred or so passengers alighted before the screwed up, tearful face of his younger son appeared under the lamplight. Mr Pan hurried up and, after being swept back several times by alighting passengers, picked up his son in his left arm and set him down on the platform. Another short wait and Mrs Pan and the eight-year-old emerged. Panting heavily and uttering groans of pain, she turned her mournful gaze to her husband's face, like a child seeking consolation.

Mr Pan was after all a man with some presence of mind. Now that his forces had been reassembled he issued another order, "We must link hands again. See what a crowd there is on the platform and look at that bottle-neck at the exit. If we don't hold on together we're bound to lose each other."

The six-year-old had had enough. Hugging his father's legs, he said, "Carry me, Daddy."

"You little nuisance!" Mr Pan was exasperated, but he restrained himself and, stooping down, picked up the child. He told his older son to hold on to the tail of his long gown with one hand and on to Mrs Pan with the other.

Never before had Mrs Pan been through an ordeal like this. The prospect of an even greater crush was more than she could bear after the effort of getting off the train. "If I had known it was going to be like this," she grumbled, "I'd have stayed at home and waited for death rather than come out and be a refugee."

"What's the use of regretting?" Mr Pan's annoyance was tinged with sympathy. "Now that we're here, why regret? Besides, at least we're safe here. Let's go now. Mind your steps!" And all four together, they staggered into the crowd.

A frantic rush and Mr Pan emerged as if from a dream through the narrow exit guarded by the ticket collector. Like a drop of water in a torrent, he had no alternative but to be swept along by the multitude around him, his feet barely touching the ground. In a moment he had cleared the wire fence of the railway station, stepped across the tramway and arrived on the cement pavement of the street outside. Turning round hurriedly, he saw countless faces pale in the lamplight and numerous bags and bundles rolling in his direction. Suddenly he realized that the little hand that had been clutching the tail of his long gown was no longer there; he had no idea when it had let go. An indescribable sorrow filled his heart and he automatically turned his head round. But there was no sign of his wife and son. He felt he had lost his family. The lights and figures round him began to swim as tears filled his eyes.

Fortunately the child in his arm had sharp eyes. "Mama, there she is," he pointed. He had spied and recognized the fringe over his mother's brows.

Mr Pan was overjoyed. He first rubbed his eyes on the child's clothes before he looked in the direction pointed out for he hardly dared to believe the good news. After a slight search, he saw his wife darting left and right in the crowd, her hands held protectively round their older son. They were still on the other side of the tramway. "Ada!" he hailed and hurrying over brought them back to where he had been standing on the pavement. Putting down the six-year-old at last, he breathed a sigh of relief. "Now, all's well!" he said, mopping his face. Indeed all was well, for once they crossed that wire fencing* they were insured against war, fire and robbery. Besides, he had found his lost son and wife. It was as if from the jaws of disaster he had rescued four lives and one black bag. All was well, indeed. Authoritatively, Mr Pan shouted,

---

* Meaning that they have entered the foreign settlement.

"Rickshaw!" Several rickshaw men pulled up clamouring to know where he wanted to go. He raised his head slightly as if to add dignity to his words and waved two fingers, "Only two, we want only two." Then, having given the matter some thought, he continued, "Ten coppers. Who'll go to Fourth Avenue for ten coppers?" This ought to show them he knew his way around in Shanghai.

After a fairly long argument they got two rickshaws for twelve coppers apiece. Mrs Pan got into one with the older boy and Mr Pan climbed into the other with the younger child and the black bag.

The outstretched arm of an Indian policeman shouldering a gun blocked the way just as the rickshaw man straightened up to go. This fearful apparition made the child on Mr Pan's knee hide his head in fright.

"There's nothing to be afraid of," said his father. "That's only an Indian policeman. Look at his handsome red turban. We have to come here because we don't have policemen like him at home. He'll use his gun to protect us. His beard is interesting, look at it, like that of the arhats in the temples."

The child was too frightened to look even at a beard like that of an arhat. Only when the clanging of a tram caught his attention did he peep out and find that a very brightly lit room had swept past in a flash. On the other side of the road were also brightly lit houses full of dazzling objects. He finally raised his face from his father's chest.

When they reached Fourth Avenue they asked for a room at half a dozen hotels, all of which had a big sign with the words "House Full". One glance was enough to assure them that it was no use trying to coax the manager into letting them have a room because temporary beds had been set up even in the lounge. Obviously the hotels were really full. At last, at one hotel they were met by a clerk who drawled lazily, "Want a room?"

"Yes, we want a room. Have you got one?" A ray of hope shot through Mr Pan making him feel he had reached haven.

"We do have one. The last occupant vacated it only a moment ago. He has rented a house for himself. If you had come a few minutes later, it would have been snapped up."

"Let us have that room." Mr Pan put his younger son down and turned back to help his wife and older son alight. "We are in luck after all," he told them. "We've finally got a room." When it came to paying off the rickshaws he generously offered one copper more than the agreed fee. It was his belief that if you treated others well when luck was with you, your luck would continue. But the rickshaw men turned out to be very ungrateful. They declared that they had spent a great deal of time taking them from one hotel to another so Mr Pan must pay them five coppers extra each. In the end, the hotel attendant came out to mediate and Mr Pan parted with four extra coppers.

The room was on the ground floor. Besides a bed, a lamp, a table and two chairs, it contained nothing but smoke. When Mr Pan took his family inside, his nostrils were immediately assailed by the pungent odour of fried fish mixed with the stink of urine. "What a foul smell!" Mr Pan muttered with annoyance. From next door came the sizzling of food frying in hot oil, the kitchen was obviously only a wall away. However unpleasant the stench, it was better than getting shot at or sleeping without a roof, Mr Pan decided, immediately feeling better. He settled himself comfortably in one of the chairs.

"Want some supper?" asked the hotel attendant putting down the black bag.

"I want ham soup with my rice," announced the younger child sucking his fingers.

His mother gave him a severe look. "Ham soup with rice indeed! We are refugees, lucky to have anything at all to eat. How can you ask for this or that!"

The older boy was no better than his brother. "Now that we're in Shanghai," he begged his father, "I want to try some European food."

Mrs Pan was furious now. Rounding on her firstborn, she said scathingly, "The idea! You deserve to have nothing to eat. You should simply starve. . . ."

Mr Pan was embarrassed. "Children don't know what they're talking about," he said, trying to smooth things over. He told the attendant, "We had something on the train. Just bring us two orders of fried rice and eggs."

The waiter nodded in a non-committal way and left. He had no sooner got out of the door than Mr Pan called him back. "Bring me a catty of Shaoxing wine and ten cents of smoked fish."

When the sound of the attendant's footsteps died away, Mr Pan, looking relieved and uplifted, said to his wife, "Now we ought to relax a little and have a drink. Just think, we got away from a place fraught with danger to this haven where no harm can come to us. This is something to celebrate. Just now you two were lost and I had a hard time finding you. I was nearly frantic with worry. But Aer was sharp." Mr Pan pulled his son closer and gently stroked his head. "He spied you at once and I was able to find you. That's another thing to celebrate. Everything's wonderful so let's relax and enjoy a few cups." Beaming with pleasure, he raised an imaginary cup to his lips.

His wife did not reply. She was thinking of home. True, they had packed their valuables away and deposited them for safe-keeping in a church, but there were still a number of things left in the house. She was not at all sure whether Wang, the maid, was reliable. She also wondered whether their poor neighbours knew that her whole family was away with only the maid to watch over the household. She wondered whether the maid would remember to close all the doors and windows at night. She also remembered her three fat hens in the backyard, the pair of trousers she was working on for her younger son, the bowl of braised duck in the kitchen.... These considerations, flashing through her mind, made her extremely uncomfortable. "I wonder what sort of mess they'll make of the place," she sighed.

A feeling of disappointment swept over the children. Vaguely they sensed that this Shanghai where they had just arrived was not as interesting and fascinating as that Shanghai they had heard so much about from their parents.

Raindrops drifted in through the window. "It's really raining. Lucky it didn't start any earlier," cried Mr Pan standing up to close the window. Suddenly he caught sight of the hotel notice on the wall which had been half hidden by the opened window. Remembering a most important thing, he fixed his eyes unblinkingly on the piece of paper.

"My, my! Two dollars, no less," was his startled cry and he turned round to look significantly into his wife's eyes, gasping at what he had discovered.

2

When the next day dawned, the hotel attendants were still curled up in deep slumber on a few benches put together in the hallway. The narrow skylight did not let in much light. Dim yellow lamps were still burning in several hotel rooms. But Mr and Mrs Pan were already talking things over. The two boys, hoping that today's Shanghai would turn out better than the Shanghai of yesterday, had been awake for some time. Their parents asked them to sleep a little longer so they were still in bed tickling each other.

"I think you'd better not go back," said Mrs Pan, very worried. "How can you be sure what they say in the papers is true? Since we went through so much difficulty to get away, there's hardly any sense in your going back right away."

"Actually, I had some idea that this might happen. Director Gu was never one to let things go. 'Since there's no fighting here, the schools must naturally start as usual.' Yes, that sounds like him all right. I know this correspondent too. He happens to work in the Bureau of Education. So, there's no question about the authenticity of his report. I'll simply have to go back."

"Don't you know it's dangerous going back?" Mrs Pan's tone was quite tragic. "Maybe in two or three days they'll be fighting in our parts. Suppose you went back and got the school started, do you think the students will come to school? Besides even if the fighting doesn't spread to our parts, you'll have a good answer for the director of education if he wants to know why you didn't start school. You have only to ask him: What's more important, the school or human lives? He is not immortal himself, he could hardly blame you for not going back."

"You don't understand," said Mr Pan with some contempt. "This is the kind of argument that only silly women like you, safe at home or in bed, can use. You don't expect me to go and say something like that? Now, don't try to stop me." His tone had become quite conciliatory. "For back I must go. There won't be the least danger. I know how to keep out of harm's way. Besides," Mr Pan smiled at his own diplomacy, "weren't you worried just now about the things we left at home? Once I'm home I'll be able to keep an eye on them so you can stay here without worrying. When things settle down a bit I'll come promptly to fetch you and the boys home."

Mrs Pan knew now there was absolutely no way to prevent her husband from going back. It would be nice to have him at home and keeping an eye on things but, in these uncertain times, once he left he would be like a pearl cast into the sea, she might never get him back. The sorrows of parting and fear of death overwhelmed her. Tears stung her eyelids and came so near to trickling out that she dared not even glance at her husband. It struck her at once that tears at this moment were a bad omen, nothing tragic had happened and she should not be weeping. Holding back her tears with an effort, more to comfort herself than in real earnest she said, "Then, just go back and see how things are. If the Bureau of Education doesn't say anything about starting the school according to schedule you just come right back, catching the afternoon train if you can and if not the early train the next morning. You see," here she could no longer restrain herself and one tear dropped on the back of her hand, to be hastily brushed away — "I worry about you so!"

Mr Pan was feeling very vexed himself. Since the director of education wanted the schools to start as usual, he himself had no reason whatever to insist that they should remain closed. It followed naturally that he should go back. But how could he not worry about his family here? He noticed the look of gentle sorrow on his wife's face. It seemed heartless to leave a woman with two young children, so weak and helpless, without anyone to rely on. How could he be sure nothing untoward would happen to them? All this made him angry and disturbed. He was angry at those sending troops out to fight this army or that, angry at the director of education who talked about starting school without delay, angry at himself for not having a grown-up son who might have helped him out.

Nevertheless, he was not a woman, he had to look ahead. He knew that going back was the right thing to do. Forgetting his anger and without showing a trace of his inner disturbance, he nodded to show that he agreed with her. "If I find that the director has no intention of starting the schools, I'll do as you say and come back by the afternoon train," he said soothingly.

The children had overheard this last remark. The younger boy, his head half buried in the pillow, lisped babyishly, "I wanna go back too."

"Mama and Daddy and I are going back and we'll leave you here all by yourself," teased the older boy, making a face.

The younger boy started to wail at the top of his voice, rubbing his eyes vigorously although there was not a single tear in them.

"You will both stay here with Mama," said Mr Pan raising his voice. "No more nonsense now. Get dressed and ready for breakfast." After a few more words with his wife, Mr Pan set out for the station.

On the way, he heard passers-by commenting on the fact that trains were no longer running. "If the trains have stopped that settles the question for me. Even if they decide to fire me for staying away, I can't help it." The news gave him a let-down feeling. But if his luck held, it might prove no more than a rumour. To find out the true situation he was anxious that the rickshaw man should go faster.

His luck turned out to be good. There was no sign posted at the station saying that trains were suspended. On the blackboard a notice declared that the night train would be four hours late. It was still not in yet. The ticket window was far from crowded. From time to time one or two people stepped up to buy tickets. The crowd in the station was made up half of people awaiting travellers, half of spectators. Some carried cameras and were waiting to snap the bustle accompanying the arrival of the night train so that the pictures could be used in some future "History of Wars and Changes". The baggage room was filled with an assortment of bags and cases piled so high that they nearly touched the ceiling.

He felt both relieved and depressed. After a slight

hesitation he bought himself a third-class ticket and boarded the train. The clear sunlight made the whole compartment bright but not hot. There were plenty of empty seats. Had he wanted to, he could have lain down. He thought, "This is unusual. If I were in a better mood this could have been a very pleasant trip."

The train was held up at various stops to give right of way to troop trains. By the time he got into Rangli, it was past three in the afternoon. Mr Pan hurried home and found his gate tightly closed. The tension in his heart eased a little for this precaution was one thing he had tried very hard to impress on Wang, the maid, before he left.

He had to knock a number of times before the maid appeared. She exclaimed in surprise at sight of Mr Pan, "Is that you back, sir? Is there no need to run away now?"

Mr Pan muttered a vague answer as he rushed in and looked around. Then he unlocked the door to his room, strode in and examined it with care. No change. There was no change at all. Everything was as he had left it the day before. His heart which had been palpitating relaxed somewhat but he was not yet fully assured. He locked the room again and turned to go. "See that the gate's properly locked," he told the maid.

The maid was very puzzled. Having closed the gate, she went in and began to wonder. The master and mistress must still be somewhere in town. Perhaps they were afraid she might want to go with them and had only pretended to run away to Shanghai. "Otherwise, why is the master back so soon? The mistress and the boys are not with him. Where can they be hiding themselves? But why didn't they want me with them?

Of course, it's because they didn't have room for so many. They are probably in that red building belonging to the foreigner. Those soldiers are all in the know; they will not touch that red building even when they are fighting. Actually they could have told me the truth for I wouldn't have been keen on going even if they had asked me. I'm not a bit frightened. Even if fighting breaks out here, my burial costume has been ready a long time." She saw in her mind's eye the beautiful embroidered burial shoes presented to her by her niece and felt sure these would make the King of Hell treat her with respect when she went to the nether world. This reflection gave her a subtle pleasure which kept her mind off the question of where her master and mistress were.

Mr Pan went to see the correspondent who was a member of the Bureau of Education to ask whether the director really intended the schools to start as usual. "But certainly," the man answered. "He also said some teachers were so busy getting themselves out of harm's way they quite neglected their duty. It just showed they were unworthy to work in the field of education and this was a good chance to eliminate some of them." This announcement made Mr Pan sit up to take notice. At once he congratulated himself on his wisdom in coming back from Shanghai. He made straight for the school, picked up a writing brush and drafted a circular to the parents of the students. War and fighting might be worrisome, he stated, but the education of young people was like food and clothing which could not be dispensed with for a single day. Now that the summer holidays were over, the school would start as usual. In the time of the great war in

Europe, a net was spread in the air to prevent bombing so that teaching might continue uninterrupted. This kind of heroism, the notice went on, should not go unrivalled. It was to be hoped that the parents would understand, and in this spirit would send their children to school as if nothing had happened. All this was in the interest of both the school and the students and also for the honour of the town and the country.

After reading the draft three times, he was finally satisfied that there was nothing more he could add. When the director of education saw this circular the least to be expected was the remark, "He thinks like me." In a mood of complacency, Mr Pan cut the stencil himself and mimeographed more than a hundred copies which he dispatched through the school janitor. Now that he had done his duty by his work he let his mind return to his private affairs. Since the school must start, he could hardly go to Shanghai again. But his wife and children would have a hard time all by themselves in the hotel. There was nothing he could do about that, he must tell them to be careful and remain there without worrying. He used what ink there was left after drafting his circular to write a letter to his wife.

The next day in the teahouse he got authentic news that the railway was cut. His heart sank. Somehow, his beloved wife and two sons seemed to have drifted away on the wind to a distant land, out of his reach. In a sad state of mind, he strolled to the school where the janitor reported on his mission the day before. "When I took the circular around I found more than twenty households with doors tightly locked and no one round to answer my knocking. I had to slip the circular in through a slit in the door. About thirty households had only servants at home; the masters had run away to Shanghai taking their children with them, of course. No one knew when they'd be back for school. The rest all took the circular but a few said since they were not sure how long they'd be alive the question of schooling had better wait for the time being."

"I see," said Mr Pan, his mind not on these matters at all but troubled by gloomier thoughts. After a cigarette, he reached a decision. He went to the branch office of the Red Cross Society.

Hc proclaimed himself willing to become a member of the Red Cross and paid his fees. He said his school had fairly spacious premises and he wanted the Red Cross to use it as a home for women refugees in case of emergency. Such a charitable offer was of course warmly accepted. Besides, Mr Pan was a well-known and respected figure in the town. The branch office gave him a Red Cross banner to be hoisted up at the school entrance and a Red Cross badge to show that he was a member of that organization.

Mr Pan held the flag and badge in his hands as if they were a talisman, a guarantee of life and security. A mysterious sense of satisfaction stole into his heart. "Everything is safe now. But. . . ." He turned back to the man in the branch office with a smile. "Give me an extra banner and a few more badges, will you?" His reason was that the school had a back door and the badge was so small he might easily lose it so it was better to have a few to spare.

"This isn't something you can eat," said the Red Cross man jokingly, "and you can hardly use it as a plaything! Even if you take more than one badge, you're still only a member, so why ask for more than one?" But in the end he gave Mr Pan a few spare ones to make him happy.

Both Red Cross banners were soon fluttering in the light breeze of early autumn but neither of them was near the school's back entrance. The second banner had been placed over Mr Pan's own door. One Red Cross badge glittered with the solemn light of charity on Mr Pan's lapel, giving its wearer a new kind of courage. As for the rest, these were kept with care, wrapped in paper, in the pocket of Mr Pan's shirt. "One is for her," he thought, "one is for Ada and the other for the little one." Although they were still in distant Shanghai, out of his reach, the badges were a sort of double insurance for their safety which should give them a new courage too.

3

The two armies opened fire at Bizhuang.

Very few households in Rangli kept their doors open; the shops naturally all remained closed. Soldiers marched past in the streets frequently. They would soon be going to the front and felt that they were endowed with the highest authority; nothing was of any account in their eyes. They could trample whatever they liked underfoot. This was how the press-gang started. To prevent those forced into the army from running away, the conscripts were bound and marched along in a line with soldiers escorting them. Thus it came about that people were afraid of going out on the streets. When it was absolutely necessary to leave their houses, they went by small paths and byways. Even people like Mr Pan, who were armed with Red Cross badges, were rather wary and dared not strut about openly. The streets of Rangli seemed quiet and very desolate.

For several days now, the Shanghai papers had not come. The local army headquarters, however, sometimes posted battle news which usually said that the enemy had been routed and our troops had advanced several *li*. When a fresh bulletin appeared on the street corner, a small group would gather slowly to read it carefully. They were not altogether convinced by what they read for they felt there were many things unsaid. They would disperse with a feeling of foreboding, their brows still tightly knit.

Mr Pan had been downcast for the last few days. He worried most about his absent wife and children of whom he had no news. It seemed he might never be able to get in touch with them again. And then there was the question of his own safety. "It's only a march of a hundred *li* or so from Bizhuang. Although the Red Cross badge may serve some purpose, nobody ever wrote me a guarantee, so who can I ask for compensation if it turns out to be useless after all? Bullets, shells, robbers and fire are no laughing matter. I'll have to make more inquiries and find some other means to ensure my safety." So he asked here and there for news about the front and was sure there was a grain of truth in whatever news he got that was different from the current rumour. He then calculated its effect on his own interest. The sight of anyone rushing along the street with a look of panic would startle him for he was sure the man had learned some reliable but fearful news.

Only the fact the man was a complete stranger prevented Mr Pan from accosting and questioning him.

The Red Cross sent people to the front to look after the wounded; some of them came back frequently in army transports. The Red Cross was naturally the most reliable source of news. Although Mr Pan belonged to the Red Cross he did not often go there for news for he was ashamed to admit his fear in public. Nevertheless, the Red Cross was a source of reliable information and it would be foolish to ask for news elsewhere. The result was Mr Pan went at dusk every day to the house of Wu, a man who worked in the Red Cross office. Wu would tell him there was no news or that this side was doing all right at the front, after which Mr Pan would go home with a sigh of relief.

One evening Mr Pan went again to Wu's house. He had to wait a long time before Wu came back.

"Nothing new, eh?" asked Mr Pan eagerly. "According to the bulletin, we launched a general offensive yesterday."

"Bad," said Wu looking worried and toying with his moustache.

"What?" Mr Pan's heart skipped a beat and he felt trapped.

As if afraid of being overheard, Wu answered in a low voice, "The reliable news is that Zhengan, a town eight *li* from Bizhuang, fell to the other side this morning."

Mr Pan uttered one desperate cry, paused for a second or so and turned to leave, muttering as he went, "I'm going."

The street lamps seemed particularly dim that evening. Mr Pan felt as if he were being chased from behind. Frightened and worried, he stumbled home as quickly as he could and told the maid, "You lock the doors and go to sleep. I'll be busy tonight and will not come back for the night." He saw there was an old padded silk gown in the wardrobe; they had forgotten to pack it in the suitcases which had been deposited for safe-keeping. It would be a pity to lose it. There were also a few of the boys' lined cotton tunics. A close scrutiny showed that they were still wearable. There was also an old silk skirt which his wife would probably be loath to part with. He tied them all together and went out with his bundle.

"Rickshaw! The red building in Fuxing Lane. Ten cents."

"Whoever heard of ten cents?" drawled the rickshaw man. "How many rickshaws are out these days! Who would be out here risking his life for a few cents unless he needed them to keep alive? Thirty cents. Take it or leave it."

"Thirty cents then." Mr Pan hurried over and stepped into the rickshaw. "But you must also do as I ask, go faster."

"Hey, Mr Pan, where are you going?" a colleague by the name of Huang saw him and called out.

"Uh, Mr . . . over there. . . ." Mr Pan in his panic was not quite sure who had spoken to him. Suddenly he realized it would be a waste of breath to answer for the rickshaw was going too fast to allow the other to chase after him to demand an answer. He swallowed the rest of his words.

The red building was full of people most of whom had moved in ten days ago. Children cried and people talked, lights were lit in many rooms so that there was even an atmosphere of cheer and bustle. "There is no vacant room here," his host told Mr Pan. "But since all your things are here I can hardly turn you away. Just now, several others arrived unexpectedly too, and as I could not refuse them I've put them in a side room ordinarily used as a kitchen. I'll go and see if they couldn't take in one more."

"Oh, yes, surely they can take in one more." Mr Pan felt comforted. "Besides, at a time like this, I don't intend to sleep through the night; a place to sit would be just fine."

When he stepped into the side room, his bundle on one arm, he thought at first that all this fear and panic were giving him hallucinations. He closed his eyes and opened them again but what he saw did not change. There, sitting by the window with a thick moustache twitching over his upper lip as he talked to someone opposite him, was none other than the director of the Bureau of Education.

Mr Pan hesitated, the foot that had stepped over the threshold wavered; he meant to withdraw but thought better of it. The director had seen him too. "Ah, Mr Pan, there you are," said he, smiling to cover his embarrassment. "Come in and sit down." When the host realized that they were acquainted he withdrew to attend to his own business.

"So you're here too, director. Can you accommodate one more in this room?"

"There's only the three of us here, of course we can. We brought along a mat so we could take turns lying down a bit. Good thing it's not too cold yet."

Mr Pan felt that the director was extremely affable that night, not at all his usual stern and dignified self.

Forgetting his restraint, he strode in. "Then allow me to come in and keep you three company for the night."

The room was far from spacious. A middle-aged man with glasses sat on a mat spread on the floor. There was a look of fatigue on his face but he showed no inclination for sleep. The stove and pots and pans were placed against one wall. Near the window stood three chairs in a row; the director occupied one, the director's cousin, a young man in his twenties with sleek hair, another, the third one was empty. In one corner were an osier suitcase and three bundles — probably the three men's luggage. The few things were enough to clutter up the room, there was hardly any vacant space left. The coat of dust on the electric bulb made everything in the room hazy.

Mr Pan put his bundle down with those of the others. He took the vacant seat with an air of apology. After the director had introduced him to his companions, he asked, "Have you also heard the news about Zhengan?"

"Yes. With Zhengan lost, Bizhuang is in great danger."

"Our side must have been careless along the southern route, the loss of Zhengan is a sign of this. It's the easiest thing for the other side to steal up to Bizhuang from Zhengan. At this very moment they may have got in. If so, I dare not think what will happen here!"

"If so, chaos will reign."

"But Commander Du on this side isn't a fool you know, he's noted for strategy. He's probably foreseen all this and has plans to forestall the other side. Maybe he'll turn the tables at this juncture and take up the offensive, attacking the enemy in its lair."

"If that happens there'll be an end to hostilities and

that'll be great. We, in the field of education, can then start school and carry on as usual."

The director promptly became conscious of his dignity at the mention of the word "education". Twisting his thick moustache, he said with a sigh, "This fighting has certainly caused a loss to students of different ages, to say nothing of other people." He forgot his cramped and uncomfortable position in the tiny room and felt as if he were back again in the dignified office of the Bureau of Education.

"Commander Zhu of the other side is really hateful," said the middle-aged man on the mat with some indignation. "Why must he resist when this side attacked? He's bound to be defeated. If he'd been smart and offered no resistance, all this fighting would not have occurred."

"He's a fool," the director's cousin agreed. "He won't give up till the end. And in the meanwhile we have to suffer cooped up in this small, dark room!" His tone was not serious.

Mr Pan's thoughts went to his wife and children in Shanghai. He wondered if they were all right, if they had kept out of trouble. Were they asleep at this moment? Since he could not feel them near him and his imagination conjured up only a very hazy picture, he felt that the fighting had injured him more than any of the others. He let his eyes rest mournfully on the little courtyard outside the window and stayed silent.

But then his thoughts turned to the terrible news he had heard from Wu and the threat of danger to follow. "I wonder what is really happening!" he exclaimed.

"Hard to say!" the director spoke knowingly. "In war, everything depends on making use of the right moment. The tide may turn any time and things may not happen as we thought. Perhaps at this very moment . . . we. . . ." He smiled at the middle-aged man.

All the others in the room, the man on the mat, the director's cousin and Mr Pan caught the significance of his smile. Assured that they were safe enough where they were, they also smiled with satisfaction.

The little yard overgrown with weeds provided a comfortable haven for mosquitoes and small insects of all descriptions. The lamp in the room drew the insects in swarms and the four frightened men had a bad time of it. Midges attacked their faces; a sudden sting from a particularly venomous mosquito kept making one or the other jump. From time to time they stopped talking to listen with trepidation for the sound of shooting or the clamour of frightened people. Sleep was out of the question, of course. They merely took turns lying down a bit as the director had predicted.

Mr Pan's eyes were bloodshot the next morning and he shivered with cold. Longing to know how things were outside he slipped out all alone. The streets looked the same as on ordinary mornings. A few stray dogs, tails up, sniffed cheerily here and there. A man with drowsy eyes walked past now and then. Mr Pan turned a corner, still he neither saw nor heard anything unusual. He could hardly suppress a smile at the recollection of his own panic the night before, but on second thought he felt there was really nothing funny about it. Better, after all, to be overcautious rather than take unnecessary risks.

Three weeks or so later, the fighting came to an end. People wagged their heads and assured each other, "Now, things'll be all right. As long as there's no fighting, we'll be safe." Mr Pan, though, was not quite happy for the trains were still not running and he could not fetch his wife and children back from Shanghai. There had been two letters, both very brief, which, instead of making him feel better, only made him miss them more. He was annoyed with himself for being such a poor prophet. He could very well have saved all that extra expense of taking his family away to Shanghai, and then he need not have led this lonely bachelor's life for several weeks.

Realizing that the Bureau of Education would soon be considering the question of starting school, he went there for news. As soon as he stepped into the reception room he noticed several clerks busy cutting up large strips of paper and grinding fresh ink. It looked as if they were getting ready for some festivity.

"Here's Mr Pan, just the man we want," cried one. "You write beautifully in the Yan style. This is just the job for you."

"Yes, indeed, Mr Pan is the only one who can do calligraphy of this size well," chimed in the rest.

"Write what? I'm completely at sea about what's going on."

"We are getting ready to welcome the triumphant return of Commander Du. Four festooned archways are to be erected at the railway station to welcome Commander Du's train. We need to write inscriptions for the four archways."

"Who am I to write for such an important event?"

"We all agree you're the best man!" "You mustn't be modest," came the cry from all sides as a writing brush was thrust into Mr Pan's hands.

Mr Pan was quite overwhelmed. He took the writing brush and dipped it in the ink. After a pensive silence, he wrote, "His Deeds Surpass All Others" and on the second strip of paper, "His Might Sweeps the Southeast." On the third piece of paper he wrote, "Virtue and Benevolence So Bountiful." But as his brush formed the word "bountiful", he had a vision of press-gangs, exploding shells, houses in flame, raped women, pale-faced refugees and rotting corpses.

"This epithet shows the people's heartfelt gratitude!" cried one of the men watching, with a sigh of admiration. "The writing is more beautiful too."

"I wonder what he'll find to match this epithet," commented another man.

1924

Translated by Tang Sheng

Night

IN a lane not too clean and neat there was a two-storey house with one room downstairs and one upstairs. All the furniture in the downstairs room was in a blur as if the dim yellowish paraffin lamp on the table had darkened the room instead of giving it light. Beside the table sat an elderly woman with a child about two in her arms. There was nothing unusual about the woman's features. Though her forehead was wrinkled, she did not look old or feeble. Only her reddened eyes were a little strange, staring fixedly from their deep sockets at the child's face. She looked sad and lost, noting how the colour had faded from the little boy's cheeks and how weak he was after his recent shock.

Of late the child had cried as much as six months ago when he was being weaned. He would burst out crying abruptly just as if someone had hit him. Once he started he would go on endlessly, like cicadas chirping in summer. The woman tried her best to soothe him, recalling all the phrases she had used to comfort babies in her younger days, but all to little avail; perhaps the child found them too outlandish or old-fashioned. Only after he had exhausted himself by sobbing would his eyelids begin to flutter until finally they closed altogether.

Tonight the woman felt relieved because, for a change, the child had not started crying. If he should go to sleep like that, wouldn't it be a rare quiet night? But on the other hand, she was wondering uneasily what news her younger brother would bring back, what he had learned of her poor darling who had been in her thoughts day and night.

These evenings had been torture to her, apart from the child's crying, for she seemed to see so many shadowy pictures in the dim lamplight. First here, now there, she could have sworn she glimpsed pools of bright red blood! As cars sped by or heavy trucks thundered steadily past outside, she seemed to see the two of them in a car with heavy clanking chains on their wrists and ankles. When footsteps — heavy or light, slow or quick — passed by her door, she was afraid the police had come for her and the baby. The ringing of her neighbour's doorbell set her heart throbbing. Already of the age when one sleeps little, she could not fall asleep at all now for terror. When she went to bed she dared not light the lamp for fear the light upstairs would attract attention and cause trouble. Besides, she preferred to see nothing, to be in sheer darkness. But no! The flickering shadows appeared just the same: the red pool like the setting sun even seemed to be spreading. All she could do was to hug the child who often sobbed in his dreams....

She kept gazing at the child. Weak and stricken, she did not know which way to turn. The future loomed before her like a sea of mist which surely hid wild beasts or pitfalls. And her only companion in danger was this small child. She was virtually alone. She dreaded to think more and, wanting something better to do, she asked the child, "Big Baby, precious, what's your surname?"

"Zhang," he replied. Not knowing what a surname means, a child simply repeats what he is told just as he is taught to say papa and mama.

"No, no," the woman scolded him mildly, a little worried because he had not learned his new lesson well. "Don't say that, nobody's surname is Zhang. Listen, Big Baby's surname is Sun. Remember, Sun, Sun. . . ."

"Sun," the child did not insist but repeated after her in his babyish tone, looking up into her face.

She shut her eyes tightly twice. Her tears had nearly run dry but she felt close to sobbing. "That's right. Sun, Sun. Now again, what is your surname?"

"Sun," repeated the little boy mischievously, reaching out for the green jade hairpin in her hair.

"Good, Big Baby's a dear!" She held the child tightly, her face brushing against his cotton shirt. "Whoever asks you, your surname is Sun, Sun. . . ." Her voice, tinged with sadness, died away.

The child, his arms pinioned, was unable to reach the hairpin. Suddenly he burst out crying, struggling with all his might, tears streaming down his face.

She knew what this meant — the normal routine had started, no chance of a quiet evening! In a very gentle voice she crooned, "Big Baby, precious, don't cry! . . . A nice doll's coming to see Big Baby. . . . She's in a red sedan-chair . . . in a pretty carriage. . . ."

The little boy as usual paid no heed but cried even louder. "I want . . . my mam. . . ."

More distressed and frightened than ever, the woman felt his cries were piercing her heart like sharp needles and worried lest the neighbours hear through the thin walls and become suspicious. But it was not easy to appease him. Fully aware that what she was saying was no use, still she repeated again and again in a trembling voice, "Mama will be back soon." At that the child only cried louder, opening wide his tearful eyes and looking around for his mother.

She stood up and started pacing the floor, holding the child in her arms. Her slow, heavy steps showed her age. She paced to and fro, reciting those outlandish, old-fashioned expressions meant to soothe a child. The furniture in the room seemed to be vibrating with the child's crying, the wick of the lamp seemed to be expanding, expanding . . . and ah, a pool of blood! She shut her weary eyes, not daring to look again. Although the child's cries were piercing her ears, she felt she was alone on a strange mountain, in surroundings so weird that her blood was turning cold.

Tap, tap, somebody was knocking at the door. At the same time the scabby brown dog across the lane started barking. She started, then recognized the familiar knock. Her younger brother had come back. She hurried to open the door.

The door had barely opened a crack when in slipped the man outside. Swiftly and softly he turned back to close the door as if shutting out something that was after him.

"Well?" asked the woman eagerly in a low voice. She wished she could see into his heart, to share all he knew.

Her brother walked in, glancing around and taking a seat, gasping. He looked like a merchant of about forty, fine wrinkles around his narrow eyes making it seem as if he were always smiling. His nose was not big either. Sweat glimmered on his forehead, yet he was shivering. The child's crying reminded him of a few water-chestnuts he had in his pocket. He took them out and handed them to the child, saying, "Eat these! Don't cry!"

Tired already and attracted by the water-chestnuts, the child took them and fell to nibbling them between sobs. Only then did the woman sit down again by the table.

"Well, I saw what I went for," said her brother faintly. Hand on forehead, he looked crestfallen and exhausted.

"You did?" The woman's eyes were dilated, her heart racked by a feeling stronger than grief.

"Yes, just now."

Only fear prevented the woman from dragging him out to show her. She uttered a cry of despair.

"Sister, nowadays there is hardly a good-hearted person to be found. But the fellow I met today, he is a good sort." Her brother stuck up one thumb in admiration.

"The one you went to look for?"

"That's right. I found him, at a small teahouse. I approached him in a friendly way, saying there were these two people he probably remembered. Now they were finished, but I begged him to have a heart and show me their coffins." He knitted his brows, making the wrinkles around his eyes more conspicuous, scratched his head and pursed his lips to show that it had not been easy. "At first he paid little attention to me, just told me to forget it. So many people were finished, male and female, in long gowns or in short coats, how could he remember any two of them? Anyway, it was forbidden to see the coffins, he said. But as I had found the fellow, I would not give up. I tried again, telling him how sad their case was, a husband and wife, the woman leaving an old mother and a baby crying for Mama day in and day out in its grandmother's arms. . . . I begged him to take pity on the old and the young. . . . In fact, I did everything I could short of kowtowing to him."

The woman listened, sadly casting down her eyes to watch the child who was falling asleep. The water-chestnuts had dropped on to her lap.

"My pleading moved him," her brother continued in a proud tone, a genuine smile appearing for one brief instant on his seemingly eternally smiling face. "After all, everybody is human. Appeal to someone as a fellow man and he's bound to be touched. He stopped holding aloof, thought for a while and sighed, 'There was a couple like that. Naturally, everyone is dear to his parents. Since you made it out such a sad case, I'll show you the place. But why should a young married couple do such things instead of leading a quiet life?' I told him I didn't know. We merchants couldn't understand those scholars. Probably. . . ."

The woman heaved a sigh from the depth of her aching heart. Like her brother, she did not know the mind of her daughter and son-in-law either. But of one thing she was certain: they did not belong to the same category as those prisoners with ferocious looks and rough voices. Not the same category, yet the same fate, why? Recently she had been pondering this painful problem but she could not solve it. Nobody was there to give her an answer either.

"He told me to meet him at six o'clock at a street corner. I of course thanked him again and again and went to the appointed place ahead of time to wait for him. After six he turned up, in ordinary civilian clothes. He led me to the fields, talking to me as we walked. Ah. . . ."

He stopped, afraid of what came next. The fearful, ugly recollections refused to be brushed aside. But could his sister bear to hear? Perhaps she would faint. . . . The two of them had walked towards the open country. . . . There was no street light, no moon and no stars in the sky, the oppressive darkness weighed heavily upon them. The black shadows of distant trees and nearby buildings in the deathly silence seemed like monsters forming ranks. Occasionally two or three fireflies floated up and down as if ghosts were blinking their eyes with joy as they danced! The dogs' barking and the automobiles' honking in the distance sounded as if they came from beyond the horizon. But the faint droning in the air emanated from scores of small ephemeral insects. It had rained in the morning and the ground was muddy and slippery. He stumbled along in the dark. The other, a cigarette between his lips, said slowly, "They seemed kindly folk. They came to this place full of indignation yet they still looked kindly. Each eyed the other, then both lowered their heads, as if they wanted to say something yet could not. You know, that is the type we are afraid of. We don't mind fighting, we can raise our guns and open fire. I suppose you could, too, provided you were strong enough to carry a gun. Before you is the enemy, whether you hit him or not, you don't know what he looks like. But if someone is bound and placed before you so that you see even his hair and eyebrows clearly, then it is hard to pull the trigger! After all, he's a human being. It's especially hard with those kindly ones, who look delicate enough to fall at a breath. That day the one given the job backed away several times and then — orders are orders! — tightly knitting his brows he fired. For some reason he missed. The man was hit in the arm and he writhed in pain. The woman, seeing that, screamed like mad. To tell you frankly, I felt so bad that I turned away. Three more shots and the thing was finished. The two of them were covered with blood." As he listened, holding his breath, his legs grew numb and he hardly dared move for fear he might tread on a skeleton. So he followed closely, his chest almost brushing against the other man's back.

The woman saw that her brother was in a sort of trance, his small eyes bulging, scratching his head. She knew there must be something more. "What did he say?" she asked. "Did he see the end?"

The "end" was something which had been on her mind for days and nights. But she could not picture it to herself. Guns she had seen on the shoulders of soldiers and policemen. Was that dark glistening tube the thing which had finished her daughter and son-in-law? No, she could not believe it! She could see the young couple as clearly as in life. In what way did they deserve to be shot? She could not understand. How did their breath cease and vanish into thin air? There was something so dreamlike and unreal about this that she sometimes felt her daughter and son-in-law had not been "done for". One day the door would open to their familiar knock and the dear young pair would come in, full of life, shoulder to shoulder. But this feeling was equally dreamlike and unreal.

"He didn't see the end," her brother hastened to

reply. "He said the man was very generous, giving away his clothes. That's how he got the pair of foreign-style trousers he had on."

"A light grey pair, made last August," murmured the woman, gazing at the lamplight, screwing up her eyes.

"I couldn't see clearly because it was dark and the ground was slippery. Several times I nearly fell. If I hadn't been wearing shoes with leather soles, my feet would have been soaked. We came to a spot and he said that was the place. I looked around. There were a dozen or so big dark trees under which were some dead white coffins." The brother lowered his head, and his bald spot glimmered in the lamplight. He had not the heart to tell her his sensation when he was told to look for coffins "numbers 17 and 18". Words would fail him to describe it. He had felt that all kinds of corpses — some frowning or gritting their teeth, some with shoulders or breasts shot through, some with broken noses or limbs — were about to kick off the coffin lids and dash at him. He was almost paralysed with horror. His guide struck several matches and said, "Look here, 17 and 18." The white coffin lids showed dimly in the match light. At first they looked like creeping snakes, but when he could fix his eyes on them, they stopped moving and he saw the two Arabic numbers, 17 and 18, written with a Chinese brush. "I've come to see you, niece!" he invoked her under his breath, praying that she would not follow him. Then he quickly fled back to the path. But this was not suitable for his sister's ears. He continued, "That fellow said the numbers were written on the coffins, and he remembered clearly their numbers were 17 and 18. We searched through the coffins one by one till we found them, one straight and one lying crosswise, I recognized the numbers on the coffins."

"Seventeen! Eighteen!" cried the woman in spite of herself, pale in anguish, her eyes shining with tears. Just as on that night when someone had slipped in to break the awful news, she felt aghast, stunned and cold, her mind a blank, with a strange sinking sensation. No more would she hear their familiar knock or see the dear young pair come in, full of life, shoulder to shoulder. They were gone beyond recall. Numbers 17 and 18 — there was evidence solid as iron! Hatred blazed from her empty heart, a fierce glint came into her eyes. "I could kill them!"

Seeing his sister in such a state, the brother turned away listlessly and said with a sigh, "I saw that the coffins were passable, not too thin. . . ." Obviously just a well-intentioned lie. All of a sudden, for no reason at all, he was gripped by a wild suspicion: What if that man had remembered the wrong numbers? It was not likely. Still the suspicion kept gnawing at his heart like a poisonous serpent.

"Listen!" the woman told him, gritting her teeth and trembling violently. The sleeping baby stretched as if he were waking up but simply turned over. Smoothing his cotton shirt, she continued, "I'm past caring! I don't mind whether I die tomorrow or this instant. I'm so old and my fate is hard." She went on between sobs, "The year that your brother-in-law died your niece was only five. Bringing her up wasn't easy for me, a poor widow all on my own. When she married a handsome, educated man, I was happy. I was happy when she gave birth to a son, a lively lovable boy." Her right hand unconsciously caressed the child's head. "The two were both teachers, doing their jobs gladly, loving and respecting each other. So much the better: that made me all the happier. But now what's become of them — 17 and 18! It's as if the sky had fallen suddenly, it's terrifying! What did they do? They were my daughter and son-in-law. I have a right to know. But I was told not to ask. Even you, you told me not to ask, saying that asking would bode no good. . . . What was there to be afraid of? I was Yingchuan's mother, Zhang was my son-in-law. I'll shout through the streets and see who dares do anything to me!" Her whole being burning with anger, she had raised her voice by the end in passionate protest for no longer was she afraid. Patting the child's back, she cried, "Who says your name is Sun? Our Big Baby's surname is Zhang, Zhang! If only I could kill those fiends, to take revenge for my young daughter and son-in-law!"

Dazed and frightened by this outburst, her brother strained his ears to hear if there was any sound outside. Then he muttered feebly, "Why, why, what does it matter to say his surname is Sun? Ah, there's something I forgot." He fumbled in his pocket, remembering the piece of crumpled paper the man had handed to him in the dark on the road, saying that he had been asked to deliver it to the young couple's family, but he had slipped it in the pocket of the trousers and nearly forgotten it. As if it were something monstrous, the brother hesitated at first to accept. But he had to let it be put in his palm and, loosely crumpling it, he thrust it into his pocket like a thief, feeling more alarmed than ever.

"They've left a note!" he said, copper coins tinkling in his pocket.

"Ah, a note!" The woman straightened up in high tension. Expectation fervent as is felt by a woman running to open the door for her beloved took possession of her for a moment.

Though it was less than ten days since she was cut off from her daughter and son-in-law, she felt she had not seen their smiles or heard their voices for years. Now this note would tell her everything about them, answer all her questions, and link her heart to theirs. Naturally it meant the whole world to her in that instant.

The note was produced. It was a torn cigarette packet with several finger-prints and a burnt spot on it. On the inner side was scrawled a message in pencil.

Screwing up his small eyes and holding the note near the paraffin lamp, the brother read aloud, " 'We are dying with no regret. Don't grieve over us.' What strange talk! Dying with no regret! 'Please take good care of Big Baby, we shall live in him!' Well, they want you to take good care of Big Baby, because he's them; if Big Baby is all right, it is as good as if they were alive themselves. But this business of 'no regret' is really queer, queer!"

"Let me see it!" The woman snatched the note and fixed her eyes on it like an intent reader ready to devour a favourite book although actually she was illiterate.

It was very still in the room. The child's deep breathing was hardly audible.

Though illiterate, the woman understood that note. Not just the words, but the meaning hidden inside. For the first time she saw into the mind of her daughter and son-in-law. A new strength flowed through her whole being and her heart felt lighter. The furniture in the lamplight looked as quiet as usual. Outside she could hear nothing except distant singing accompanied by a fiddle played by an adept hand.

"Big Baby, my darling, go upstairs and sleep." She stood up and made for the stairs, her lips touching the little boy's head, the note pressed against his breast. Her tired eyes were glowing with maternal love, her steps were lighter than before. She had courageously made up her mind to take up a mother's responsibilities once again.

The child, jogged awake, without opening his eyes screwed up his little face and cried, "Mam. . . ."

1927

Translated by Zhang Su

A Declaration

THE school principal received a telegram. As his habit was, he looked first at the end where he saw "Education Bureau" and the date. Next, his eyes flashed to the beginning of the telegram and travelled slowly over the mimeographed blue characters. Ah, it was nothing serious. He breathed more freely.

The telegram merely instructed him to find out and report back immediately who had drafted the declaration issued recently by some teachers in his school.

"I saw the declaration in the papers, but I don't know who wrote it," thought the principal. "I must be the only one kept in the dark. More than fifty teachers from different schools signed the declaration. All twenty or so of my staff, except for the civics teacher, put down their names. Yet no one mentioned anything to me. They behaved as if nothing had happened even when it was published in the papers. I remarked, 'So you've made a declaration.' Mr Zhang, sitting opposite me, answered with his eyes on the wall, 'Yes, we've made a declaration. We are so fed up with this mess that we had to say something to make ourselves feel better.' The others went on reading their textbooks and making notes as if they had heard nothing. Two hurried away pretending to have remembered something. In a word, they didn't want to discuss it with me. I'm not a fool, I can see clearly. Why should I insist on talking about it?"

But the telegram in his hands said the Education Bureau was waiting for a reply. He must have a talk with his staff. He could find out by other means, of course, but that would take longer, and making inquiries among the teachers of other schools would be more awkward than among his own. There were more than twenty of them. Whom should he ask? Not those tiresome fellows who had pretended not to hear him. Perhaps Mr Zhang would do. Although he kept his eyes on the wall he had at least answered him. All the principal wanted from him was the name of the man who had drafted the declaration. He would report this to the Education Bureau. Then his task would be done.

So Mr Zhang the drawing master was summoned to the principal's office and asked to sit down. "I want to know who drafted your declaration. Can you tell me?" This was a simple enough question.

"It was Mr Wang Yongyi," Mr Zhang answered without hesitation.

"Mr Wang? You don't say!" His task was not so very simple, it seemed. The principal felt as if an invisible noose was falling over his head.

"Though he drafted it, the content was decided by us all," explained Mr Zhang, running his fingers through his long hair. "We had a meeting to discuss it. Different people raised different points. After talking them over we put our ideas together. Somebody suggested, 'Let Mr Wang Yongyi do the writing. He is the language teacher. He writes well.' Mr Wang did not refuse and brought his draft to our next meeting."

Tap, tap, tap! Drumming on the desk, the principal gazed fixedly at a couplet written by Zhang Binglin in the style of ancient inscriptions. "It doesn't look too good," he murmured, then checked himself. Regret showed on his face. After half a minute's consideration, his gaze fell on Mr Zhang. "The Education Bureau has sent a telegram asking me to find out who made the draft," he said softly.

"Find out who made the draft? What does that mean?"

"Who knows? But I can assure you that they are not going to ask him to be their secretary general because they like the style of the declaration! Mr Wang ought not to have done it. There are language teachers in the other schools too. Why should an old man like him look for trouble?"

"But there was nothing wrong in making the draft."

The principal looked at the drawing master who had been a student himself not long ago and sighed. "You are too naive, Mr Zhang! You would think differently if you had been a teacher longer. You say there is nothing wrong? This investigation proves there is something wrong — how serious, we don't know. Even if it is only a little thing, how annoying to have this happen in our school!"

"Is that so?" Bewildered as well as indignant, the drawing master was lost for words.

"Well, I have to report the truth. But I will warn Mr Wang," said the principal to himself. He rang for the usher and told him to invite Mr Wang over.

Mr Wang arrived and sat down, tugging at his beard as usual. His threadbare, shiny cuffs were stained with red ink. He flushed and showed a trace of agitation when he heard what the principal had to say, but he replied calmly, "Yes, I made the draft. You can report it to the Education Bureau. There is nothing outrageous in a declaration which merely expressed our wish to maintain our territorial integrity and sovereignty. Every Chinese, every right-minded Chinese, must cherish the same thoughts day and night."

"A few days ago, the professors from more than twenty universities in Beijing issued a simple straightforward declaration, quite similar to ours," put in Mr Zhang. "That is to say, we all feel the same."

"It may not be appropriate for middle-school teachers to say what the professors say. You ought...." Thinking better of it, the principal changed the subject. "Since you drew up the draft, Mr Wang, I cannot but report the truth. It is good to find you so understanding. But by way of extenuation we might add that you simply recorded the consensus of opinion." This was said in a tone of concern, while the principal peered sympathetically through his large glasses at the somewhat uneasy face of Mr Wang, as if he were a small boy who had misbehaved.

"All right," said Mr Wang, and withdrew with Mr Zhang from the principal's office.

That same evening, after telegraphing his reply the principal received another telegram instructing him to send express to the bureau the composition books of the two forms Mr Wang taught. "Just as I feared!" He shuddered, as if a noose were tightening round his neck. This was not an ordinary check-up on the work. It presaged calamity. If this calamity, like a shower of meteors, fell not on one individual but on the whole school, the result would not bear contemplating! The night was chilly and he turned icy cold as if he had changed suddenly into thin clothes.

Mr Wang collected the composition books from his

pupils. The principal suggested that they work all night on them.

"Do you mean we should go through all these exercise books? I don't think it's necessary," said Mr Wang who was quite sure of himself. "I've confidence in my corrections — they're carefully done."

"It's not that, Mr Wang. Just think how serious it would be, especially for you, if there were anything wrong with these compositions!"

"Anything wrong?" Mr Wang laughed. "I assure you I am most careful and our boys have always been taught to behave themselves. How could 'anything wrong' crawl like worms into these exercise books?"

"Discretion is always necessary. We must be discreet in everything." The principal felt not a little embarrassed, but he was determined to carry out his plan. "As the principal, I ask you to have some consideration for our school and look over these exercise books with me," he insisted.

There was no escape for Mr Wang. The two men sat up all night, not reaching the end of their laborious task till the early sparrows were cheeping on the eaves at the break of day. By then characters were reeling before their eyes like flies swarming round a garbage can or crows wheeling in the evening sky. Mr Wang had read each composition first, then passed it on for the principal to check. Carefully, the principal chewed over every phrase and sentence for a hidden meaning, not going on to the next expression until he was certain that this one was genuinely correct and loyal. The result of a whole night's work was the discovery that in writing an essay entitled *The Countryside in Autumn* seven boys had referred to peasants harvesting rice with "sickles". This struck the principal as improper, and he changed all seven sickles into knives.

"Nothing else wrong, is there?" said the principal, yawning and turning out the light.

Mr Wang, tired out and thoroughly annoyed, reflected that one minute would have sufficed to change seven "sickles", instead of sitting up, shivering all night. "Not after you've read them, sir," he replied indifferently.

Rousing his secretary out of his warm bed, the principal told him to wrap up the composition books and send someone with them at once to the post office. They were to be dispatched express as soon as the post office opened.

News of the two telegrams soon spread among the teachers, who felt sickened by it, as if smeared with slime and unable to wash themselves clean. This was the chief topic of conversation in the staff room.

"They want to look at the compositions he corrected just because he made the draft. Any fool can see there's something wrong with the declaration."

"What's wrong with it? It says no more than you can find in the papers. Why shouldn't we say what educational circles elsewhere and the Beijing students are saying?"

"Have you seen yesterday's newspaper? The Shanghai students have published a similar statement."

"That's just the point. How can the teachers take the part of the students? The Beijing students are being arrested and beaten. Now that we have made a declaration we should expect to be investigated."

"You mean that teachers should take the opposite stand from the students?"

"Precisely! That's how it is today. If we don't take the opposite stand, how can we teach? If we want to keep our jobs we must join the opposition. . . . I am not pulling your leg. This is the truth, whether you like it or not."

"Then we ought not to have made any declaration?"

"That's another thing. We have a dual personality, being Chinese as well as teachers. As Chinese we must speak, be there listeners or not. But a teacher, like a soldier, must obey orders. No freedom of speech for us! Has anyone ever seen a declaration issued by a platoon of soldiers in such-and-such a company?"

"All we did was sign our names. We didn't say we were teachers. That meant we were signing as Chinese."

"What if others classify us as teachers?"

"Then we're in for disciplinary action!"

Here the conversation stopped. The ticking of the clock was suddenly heard. Indefinable doubts and misgivings filled their minds.

"What if Mr Wang is the only one penalized?" asked the drawing master Mr Zhang eagerly, looking at the faces around him.

"We'll stand up for him. He has done nothing wrong."

"He only put down what everyone agreed on. All of us should be responsible if we were in the wrong."

"Why should we say we were wrong?"

"Let's get everyone who signed to go in a body to the commissioner of education and tell him that all we did was to voice our love for our country. Are we not allowed to love our country? . . ."

Just then the principal's shadow, obliquely framed

by the doorway, fell on to the floor. The ticking of the clock was heard once more.

Two days later the third telegram arrived from the Education Bureau. The principal opened it with trembling fingers. A long sigh of relief escaped him, the noose round his neck seemed to loosen.

The telegram read: Nothing improper was found in Wang Yongyi's composition books. Dismiss him immediately. No reprimand.

The principal showed Mr Wang the telegram to save himself the trouble of talking. With a sinking heart Mr Wang saw in his mind's eye his homeless compatriots in the northeast, refugees suffering hunger and cold in the Yellow and Yangzi River Valleys, the unemployed in the big cities . . . and among these scenes of desolation he glimpsed himself. Coming out of this daze, he quietly took his luggage and left the school without once turning his head. He took a rickshaw to the station which was crammed with passengers waiting for various trains. They were saying that no trains were likely to come because the Shanghai students were on strike. Yet still they waited. From time to time they went to the edge of the platform, braving the cutting wind, to look at the motionless signal. Mr Wang joined these passengers and, tugging at his beard, waited disconsolately with them.

When news of Mr Wang's departure reached the staff room, the disgust in each mind was tempered by the dubious speculation: "Suppose I'd been the one to draft that declaration!"

Translated by Yu Fanqin

Xu Dishan

XU Dishan (1893-1941) was born in Taiwan Province. He entered Yanjing University in 1917 and was active in the 1919 New Culture Movement. Along with the celebrated writer Mao Dun, he was one of the founders of the Literature Research Society. After graduating in 1922, he went abroad to study, first in the United States and then in Britain. Following his return in 1927, he became a lecturer at Beijing University. He died of illness in Hong Kong in 1941.

His first work was published in 1921 and his next twenty years were spent writing mainly about young people and their struggles against the old order. His compelling, romantic stories exhibit a deep sympathy for the plight of ordinary people and his innovative style has always been popular with the general public. "Big Sister Liu" is one of his representative works.

Blooms on a Dried Poplar

SECONDS, minutes, years
  Are mechanical calcu'ations of Time.
Grey hair, wrinkles
  Are Time's marks upon us.
But who has ever seen a grey-haired heart,
  A heart with wrinkles?

The heart never ceases to flower.
  Though lodged in an aged and ailing body,
It never loses its shining glory.
  Who says ancient poplar blossoms cannot last?

"The body is but earth," they say,
  Yes, earth to nurture the blossoms of our hearts.
As humble soil can bring forth lovely flowers,
  So can old bodies bear long-living heart-fruit.

Everyone in the little fishing village was used to life on the sea. Even the women sometimes went fishing with their menfolk and lived for days in the floating, tossing craft. But some of the women, though they were quite willing to share their husbands' dangerous lives, had no chance to do so, for their men were far from home. After a long, long absence, a man might return with the swallows, only to depart again a few months later. The lucky swallows always flew in pairs, but the man who left his native village to travel in distant places, whether setting out or coming back, except for his baggage was very much alone.

Deep in the shade of a banian tree in a narrow lane lived a family named Jin. Only an old woman and her daughter-in-law were at home. The son was many miles away, and there had been no news of him for several years. Time, flowing on tirelessly, had steeped the hearts of the old woman and her daughter-in-law in anxiety and melancholy. Like a cliff beside a stream, they were washed bare of their bloom and bedecked with dirty flotsam brought down from the stream's upper reaches. Many were the vain hopes and useless inquiries these two mournful women had expended on their man.

Because the village was sparsely populated and everyone's life there was pretty much the same, the blind fortune-teller seldom called. Whenever the old lady heard the sound of his gong, she hurried out to wait for him and ask him to predict the luck of her distant son. She was even more concerned about this than her daughter-in-law, for a reason that she alone knew. The blind man always foretold the same thing — he saw nothing but peace and good fortune for the son. What he did not know was when the son would attain them.

One day, the soft sound of the gong again announced the visit of Master Blind Man. As usual, the old lady was waiting for him at her door. "Do you want me to tell the fortune of the traveller today?" he asked her.

"Every day that he's away from home, I'm afraid I must trouble you. But I'm beginning to doubt your predictions. All these years you've been saying that we'll be able to be together again. But we haven't even had the sign of a letter from him. I think you'd better turn your gong over to me and take up another trade," she said jestingly. "You're a very unreliable fortune-teller!"

Master Blind Man joined in her laugh. "You're teasing me. But that's the way your son's fortune is — for the good, you'll have to wait; for the bad. . ."

"What about the bad?"

"You can learn the bad part immediately. For the good, there's nothing to do but wait. Even if you took my little gong and smashed it, you couldn't make his good fortune come a minute sooner. But if you want to see him, you don't have to wait till then. All you have to do is go to him. You've been to his place several times, haven't you?"

"Of course I can see him if I go there. Do I need you to tell me that!"

"I'm only reminding you because you're so impatient. I think the best thing would be for you to go. I won't tell his fortune today. If you can't find him when you get there, it still won't be too late for you to take my little gong away when you come back. I'll admit that I'm not psychic and not fit to be a fortune-teller."

Although Master Blind Man's reply was something of an evasion, it reminded the old lady of her desire to seek her son.

"Very well," she said. "Unless there's news from him in another month or so, I definitely will go. But just you wait. Beware that I don't smash your little gong if I can't find him."

"It won't come to that, it won't come to that," Master Blind Man murmured. Holding his bamboo staff, he followed the path along the edge of the pool. The sound of his gong gradually drifted beyond the shade of the large banian.

One month, two months, flew quickly by, and still no news from the son. Setting out with her daughter-in-law, the old lady took to the road. Their trials and hardships *en route* I don't have to tell you — they had more than their share. The old lady had made this trip two or three times before, and she knew the way well. At last she again recognized the familiar gate and walls, only this time they appeared more resplendent than before. "You see, your son has become rich!" they seemed to say.

She had long suspected that her son had prospered and forgotten her. Now, coming in sight of this pleasant view, she said reproachfully to her daughter-in-law:

"You're always defending him. Today you can see for yourself."

The gate was closed but not barred. Pushing it open, the old lady stepped into the compound.

"Maybe someone else lives here," suggested the daughter-in-law. "Maybe this isn't the right place."

The old lady took the younger woman abruptly by the hand and pulled her along. "How could it be wrong?" she demanded. "I've been here lots of times." The daughter-in-law had nothing more to say, and she followed the old lady in.

Before them lay a small garden. Pretty flowers postured and gestured to them seductively. On each side of the path from the main gate to the house was a row of evenly trimmed shrubs called "Fickle Singsong Girls". Daughter-in-law had never seen this kind of live, growing railing before, and she brushed her hand back and forth over the top of it as she walked.

"The young wretch knows how to enjoy himself alright," the old lady muttered. "This courtyard used to be a field of rubble and now look at it. He's lavished plenty of money on himself, without a thought for his old mother who spent her every penny to pay for his education. Of course he couldn't save anything while he was in school those ten or twelve years. But now that he's able to put something aside, he can only think of spending it on himself!"

By then the women had reached the house. They could see a painting of some flowers hanging on the wall inside, and they recognized it as a picture the son had taken from home. Reassured that they had come to the right place, they sat down in the anteroom. The old lady kept peering toward the interior of the house, but there was no sign of her son.

"Is anyone at home?" she called out finally, in some annoyance. "I've been waiting here a long time. Why hasn't there been even half a shadow of a person come out to greet me?"

This wave of sound brought forth a young servant. "Who do you wish to see?" he inquired.

"Who do I wish to see!" the old lady retorted angrily. "Are you pretending you don't recognize me? Hurry and ask your master to come out."

The old lady obviously was no one to be trifled with when she was aroused. "Madam is some close relative of his excellency, then?" the servant asked respectfully.

"'Excellency' indeed! The nerve of him — putting on airs before his own mother!"

This came as a surprise to the young servant, for his

master's mother was living right upstairs, and now here was another one.

"But madam surely can't be my Master Xiao's —"

"Master Xiao? My son is Master Jin."

"Perhaps madam has come to the wrong gate. My master's name is Xiao, not Jin." The exchange grew livelier, with both sides becoming more and more confused, until the noise brought out another servant. He recognized the old lady.

"Why, how are you, madam?" he cried. He was the son's cook.

"So you're still here, Song," the old lady said to him. "This hateful little flunkey insists his master's name is not Jin. Don't tell me my son has changed his name?"

"Doesn't madam know?" asked the cook. "The young master hasn't been living here since the beginning of last year. He sold all these things to the new owner. I'm not working for him any more either. The owner of this place is named Xiao."

It seemed that Chengren, the son, had been engaged in business and doing fairly well. But times had changed, and soon he was reduced to living from hand to mouth. Sometimes two or three days went by with no smoke rising from his kitchen stove. Although he obviously couldn't go on like that, he was ashamed to tell his family. Finally, he sold the house and furniture for whatever he could get.

The old lady asked for his present address. "I haven't seen the young master for more than a year. I really don't know where he is now," said the cook. "I remember him saying he wanted to leave this town."

The cook saw them to the gate and gave them directions to the main street. They walked aimlessly for a while. "Now where are we going?" said the daughter-in-law in a tearful voice. The over-sensitive old lady thought she was ridiculing her. "We'll just follow our noses!" she snapped. Daughter-in-law dared say no more. She continued to support the old lady down the street in silence.

Having failed to find their relative and being unfamiliar with the town, the two country women, each carrying a small bundle, could only wander from street to street. When the old lady had walked almost to the point of exhaustion, she turned to her daughter-in-law and said:

"We had better find a place to put up for the night. But whether there is an inn around here. . . . I have no idea."

"Then what shall we do?"

They had stopped on a street corner to talk things over. At that moment, a motor-cycle drove slowly by. Because it had sounded its horn, they glanced in its direction while stepping to the side of the road. Everything would have been alright if the old lady hadn't noticed the rider, but when she saw him, she gazed at him in stupefaction, and the daughter-in-law did the same. Before they had a chance to cry out, the vehicle was already far down the street.

"Riding that motor-cycle — wasn't that your husband, Chengren? How could you be so slow-witted? Why didn't you call to him to stop?"

"Oh, it was such a shock! Besides, how could I just call out like that on a public street?"

"So you wouldn't call! Well, now we'll see where you sleep tonight."

The passing motor-cycle had produced a different

reaction in each of the women. The mother thought the son had become rich and no longer cared about her; that he had told the cook to fool her with stories of his poverty. The wife thought the husband had found himself a pretty new wife in town and couldn't be bothered with a simple country woman any more. She bemoaned this unlucky destiny which Fate had bestowed upon her.

But a busy street corner was no place for idle speculation. In any event, the women had to find somewhere to stay. The sun was already low in the west. If they delayed much longer, they'd have to spend the night in the open. While they were trying to sort out their thoughts, a policeman, twirling a big black club, came ambling down the street, whistling a vulgar ditty. Observing these odd-looking women, he walked over to question them. When they told him they were looking for lodging, he pointed to a building a distance off and said, "That place over there is an inn." Too tired to walk any farther, they went in the direction indicated.

The women assumed that the streets of a big town were as simple as those in their little village, that everyone took the same route every day. And so the next morning, before she had even washed her face or combed her hair, the old lady hurried to the corner where she had seen the motor-cycle the previous day. She had some difficulty in finding the place, for she didn't know the town. She stood on the corner for hours, and though many motor-cycles passed, none of them was ridden by her son. Finally, the policeman again came up and questioned her. She replied excitedly, with many vigorous gestures, but the policeman couldn't make head or tail of what she was saying. He had to ask her to move on and not block the busy intersection. Muttering under her breath, the old lady slowly returned to the inn.

The daughter-in-law had been sitting in the doorway for a long time, eagerly awaiting good news from the old lady. She remained at the gate all day, her eyes never leaving the street. When she saw the old lady coming back alone, her eyes glazed. Such disappointments are not unusual. We meet them often in our daily life.

The old lady came in the door and sat down, breathing hard. For several minutes she did not speak, but only shook her head. "Come what may, I must find him," she said after a long silence. "How hateful that a man should forget his family when he prospers. I'll get hold of him and make him give an account of himself if it's the last thing I do."

Although the daughter-in-law was feeling upset, she suppressed her own emotions and made an effort to comfort the old lady. "We're sure to find him sooner or later," she said. "But I don't think we can do it by standing on the street corner every day. Wouldn't it be better to hire someone to make a search for him?"

"You hire someone, if you're so rich!" retorted the old lady angrily. After a pause she said, "I know that street now; tomorrow I'm going to wait there again. It was dusk when I saw him the other day. If I go in the afternoon the next time, I'll be able to find him."

"You ought to let me go," the daughter-in-law urged. "I'm stronger and can stand a longer time."

The old lady shook her head. "No. People's hearts here are very wicked. The less a young woman goes out alone the better."

"You scolded me that day for not calling the motor-cycle to stop," the daughter-in-law said in a low voice. She was very disappointed. "Now you won't even let me go out."

The old lady's face hardened. "Talking back to me again, and at a time like this."

The daughter-in-law was afraid to say any more.

They talked of various possible methods to seek the missing son. But the old lady was very stubborn. She insisted on waiting on the same street corner every day.

And so each day she stood on the corner, but the motor-cycle she had seen before never came her way. A month quickly passed. They were running out of money and would soon have to leave the inn. The old lady decided to return home first and then make further plans. The daughter-in-law didn't want to leave immediately, but knowing the old lady's stubborn disposition, she could only swallow the protest that was on the tip of her tongue.

When they went on board, they were given a small cabin near the side of the ship. Not long after they set sail, a strong wind began dashing spray against their cabin window. The ship rolled and tossed until they were dizzy. The second night at sea, they were wrenched from their dreams by a loud sudden crash that was followed by terrifying cries. The daughter-in-law leaped from her bunk and ripped open the cabin door. She could see passengers dashing madly about the deck like mice in a cage. Hastily returning to the cabin, she cried to the old lady:

"We must get outside, quickly!"

The two women rushed out of the cabin, tightly

holding hands. Frightened passengers crowded and pushed one another on the wet, slippery deck. Because of the gale and the angry waves, many of them lost their footing and rolled into the sea. The two women stumbled, and the old lady let go of her daughter-in-law's hand to steady herself. In the next instant the younger woman was swept away in the milling crowd. A young man helped the old lady up and she threw her arms around a mast. Not daring to release her grip, she cried aloud for her daughter-in-law. But not even thunder or the roaring of a lion could have been heard above that raging storm.

At dawn the stricken vessel was still afloat. It had run aground on a reef, and its entire stern was under water. Because of their panic-stricken jostling, people crowded on the forward deck were falling off and sinking into the sea much faster than the ship itself. The old lady wandered about, distractedly seeking her daughter-in-law. There's no telling how many were lost the night before; the daughter-in-law was not the only one. Although the old lady wept bitterly, no one tried to comfort her. Each was bewailing his own personal tragedy, and heart-broken weeping was common enough.

For several days the ship remained on the reef. The storm gradually abated, and a hope sprang up in the survivors that another ship might pass and save them. Sometimes hopes are fulfilled. When the passengers saw a column of black smoke coming nearer from the horizon, the old lady forgot her loss and joined her voice to their pleading shouts.

It was after she and the others were taken aboard the rescue ship that she again thought of her daughter-in-law. Simple people always hark back to an event after the time of stress has passed. She knew that the ship was bearing her back to the port she had just left, a place she didn't want to go to, and this upset her still more. She had left there a few days before because she had no alternative, and now she was being returned to the same place. The old lady couldn't restrain her tears.

She was the only unhappy person on board, and several of the passengers came to comfort her. An old gentleman named Mr Zhu was particularly kind. On hearing the old lady's story, he felt very sorry for her and invited her to stay at his home after they landed; there she would be able to rest and make inquiries about her son.

Old folks are the only real selfless philanthropists. Young people perform good deeds mostly to please themselves, or to earn fame and respect in society. Mr Zhu was quite sincere in bringing the old lady home and introducing her to his wife, to whom he explained the situation. The wife, also a very generous person, hurried to prepare a room for their guest, and saw to it that the old lady had everything she needed in the way of food and other necessities.

Mr Zhu did his utmost to help find the son, but with no success. Though the old lady found it rather embarrassing to stay so long in another person's home, she had no way of returning to her own village. She was really too old to look after herself. Before, her daughter-in-law had taken care of her, but now the daughter-in-law was gone. The mists in the evening of life were indeed frightening, painful. In her youth she had been aggressive, positive, unwilling to rely on anyone. But now she was old. Besides, her aged host and hostess were happy to have her and did everything to make her forget her troubles.

People all have many hidden thoughts, especially old folks. Although the old lady didn't like the big town, her heart was always there. For her the most important thing in life was to go to the town and see her son's face again. Why this was so urgent her daughter-in-law didn't know — neither did her son. For this was the old lady's most closely guarded secret. Wanderers cannot be satisfied with their life away from home, and the old lady's secret coiled around her heart like a poisonous snake. She had the heart of a young woman. She wasn't at all like an old lady reaching the end of her days. The serpentine secret bit deeply into her mind.

Mr Zhu, whose love extended to all passers-by, of course bought her medicine. But there is no medicine which can ease a sickness of the mind. He could only beg her to tell what was troubling her, so that he might find some way to help. But there are some things that are not easy for a woman to say, and she wasn't sure that speaking would do any good. In the end she said nothing.

The days slipped by. Mr Zhu was a worrier over others' worries, and he grew more upset with each passing day. His wife, an intelligent woman, reminded him:

"Didn't you say she's from the village of Canghai? My sister's husband is also from Canghai, and his name is Jin too. Maybe they're related. Why not ask him about her son?"

"According to your brother-in-law, Canghai is full of people named Jin, and many of them travel to all parts of the land. They may not be close relatives. If they're distant relatives what good will it do? I've asked Mrs Jin if she knows Sijing, and she says there was never anybody by that name in her village. Sijing left there over forty years ago and has never gone back. He might not recall her anyhow."

"There's nothing strange about her not remembering his name. Country boys always go by some nickname or other, but they adopt a proper name if they leave their native village. How could you expect her to remember him? It's much easier for a man to recall a girl's name, which doesn't change. Since Canghai is a small place, he's sure to know her. She's over sixty now. That means she was about twenty-five or six when Sijing came here. Right? I still think you'd better ask him."

After talking the matter over, it was decided that Mr Zhu would call on his brother-in-law, Sijing. Although the two were related by marriage, they seldom met. Sijing's wife, younger sister of Mr Zhu's wife, had died many years before. She left only one child, a son named Lisheng. Because there were no women in Sijing's house, except for the traditional exchange of gifts at New Year's time, there was little visiting between the two families. Sijing was a very affable fellow with a fine sense of humour. After his wife died, he turned all of his affairs over to his young son and retired to a country retreat outside the town. He called the place "Fairy Villa of the Little Waves". He had been living there for the past fifteen years. Men of his sort, who build up their families with their own hands, as a rule always want to keep climbing higher.

He was one of the few who knew how to relax and enjoy life.

The "Fairy Villa of the Little Waves" was hidden in a dense grove of bamboos which was surrounded by a meandering stream. It was virtually a small island, and you had to cross a little bridge to reach it. Mr Zhu, entering the bamboo grove after walking across the bridge, came upon three or four tame deer. Evidently hoping to be fed, they trotted toward him. The grove was full of the insects of late autumn. Their droning blended with the sound of the drumming hoofs of the deer. Mr Zhu was an infrequent visitor and, to him, seeing the lovely grove was like seeing its master. He wandered about the leafy glade for some time.

Sijing's country house was no glittering tower of gold and jade, but a simple thatched-roof cottage with only a few rooms. Instead of rare treasures it was stocked with a small number of well-thumbed books and some old painting scrolls. As the old gentleman approached the house, the cheerful Sijing came smilingly out to greet him.

"It's been a long time, brother-in-law!" cried the host. "There must be something special to make you come all the way from town and honour me with a visit."

"Naturally, 'One doesn't disturb an important personage without real cause,' " said Mr Zhu with a smile. "There's something I have to ask you about. But you haven't been back there for so many years, perhaps you don't know."

"Is it something to do with my native village?"

"Yes. I haven't told you yet: This summer when I

was coming back from Hong Kong, my ship rescued several dozen people from the sea."

"I heard about that. My son Lisheng told me. I instructed him to call on you and inquire after your health."

Mr Zhu was surprised. "Oh? But he never came to see me."

"He still hasn't called? The longer that boy studies the less propriety he seems to understand!"

"No, don't blame him. He's very busy. What I want to talk to you about is this: On the boat I brought back a woman with me —"

The humorous Sijing laughed gaily. "Who would have believed that an old gentleman like you would have a heart so young?"

Mr Zhu smiled. "You haven't let me finish. The woman is over sixty. She came here recently to look for her son. Unfortunately she couldn't find him and started to return home with her daughter-in-law. During the voyage the ship was wrecked by a storm and the daughter-in-law was lost. Because she was all alone, I brought her home to live with us temporarily. She says she's from Canghai. My wife and I have been very worried about her these past few months. If she goes home, there's no one to look after her. But staying here and not being able to find her son has made her ill with anxiety. When I ask her about her family affairs, she answers in a very confused manner. So I've come to ask for your assistance."

"I was never an official of Canghai. I may not necessarily know her. Still, someone about sixty — I ought to know quite a few of that age. What's her name?"

"Her name is Yungu."

Sijing's interest mounted. "Is she the Yungu who married Riteng? I knew a Sister Riteng once. Her own name was Yungu. But if her son came here I certainly would have known it."

"She hasn't said whether she was known as Sister Riteng. But her son's name is Chengren. She told me so herself."

"Say, that's right. Sister Riteng did have a son of that name. I'd better go and see her. Then we can be sure."

Sijing was even more eager than Mr Zhu. In less than ten minutes he was ready and hastening the old gentleman back to the town.

As they were entering the door, Mr Zhu said to him, "You wait in the study. Let me tell her first."

Mr Zhu hurried to the guest's room where he found his wife seated on the edge of the bed, keeping the ailing Yungu company.

"Brother-in-law is here," he said to his wife. "It's a remarkable coincidence. He says he knows her." To Yungu he said, "You say you don't remember anyone called Sijing, but he remembers you alright. He's already come. I'll bring him in to see you in a minute."

The old lady still maintained that she didn't know him. When he came in the door and asked her, "Aren't you Sister Riteng?" she was startled. She stared at this old man with the grey hair and grey eyebrows for a long time.

"You're not Brother Rihui?" she asked finally.

"Of course I am!" Sijing's grey brows danced delightedly.

Yungu seemed to be suddenly restored to health. She sat up and gazed long at the old man standing before her. "Ah, you've aged so," she said, shaking her head.

"Me? Old?" Sijing replied with a laugh. "I still expect to live another thirty years. But I never thought I'd see you again in this world!"

Tears ran down Yungu's old cheeks. "Nor I," she said. "After you left, you never wrote. If I had known you were here, Chengren wouldn't be lost today."

Mr Zhu and his wife looked at each other in bewilderment. They hadn't the faintest idea what this was all about. Sijing sat down.

"You two must be quite surprised. Let me explain. She and I are relatives. We're both well along in years now; there's no harm in telling something that happened in our youth. All my life I never loved and respected any woman more than Yungu. Her husband and I were clan brothers. He was my elder, but she's five years younger than I. Less than a year after her marriage, her husband died. Shortly afterwards, she gave birth to a son. I knew her before she was married. We were always together. I went to see her often after her marriage too." Sijing paused a moment, then went on:

"We lived at opposite ends of a small lane. Whenever I went out I had to pass her door. After she lost her husband, she became rather high-strung, often getting very angry over trifles, and I stayed away from her. But the world is full of coincidences. When her son Chengren grew to be five or six, he began to look the very image of me."

"Then when she thought she saw him here," Mr Zhu interrupted, "it must have been your boy Lisheng who went by on the motor-cycle."

"Oh, you've seen Lisheng?" Sijing asked Yungu. "He doesn't know you. Even if he had seen you, he wouldn't have known who you are." Turning to Mr Zhu, he continued, "I've told you that the people in my village were very ignorant, and they loved to gossip. I was the only son of a declining family. There were many in the clan who were always looking for a chance to take advantage of me. A couple of rascals used Chengren's resemblance to me as a means for blackmail. They threatened to 'expose' me before the magistrate for getting gay with a widow, for ruining her faithfulness to her husband's memory. For the sake of us both, I took a bit of money with me and ran away to this place. Actually I had never been a merchant. It was just luck that I was able to set up in business here. Anyhow I never went back. I was afraid of being blackmailed again."

Sijing looked at Yungu. "Since you've come, there's no point in your going back. I'll prepare a place for you to live, then I'll think of some way to find Chengren."

He didn't talk much longer, for he wanted to let Yungu get some rest. Following Mr Zhu out of the room, he told the old gentleman he would move her to his country retreat. Since the two were relatives in the same clan, Mr Zhu of course couldn't insist on her remaining. Yungu was very happy, but she was still sick in bed and couldn't travel immediately, so she continued living with the Zhus for the time being.

For the bed-ridden old lady, this sudden meeting with the lover of whom she often thought but never could speak, the man she had so longed for in her youth, was the best possible medicine. The frown was erased from her brow. No one knew how happy she was. Only the animation of her face gave some hint of her feelings.

Lying in bed, she mentally turned back through her history to its most interesting page.

She remembered the period after her husband died. She was only twenty. Although she had a child, it was difficult for her to remain faithful to her husband's memory, especially since there was another man who was always in her thoughts. She saw him every day. A widow's existence was becoming increasingly harder to bear.

Operas were performed every year in the courtyard of the temple in the neighbouring village, and everyone took this opportunity to relax a bit. When the show started, men and women from miles around gathered before the temple's outdoor platform. They watched the performances from noon until dawn the following day. One night, Yungu also sat among the audience. But she tired of the play before midnight and returned home, depressed and irritable.

She found the baby sleeping peacefully. The room was hot and, as was her custom, she took a little stool and sat outside the door to get some fresh air. The lane was deserted. Her only company was the reflection of the moon in the nearby pond. Voices and the clash of cymbals occasionally drifting over from the neighbouring village where the opera was being staged seemed to add to her misery. Facing the small pond, she wept silently.

The echo of footsteps in the lane made her turn her head. A man was approaching, smoking a pipe. She recognized Rihui, and at once her heart was eased. Rihui was then a refined, bookish student. He lived near the end of the village and he had to pass down this lane every day. As he came nearer, he saw Yungu sitting alone, moonlight glistening on the two streams of tears that ran down her cheeks. Weeping widows are difficult to console. He sucked noisily on his pipe and stopped beside her.

"Not asleep yet? Now what's troubling you?"

She made no answer, but grasped his hand in hers. The inexperienced Rihui was beside himself with embarrassment. After a long silence he said:

"Does holding my hand help you not to cry?"

"Tonight, I'm not going to let you go."

Rihui was very frightened. His pulse quickened; his pipe dropped to the ground. He spoke very seriously:

"Perhaps the opera tonight has made you unhappy. It's not that I don't feel the same as you. But I'm the only scholar in the village. If I do anything even three-tenths out of the way, I'm criticized for the other seven-tenths as well. When you married my clan brother that made us relatives, and men and women relatives are not supposed to be intimate with each other. What's more, the clan has high hopes that you'll remain a chaste widow the rest of your life. So even though my heart is burning with desire for you, I can't let myself assuage the anguish with the bit of cool water you're offering me tonight. You know that if my parents had been alive to speak for me, you would have been my bride long ago and we wouldn't be suffering now. But don't fret; I'm sure to find a way to comfort you. I'm not afraid of ruining your reputation, or being accused of incest.* We grew up together. Our love is more im-

* In feudal China a love affair with a relative by marriage was considered equally incestuous as an affair with a blood relative.

portant than all those other things. I'm only worried about your son. He's still a baby, and if a storm should break over our heads, wouldn't that be harming him? Why don't we wait another few years? After I've come up in the world a bit, then —"

The baby began to cry, and Yungu had to let go of Rihui's hand to hurry into the house. When she came out again, Rihui was gone. As she stared down the lane into the darkness, someone's arms suddenly embraced her from behind. Twisting her head, she saw Stinking Dog, a village rascal.

"What are you trying to do, Stinking Dog?"

"I heard everything you two said. You wanted him to spend the night. Why not me?"

Yungu was frantic. She wanted to cry out.

"If you scream I'll drag Rihui back here and confront him," Stinking Dog warned. "I'll accuse him before the clan council. I'll tell the prefect not to guarantee him when he wants to sit for his official examination. He'll never get to be a *xiu cai*." As he spoke, he ran his hands boldly over Yungu's bosom.

Unable to call for help, she tried soft talk as a last resort. "You can't get what you want unless I agree. You can hold me from now until tomorrow, but unless I'm willing, what good will it do? But if you let me go a minute, I'll move the baby into the next room —"

Stinking Dog eagerly released her before she had even finished her sentence. "And then you'll be willing," he said fawningly.

Yungu glanced at him coyly, then ran into the house and grabbed the door. Seeing that she was getting away, Stinking Dog thrust a foot over the threshold. Yungu closed the door hard, and put her whole weight against it, pinning Stinking Dog's foot in a painful vice. Howling with agony, he begged for forgiveness.

"So you thought you could get something cheap, Stinking Dog, you scabby toad. The scabby toad wants to eat the flesh of the high flying swan, does he? Stinking fool, how can he leave the mud if he has no wings? Come on in — if you can! Shameless, stinking monster. You stink worse than any real dead stinking dog."

Outside, pleas for mercy; inside, curses and unrelenting anger. Only when the young woman's strength was nearly at its end did she finally let him go.

That night taught her a lesson. Thereafter she never sat alone on the doorstep to enjoy the evening breezes. Stinking Dog, unable to eat the flesh of the "high flying swan", waited for a chance for revenge.

A few years passed. Chengren was now nearly five. He looked remarkably like Rihui. The village gossips — Stinking Dog among them no doubt — insisted that the child's parentage was doubtful. Rihui was very face-conscious. A thousand evil tongues put the blame on him, besmirching his good name. It was more than he could bear.

One night there was a heavy thunderstorm. Frightened, Yungu had closed her door and windows tight, and lay down on the bed beside her child. In the early hours of the morning, she heard a light tapping on the little window facing the lane. Yungu was too afraid to ask who was there, but then someone called her name and she recognized that refined and agitated voice. She opened the window.

"It's you. I couldn't imagine who it was! Wait a minute. I'll light a lamp and open the door."

"No, it's too late at night. I won't come in. We

don't need a lamp either. I'll just stand here and tell you something. I'm leaving tomorrow, first thing in the morning." There was a flash of lightning, and Yungu could see that his face and clothing were soaking wet. Before she had a chance to see whether those were tears or raindrops on his cheeks, Rihui continued, "For your sake, I can't stay in this village any longer. Anyhow, here I can have no hope for my future."

As the woman looked at him, he drew a title-deed from his sleeve and handed it to her through the window. "This is all I can give you now. The deed says that I've sold my land to Chengren. I've already spoken to the county Land Registrar about it. It's all right. When Chengren grows up you can sell it for his tuition."

After giving her the deed he started to withdraw his hand. But it wasn't the deed she wanted; it was the hand she hastily grasped. The deed fell to the floor, but the woman seemed to be unaware of it. She kept caressing Rihui's hand, not saying a word.

"Have you forgotten that I'm standing out here in the rain in the middle of the night? Let me go back. If someone should see us, it wouldn't be good."

The woman wouldn't release him. After a long time, she said, "I was going to ask you something, but I've forgotten. . . . Oh, that's right, you haven't told me where you're going."

"I can't really. I have to make some inquiries in Xiamen first, then I'll be able to decide. I used to think of going to Nagasaki or Shanghai, but lately I've been wondering about Singapore. So I'm not sure, yet."

"When I let go your hand it will be like letting go

the string of a kite," the woman said in a stricken voice. "I won't know where to look for you again."

She released his hand, and the man stood numbly. He seemed to want to say something more. The woman gazed at him in silence. Rain pelted the man standing outside; lightning startled the widow within. Yet neither of them noticed. In the darkness, the woman heard him say:

"When Chengren is older, you must send him to school. Bring him up well, and some day he'll bring honours to you."

Without waiting for her reply, he opened his battered umbrella and walked away.

More than forty years they had separated, with never a letter from him. The woman felt as if she had refound a lost treasure. No message or news, no son or daughter-in-law, could have moved her as this reunion did. Her happiness soon cured her illness.

When Yungu was able to leave her bed, Rihui, or Sijing, as he was now called, came for her in a car and brought her to his country retreat. In the bamboo grove of droning insects and pattering deer hoofs the old couple at last began the life they had always longed for. Yungu upbraided Sijing for never having sent her any word.

"I didn't want to cut myself off from you," he replied. "But if I told you where I was then, it might not have been to our benefit. I thought to myself — you had Chengren; there was sure to be a lot of gossip after I left. If I went back to see you, I knew you wouldn't let me go so easily again the next time. If I insisted on staying with you, I'd be brought up on charges. Leaving you again — that would be unthinkable.

"After I took a wife, I forgot you. I didn't really forget you, but since thinking of you made me miserable, I learned to pretend that you didn't exist. And because I was married, I all the more didn't dare go back to see you."

As Sijing was talking he saw his son Lisheng stop his motor-cycle on the edge of the grove. "The 'Chengren' you saw that day is here," he said to Yungu.

Lisheng entered. Sijing told him to greet Yungu as "mother". To the old lady he said, "Doesn't he look like your Chengren?"

"Yes, very much. No wonder I mistook him. But looking at him closely, I can see that he's much younger."

"Naturally. Chengren is more than ten years older. Lisheng is only thirty-four."

At the mention of her son, Yungu again felt distressed and her eyes wandered vacantly. Sijing consoled her: "Anyhow, my son is yours. Sooner or later Chengren will be found. We'll give the job to Lisheng. Let's spend our old age in carefree pleasure."

Hearing this, Mr Zhu, who was present, laughed heartily. " 'Who would have believed that an old gentleman like you would have a heart so young?' Who's the old man now?"

Sijing smiled. "I'm her brother-in-law. It's quite right that I should look after my widowed sister-in-law. Would you have me send her to a home for the aged?"

The indulgent talk of these elderly people embarrassed Lisheng. He excused himself, saying that he wanted to order a celebration banquet sent out from town. Mounting his motor-cycle, he rode off.

The chime clock on the wall struck the hour, and its musical clang reminded Yungu of the gong of the blind fortune-teller back in Canghai. "Now you've found everything," she seemed to hear him say. "You ought to pay double for my prediction about the traveller. And I don't suppose you dare say anything about breaking my little gong any more!"

Of course the banquet that night was a very special one.

Translated by Sidney Shapiro

Director Fei's Reception Room

EVERYTHING in Director Fei's reception room testifies to his being a warm-hearted philanthropist with many good works to his credit. From the rafters hang two placards inscribed "Zealous for the Public Interest" and "Sharing Benefits with All Men". The "presidential seal of honour" with which they are stamped makes it clear that these were given him by the first and second presidents of the republic. Between them hangs the motto "Hall for Appreciating Poetry and Discussing Ceremony" written, they say, by the venerable Mr Kang Youwei* in return for several hundred silver dollars. It was to get the maximum of Mr Kang's calligraphy that the director gave this room such a long name. The four walls are graced with certificates of merit, scrolls of maxims, the painting *Blessings Bestowed by Heaven* and a variety of handsome mirrors. Indeed the room seems full of mirrors, the largest of which, a western looking-glass, hangs opposite the window by the street. All the furniture is of the finest mahogany. Set out on the tables are genuine and fake antiques as well as clocks of all kinds from East and West. The bookcase in one corner, in addition to *The Classic of Filial Piety, Maxims for Regulating the*

* 1858-1927. A bourgeois reformist who advocated constitutional monarchy; after the 1911 Revolution led by Dr Sun Yat-sen, he became a reactionary monarchist.

Family, the *Neo-Confucian Compendium** and some newspapers, holds albums of subscribers' names and albums of tributes penned by celebrities.

A manservant ushers in a visitor with a moustache, wearing a western-style suit.

"Please take a seat, sir," he says. "The director will soon be here."

As the guest sits down the servant slips out to tell a maid:

"Go and let the master know a Mr Huang has called."

A woman's voice can be faintly heard:

"Cuihua, the master's with the fifth mistress."

This brief exchange informs us that Director Fei is a polygamist with at least five wives, not to mention maidservants. Not that this is in any way reprehensible. In fact, in this civilized Confucian country, at a time when most notables and government officials advocate the "old morality", a few extra concubines add tone to your family and aid social intercourse. If even those in humble circumstances are laughed at for having only a single wife, how much worse would be the case of Director Fei who is always donating money to charities!

Fifteen minutes pass and the visitor is surveying his surroundings when in walks his host adjusting his long gown. Clasping his hands in greeting, he exclaims:

"Excuse me for keeping you waiting."

Mr Huang of course makes haste to return his greeting and protests, "This is an honour."

After the usual exchange of courtesies the visitor broaches the reason for this intrusion.

---

* All these are works advocating feudal morality.

"I have set up a charity works for women in my home town. And having heard so much praise of the one you run, sir, I have to ask permission to see over this admirable institution. There must be much in it that my humble establishment should emulate."

The director is of a scholarly build with a delicate frame in keeping. His mottled, discoloured teeth are evidence of his wealth. For nothing but several pipes of opium daily could turn teeth so black and yellow. Very modestly he outlines to the visitor his aim in setting up the People's Welfare Factory for women and recent developments there. From his account it emerges that the funds for this plant are contributed by the public. The factory hands are girls from the villages. And they are taught to weave stockings, embroider, make clothes and carry out various other light tasks requiring a certain skill. The output of the plant is large and its products sell well, yet instead of the profit you might expect, according to the director, he has to make good a deficit of over ten thousand dollars every year.

The director orders one of his men to telephone to the factory informing them of Mr Huang's visit, and he scribbles a line on a card for him by way of introduction. With every sign of gratitude, Mr Huang rises and bows in farewell while his host invites him to come back for a simple meal that evening.

While seeing his visitor out, the director switches off the electric fan, but for a few minutes longer it continues to ruffle the pages of *The Classic of Filial Piety* and other books. He has gone, to smoke opium no doubt with one of his concubines, and quiet reigns again in the reception room. But inside a girl can be heard sobbing and protesting, "I've a husband of my own. . . Not for all your money. . . ."

Just after lunch the servant ushers in another caller, serves him tea and goes upstairs to announce, "Second Master is here."

Second Master is Director Fei's sworn brother. Although actually a few years older than the director, he insists that he is the younger by two or three years, preferring a junior status perhaps because he is the second son of his family. He looks thoroughly wrought up and anxious to see the director without delay.

This visitor is not kept waiting long. The director, not troubling to put on his gown, comes in holding a water-pipe and blowing on a paper spill.

"Have you lunched, second brother?" he asks. "What's on your mind?"

"Elder brother, I'm afraid our factory's in for trouble this time. Someone went south to report that we're bad characters, and I hear they're going to make an investigation. This business has kept me on the go all morning. I haven't had lunch yet. If they find out we're using funds from the People's Welfare Factory to run the Xinghua Company, what can we do, elder brother? We'll be sentenced to hard labour for life, if not shot!"

The director answers calmly and confidently, "Don't worry, second brother. Let me order a meal for you, then we'll talk this over." He rings the bell and orders rice and some dishes, then turns back to Second Master.

"You lose your head too easily over trifles. How can they call philanthropists 'bad characters'? If inspectors come, bring them to this Hall for Appreciating Poetry and Discussing Ceremony to see our subscription lists, accounts and certificates of merit. It's all open and above board, what fault can they find? Naturally we won't admit that the company's capital comes from donations to the factory. There's no rule forbidding philanthropists to run a business. We've not broken any law."

"I'm afraid they'll discover we can account for our income but not for our expenditure. What am I to do, elder brother? By helping you run your charity I've involved myself in crime. What shall I do?"

"Don't get so worked up. If that happens I'm ready for them. We've never transferred funds directly from the factory to the Xinghua Company. In a factory run as a charity there's bound to be some waste, and we can cook the accounts so as to get by. Actually, which of our contributors is going to look into our books? Those who donate several hundred or a thousand only do it to give us face, not to help a good cause. They're ready to lose money at mahjong, so why not donate it to us? And they're quite satisfied when they come to the works and see their names inscribed on the roll of benefactors in our meeting hall. The anonymous donors of a hundred dollars or less are easy to handle too. There are forty or fifty of them but we need only own up to three or four, and each will think he's meant by those mentioned in our report. That will help us to make up leeway. As for those who contribute a dollar or a few cents, if they want to check our books we'll just ask them who they think they are."

"What about the factory's reserve fund?"

"We can account for that by our losses on the Stock Exchange last year. If they do investigate that, the worst charge they can bring against us is 'incompetence' and you can't be penalized or arrested for that. Besides we can make it seem that our Xinghua Company was set up to dispose of the factory's products and serve it in other ways. Neither you nor I have ever been shareholders, and it's surely no crime for our concubines to run a company? In a word, we've nothing to be ashamed of. You've no call to panic." With this, he sucks on his water-pipe till it bubbles.

Second Master has been nodding repeatedly. "Quite right, quite right," he says. "We've nothing to be ashamed of in our factory. If inspectors come they'll discover nothing that isn't to our credit. . . . But we've another problem not yet settled, elder brother. Remember last year when the students came to inspect the factory goods, two of them were killed by our guards. If this comes out in an investigation there'll be the devil to pay. Yesterday I heard that the students' association has declared us both criminals, and they mean to post up slogans in the streets. Worse still, they're threatening to expose our guards passing themselves off as Japanese.* This strikes me as more serious than the question of the factory. Not only will it ruin our reputations, our property and lives are in danger too."

Although inwardly perturbed, the director says calmly, "I've asked Guoren to take that matter up. I can't say for certain what the outcome will be, but I don't anticipate any serious trouble. Guoren has a lot of pull down south. A word from him to the authorities there and some judicious greasing of palms should smooth matters over."

"You really think we can buy them off? They're so

* In old China the foreign imperialists often broke the law with impunity. Hence thugs and bullies sometimes posed as Japanese.

strongly against corruption they'd never accept a bribe, would they?"

"You're too naive, second brother. Not many people in this world practise what they preach. In any case, it's honest government they advocate, not honest individuals. Of course the government won't accept a bribe — what government ever has? But officials are only human, and who doesn't like money? So long as we find a plausible pretext, they'll take it. If you're worried, why not call on Guoren now and find out how things stand?"

"Yes, I'll do that. I can't help being afraid this is something money won't settle."

The director naturally wants him to leave at once to save the expense of a meal and procure the latest news about this case.

"You'd better lose no time if you're going," he suggests. "Guoren often goes out after lunch. Get yourself a snack outside. Confound that cook! What makes him so slow?" He calls a servant in and swears at him before ordering him to hire a rickshaw for Second Master.

When the rickshaw comes Second Master rises to leave. "Is it all fixed up about Furong?" he asks casually. "Congratulations on your new concubine."

The director's face clouds over. He replies:

"I've no time to go into that now. I'll tell you later. Don't delay, and come back to dine here. I've invited a Mr Huang whom I want you to meet. If Guoren is free, ask him too."

Second Master makes haste to mount the rickshaw and leave. The director does not trouble to see him out but, puffing at his pipe, goes back to his room again. A servant comes in to empty the teacups and replace them on the shelf. All is still once more in the reception room except for the mirror's reflection of passers-by in the street. A fashionable lady drives past in a car, her pet dog seated beside her. Oddly enough the dog keeps putting his head out of the window to bark at pedestrians, thus showing them that he is a rich lady's dog. His bark can be heard in the reception room.

On the stroke of three the room comes to life again. Mr Wei, business manager of the factory, brings in a couple of villagers to see the arrangements of this room. The two tablets remind them of two similar objects in their ancestral temple, said to have been conferred by an emperor on one of their ancestors. The clocks large and small, the antiques genuine and faked, and everything else make such an impression on them that they think the emperor's palace can hardly be grander.

They sit down and the elderly woman fingers the things within reach admiringly.

"You wouldn't believe me," says Mr Wei, "but now you can see for yourselves. Our director is a most respected and wealthy man. You're lucky that he's taken a fancy to Furong. If she becomes the director's concubine, you'll never lack for food, clothing or shelter, and your son Xiaogou may become a magistrate too."

"That's all very well," says the old man. "But we brought Furong up from a child to marry Xiaogou. If we let her go her family will have the law on us."

"We sent her to the factory to learn a skill and earn more money for us," puts in his wife. "If this rich director wants her, that's just Xiaogou's bad luck. If this rich director can pay for the lawsuit and will promise to make our son a battalion commander, we can buy him another wife. Tell me, Mr Wei, sir, isn't a battalion commander better than a magistrate? You said this rich director could make Xiaogou a magistrate, but I think an army commander would be better. Nowadays magistrates have a lot to put up with, and I've heard a battalion commander may rise to be a commissioner."

"So long as you agree," says Mr Wei, "the director can cope with even the biggest lawsuit. Not one of his concubines' relatives but has a well-paid job. If Xiaogou makes over Furong to the director, of course he'll get a good post. Battalion commander or anything he wants."

The old man is a reasonable soft-spoken peasant. Much as this goes against the grain he has not the courage to contradict Mr Wei. "Well," he says, "this isn't for my wife and me to decide. We must see Furong and ask if she's willing or not."

"She's certainly willing," is Mr Wei's prompt reply. "All that's lacking now is your approval. Furong spent last night here. She'd hardly have done that if she wasn't willing."

This information incenses the old man. Mr Wei, gauging his displeasure, makes haste to explain that it is quite customary for the factory hands to undertake work outside. The director is entitled to transfer girls to his house. Cuihua and Linghua are working permanently for him. The previous evening it so happened that Mrs Fei had a job for Furong to do, for which reason and no other she spent the night there.

The old couple ask to see Furong to clear this up and find out her real inclinations. Presently Cuihua brings her in. At the sight of her in-laws she falls to her knees and bursts into a storm of weeping. "Take me home, dad, mum!" she sobs. "Don't leave me here at his mercy.... I've a husband already. I refuse to stay here. He may have money but he can't buy me...."

Because her cries must be carrying out to the street, Mr Wei urges her to calm down and not weep so loudly. The old woman helps her up and Furong, worn out by her own indignant protest, finally subsides into silence.

The old woman, who hankers after riches and rank, draws her daughter-in-law to her and softly explains the benefits that will accrue to the family if she marries this rich director. But the girl is adamant. She will not hear of becoming a concubine, she wants to go back to Xiaogou.

Mr Wei, though unable to persuade her, admires her spirit. After a heated argument Furong leaves for home with her in-laws. Then Mr Wei asks to see Director Fei and explains that this girl is such a shrew he is better off without her and there are plenty of prettier girls in their works. The director inveighs against her stupidity too, describing the scene she made last night and this morning. On his way back from speeding a parting guest, she called him filthy names. If he hadn't meant to make her his concubine, he'd have killed the ungrateful bitch. He tells Mr Wei to go back to the factory and strike her name off their roll, then buy her family's silence with a few dozen dollars from the special fund.

It is after five. Some policemen come to the gate, making the whole household break out in a cold sweat. Have Furong and her in-laws reported them to the authorities and are these officers here to make an arrest? But it seems this is not the case. The police announce:

"The order has come to welcome the commander-in-chief and chief-of-staff tomorrow. Every house must put up flags."

The Fei household breathes again.

One servant protests, "A few days ago you made us put up a flag to farewell a general. Tomorrow we've to put up another for this commander. What's the point of all these flags?"

"We're just passing on orders from above. Mind you don't hang five-coloured national flags tomorrow. The naval flag's being used now as the national flag."*

"Where are we to find a naval flag? You police are the limit, making people hang one flag today and a different one tomorrow."

"It's not our doing. If the higher-ups order a dragon flag we ask for a dragon flag** too. If they order army flags, we ask for army flags."

Having transmitted these orders the police move on. The big looking-glass in the reception room already reflects two huge Kuomintang Party flags twenty-four feet in length hanging over the newly opened hairdresser's opposite and trailing to the ground. They are larger than the flag usually flown over the Xinhua Gate.*** From a distance you would suspect that this saloon was a vitally important government office.

Lighting-up time has come. A feast is spread in the reception room for Mr Huang after his visit to the

---

* The five-coloured flag was first used after the 1911 Revolution converted the old monarchy into a republic. In 1928 when Chiang Kai-shek came into power he made the old naval flag of the republic the new national flag.

** The dragon flag was the national flag of the old monarchy.

*** Gate leading to the former palace grounds of the Qing Dynasty, which at that time was the warlord government house.

factory. Mr Wei the business manager is the first arrival. He has carried out all the director's instructions. And he reports that he has bought two new flags. The director reproaches him for wasting money on new ones and says he should have looked in a second-hand shop. Evidently the director imagines you can find the new national flag among second-hand clothes.

Second Master makes his appearance. His relaxed air proclaims him the bearer of good news. Producing some books from his sleeve he tells the director, "Guoren couldn't come as he's taking the special train tonight to Baoding to meet the commander. He told me to bring you these books. From now on, he says, anybody socially active will have to learn these off by heart. They're the new *Sacred Canons,* and not a word can be changed."

In spite of this build-up, the director leafs through the books very casually until he lights on the words "the principle of the people's welfare",* which send him into raptures. He asks Second Master, "Isn't our People's Welfare Factory in line with the principle of the people's welfare?"

"Quite right, quite right! So our views coincide with those of Sun Yat-sen." Second Master informs the director that Guoren has settled their problem satisfactorily, and it seems they have nothing to fear.

The director lays these new books on top of *The Classic of Filial Piety* and *Maxims for Regulating the*

---

* One of the Three People's Principles — the other two were Nationalism and Democracy — proposed by Sun Yat-sen (1866-1925) who was the leader of China's democratic revolution. These later became the official doctrine of the Kuomintang.

Family. Evidently that case in the corner contains his whole library. He has nowhere else to keep books.

Mr Huang arrives now, brimming over with admiration. After modestly disclaiming any credit, the director tells him the relation between his factory and the principle of the people's welfare. Mr Huang is more impressed than ever by this modern social reformer and great philanthropist, since he is also a comrade of Dr Sun Yat-sen. The overwhelming privilege of sitting at the same table with such a man will be recorded in the account of his travels which he intends to publish. It goes without saying he is also consumed with envy of the director's wealth. He reflects that only a rich man could be such a philanthropist, and reaches the conclusion that none but the rich are qualified to be philanthropists. Very true, indeed!

Host and guests take their seats and feast convivially until nearly ten o'clock, when the party breaks up. Only a few servants are left to clear the table in the reception room. The clatter of crockery mingles with gramophone music from the new hairdressing salon.

1928

Translated by Gladys Yang

Big Sister Liu

SUMMER was unusually hot in Beijing that year. Although the street lamps were already lit, the man who sold cool crab-apple cider on the corner of the lane was still announcing his wares with a rhythmic clanging of two small brass bowls, like the accompaniment women ballad reciters use to punctuate their stories. A woman with a large basket of scrap paper on her back passed before the cider vendor. A large battered straw hat obscured her face, but when she hailed him, you caught a flash of even white teeth. Her burden weighed her down heavily. She walked placing one foot solemnly in front of the other, like a camel, until she entered her own gate.

Beyond was a small compound lined with one-storey buildings built in a hollow square. The woman lived in two dilapidated rooms on one side of the compound. Most of the yard was strewn with rubble, but before her door was an arbour of cucumbers and a few stalks of tall corn. Tuberoses grew beneath her window. A few rotting timbers beneath the arbour evidently served as seats. As she neared her door, a man came out and helped her lower the heavy basket.

"You're late today, wife."

The woman looked at him in surprise. "What do you mean? Have you gone out of your mind, wanting a wife? Don't call me that, I tell you." Entering the room, she took off her battered straw hat and hung it behind the door. Then she scooped water from a large earthen vat several times in succession with half a segment of bamboo, drinking so rapidly she couldn't catch her breath. After standing a moment, gasping, she walked out to the arbour, pulled the big basket to one side and sat down on a rotting timber.

The man's name was Liu Xianggao. He was approximately the same age as she — about thirty. The woman's surname was also Liu. But, except for Xianggao no one knew that her given name was Chuntao, or Spring Peach. The neighbours all referred to her as Big Sister Liu the scrap paper collector. That was because of her occupation — poking through rubbish heaps on street corners and lanes' ends to earn a living, buying old written matter for which she gave boxes of matches in exchange. From morning till night, beneath the blazing sun or in the icy gale, she tramped the streets, eating her full share of dust. But she had always loved cleanliness. Winter or summer, each day when she returned home she washed her face and bathed her body. Xianggao never failed to have a bucket of water waiting for her.

Xianggao had graduated from a rural elementary school. Four years ago, soldiers were marauding through his native region, and his whole family was forced to flee and scatter. On the road he met Chuntao, another refugee. They travelled together several hundred miles, then separated.

She went with a group of people to Beijing and found a job as nursemaid in a family of foreigners whose mistress was looking for an inexperienced country girl. Because she was clean and pretty, her mistress became very fond of her. But country people don't make good servants; they can't get used to being scolded. In less than two months, Chuntao quit. Her finances at a low ebb, she decided to try collecting scrap paper. In this trade she was able to earn enough to live on.

Xianggao's story, after he parted from Chuntao, was quite simple. He went to Zhuozhou to look up a relative, but the man was gone. Family friends, hearing that he had come as a penniless refugee, were not very cordial. He drifted to Beijing where someone introduced him to Old Wu, who sold crab-apple cider on the street corner. Old Wu loaned him his present quarters in the run-down courtyard, on the understanding that if anybody wanted to rent them, he would move out. Xianggao had no job, so he helped the old man sell cider and kept his accounts for him. He paid no rent and Old Wu gave him nothing for his work, but supplied him with two meals a day. Chuntao wasn't doing too badly at her paper collecting, but the people with whom she was staying wouldn't allow her to store her merchandise. She went looking for a place along the north city wall and the first time she rapped on a gate, Xianggao came out. Saving herself a lot of formalities, she rented the rooms from Old Wu and kept Xianggao on as her helper.

That was three years before. Since Xianggao could read a bit, he was able to sort through the paper that Chuntao collected and pick out the relatively valuable pieces, such as inscribed paintings or letters or scrolls written by some famous figure. With the two cooperating, business improved. Occasionally, Xianggao tried to teach Chuntao to read and write, but without much success. He couldn't read very well himself and had even greater difficulty in explaining the words to others.

Their life together, while perhaps not as idyllic as that of the mandarin duck and drake, famed symbols of connubial bliss, was in any event as cheerful as the union of a pair of common sparrows.

But to get back to the present. As Chuntao came into the room, Xianggao followed behind her with a bucket of water.

"Wash up, wife," he said happily. "I'm starving. Let's have something good tonight — onion griddle cake, alright? If you agree, I'll go out and buy the fixings."

"Wife, wife! Why can't you stop calling me that?" Chuntao demanded impatiently.

"If you'll only answer to it — just once — tomorrow I'll buy you a good straw hat in the second-hand market. Haven't you been saying you need one?" Xianggao pleaded.

"I don't like to hear it."

Seeing that she was a little annoyed, he changed the subject. "Well, what do you want to eat?"

"Whatever you like. You buy it and I'll make it for you."

After a while Xianggao returned with some onions and a bowl of sesame seed sauce, and placed them on the table. Chuntao had finished washing. She came in holding a large red card.

"This must be some big official's wedding certificate. Don't sell it in the Small Market this time. Better have someone take it to the Beijing Hotel. We'll get more for it there."

"That's ours. Otherwise what right would I have

to call you wife?" replied Xianggao playfully. "I've been teaching you to read for nearly two years and you still can't recognize your own name!"

"Who can read so many words? And cut out this wife business. I don't like to hear it. Seriously now, who wrote this thing?"

"I did. This morning a policeman came around to check up on the tenants. He says the martial law has been stricter the last two days. Every family has to report exactly who's staying with them and their relationship. Old Wu said that if I said we were husband and wife it would save a lot of trouble. The policeman, too, said it wouldn't look good if he wrote down that a man and a woman, unmarried, were living together. So I took that blank wedding certificate we couldn't sell last time and filled in that we were married in 1919."

"What? 1919? I didn't even know you in 1919. You'll get us into an awful mess. We never worshipped Heaven and Earth together, we never drank from each other's wine cups. How can anyone say we're husband and wife?"

Although opposed to the idea, Chuntao spoke calmly. She had changed to blue cloth trousers and she wore a white tunic. Even without make-up, her face had a fresh natural beauty. Had she been willing to marry, the local matchmaker could easily have passed her off as a young widow of twenty-three or four. Chuntao could have commanded at least a hundred and eighty dollars under prevailing market conditions.

Laughing, she folded the card down the middle. "Don't fool around. A fine wedding certificate. Let's make our griddle cakes and eat." She lifted the stove lid and thrust the card into the flames. Then she walked to the table and began to knead some dough.

"You can burn it if you like," said Xianggao with a grin. "The policeman has already registered us as husband and wife. If they make an official check, I'll say we lost it when we were refugees on the road. From now on, I'm going to call you wife. Old Wu recognizes our marriage; so does the policeman. I'm going to call you wife whether you like it or not. Wife, wife. Tomorrow I'll buy you a new hat. I'm afraid I can't afford a ring."

"Keep that up and you'll make me mad."

"Looks like you're still thinking of that Li Mao." Xianggao was not quite so high-spirited as he had been a moment before. He said it under his breath, but Chuntao heard him.

"Think of him? Husband and wife for one night, then separated for nearly five years, with no news all that time. What's the good of thinking?"

She had told Xianggao what had happened on her marriage day. When the flowery sedan-chair brought her to the groom's home, before the guests even had a chance to take their seats at the wedding feast, a man came rushing in to announce that an army of many soldiers had arrived in the two neighbouring villages. They were grabbing men to dig trenches and everybody was running away. The new couple hastily bundled their belongings together and fled toward the west with the rest of the villagers. Their second night on the road, they suddenly heard people ahead shouting, "The bandits are coming. Hide, quickly, hide!" There was a wild scramble to get out of sight. No one had time to think of anyone but himself. When the sun rose the next morning, a dozen people had disappeared, Chuntao's husband Li Mao among them.

"I think he must have been taken by the bandits," she now said. "Maybe they killed him long ago. Forget it. Let's not talk about him."

She finished making a griddle cake and put it on the table. Xianggao scooped a bowl of cucumber soup from the crockery pot. The two sat down and ate in silence.

When the meal was over, they sat beneath the arbour and chatted. A cool breeze brought tiny fireflies descending on the arbour like a myriad of falling stars, while countless real stars flashed and twinkled among the leaves of the cucumber vine. The night-blooming tuberoses slowly opened their petals and filled the garden with their perfume.

"How lovely they smell," said Xianggao. He plucked one of the flowers and put it in Chuntao's hair.

"Don't spoil my tuberoses. Wearing flowers in the hair at night — I'm no prostitute." She took the flower out, inhaled its delicate scent then placed it on the timber seat beside her.

"Why were you so late today?"

"Huh! Today I did a good piece of business. As I was coming home this afternoon, passing the Houmen Arch I saw some street cleaners pushing a big cartful of scrap paper. I asked them where they got it. They said it came from the Shenwu Gate of the old Imperial Palace.* I saw that it was full of official-looking red and yellow documents. I asked them whether they'd sell it to me. They were very polite. If you want it,

* The paper was sold by museum employees to pay their salary, which was months in arrears.

they said, we'll give you a special price, and you can take it away." Chuntao pointed at the big basket resting beneath the window of the house. "I only spent a dollar for all that! Maybe it's money thrown away, I don't know. We can go through it tomorrow and see."

"You can't go wrong on things from the palace. It's only stuff from the schools and the foreign business firms that I'm afraid of. Their paper is heavy and it smells bad. You never know what you're getting."

"All the shopkeepers have been using foreign paper for wrapping paper the last few years. I can't imagine where it all comes from. None of the collectors like to handle it. We have to pay more for it because it's heavy, but when we sell it we get very little."

"More and more people are studying foreign languages. Everybody wants to be able to read the foreign newspaper so that they can learn how to do business with the foreigners."

"Let them. We'll stick to picking foreign paper."

"Looks like everything will have to have a foreign label from now on. We've got 'foreign' clothes and 'foreign' hats and 'foreign' cloth. The next thing you know we'll be using 'foreign' camels!"

Chuntao laughed. "You shouldn't talk about others. If you had money you'd probably want to study foreign books too, and get yourself a foreignized wife."

"The Lord of the Heavens knows, I'll never get rich, and even if I did, I wouldn't want a foreignized wife. If I had a little money I'd go to the countryside and buy some good farm land, and we two could till it together."

Ever since Chuntao had been forced to flee from her home and lost her husband, the word "countryside" had unpleasant associations for her. "Is that what you want?" she demanded. "Before you'd even have bought your land, both you and your money would be gobbled up. The countryside's a hell. I wouldn't go back even if I were starving here."

"I'd like to see our Jinxian County again."

"The countryside's the same wherever you go. If it's not marauding soldiers then it's bandits on a raid. If it's not the bandits, it's the Japanese. Who dares go back? We're much better off right here, picking scrap paper. What we need is another person to help us. If we had someone to take your place at home going through the pickings, you could set up a stall during the day and sell direct to the customers. Besides cutting out the middleman, we'd be less likely to pass over any good items."

"Another three years at this trade and I'll be alright. If we pass over any good items, it's nobody's fault but my own. I've learned plenty the last few months. Used postage stamps — which ones are worth money, which ones aren't — I pretty near know them all. I'm beginning to get the hang of spotting the writing of famous men. A couple of days ago I found something by Kang Youwei.* Guess how much I sold it for today." Xianggao happily held up a thumb and an index finger. "Eighty cents!"

"You see! If we could pick eighty cents out of our heap of scrap paper every day, that wouldn't be so bad. Why go back to the countryside? Wouldn't that just be looking for trouble?" Chuntao's cheerful tones were like the throaty warble of an oriole in late spring. "I gua-

---

* Qing-dynasty scholar and statesman.

rantee you'll find plenty of good stuff in the paper I brought home today. I hear there'll be even more coming out of the palace tomorrow. That street cleaner told me to wait for him at the Houmen Arch first thing in the morning. He says all the things in the palace are being crated and sent south, but nobody wants the old paper. I saw a lot outside the Donghua Gate of the palace too. They're practically giving it away — whole sacks of it. You go down there tomorrow and ask about it."

Before they knew it, it was almost midnight. Chuntao stood up and stretched. "I'm tired. Let's get some rest."

Xianggao followed her into the house. There was a brick oven-bed against the window wide enough to sleep three. In the tiny light of an oil lamp, the two pictures on the wall were dimly visible. One was "Eight Fairies Playing Mahjong", the other was a cigarette advertisement with a beautiful girl. It seemed to Xianggao that if Chuntao took off her battered straw hat and put on a decent gown and sat on a grassy knoll, she wouldn't look much different from the fashionable young lady in the cigarette ad. That was why he liked to tease Chuntao and say that the advertisement was her photograph.

Chuntao undressed, draped herself in a thin coverlet and lay face downwards on the bed. According to their nightly habit, Xianggao massaged her back and legs. As usual, she gradually relaxed, a faint smile on her lips, as Xianggao kneaded her weary muscles in the light of the oil lamp's flickering little flame.

Already half asleep, she murmured, "You come to bed too. Don't work tonight. You have to get up early tomorrow."

Soon the woman was snoring faintly. Xianggao put out the lamp.

At dawn they rose promptly, and set off on their respective missions like a pair of ravens leaving their nest in search of food.

Just as the noon cannon sounded, and the drums and cymbals of the fair grounds on the shores of the Ten Monasteries Lake were at their noisiest, Chuntao came through the Houmen Arch, bearing a basket of paper on her back, and headed west toward the Buya Bridge. As she neared the fair grounds, a man by the side of the road hailed her:

"Chuntao, Chuntao!"

Even Xianggao seldom addressed her by her given name. In the four or five years since she left the countryside, certainly no one had ever shouted it out like that in public.

"Chuntao, don't you remember me?"

She turned to see a beggar sitting by the roadside. The piteous cry had come from him. His face was heavily bearded. He was unable to stand because he had no legs. The white metal buttons of his tattered grey uniform were already rusting and his skin showed through the splits in his shoulder seams. A nondescript army cap devoid of any insignia perched askew on his head.

Chuntao stared at him wordlessly.

"Chuntao, I'm Li Mao!"

She took two steps forward. Grimy tears were running down the man's cheeks into his tangled beard. Her heart beat wildly. For several minutes she was unable to speak.

"Mao, you're a beggar?" she said finally. "How did you lose your legs?"

He sighed. "It's a long story. How long have you been in Beijing? What are you selling?"

"Selling? I collect scrap paper. — We can talk after we get home."

Chuntao called a rickshaw, raised Li Mao in and put her basket on the vehicle's floorboard. While the rickshaw man pulled, she trotted along behind and pushed. Old Wu, standing at the head of her lane near the north wall clanging his little brass bowls, hailed her as they went by:

"You're home early today, Big Sister. Business must be good!"

"A relative's come from the country," she shouted back in reply.

At the compound gate, the rickshaw man helped Li Mao down. Chuntao opened the gate with her key, then led Li Mao in. He crawled forward on his hands, like a performing bear, his amputated legs dragging behind him.

She brought out a suit of Xianggao's clothing and drew two buckets of water from the well, just as Xianggao did for her every day. She poured the water into a wooden tub and told Li Mao to bathe. After he finished, she filled another basin so that he could wash his face. Finally she helped him to a seat on the oven-bed, then went into the next room to bathe herself.

"Your place is nice and clean, Chuntao. Do you live here alone?"

"My partner stays here too," she answered without any hesitation.

"Are you in business?"

"Didn't I tell you I collect scrap paper?"

"Collect scrap paper? How much can you earn in a day doing that?"

"Never mind questioning me. Let me hear about you first." Chuntao spilled out the bath water and came into the room, combing her hair. She sat down opposite Li Mao.

Li Mao began his story:

"Chuntao — ah, it's too long. I'll just tell you the main things. — After the bandits captured me that night, I hated them because they had made me lose you. I watched for my chance, grabbed one of their rifles, killed two of them and ran for my life. I managed to get to Shenyang just when they were recruiting for the army, and I joined up. All during the next three years I kept trying to get news from home. People said our village had been razed to the ground; no one knew what had happened to the title-deed to our bit of land. I had forgotten to take it with me when we ran away. And so I never asked for leave to go home for a look around. I was afraid if I did, I'd lose the few dollars' pay I was drawing every month.

"So I settled down to being a soldier, just living for pay day. As for becoming an officer, I had no hope of that. Then, last year, something happened — I must be fated to a life of bad luck. The colonel of our regiment issued an order saying that any man who could hit the bull's-eye nine shots out of ten would get double pay and be promoted. In the whole regiment, not one soldier was able to hit the target more than four times in ten, and even those shots weren't in the middle. But I sent nine bullets right into the red ball, one after another. Then to show how good I really was, I turned my back to the target, bent down and fired the tenth shot from between my legs. It hit the bull's-eye exactly in the centre.

"When the colonel sent for me, I was very happy. I was sure he was going to praise me. Instead the pig became very angry. He swore I must be a bandit, and wanted to have me shot. He said nobody but a bandit could shoot so well. My sergeant and my lieutenant both pleaded for me; they guaranteed I wasn't a bad man. Although they convinced him not to shoot me, I lost my private's rank; I wasn't even a private second class. The colonel said an officer was bound to hurt the feelings of his men sometimes, and with a sharpshooter in the ranks, during battle he'd run the same risk of being shot from behind as in front; that although he'd be killed in either event, he'd rather not lose his life for the sake of someone's revenge. Nobody had any answer to that one. People could only urge me to quit the army and find some other trade.

"Not long after I left, I heard that the Japanese had occupied Shenyang and that dog of a colonel had led all his troops over in surrender. I was boiling mad. I swore I'd get the bastard. I joined the Volunteers and fought outside of Haicheng for the next few months. We gave ground slowly, retreating south toward the Great Wall. Two months ago we were northeast of Pinggu and I was on patrol duty. I ran into the enemy and was hit in both legs. I was still able to walk then and took cover behind a boulder and killed a couple of them. When I finally couldn't hold out any longer, I threw my rifle away and crawled into the fields. There I hid one day, two days — with still no sign of our stretcher-bearers. My legs were swelling badly. I couldn't move. I had nothing to eat and nothing to drink. I just lay there and waited to die. Luckily a man came by with a big cart. He picked me up and brought me to a first-aid tent. They took one look at me and rushed me to a field hospital in Beijing. But it was already the third day. My legs were too far gone. The doctor had to amputate.

"I was in the hospital for more than a month. I pulled through alright, but my legs are gone. I thought to myself — In this town I haven't a single relative or friend and I can't go home; even if I could, how can I till the land without any legs? I begged the hospital to keep me on and give me a small job — any kind. The doctor said the hospital cures people but it doesn't support them and it's not its duty to find work for them. This city has no soldiers' sanatorium so all I could do was beg on the streets. Today is exactly the third day. Lately I've been thinking I can't stand this much longer; it would be better to hang myself and get it over with."

Chuntao listened intently. Her eyes were moist but she said nothing. Li Mao paused to wipe the sweat from his brow.

"And what about you?" he asked. "Though this place is kind of cramped compared with our broad, open countryside, from the looks of things you're doing all right."

"Who's doing all right? No matter how bad things are, a person still has to live. You can see people with smiles on their faces even at the gates of hell. I've been collecting scrap paper for a living, the past few years. A fellow by the name of Xianggao is my partner. He and I share everything, you might say. We can get by in a pinch."

"You and he live here together?"

"Yes, we both sleep on this oven-bed," Chuntao replied without the least hesitation, as if she had definite views on the subject for a long time.

"Oh, then you're married to him."

"No, we just live together."

"In that case, are you still my wife or aren't you?"

"No, I'm not anybody's wife."

Li Mao's pride as a husband was hurt, but he couldn't think of what to say. His eyes were fixed on the ground, not that he was looking at anything of course, but because he was rather ashamed to face his wife.

"Everyone must be laughing at me for being a cuckold," he said at last in a low voice.

"Cuckold?" The woman's face hardened a bit at the word, but she spoke without rancour. "Only people with money and position are afraid of being cuckolds. A man like you — who knows that you're even alive? Besides, cuckold or not, what's the difference? I'm independent now. Whatever I do can't have any effect on you."

"But we're still married, after all. As the old saying goes. 'One night of marriage, a hundred days of bliss —' "

"I don't know anything about any hundred days of bliss," Chuntao interrupted. "Several hundred days of bliss have passed since then. Nearly five years without a word. I'm sure you never dreamed we'd meet again either. I was here alone. I had to live. I needed someone to help me. After living together with him all these years, of course I don't feel the same about you any more. I brought you home today because our fathers were friends, because we come from the same village. You may claim I'm your wife, but I deny you. Even if you take the case to court, I'm not so sure you'll win."

Li Mao fumbled at the pouch in his belt as if searching for something. But then he stopped and stared at Chuntao, and his hand dropped back and rested on the mat covering of the brick bed.

Li Mao was silent. Chuntao wept. The shadows on the floor softly lengthened.

"Alright, Chuntao, if that's how you want it. I'm a cripple. Even if you came back to me, I couldn't support you," Li Mao said sensibly.

"I can't throw you over because you're crippled. But I can't give him up either. Why don't we all just live here, and no one think about who's supporting whom, what do you say?" Chuntao, too, spoke the words that were in her heart.

Li Mao's stomach rumbled faintly.

"Oh, here we've been talking all this time and I haven't even asked you what you'd like to eat. You must be terribly hungry."

"Anything at all. I haven't eaten since last night. I only had some water."

"I'll buy something." As Chuntao hurried from the house, Xianggao gaily entered the courtyard. They collided under the arbour.

"What are you so happy about?" she asked him. "Why are you home so early?"

"I did some good business today. This morning I went through that load of paper you brought home last night, and what did I find but some Ming-dynasty petitions sent to the emperor of China by the king of Korea — ten of them, worth at least fifty dollars apiece!

I just brought a few down to the exchange to see what they'll bring from the customers: I'll take some more down later. I also found two stamped sheets of paper that the experts say are Song Dynasty. I've been offered sixty dollars for them already, but I was afraid to sell. Maybe that's too cheap. I brought them back to let you take a look. See. . . ."

He undid the cloth wrapper of his bundle and took out the documents and the stamped paper. "This is the imperial seal." He pointed at the stamped imprint.

"Except for that mark, I don't see anything special about this paper. Fine foreign paper is much whiter," said Chuntao. "Those palace officials must be as blind as I am."

Xianggao laughed. "If they weren't a little blind how could people like us earn a couple of dollars now and again?"

He retied the bundle. "I say, wife —"

Chuntao glanced at him sharply. "I told you not to call me that."

Xianggao ignored her tone. "You've come home early too. Business must be not bad."

"I bought another basketful, the same as yesterday's."

"Didn't you say there was a lot more?"

"They sent it all to the Morning Market to use for peanut bags!"

"Never mind. We've done very well today. It's the first time we've done more than thirty dollars' worth of business in a day. Say, it isn't often that we're both home together in the afternoon. Why don't we take a stroll around the fair grounds at Ten Monasteries Lake? It's nice and cool there."

He went into the house and put his bundle on the table. Chuntao followed him in. "We can't," she said. "We have a visitor today." Raising the door curtain of the inner room, she nodded to Xianggao, "Go on in."

He walked into the next room with Chuntao right behind him. "This is my former husband," she said to Xianggao, and to Li Mao she said, "This is my partner."

The eyes of the two men met. If the pupils of each man's eyes were spaced equally far apart, the lines of vision would have been exactly parallel. Neither man spoke. Even the two flies resting on the window-sill were silent. The room remained hushed for several moments.

"Your name, sir?" asked Xianggao courteously. Of course, he knew very well.

They began to chat.

"I must go out and buy a couple of things," said Chuntao. "You probably haven't eaten either," she said to Xianggao. "Will griddle cakes be alright?"

"I've eaten. You stay here. I'll do the buying."

Chuntao pushed him to a seat on the brick bed. "You stay here and entertain the guest," she insisted with a smile. She went out.

The two men were left alone in the room. In a situation like that, if they hadn't liked one another on sight, they might have fought to the death. Fortunately, they had formed a mutual liking. We needn't think because Li Mao had lost his legs that he couldn't fight. We must remember that Xianggao's only exercise the past four or five years had been wielding a pen. Li Mao was strong enough to have killed him. If he had a gun, it would have been even easier. One crook of the trigger finger and Xianggao would have crossed the Bridge to the Outer World.

Li Mao told Xianggao that his father used to help Chuntao's father on the farm during the busy seasons, and that the two were good friends. Because Li Mao was a crack shot, Chuntao's father was afraid he would go off and join the army. To make sure he would stay and protect the local peasants, the old man gave his daughter to Li Mao in marriage. This was something Chuntao had never mentioned to Xianggao before. Li Mao then told him of the conversation he had just had with Chuntao, and the talk came around to the question that affected them both so vitally.

"Now that you husband and wife are reunited again, I'll leave, of course," said Xianggao reluctantly.

"No. I've been away from her so long. And now I'm a cripple. I couldn't support her. It wouldn't be any use. You've lived together all these years. Why break up? I can go to a home for the disabled. I hear there's one here. I can get in if I can make the right connections."

Xianggao was surprised. He hadn't expected such magnanimous conduct from a man he had considered a rough soldier. But though his heart agreed, his mouth continued to refuse. This is the courteous hypocrisy known so well by all who have had some book-learning.

"That's not right," replied Xianggao. "I don't want to be known as a wife-stealer. And, thinking of it from your angle, you shouldn't let your wife live with another man."

"I'll write a paper disowning her, or I'll give you a bill of sale. Either way will do," Li Mao said with a smile. But his tone was quite earnest.

"How can you disown her? She hasn't done anything wrong. I don't want her to lose face. As for buying her — where would I get the money? Whatever money I have is hers."

"I don't want any money."

"What do you want?"

"I don't want anything."

"Then why write a bill of sale?"

"Because if we just agree verbally you won't have any proof. I might be sorry later and change my mind; that would make things awkward. Excuse me for talking so frankly, but that's the best way to get this thing settled. We can save the polite chatter for later."

Chuntao returned with the sesame seed buns she had bought. Seeing the two men talking together so freely, she was very happy.

"I've been thinking a lot lately about finding another person to help us," she said to Xianggao. "Now, by a lucky coincidence, Mao has shown up. He can't walk, but he'll be fine at home, sorting through the paper. You can be our outside salesman. I'll still do the collecting. The three of us will be a business company."

Li Mao made no reply, but picked up a sesame seed bun and began wolfing it down. It was as if he had just come back from the world of the starving and had no time for talk.

"Two men and a woman form a company? And you put up the capital?" Xianggao asked needlessly.

"What's the matter? Don't you agree?"

"Of course, of course. I haven't any objections." Xianggao couldn't bring himself to say what he was thinking.

"What can I do? What use will I be, sitting around

the house all day?" Li Mao was rather hesitant too. He understood Xianggao's meaning.

"Now both of you just take it easy. I've got it all figured out."

Xianggao uneasily moistened his lips. Li Mao continued eating, but his eyes were fixed on Chuntao. He waited to hear what she had to say.

Collecting scrap paper is probably an occupation in which women play the leading role. Chuntao had already evolved a plan. Li Mao would stay home and pick out the used postage stamps and the picture cards in the empty cigarette packs. The job required only eyes and hands, and he could do it. She calculated that if he could find a hundred and some odd cigarette pack pictures every day, that would cover the cost of his food. If, each day, he could also find even two or three good, relatively rare, stamps, that would be even better. About ten thousand packs of foreign cigarettes were sold in Beijing daily (the foreign cigarette packs were the ones containing the premium picture cards). Chuntao thought that she could collect, say, one per cent of these without much difficulty. Xianggao would concentrate on looking for letters of famous people and other comparatively valuable items. Needless to say, he was already an expert, and needed no further guidance. Chuntao herself would do the heavy work. Unless there was a big rain storm, she would go out every day, regardless of the wind or cold. In fact she would make a special point of working in the bad weather, because on such days some of her competitors were likely to stay home.

Glancing at the sun through the window, she estimated it was not yet two o'clock. She went out into the courtyard, put on her battered straw hat, then called through the door to Xianggao:

"I must inquire whether there's anything else being thrown out of the palace. You look after him. I'll be back tonight and we can talk some more."

Xianggao knew it was hopeless to try and detain her. He let her go.

Several days went by in silence. But two men and a woman sleeping together on a single brick oven-bed of course was very awkward. The institution of polyandrous marriage after all hasn't too many adherents in the world, one of the reasons being that the average man cannot rid himself of his primitive concepts regarding his rights as a husband and father. It is from these concepts that our customs and moral codes arise. Actually, in our society, only the parasites and exploiters observe the so-called customs; people who have to work for a living have very little respect for them in their hearts.

Take Chuntao, for instance. She was neither a well-to-do matron or a fashionable young miss. She was not likely to go dancing at some glittering ballroom, nor would she have any opportunity to play the hostess at a big society function. No one criticized or questioned her conduct. Even if they had, it wouldn't have bothered her a whit. Only the local policeman was concerned with her comings and goings, and he was quite easy to handle.

The two men? Xianggao, with a few years of schooling, had a vague idea of the precepts of the ancient feudal philosophers. But except for a mild interest in preserving appearances, he was the same as Chuntao. From the time he moved in, he was completely dependent on her. To him, her word was law. He obeyed her because it was to his benefit to do so. Chuntao told him not to be jealous, so he cast aside even the seed of jealousy.

As for Li Mao, his demands were simple. If Xianggao and Chuntao would let him live with them for a day, he would stay for a day; if they treated him as a relative, he would be quite satisfied. Travelling around so much, a soldier always loses a wife or two. Li Mao's problem was also one of appearances.

Nevertheless, although Xianggao was not jealous, a number of other disturbing things kept coming between the two men.

The summer days were still stifling hot, but Chuntao and Xianggao were not the sort of people to go to exclusive vacation resorts. They had to get on with their work. At home, Li Mao was beginning to learn the trade. He could already distinguish between which paper should be sent to the toilet paper makers and which he should keep for a final appraisal by Xianggao.

Coming home one day, Chuntao found Xianggao waiting for her as usual. It was already late, and as she entered the house she could smell incense burning.

"When did we take to burning mosquito-repellent incense?" she called to Xianggao, who was sitting beneath the arbour. "You're liable to burn the house down too, if you're not careful."

Xianggao made no reply, but Li Mao said, "We're not trying to drive away the mosquitoes, we're just purifying the air. I asked Brother Xianggao to light it for me. I'm figuring on sleeping outside tonight. It's too hot inside. With three people sleeping together, it's really uncomfortable."

"Who does this red card on the table belong to?" Chuntao asked, picking it up.

"We talked it over today," said Li Mao from the brick bed. "You go to Xianggao. That's the contract of sale."

"Oh, so you've got it all settled among yourselves! Well, and I say it's not up to you two to dispose of me!" She walked over to Li Mao with the red card. "Was this your idea, or his?"

"It's what we both want. The way we've been living, I'm not happy and neither is he."

"We talk and talk and it's still the same question. Why must you two always think about this husband and wife business?" Angrily, she tore the card to bits. "How much did you sell me for?"

"We put down a figure just for the looks of things. No real man gives his wife away for nothing."

"But if he sells her, that makes everything alright, does it?" She walked out to Xianggao. "You've got money now. You can afford to buy a wife. Why not spend a little more and —"

"Don't talk like that, don't talk like that," Xianggao pleaded. "You don't understand, Chuntao. The last few days, the people in the trade have all been laughing at me —"

"Laughing?"

"Yes. . . ." Xianggao's voice trailed off. As a matter of fact, he didn't feel very strongly about the matter. Nine cases out of ten, he did whatever Chuntao wanted. He didn't know why she had such power over him. At times he thought a certain thing should be done this way or that, yet when he came face to face with her, she was like a queen whose every command he had to obey.

"So you can't forget you're a scholar — just because you've read a couple of books. Scared to death that someone will scold you, laugh at you."

From the earliest days, real control over the people has been exercised not through the teachings of the sages but by cursing tongues and blows of the whip. Curses and blows are what have maintained our customs. But in Chuntao's state of mind she was ready to return "a curse for a curse, a blow for a blow". No weakling, while she didn't pick on anyone, she wouldn't take abuse from others either. Just hear how she instructed Xianggao, and you'll see:

"If anyone laughs at you, why don't you hit him? What are you afraid of? What we do is nobody else's business."

Xianggao was silent.

"Let's not talk about this any more. Why can't the three of us go on living as we are?"

The room was still. After the evening meal Xianggao and Chuntao sat beneath the arbour as usual, but both were unusually quiet. They didn't even recite any passages from the scriptures of the day's business.

Li Mao called Chuntao into the house. He urged her to become Xianggao's wife officially. He said she didn't understand a man's psychology. No one wanted to be a cuckold; nor did anyone want to become known as a wife-stealer. Taking out a red card which was already turning brown, he handed it to Chuntao.

"This is our marriage certificate. That night we fled, I took it from the shrine and put it in my shirt. I'm giving it back to you, so now we can be considered no longer married."

Chuntao accepted the card from him without a word, her eyes fixed on the torn mat covering the brick bed. She sank to a seat beside her crippled husband.

"Take it back, Mao dear, I don't want it. I'm still your wife. 'One night of marriage, a hundred days of bliss' — I can't wrong you like this. What kind of a person would I be if I threw you over because you can't walk or work?"

She placed the red card on the brick bed.

Li Mao was deeply moved. "I can see that you like him a lot," he said in a low voice. "You'd better live with him. When we get a little money scraped together, you can send me back to the country, or to a home for disabled soldiers."

"It's true these last few years we've been living together, we've been getting along fine," Chuntao replied softly. "If he were to go, I'd miss him terribly. Let's ask him in and see what he thinks."

"Xianggao, Xianggao," she called from the window. No response. She went outside. Xianggao was not there. This was the first time he had ever gone out at night alone. Chuntao was stunned. She called toward the house:

"I'll go look for him."

She was sure Xianggao had only gone up to the corner. But when she asked Old Wu, the old man said he had seen him going toward the main street. She went to all of his usual haunts, but Xianggao was nowhere to be seen. It's very easy to lose a person. Once they get out of sight, they disappear without a trace.

It was nearly one in the morning when Chuntao, heavy-hearted, returned home.

The oil lamp in the room was already extinguished.

"Are you asleep? Has Xianggao come back yet?" she asked. Striking a match, she lit the lamp and peered at the brick bed. A chill of terror ran through her veins. Li Mao had hanged himself with his belt from the top of the window lattice. She managed to control herself sufficiently to climb up and lower him to the bed. Fortunately, the time had been short and it wasn't necessary to call for help. By kneading his chest, she gradually was able to revive him.

Taking one's own life for the sake of another is the deed of a knight-errant. If Li Mao hadn't lost his legs he would not have had to resort to such a measure; but for the past few days he had been thinking there was little hope in store for him, that it would be best to do away with himself and let Chuntao live in peace.

Although Chuntao didn't love him, she had a strong sense of duty to him. She comforted and reassured him, talking to him until the sky turned light. At last he slept and Chuntao got down off the bed. On the floor she saw the charred remains of a red card — their marriage certificate. Transfixed, she stared at it for a long time.

All that day she didn't go out of the door. In the evening, she sat beside Li Mao on the brick bed.

"Why are you crying?" she asked him. Tears were rolling down his cheeks.

"I've wronged you. What did I come here for?"

"Nobody's blaming you."

"Now he's gone, and I haven't any legs —"

"You mustn't think like that. He'll come back."

"I hope so."

Thus another day passed. When Chuntao arose the next morning, she picked a couple of cucumbers from the vine and peeled and sliced them. Carelessly mixing a few ingredients, she grilled a big griddle cake, and brought it with the cucumbers to a small table on the brick bed. She and Li Mao ate together.

Then Chuntao donned her battered straw hat and fastened her basket on her back.

"You're in low spirits today, don't go out," Li Mao said to her through the window.

"I feel worse sitting around the house."

Slowly, she walked through the gate. Work was part of her very being. Even though she was depressed and unhappy, she still wanted to work. Work is the only thing Chinese women seem to understand. They don't seem to understand love. All their attention is concentrated on the routine problems of life. Love's flowering is only a blind, stifled stirring in their hearts.

Of course love is merely an emotion, while life is tangible and real. The art of talking learnedly of love while reclining behind a silken curtain or sitting in a secluded forest glade is an importation brought on ocean-going steamers — the "Empress" of this, the "President" that. Chuntao had never been abroad, nor had she ever studied in a school run by blue-eyed foreigners. She didn't understand fashionable love. All she knew was a dull, unaccountable pain.

She wandered from one lane to the next. Endless dust, endless streets engulfed the downcast young woman. "Matches for scrap paper!" she called occasionally. Yet at times she walked by a pile of discarded paper without giving it a glance. Once or twice, when she was supposed to give two boxes of matches in payment, Chuntao gave five. After muddling through the day, she returned home with the black-cloaked ravens, those rascals who are good for nothing but cawing raucously and stealing food. At the gate she saw the new residents' identification card which the police had posted, stating that Xianggao and she, his wife, were the residents-in-charge. The pressure on her heart grew heavier.

As she entered the courtyard, Xianggao came running out of the house.

Chuntao's eyes went wide. "You've come back! . . ." she cried, and then she couldn't speak for the choking tears.

"I can't leave you. Everything I have I owe to you. I know you want me to help you with your work. I can't be so callous. . . ."

He had been drifting about aimlessly for two days. His feet seemed to be dragging heavy iron fetters, fastened at one end to Chuntao's wrist. To make matters worse, wherever he went he saw the cigarette ad with the girl who looked just like Chuntao. He was so miserable, he didn't even know he was hungry.

"Brother Xianggao and I have talked it over," said Li Mao. "He's the resident-in-charge, I'm the subtenant."

Xianggao helped her take off the basket, as in the old days, at the same time wiping the tears from her face. "If we all go back to the country," he said, "Li Mao will be the resident-in-charge and I'll be the sub-tenant. You're our wife."

She made no reply but went into the house, hung up her hat, and took her daily bath.

Once again Chuntao and Xianggao began reciting passages from the scriptures of the day's business under the cucumber arbour. They agreed that after they sold that paper from the Imperial Palace, they would use some of the money to set up a stall for Xianggao in the public market; perhaps they could also find a somewhat roomier place to live, too.

A moth, flying into the house from the arbour, snuffed out the oil lamp's tiny flame. Li Mao was fast asleep, for the Milky Way was already low in the sky.

"We ought to sleep too," the woman said.

"You get into bed first. I'll come and massage you in a minute."

"You don't have to. I didn't walk very far today. We have to be up early tomorrow. Don't forget to take care of that business. We haven't shown a profit for days."

"Say, I forgot to give it to you. On the way home today, I made a special trip to the second-hand market and bought you a hat that's practically new. What do you think of it?" Groping, Xianggao found the hat and handed it to her.

"How can I see anything in the dark? I'll wear it tomorrow anyhow."

A hush fell on the courtyard. The scent of tuberoses wafted lazily on the night's gentle breeze. In the room soft voices could be faintly heard.

"Wife. . . ."

"I don't want to hear it. I'm not your wife. . . ."

1934

Translated by Sidney Shapiro

The Iron Fish with Gills

IT was afternoon and the all-clear had sounded. A busy thoroughfare in a south China city was lined with solemn spectators as the men recruited to defend the nation marched past. Not one of these conscripts, strange to say, had a gun. In their bamboo hats and grey uniforms they seemed neither soldiers nor peasants. And this parade had no apparent purpose, except to impress the local populace.

As soon as the troops had passed, an old man stepped into the road alongside the harbour. His hair was a tousled mop and although he wore a western suit it was patched and shapeless. Some rolled up papers in one hand, in his haste he collided with another man.

"You're in a hurry, Mr Lei!"

The old man looked up and recognized an acquaintance. Mr Lei, as a matter of fact, had no close friends. The man he'd bumped into was also hastening home after having been delayed by the parade. Lei felt constrained to stop and reply:

"Why, it's Mr Huang. I've not seen you for some time. Have you just left the shelter too? While they have their mock fights useless people like ourselves can only practise mock flight."

"That's a fact," agreed Huang, smiling.

They stood chatting for a while and Huang asked what the old man was carrying.

"The labours of a lifetime," was Lei's reply. "It's a long story. If you are interested, come back with me and take a look. I'd like to have your opinion."

Huang knew he had been one of the first students sent abroad by the government to learn gun-making. But as China had no arsenals with gun factories, he had been a square peg in a round hole since his return. He'd taught English and mathematics and served as a factory manager for some years. Eventually he'd taken a job in a naval dockyard on an offshore island ceded to a foreign power, but he had long ago left that employment. The old fellow's one passion in life was the study of new weapons. Huang was curious to see the papers in his hand which must be the blueprints of weapons he had invented. With a smile he asked:

"Mr Lei, am I right in supposing that those are blueprints for super-weapons like death-rays or rockets?" There was a sceptical note in his voice, for none of the designs submitted by Lei to the military authorities had been adopted. Those who called him visionary or incompetent were not necessarily right, but the fact remained that he had nothing to show for his work.

"No, no, this is something still more important," was Lei's answer. "I don't suppose it would interest you. Goodbye."

But Huang's curiosity was fully aroused. He followed Lei, protesting, "Of course I'd like to see your new invention. My place isn't far. Why not come in for a chat?"

"I don't like to trouble you, and just the design would hardly interest you. I've made a small model, though. Come back with me and I'll give you a demonstration."

Without further ado Huang walked back with him to his home. Slightly out of breath, Lei ushered him inside, put his blueprints on the table and sat down. This was Huang's first visit here. The walls were covered with blueprints of various kinds, but he could make neither head nor tail of them. Neatly set out on a work bench at the back were saws, pincers, screws and the like. Elsewhere there were boxes on shelves.

"Here's the model of the submarine I've designed." Lei went to the shelves at which his guest was looking, lifted down a box about three feet long and produced an "iron fish".

"I've been working on this for several years. The distinctive thing about this submarine is that it has gills — it can breathe just like a fish."

He led Huang to a back yard where stood a tin tank eight feet square reinforced with wood, obviously constructed from three large packing cases. Inside there was a good four feet of water. Before putting in the iron fish, Lei opened its lid to show Huang the mechanism, explaining that his air supply was unlike any method now used. His iron fish could absorb oxygen from the water just like real fish, which meant it could remain submerged for several days at a time. With this he unrolled his designs and displayed them one by one. This was all he had taken to the shelter when the air-raid warning sounded. He claimed other merits for his invention too.

"My vessel has so many 'floating eyes' that even if it reaches a depth at which ordinary periscopes are useless, it can float some 'eyes' up to the surface and by means of an electric current reflect movement on the surface or in the air on to a screen in the submarine.

These small eyes can be made in so many different shapes that low-flying aircraft can't easily detect them. And the fact that the torpedo tube is outside the submarine means that torpedoes can be discharged in any direction without the vessel having to change course. Furthermore, discharging torpedoes is not the dangerous business it is in other old-fashioned submarines. All the crew are equipped with artificial gills too, so that if any accident happens to the submarine they can escape quickly through the emergency exit and float up to the surface."

To illustrate this he opened a sliding dome-shaped port in the model. But Huang's patience was rapidly becoming exhausted.

"I can't understand these technical terms," he said. "Won't you give me a demonstration before you explain?"

"Very well." Lei switched on the motor, snapped the cover down and lowered the model into the tank. It submerged and soon discharged a small torpedo. "This still doesn't show you how the gills work," he said. "Come inside and see another model."

He carried the submarine in and laid it on the table, then steered Huang to the shelves and took down another box containing a model of the iron gill. This was like a goldfish tank bisected by two sheets of glass with an ingenious mechanism between them. Lei plugged in an electric wire and poured water into one compartment. Fine long cracks in the glass partition on that side allowed the water to seep through, and presently the pistons of the small central mechanism were in motion. The compartment free from water represented the submarine's interior and some pistons there were attached to tubes in the partition. Lei explained that this artificial gill extracted oxygen from the water and simultaneously pumped out carbon-monoxide. There was also a mechanism to regulate the air to the crew's satisfaction. As for the question of underwater pressure, Lei explained that military submarines need not go down to any great depth. He was working on a vessel to explore the ocean bed, but had not yet made much headway.

Much of this was incomprehensible to Huang, but not wanting to ask questions he let the old man run on. When at last Lei rolled up his blueprints and put his models away, they sat down again and Huang tried to change the subject.

But the old man, still engrossed in his iron gill, held forth at length about this discovery's value and potential contribution to China's naval defence.

"You ought to send your discoveries to the authorities. Someone might take this seriously and let you build a trial boat in the shipyard." Huang rose to his feet.

Lei saw that he was leaving and protested, "What's the hurry, Mr Huang? Let me take you to have a snack at the tea-house later."

Huang knew that the old fellow was hard up and did not like to put him to any expense. He sat down again saying, "No, thank you all the same. I've another engagement. But let's talk a little longer."

They discussed the theory of ship-building and some practical problems involved.

Lei told Huang that since his return from studying abroad he had never really had a chance to use his knowledge. Some people failed to use what they had learned, but in his case he had no opportunity.

"The naval docks ought to be interested in inventions like yours. Why did they let you leave?"

"Don't forget those aren't Chinese shipyards. As a matter of fact it was while I was there that I started taking an interest in submarines. Before that I managed a hosiery works. That plant went bankrupt just at the time when the naval docks wanted new mechanics, and I was taken on as a skilled hand. Naturally I kept quiet about my specialized training. All they wanted were skilled workers."

"If you'd told them your qualifications they might have given you a better job."

"Not likely!" Lei shook his head. "I'd have been turned down. I've always been satisfied with a bare subsistence. Thirty foreign dollars a month was more than enough for me. It didn't take them long to spot my skill in repairing big guns and motors. I was always being sent to work on warships and submarines. Of course what I'd learned scores of years before wasn't much use, but I picked up quite a bit from the instructions of the chief engineer. I never used technical terms with those foreign engineers, for fear they might suspect me. As it was, they were surprised I didn't use the local pidgin English and asked me several times where I'd been to school. I fooled them by calling myself an overseas Chinese from Canada."

"Why did you throw up the job?"

"For a very simple reason. Because I was studying submarines, each time I worked on one I got talking with the crew and asked all sorts of questions. One day an officer caught me at this, and that was my last job on a submarine. They suspected me of spying. I'd taken good care to hide my drawings elsewhere in case they searched my lodgings, for otherwise I could have been in serious trouble. And I saw no reason to make them a gift of my blueprints. My own country comes first with me. That's why I threw in the job and left the dockyard."

"The ideal thing would be for you to work in a Chinese dockyard."

Lei shook his head impatiently. "Out of the question. Don't you realize that our shipyards, such as they are, are controlled by vested interests? From what I've seen of them, you won't get a decent job there unless you're related to one of the bosses or connected with him by marriage. Suppose I did get taken on, put forward some proposals and was actually allotted funds to experiment? There'd be precious little of the money left by the time I wanted to use it. And a failure wouldn't only make people sneer — it might land you in gaol. Who's going to risk that?"

"But it seems to me your inventions are very important. Quite a few higher research institutes have been set up recently. Why don't you bring your ideas to their attention? Demonstrate your model to them."

"There you go again. A man in his seventies like me has lost all desire to show off. There are too many self-styled inventors who entertain reporters right and left or lecture to college students posing as superior to Edison or Einstein. People are sick of them. Most research institutes are headed by young second-rate scholars, who aren't modest enough to learn but jump to conclusions. Besides they all seem to belong to various cliques. No outsider stands a chance with them. There's nothing I dislike so much as rubbing shoulders with those pseudo-scholars. I'm beneath their notice. Why should I send them my work to waste their energy debunking me? Why lay myself open to a snub like that?"

Huang glanced at his watch and stood up. "You're too cynical, sir," he protested. "At this rate you'll never have a chance to win recognition."

"I know, but what can I do? No individual can help. A heavy investment is needed and not just anyone can manufacture arms. I only hope I live to see the day when the country needs me and can trust me."

"Goodbye," said Huang, already in the doorway. "I hope that day comes too."

The inventor was so blunt that anyone not well acquainted with him might think him unbalanced, and some people did refer to him as "that crank Lei". He was alone in the world except for a widowed daughter-in-law now teaching in Manila and a grandson studying there. In the ten years and more since he left the dockyard his daughter-in-law had been supporting him. His need for a little workshop made it impossible for him to live on the island. Constructing model machines was this healthy septuagenarian's only hobby. He was not a smoker and his tastes were simple. But he often regretted giving up his job because now he depended on his daughter-in-law. Another year's work would have made him independent. His only consolation was the fact that he had quit shortly before a big strike in the docks, and during that high tide of patriotism he had felt it was important to leave and wait for an opportunity somewhere else. He had quite a library of books on ship-building which he tried several times to sell, but there were no buyers. His wife had long since died and the old maid Laixi, who looked after him had come to his house fifty years ago with his bride, left them at her marriage and returned again after the death of her own husband. She accepted no wages but ran the house for him, and Lei had to ask her for what money he needed. They had lived in this mutual dependence for twenty years and more.

After Huang had left, Laixi brought in a meal and they had supper together.

"There are disturbing reports about," Lei told her. "The Japanese may be coming. We'd better be prepared so as not to be caught unawares."

"People say we needn't worry. Most officials and their families are still here. I can't believe things will get out of hand."

"How are we to know what officials have gone? You can't trust public announcements or newspapers. Most people have too much faith in the printed word. I tell you, the powers that be are mostly cowardly fools, out for money or power. If they don't surrender territory outright to the enemy like Shi Jingtang, they count as patriots. You've read enough old books and plays to remember how Shi Jingtang gave away sixteen districts."

"Yes, I remember that." The old woman nodded. "But after handing over sixteen districts Shi Jingtang became emperor."

"You've no sense of history," exclaimed Lei impatiently. "Well, never mind that. Tomorrow you start sorting out our things and I'll write to my daughter-in-law telling her maybe we'll have to go to Guangxi."

After supper he put the model submarine back in its box and tidied away various other odds and ends. He was interrupted by Laixi, come to remind him, "Your daughter-in-law hasn't sent this month's remittance yet. We haven't enough for the journey unless the money arrives in the next few days."

"How much have we left?"

"Less than fifty dollars."

"That's enough. It won't cost thirty from here to Wuzhou."

But they had left it too late. In less than three days the invaders' tanks were rumbling down the highway on the dike. The local people, taken by surprise, embarked on the first boat they could find, leaving most of their possessions behind them. There were fires on every side, no trains were running. Lei and Laixi, each carrying a bundle, rushed to the river and boarded a boat without asking its destination. So many other refugees swarmed aboard that in a few hours they capsized. Luckily the river was not deep and most of the passengers were saved and put ashore by sampans. But Laixi was not among them. She had either drowned or been strafed by the Japanese planes.

Lei, stranded with less than twenty dollars, made his way to the island where he had been employed. It was an indescribably difficult journey, but the old man had plenty of determination. He discovered after his long absence that the old workmates whom he succeeded in tracing were in no position to help him. Going on to Wuzhou was out of the question. He had not enough money to rent a room in a hotel. With some other refugees he slept on the ground by the West Market. His neighbours were a middle-aged woman and two children who had also fled from the city when it fell.

A few days sufficed to acquaint him with the owner

of a small snack bar. He wrote to his daughter-in-law of his misfortunes and asked her to send him some money care of this man.

He and the middle-aged woman became friends in adversity. Since she had cumbersome luggage and her children were small, it was difficult for her to move about; and in any case there was the danger that her place might be seized in her absence. So they took it in turns to watch. After going to the street every day for his midday meal Lei would bring her back something to eat. And when she went off to wash clothes he minded her things.

One day he happened to meet Huang in the street. They compared notes on the disaster.

"Where are you staying now?" asked Huang.

"On the pavement by the West Market."

"We can't have that."

"What else can I do?"

"Move in with me."

"We're all refugees. No reason why I should add to your difficulties."

"Two extra won't make much difference," replied Huang warmly. "I'll help you to move." He looked round for a rickshaw.

"Thank you, it's extremely good of you," said Lei hastily stopping him. "But there are too many of us. We'd be in the way."

"Don't you just have the one servant?"

"Laixi's gone. Now I'm with another woman and her two children whom I met on the way. We lend each other a hand. I can't leave her in the lurch. I must get her settled."

"That shouldn't be hard. Take her to the refugee

camp. I hear they're getting things better organized there."

Lei knew Huang was far from well-off but had felt compelled to offer him a roof over his head. And now Huang insisted on going back with him.

"This is shocking. We can't have a man of your age sleeping out," he declared. "Your daughter-in-law would be horrified if she knew."

Lei would not hear of Huang going to his bivouac. He agreed that the refugee organization was improving and said he must see his companion settled before he did anything else. Huang insisted on taking him to a small tea-house. When he asked about the inventions, the old man told him that the model submarine had been lost with Laixi, leaving him only the blueprints and model of the iron gill. These had been in his charge when they left home and he had put the rolled up designs inside his bedding. The model he had carried in his other hand. Passers-by had sniggered and thought he had lost his wits, saving nothing from his home but a wooden box.

"At least let me keep those precious things for you," urged Huang.

"There's no need. In a house with children in it, they might easily get destroyed and I could never replace them."

"They would be safe with me. I'd lock them in a trunk. Why not? What are your plans, anyway?"

"I'm still thinking of going to Guangxi as soon as my daughter-in-law remits me money. I may have to wait a month or two, then I should be able to go by way of Guangzhou Wan or some other fairly safe route."

"Let me take your valuables into safe keeping."

"Where are you staying?"

"With a relative by the sea. We'll both go there presently."

Hearing that it wasn't his own house, Lei replied firmly, "There's no need. I prefer to keep these things with me. They're no encumbrance, and it'll only be for a few weeks."

"Well, at least let me see where you're staying, so that I know where to find you."

Lei had to give in and take him to the West Market. As they passed the snack bar the owner called out, "Mr Lei! Mr Lei! Your letter's come. It's come. When I couldn't find you the postman took it away but he'll bring it back tomorrow."

Lei beamed with delight and thanked the man warmly before turning back to Huang. "My daughter-in-law's sent me money. Now everything will work out all right."

As Huang was congratulating him they reached his sleeping place.

"You must excuse me," said Lei. "My sitting-room is where you're standing. This is no place to chat, so I won't keep you. I'll call on you tomorrow after I've cashed my cheque. Just write me down the address."

Huang pulled a card from his pocket and scribbled his address, then left, saying, "I'll be expecting you tomorrow."

That night dragged slowly for Lei, who went early the next day to the snack bar. Sure enough the postman handed him a letter and asked for a receipt. Ripping open the envelope, Lei found his daughter-in-law had sent him a remittance to cover his fare to Manila and the expense of getting himself a passport. He had no wish to go to Manila, but decided to draw the money he required. When he reached the banking-house he was told he must first have his photograph taken and get a passport. Lei explained that there had been a misunderstanding, he had no intention of going to Manila and would like the money at once. The cashier refused to pay it until he had sent a cable to clear matters up. After a fruitless argument in which Lei was naturally worsted, he let the cashier send off a cable.

From there he went to inform Huang of these fresh developments. His friend was in favour of his going to Manila. But Lei replied that his inventions were his contribution to China and a day would surely come when they would need to construct submarines on a large scale. If not as a striking-force, at least to facilitate underwater transport and so frustrate an enemy blockade. To him, building the ships was only the second step. It would satisfy him if the authorities allowed him to test some small submarines in the river and the experiment proved successful. He appeared to have given little thought to ordnance problems. They could order a standard submarine from abroad and convert it by adding his iron gills, floating eyes and other improvements.

Knowing how stubborn the old man could be, Huang did not press the matter. And after a little more talk Lei took his leave.

A day or two later, when he went back to the banking-house, the cashier gave him the money with the news that a cable from Manila agreed to his doing as he pleased. Lei said five hundred dollars would be plenty to see him to the interior and had the remainder sent back. Next he went to the China Travel Service, where he learned a boat would leave the next morning for Guangzhou Wan. He lost no time in informing Mr Huang, and the two of them went to the West Market for his things. While rolling up his bedding he discovered to his anger and dismay that many of his blueprints were torn. Apparently for several days the children had been using them as toilet paper. Hastily inspecting the damage, he was relieved to find the iron-gill designs in the centre still intact. Only some less important sheets outside had been spoiled. The iron-gill model in its box was also untouched. So things could have been much worse.

He told the woman that he would be taking the boat next morning and had so much to attend to, first, he would leave his luggage in a hotel. He gave her fifty dollars and introduced Mr Huang, advising her to start a little business with the money or, failing that, to ask Mr Huang to install her in the refugee camp. The woman took the money, apologizing profusely for touching his designs under the impression that they were waste paper. Tears of gratitude rolled down her cheeks as she watched him and Mr Huang set off with the mutilated blueprints and the model in its box.

Huang saw him to the boat, where Lei urged him to find somewhere to settle down, for the further you ran the more trouble you ran into. If you halted and took a stand, you could cope with the worst. Judging by the uselessness of mock flight and flight in good earnest, he meant to do his best to remedy the situation by joining in the war effort. He hoped Mr Huang would do the same before long.

Huang waited in vain for news of Lei's arrival in Guangxi. Some days later a friend back from Chikan remarked that an old man on the last boat had dropped a box into the sea while disembarking and in desperation had jumped in after it. Huang could not refrain from tears. Perhaps this was a judgement on Lei for inventing that iron-gill fish prematurely, so it had to go to the bottom of the sea.

1937

Translated by Gladys Yang

Wang Tongzhao

WANG Tongzhao (1897-1957) was born in Zhucheng in Shandong Province. He started writing in 1919 while a student at Beijing University, where he participated in the New Culture Movement. In 1921 he helped found the Literature Research Society. He subsequently travelled to Europe to research classical literature and art. Returning to China in 1935, he taught at Jinan University and edited books for the Shanghai-based Kaiming Publishing House. After the 1949 founding of the People's Republic of China, he held leading posts in cultural organizations.

Wang Tongzhao has published many collections of poems and short stories. His most influential work is the novel *Mountain Rain* published in 1933. He is noted for his skilled and absorbing characterizations and a vivid, finely-wrought style.

The Child at the Lakeside

I seldom cared to visit the famous lake although I lived in a city along its shore. Filled with reeds and large craft, it seemed exceptionally narrow and cramped and noisy. Sometimes I went rowing with a few friends in the evening, but every night it was the same bedlam. The clash of cymbals, the high-pitched squeal of fiddles, the unpleasant singing, the men's raucous shouts, the seductive laughter of painted women with sleekly oiled hair, the cries of the vendors on the little pedlar boats . . . swept the placid surface of the lake like a huge wave.

And so, whenever I went to the lake, I would close my eyes and ears to my surroundings and withdraw into my own thoughts. Occasionally, when the sunset colours were reflected on the water, I would stroll along a quiet sector of the lakeside to enjoy the breeze. I would listen to the frogs singing in the green grass after the rain and watch the twittering birds flit among the branches of the trees. I would feel rather stimulated, moved by a profound consciousness of nature and excited by innumerable far-reaching thoughts.

One day at sunset, violet and purple rays illuminated the emerald trailers of the weeping willows on the dike. In a little pond beside a temple huge lotus leaves grew higher than a man. Although the lotus flowers, pure as carved white jade, had slowly closed their petals after noon, one or two bees, lured by their scent, still hovered, reluctant to depart. On the dark green water, scarlet clouds shimmered golden; the rapidly lowering rays in their midst were a remarkable variety of hues. Layer upon layer of colour, interweaving and interplaying, shone with a dazzling brilliance.

It had rained heavily for six or seven hours the night before. Today the sky was clear, and I walked alone along the west bank of the lake, enjoying the freshly washed scene. My leather shoes left sharp prints on the moss-covered flagstones of the inclined path.

In the centre of the lake people were shouting, quarrelling violently. I walked slowly towards the far end of the stone-flagged path. Rustling willow trailers and the water-pepper shrubs that had just come into flower beside the trembling reeds danced in the west breeze at the edge of the water. This was perhaps the coolest and most secluded spot on the entire lake. Except for the steps of an infrequent passer-by or two, the only sound was the twittering of the little birds in the trees greeting the eventide. Frogs in the tangled grass croaked a rhythmic accompaniment.

Although this made me feel somewhat more cheerful than usual, I had no desire to retain the rapidly fading scene. For it reminded me of the words, "the yellow dusk of the dying sun" — a phrase I found rather depressing.

My head lowered in thought, I walked with heavy weary tread. The violet and purple sunset rays were growing dimmer, the light of the sun having already more than half sunk in the reflecting water. Although I knew it was getting late, I did not wish to return home. I sat down on a large white rock by the lake's edge.

Listening to the last of the cicadas droning in the late summer night, I was conscious of an air of autumn in the golden haze drifting on the water's surface. I sat alone beneath the willows and watched the yellow light fading in the distance and observed far off the tiny glow of the first lamps of evening. The weather was no longer very hot during the day; with evening came a certain soft coolness. At the same time, probably because of this coolness, I was vaguely stirred by an indefinable excitement.

As I sat wrapped in idle thought, suddenly I heard a rustling behind the willows. It came so unexpectedly in the quiet darkness, I was a bit startled. A moment later, I heard light footsteps threshing through a cove of reeds. I leaped up, circled the willows and emerged on the other side of the cove. It was quite dark by then. I couldn't see clearly. On a mud bank beside the reeds I seemed to perceive a small figure.

"Who's there?" I shouted.

But the shadow made no reply.

Ordinarily, this was a very quiet spot. At night, it was even more deserted. Now, it was growing darker and darker, and the reeds and the willows were rustling faintly. I felt a bit afraid. "Who's there?" I cried again. Just as I was turning to leave, the little dark figure on the mud bank replied in a small weak voice:

"It's me, Little Shun . . . I'm here . . . fishing."

He practically swallowed the last word and his voice trembled slightly. He sounded like an eleven or twelve-year-old little boy. I was very suspicious.

"How can you fish after dark?" I asked him. "How can you see?"

Again the small shadow did not reply.

"Where do you live?"

"In Horse Head Lane. . . ."

There was something about that weak voice that sounded familiar. I took a step closer and asked, "Have you always lived there?"

"No," the little boy replied quickly. "I used to live on Peace Street. . . ."

Suddenly I remembered. "Oh! You're the Chens' little boy. . . . Isn't your father a blacksmith?"

The child pulled in his bamboo fishing pole and ran to me, barefoot, down the mud bank. "Yes. . . . Papa is a blacksmith. But who are you?"

I drew nearer and peered at the child's face. I could barely recognize him. What had happened to the darling Little Shun of five or six! His face was blackened — either by mud or soot. He wore a short homespun blue robe that was well up above his knees, and he reeked of mud and sweat. When he heard me call his name, he stared at me in astonishment. He didn't know who I was.

I remembered him when he was four or five — I was very fond of playing with children then. Whenever I passed his door I saw him sitting on his mother's lap beneath the big shady old elm tree. He always sang me his song about the little rooster.

More than six years had passed, and I was often away from home. People in my family told me that Little Shun had moved, no one knew exactly where. When I passed his house and saw someone else's name on the door I felt sorry, as if I had lost a constant companion!

Meeting him today again in the cool dusk by the lakeside, how could I help but be surprised? Strangest of all, how could the rosy-cheeked Little Shun with the clean white hands have become virtually the same as the dirty little beggar boys on the street? His father had been a respectable blacksmith, quite able to look after his child financially.

I led Little Shun over to the rock and made him sit down beside me. I told him how I often saw him when he was very young, and how I had played with him and made him laugh. He looked at me, bewildered. I began to question him.

"Where is your papa now?"

"At home, you might say. . . ." Little Shun replied hesitantly. From his expression I could see that he thought this old friend was rather peculiar.

"Is he still working?"

"What? . . . He goes out every day, but he never . . . brings home any money. . . . Working? . . . I don't know."

"What about your mother?"

"Dead," the boy retorted briefly.

I was shocked. But of course it had to be. Little Shun's mother had been a frail little woman. People said she had borne seven children in thirteen years. Little Shun was the only one that remained alive. But I hadn't thought her time would come so quickly!

"Who else do you have at home now?"

"I've got a ma, a new one. . . ."

"Oh, is your family poorer than before? You look. . ."

Little Shun had always been an intelligent child. At my blunt question, he stared off into the misty distance. Then he dropped his head. After a long time he said in a low voice:

"Sometimes we have nothing to eat. My papa is often away from home. . . ."

"Where does he go?"

"I don't know. . . . He doesn't come home till after breakfast. . . . I hear that he works in an opium den. . . . I don't know where."

His low voice spoke very slowly. I was beginning to understand. I felt compelled to go on.

"How . . . how old is your new ma? Is she good to you?"

"I hear she's only thirty. She comes from a family inside the East Gate. . . ." An uneasy expression stole over his face. I asked him:

"Does she beat you?"

"Her? No, she has no time." He said this decisively.

If the young woman was the sole support of a family like his, she obviously couldn't have much time to spare!

"And what sort of work does she do?"

"Work? She doesn't work. But she gets very busy late every afternoon. That's why I can't stay home. . . . Every evening I come out to this cove of reeds; only here . . . just here. . . ."

"What? . . ."

Little Shun had learned to take a grown-up attitude. He wrinkled his small nose and snorted: "There are always guests in our house! Sometimes two or three in one night. Sometimes not a single one shows up. . . ."

I was rather shaken. But he continued:

". . . My ma can earn money to buy us food. . . . When they come, she chases me out. She never lets me go back till very late. My papa knows. He doesn't come home at night either. . . ."

By now I knew quite well what kind of environment

Little Shun came from. It was like something in a novel: A tousle-headed child, sallow, thin, with sunken eyes, every night had to wander among the reeds, barefoot. When he grew hungry, he could talk to his friends — the birds and the frogs, or listen to the music of the wind blowing through the reeds.

His father was a waiter in an opium den. His mother — rather his stepmother — in order to keep alive did the bitterest of all things — she sold her flesh.

Only the stars kept Little Shun company when he returned home in the still, deserted night. But the following day, it was the same all over again. It was too much like a piece of fiction. I couldn't believe it. I remembered him so well as a clean, lovable child. How could he have come to this?

"What kind of people are they," I asked him, "these men who come to your house every night?"

"I don't see them very often," said Little Shun, "and then only for a moment. Some wear grey military tunics, with army caps cocked over one eye. Some smell of kerosene oil and wear thick silver watch chains on their vests. A few are dressed in long scholars' gowns. Usually we have three or four visitors a night. But sometimes not even one comes to our door."

"Why is that?"

I felt my persistent questioning was very unkind to the child. But I couldn't stop.

Little Shun laughed. "Don't you know? All the houses in Horse Head Lane are open to visitors every night! . . ." He laughed again, as if amused that I, an educated person, should understand so little.

There didn't seem to be anything else to ask him. I couldn't bring myself to make this innocent child tell any more of his tragic history. He appeared to have something on his mind; he gazed abstractedly at the stars shining palely through the dusk.

If his own mother were still alive, perhaps things would be different, I mused. The life this poor woman who is his present mother leads is no better than hell!

Ah, the family! The family organization and the pressure of the times, the urgent need to make a living! I had come for an idle stroll along the lakeside after the rain. But instead of finding relaxation, I ended with many troublesome problems knotted in my breast.

Just think of it. Suffering hunger and discomfort, a child must come to a cove of reeds at dusk and remain half the night. His mother, because the burden of supporting the whole family rests on her, must endure endlessly the worst of all humiliations. Such a life is less than human! The poor in our present society can take only this hopeless, dead-end road!

I was consumed with doubts. I felt agitated, unable to sit still. And the lakeside scene which had given me such fresh, soothing impressions had long since been swallowed up by the darkness.

Knowing that Little Shun did not dare to return home yet, I didn't have the heart to leave him to watching the starlight alone by the shore. I sat down beside him beneath the willows. Though I wanted to question him further, I felt that it would be too cruel. In silence, I reflected on the fact that a child is moulded by his environment . . . and I trembled for Little Shun and all other children like him!

Suddenly an agitated call drifted over from the opposite bank. "Little Shun. . . . Where are you? . . ." I jumped to my feet. The child was so frightened that he dropped his fishing pole into the water and began hurrying along a small path. I was completely bewildered; I didn't know what had happened. Just then a middle-aged man burst through the reeds, took Little Shun by the hand, and rushed off with him. I heard the man say:

"Your father was arrested by the police tonight. . . . They raided the opium den. . . . We couldn't tell your mother. Master Wu is calling on her. Who would dare to disturb him! . . . Child, you were the only one we neighbours could notify. . . ."

Their shadows gradually disappeared into the night, the man's voice faded away.

Slowly, I trudged home. Few people walked abroad in the dense night mists. There was a weight on my chest, as if the atmospheric pressure that evening was exceptionally heavy. The stars that guided me were very pale, not nearly so bright as usual.

1922

Translated by Sidney Shapiro

Shipwreck

"A few more hours should bring us in sight of the sea — a lovely sight, stretching off to the horizon. Don't you agree, Brother Liu? You've seen it. Sampans fly to and fro as if they had wings, and a snatch of opera accompanied by a fiddle sounds extra good out on the water. A fellow can relax out at sea and his voice carries further. . . ." Gu Bao, a tall, sturdy carter, as he pushed a large wheel-barrow was addressing Liu Erzeng who was tugging in front.

Liu Erzeng, a peasant nearing forty, had taken up barbering in his spare time and in recent years had come to be known as The Barber. On the barrow they were pushing sat his wife of forty-odd in a dark blue homespun jacket, and two children aged eight and three respectively.

"Of course! Don't forget our trip to buy fish a few years back, when we crossed the sea and strolled down that big road built by the Germans. I don't get seasick myself, but some folk daren't take a boat." After trundling the barrow for several hours, Liu was panting with exhaustion, unlike his companion who took this in his stride.

"Look at you, man. You can travel by boat but not push a cart, seemingly. It's still ten *li* to the place where we'll stop for lunch — think you can make it? That light work you're used to at home has made you flabby, yet you want to try your luck now in the northeast. You'll have to rough it there! I've been and I know. The cold's too much for anyone from our parts. You may have relatives there, but you can't live on them. Getting paid is easy, it's sweating at a job that's hard. . . ."

Panting, his eyes on the lean donkey pulling the barrow, Liu Erzeng replied, "Of course we're prepared to rough it. Heaven helps those who help themselves. Was it our fault we couldn't make a living back there? In a good year who wants to leave home and start again? It's lucky I know a trade and perhaps can find work wherever I go. The thing is, it's easy for a single man, but I've a wife and children to support."

"Don't you go pinning the blame on us!" cried his wife, in whose arms their three-year-old was sleeping. "Did we hold you back? I was all for farming the children out and going into service myself to get good food and clothes and a chance to see the world. But you wouldn't have it. You've dragged us all this way, the children too. I hope we don't come to grief." Mrs Liu was a capable woman with a sharp tongue, and her husband knuckled under at once.

Still panting, he spat in disgust at a stone by the roadside.

Gu Bao was shrewd. Pulling on the donkey's reins, he called out to slow it down, then mopped his sweating face with the white cloth draped over his shoulder.

"Forget it!" he cried with a grin. "You've been at it hammer and tongs every step of the way. 'A single tree doesn't make a wood' — married folk must stick together. You've hard times ahead and you're still a long way from Shahe. For heaven's sake call a truce!

You don't want to break up your family. I'm famished, this barrow's so heavy. Can we get a jug of wine when we stop at the tavern?"

"Of course we can." Mrs Liu laughed. "You laid by your work to see us off — why should he grudge you a drink? Tell you what: In nine or ten years when we're doing well, I'll send Azi to fetch Uncle Gu to stay with us."

"Yes, I'll come and fetch you back, Uncle Gu, in a sampan," chimed in The Barber's eight-year-old boy who was lying on the right side of the barrow.

They stopped talking then as the barrow slowly mounted a slope.

The wild mulberry woods around them were bathed in the noonday sun and their big leaves rustling in the warm, early autumn wind filled the hills with a murmur like waves washing the shore. Normally peasants came here in spring to raise wild silkworms, while by late summer and early autumn the woods were at their best, a source of riches for those living in this region. In recent years, however, the wild silkworms had greatly diminished and, although wild mulberry trees were still plentiful, not many people came up here in the spring. The stony path through the hills was overgrown with grass. Grey grasshoppers speckled with black hopped to and fro, more of them every day the dry weather held.

Beads of sweat were running down the faces of both men, whose bare shoulders appeared brown and worn with toil as they laboured along beneath the scorching sun. It was hard work pushing the barrow up that stony track and they had no energy to spare for talking.

Half an hour or so later they halted in front of a

crazily built stone inn. The donkey half closed its eyes, as if to meditate on its hard lot and the uncertain future. The children scampered off to catch grasshoppers. Liu Erzeng sank down on a rough bench in front of the inn to fan himself with his tattered straw hat and mop his perspiring face. Cheerful, talkative Gu Bao squatted under the mat that served as an awning and lit a cigarette.

The name of this inn was The Rock and it lay on the way of all travellers to the wharf at Red Stone Cliff. The faint red of the boulders and soil of the hills hereabouts seemed to typify the poverty of the region. Small villages, numbering only four or five households, were swallowed up by large-leafed wild mulberry trees and poplars. The old wayside inn had just three rooms built of stones roughly piled together. And the walls, white to begin with, were blackened by the smoke of wood fires. Above the front gate, made of brambles, a blue cloth sign hung from the projecting bough of an old locust tree, giving the place a certain old-world charm. When travellers several *li* away saw that sign, it never failed to stir their imaginations; they would often be assailed by a sense of desolation and longing but at the same time their parched lips seemed to savour the taste of home-brewed wine.

When the innkeeper had greeted these guests he went inside with their order for unleavened griddle-cakes and vegetable dishes. On the chipped table under the matting inside the bramble gate, he set an earthenware jug of the local liquor, a big packet of salted peanuts and two thick crockery winecups. The Barber sat down with his wife and friend to drink and recover from their journey.

"This is a good place, Brother Liu," cried Gu Bao cheerfully after a few cups. "If ever I get married, I swear I'll move here to live. With so few families and so many trees, you'd never go short of firewood. There are hills all around and it's only twenty *li* to the sea. Fish and prawns must be cheap in spring. . . . Say, why don't you try it out here instead of going all the way to Shahe?"

"Trust you to come up with a scheme like that, Uncle Gu," retorted Mrs Liu. "You can manage anywhere, with no wife or children. What would we live on here, I'd like to know? Eat the hills and drink the sea water, I suppose!"

After gulping down some wine the lean, sun-burned barber gazed north towards his old home, concealed by trees and clouds at the horizon. His simple heart ached with a longing that he could not put into words, making him reluctant to answer. He was thinking of his thatched cottage, the three hens he had given to a neighbour, the small courtyard in which he had grown cabbage, and his two nephews in school, two boys with shabby satchels whom he met each day when he went out with his barber's kit. More distressing still was the memory of his elder brother's parting advice and proposal that he should stay on another year. The rugged hills in early autumn brought these memories back as he sat there exhausted, and misgivings stirred in him. One glance at his firm, outspoken wife, however, induced him to hold his peace. He turned to look at the children, munching toasted buns on the grass, and two tears trickled over the dust and sweat on his cheeks.

The innkeeper came out wearing a short jacket and straw sandals and holding a bamboo pipe a good two feet in length. He walked over to the gnarled trunk supporting the matting to chat with Gu Bao, whom he knew.

He was a man of sixty, with no queue but grizzled hair three or four inches long. His withered face was scored with wrinkles. His palsied hands trembled as if he would drop the pipe.

"Where are you off to? Seeing these guests to the northeast?"

"That's right," said Gu Bao. ""I suppose lots of people are travelling this way?"

"Ah, what times we're living in! I've never seen so many people heading north. Ever since spring there's been an endless stream of carts along the road. Poor souls! Some of them, I heard, just handed their title-deeds over to the authorities and left — times are too hard." This speech was punctuated by sighs.

"Things look pretty bad. But my friends here could still manage, although feeding a family's not as easy as it used to be. They're all right, though, they've relatives up north who asked them to go. You should be doing good business. Are you making plenty of money?"

"Far from it! Not with prices soaring like this and so many mouths to feed. Private schools aren't forbidden in the villages now, but who's going to send his children to school these days? It's lucky I gave up teaching before it was too late. Otherwise. . . ."

"Of course, I'd forgotten. Ten years ago you were the schoolmaster in the North Village. What a wise old man you are! Even in business you manage better than others." Gu Bao had a ready tongue and natural tact.

This reminded the innkeeper suddenly of the time, several dozen years ago, when he had taken the imperial examinations. Now he was reduced to living in this country tavern and catering for travellers from all parts of the land. He heaved a deep sigh of regret.

"What do you young people know of the world?" he demanded. "It's a wretched life I've had. In these times of great upheavals all I can do is 'retain my integrity' in a 'world that has lost the Way'."

These literary allusions were over Gu Bao's head, but he answered at random, "True enough. If not driven by hunger and cold, who'd leave home to put up with hardships?"

The old man knocked out his pipe and walked off with a bitter smile.

A cock crowed in the woods to announce that it was noon. After stuffing himself with griddle-cakes, Gu Bao lay down on some planks and was soon sound asleep. The Barber and his wife sat facing each other in silence. He was staring at the path ahead which seemed to wind unendingly into the distance, leading him to some future as yet unknown. Lost in thought, he looked like a man scouring his memory in vain for something that eluded him.

The children had not yet tired of chasing grasshoppers, while the donkey twitched its tail from time to time to drive away the flies on its flanks.

Dusk found them in the Inn of Tranquillity at Red Stone Cliff, hurriedly packing up their humble belongings ready to take the boat the next day to Qingdao, from where they would ship for Dalian and the northeast. The inn was swarming with refugees like themselves or even worse off, while groups of boys and girls, ragged and grimy, were crying and quarrelling outside the gate. A few gaunt draught animals had left droppings all over the road. The roar of the wind and waves out at sea sounded like some evening dirge or song of farewell. The Barber and his family were shown into a large room quite bare of beds which was crowded with country women and their children. Leaving his wife to keep an eye on their things, The Barber went with Gu Bao to find out about a boat.

The accountant's office was packed with peasants in short, belted jackets and sandals, who were asking what the fare would be.

"Will you take the steamer at ten tomorrow morning? It's a Japanese boat, fast, steady, and not much dearer than a sampan. Please yourselves. With this high wind, it's not certain what time the sampans can leave." The accountant, flourishing a writing brush, was an old hand at persuading villagers.

The Barber, eager to have a quick, smooth passage, paid two dollars and more for the tickets, then went back to the big room to inform his wife, who approved of his decision on the grounds that there was less chance of seasickness on the steamer.

The elder boy, hearing that they were to sail out to sea, asked round-eyed where the steamer was and if there were any grasshoppers on board.

By supper time the sun had not set completely and Gu Bao offered to show The Barber over the steamer, on which he had travelled on a previous occasion.

So after hastily swallowing the coarse meal served by the inn, they set off together.

The inn was barely a hundred yards from the sea, and there was a wooden pier for the use of passengers or porters loading or unloading boats. Red Stone Cliff had quite a number of warehouses for such a small place, as it was an important trading port for all the counties nearby. Groundnuts, bean oil and hide stored in dozens of godowns were waiting to be loaded and shipped away. Groups of sailors in navy blue and big straw hats were cheerfully playing the finger-game while they drank together in taverns along the street. As The Barber walked down the road in the evening mist and heard the very mixed accents of the vendors of sweet potatoes and date cakes, he felt he was already far from home. To make a better impression on strangers, he was wearing the long lined gown he only put on at home when calling on clients. Many washings had transformed the dark grey cloth into a shadowy silver, and two of the buttons were missing. The evening wind from the sea swept his newly shaved head and sent a chill through his bones. Gu Bao had on the short jacket and straw sandals he wore at work every day, but he smoked a cigarette as he led the way.

This was not a clean, orderly wharf for, with the exception of one or two small foreign steamers that picked up passengers here, all the boats that put in were sampans. The sandy path by the coast was choked with cinders and weeds, and the autumn wind carried the rank smell of fish and brine. Some fishermen's straw huts stood on the cliff, their cooking fires visible through the mist that was rising from the water. All was dirt, neglect and disorder, typical of an old coastal village in the East. As The Barber followed Gu Bao down the pier, he could just see the ocean with its white-capped billows. The vast expanse of murky water inspired him with both wonder and dismay. At home he had looked forward eagerly, without any qualms, to this voyage to the northeast. Yesterday at the wayside inn a sense of desolation had stolen over him. And now that he had actually reached the ocean, could hear the roar of its waves and see its waters stretching off without end, The Barber's heart sank within him. Why had they embarked on this long and dangerous journey? But what alternative had they? He halted under a street lamp that shed a faint yellow light.

"Come on! Let's stroll over the boat!" cried Gu Bao, following some porters up the gangway to the belly of the dark monster.

A ribbon of smoke was rising from the funnel and chains were rattling as the small 200-tonner made ready for her trip the following morning.

Gu Bao walked up and down the deck as if to impress The Barber with his courage and knowledge of the sea. Gazing at the lights of vessels out in the ocean, he casually tossed a cigarette stub into the water. "Hey! Why not come aboard and see something of the boat? Come on!"

But The Barber by the lamppost shook his head, a prey to bewilderment, doubts and misgivings.

Group after group of shabby villagers were passing now in quite surprising numbers to have a look at the steamer. The same cruel winds of change had brought them to this unfamiliar coast from the fighting, brigandage, crippling taxation and natural calamities which were bankrupting the villages where they had lived so long. With their children, brothers and friends, they were prepared to let the ship of fate carry them through the darkness to unfamiliar shores far, far away.

Stern night brooded over all, while waves murmured

faintly as they lapped the shingle. At last a rather sulky Gu Bao accompanied his friend back along the bleak road to the disorderly inn.

The square doss-house, large as a barn, re-echoed with the snores of exhausted sleepers, and the paraffin lamp suspended from the ceiling shed a faint, flickering light which barely picked out the sprawled figures of weary travellers, dreaming for a while after the day's long journey. Their piles of old cases and rough clothes and quilts could hardly be distinguished in the gloom. The Barber trudged in with a heavy heart to find his eight-year-old son sleeping, fully dressed, in one corner on a thin cotton mattress, an innocent smile curving his grubby lips. He certainly was a fine, lovable little fellow, and the apple of his father's eye. The Barber's wife had their sleeping three-year-old on her knees. Her husband noticed a cold draught as he sat down and saw that some tiles were missing in that corner, admitting a faint glimmer of light.

"What's the time? When do we embark tomorrow morning?"

"At ten, they told us here," was his listless reply.

"Don't look so grumpy! One trip by sea, then another, and we'll be at my brother's house in no time. Why look so down in the mouth?"

He did not answer.

"Cheer up! Remember the Wu family of Huang Village? After less than ten years in the northeast, they came back to a house and land, good food and good clothes, so that everybody envied their luck. Why should we sweat in the fields for the rest of our days? Luck's something you have to look for, don't expect it to seek you out." As usual, she was trying to encourage him.

Crooning a lullaby to the child, she dreamed happily to herself for a while in the darkness.

"See here," she resumed. "There are richer, better dressed people than us on their way up to try their luck. I just had a talk with a woman from Yishui, a daughter of a well-to-do family, who's now a 'refugee'. They fought over a dozen battles at her home, till the house was destroyed by shells and none of their land could be tilled, yet they had to pay grain and taxes just the same. It's far worse for her than for us. Her daughter, just turned eighteen, died of fright in the fighting. Compared with her we're lucky."

"All in the same boat," replied The Barber indifferently from his pallet.

His wife, silenced for a while, started thinking over their problems amid the chorus of snoring all around. Presently she asked her husband:

"How much money have you left now?"

"How much?" Plaintively, he recapitulated their account. "You know I gave up the lease of our land and sold the two pigs. I made over that one *mu* of ours to my brother for three hundred strings of cash. The pigs fetched two hundred and fifty. I changed that into fifty silver dollars and fifty strings of cash. So far, we've used over twenty. Think, woman, one catty of griddle-cake costs one string and we have to eat. We've still a long way to go, and we're cleaned out at home."

They fell silent again, both occupied with their thoughts. Mrs Liu, with her strong, forthright character, could not help despising her husband's spinelessness. It was only at her insistence that they had left home. As for him, his thoughts were in such a tangle of regret for the past and anxiety over the future, that he could not sleep in this stuffy, disorderly doss-house.

As he turned on his side and caught sight of his elder son smiling in his dreams and his wife's face aged before its time by care, he felt that the snoring sleepers in the room and the pallid lamplight were a fantastic nightmare.

Every day the old owner of The Rock waited by his bramble gate for customers, while his elder son's wife and two children worked all day in the little stone tavern preparing food. Business was brisk, but the old man knew that the money proffered him by wayfarers had cost them blood and sweat. Because of the ups and downs in his own life, he did his best for these refugees on their way to the northeast. The food and drink here were better served and cheaper than elsewhere.

One morning three or four days after The Barber's family had passed, the old innkeeper rose early and went into the woods to gather fallen leaves for his small grandson to carry back in his wicker crate for fuel. After a light meal of congee, he sat smoking his long pipe under the matting. There had been fewer passers-by the last few days, and it struck him that no one had returned from the wharf. Not that this worried him, he simply regarded it as rather strange.

The old man had an excellent memory, the result of hard application in his youth. In those days his family had been quite well off and after studying in the village school he attended a school in town, with the result that he could recite the whole of the *Four Classics** and Zhu Xi's commentaries,** and was even word-perfect in the *Book of Rhymes.* This had won the admiration of many of his teachers and fellow candidates. So although he never passed the district examination he had something of which to be proud. When he started moving in a different world, keeping a roadside tavern, sometimes he could not resist airing his knowledge to scholars who passed that way. But in recent times scholars and country gentlemen had virtually stopped making excursions to the sea. During the fighting that raged year after year, it was only poor peasants and artisans who streamed past to the coast to find some means of livelihood in the north. For them he felt infinite sympathy and compassion. But much as he sympathized with these good, honest folk, none of them understood Zhu Xi's commentaries or the *Book of Rhymes* — their sole topics of conversation were drought, flood, fighting and natural calamities. He often reflected that the good old cultured days had gone, never to return, like his vanished youth. All men knew today was suffering and hardships and no ancient culture could alleviate their distress.

That was why, when no one was by, he stood alone gazing at the distant peaks and sighed so heavily.

It was a dull autumn day. Grey clouds raced past overhead and the sun, still below the mountains, cast no light. The forest trees bent before cold blasts of wind and whispered to their leaves so soon to fall. Mist

---

**The Great Learning, Doctrine of the Mean, Analects of Confucius* and *Mencius.*

** Zhu Xi, a Song-dynasty scholar of the 12th century, wrote commentaries on the Confucian classics.

from the far-off horizon was billowing over the whole countryside, enough to fill every heart with autumnal gloom. Dressed in a long black gown, the old innkeeper twisted his grizzled moustache as he brooded under his matting over the past. He fixed his eyes on the track leading to the wharf, the pockets of mist in the withered brown grass and the growing network of mist. He recalled the lines:

> I stop my cart at dusk to enjoy the maples,
> Their frosted leaves red as the flowers of
> spring.

A longing for the past nearly overwhelmed him. Just then a shadowy figure loomed through the mist. The old man was too lost in thought to pay much attention, until the traveller confronted him. Then he looked up and without rising to his feet said, "You're an early bird. Back from seeing your neighbours off? Have you bought no seafood this time?"

"Don't talk about seafood! Of all the damned luck! I set off before it was light and ran into this fog. First give me two jugs of wine! . . ." The new arrival had a gown over one shoulder, but his hands were empty, his face a ghastly colour.

"Heat two pots of wine, quick! Brother Gu is back and in a hurry. . . . Look sharp!" The old innkeeper tottered inside.

What had happened to make cheerful, talkative Gu Bao so frantic? The carter usually came back from the coast with a load of fish or a barrow for someone else, always as lively as could be, singing folk-songs or smoking the cheapest cigarettes. This morning the old man had hardly recognized him.

Presently amid the fumes of liquor and smoke of cigarettes the old fellow asked: "Did you see them to Qingdao? You've been gone some time. What's all the hurry today?"

"No, I didn't take the boat with them. Such a pitiful business! Little did I think I was seeing them to their graves! These days anything can happen — hadn't you heard?" Gu Bao kept refilling his cup with the newly broached liquor.

"What's that?" demanded the innkeeper. "To their graves, did you say? What's happened?"

"I tell you, there's been a fearful accident!"

"An accident? . . . That's the first I've heard of it. You don't mean the steamer? What could go wrong with that? How shocking! Were many drowned? When did it happen? No one's been this way for a couple of days, so I hadn't heard any news."

"They're done for! . . . All done for, that poor barber, his wife and the two boys you saw." Gu Bao gulped down the liquor as if seething with rage.

"What! . . . All of them lost?"

"That's the way it was. Just their luck to arrive that day and take that confounded foreign boat the next morning. Less than two hours after casting off it foundered — only its funnel left above the waves!"

"What a terrible business! And the passengers? Were none saved?" The old man was stammering in his distress.

"Some were. The Japanese lowered one of their lifeboats in time, but it was so overloaded The Barber wouldn't get in — just pushed in his eight-year-old whom he'd been carrying. I heard that from another survivor. To make matters worse, his body's never been found. His wife was laid out on the shore at Qingdao, still holding her baby tight in her arms. She was trapped in the cabin, poor soul!"

"So you went to Qingdao?"

"I'd stayed an extra day at Red Stone Cliff to buy some things to take home. The next morning I took a sampan to Qingdao to see the boat they'd salvaged and the bodies, and to get news for the folk back home."

"Well, what about the boy who's left?" In his distress the old innkeeper let fall his bamboo pipe.

"It was for him I went, the only one left of the poor barber's family! After seeing his mother's corpse, I found out that the boy had been taken in by a home. Luckily I knew the place well enough to find it. There were several poor waifs there, Azi among them, and he seemed half-crazed! He didn't know his father was lost out at sea, nor that his mother was laid out on the shore with his dead baby brother in her arms, the flies swarming round them. He couldn't talk sense and he'd lost all interest in food. He must have had a concussion. So although he's still living, who knows if he can be cured! . . ." By now Gu Bao had downed more than half of the spirits.

"Where is he now?"

"In the home. Not knowing me, they wouldn't let me take him. They said there's some relief fund too and his uncle should fetch the boy and the money at the same time. So I took the boat back yesterday evening. I shall get home tomorrow and tell The Barber's brother to go for the boy."

A short silence ensued. The matting was buffeted by a high wind and the two men felt a sense of utter desolation. The clouds drifting through the sky parted, then converged again. As Gu Bao chewed his griddle-cake, he looked up at the old man's wrinkled face. "Luck? To those Japanese, Chinese count lower than dogs! They loaded four hundred passengers on to that little boat. No wonder it foundered, in the high sea running that day! I'd warned The Barber, but he didn't want to sacrifice his tickets. Ah, grandad, isn't it all the same in the end? If you don't freeze, starve or burn to death, you'll be drowned! I reckon this was fate. Yet not one of the crew of that Japanese boat was drowned. Not because they're such strong swimmers, but because they were ready for an accident!"

The old innkeeper's thoughts had veered off at a tangent. He decided that this was the result of "forcing barbarian customs upon China". If none of those contemptible steamers touched at Red Stone Cliff, sampans might not have sunk; and even if they had, fewer lives would have been lost. To find support for this conclusion, he asked:

"How many, actually, were drowned?"

"Nearly four hundred souls, they said! Men and women, both. Some of the bodies haven't been found, they were still searching when I left. But all those were folk from Yizhou. Some of the 'refugees' were quite well-to-do. You'd be surprised what different parts they hailed from. Now they'll all go down in the same register of the dead!"

Without any comment the old innkeeper stooped to retrieve his pipe having reached another conclusion: "These disasters mean the day of doom is near!" Absent-mindedly stroking his grizzled moustache, he reflected that he belonged to a doomed generation. His eyes stung as up welled two tears of bitterness and despair.

As Gu Bao finished his hasty meal and prepared to set off again, the old man was struck by an idea and said earnestly: "Will you tell the dead man's brother to drop in here on his way to fetch the lad home? Will you do that? It's not taking him out of his way."

"Of course I will. He'll be passing here." Gu Bao slung his long gown over his shoulder again. "So, grandad, you haven't forgotten the poor little fellow who was so keen on chasing grasshoppers?"

"No . . . because, you see, he's just the age of my second grandson. . . ." But before the old man could finish, Gu Bao had gone, vanishing behind a clump of rustling wild mulberry trees.

1927

Translated by Gladys Yang

Fifty Yuan

HE left the group of people in the field and walked listlessly along the poplar-lined ditch. The afternoon July sun was like a fiery umbrella overhead. Beads of sweat rolled from his brow, soaking even the white towel slung across his left shoulder. But he was too abstracted to mop his face.

As a matter of fact, the scorching weather didn't bother him in the least. But inside him, something was crushing his heart like a smouldering grenade, making it difficult for him to breathe.

Nearly sixty, he had always been a simple obedient man who knew his place. He might have an occasional argument with a neighbour over how big the coming wheat harvest would be, or how many eggs a chicken could lay in a week. But to the long-robed gentry, he never said a contrary word. His soft voice and lowered eyes when addressing them won the approval of many.

"Never gets above himself . . . quite respectable . . . very steady . . . a fine servant!" For dozens of years this was the praise he won from masters everywhere as he stood with head bowed.

At the meeting which the ward leader had called in the field, the old man had been dealt a sudden blow. Now, no matter how he pondered, he could see no way out of the dilemma.

"Hey, Old Pu, where've you been? Just look at you — all perspiring. . . ."

A young man was crossing a half-collapsed old stone bridge at the far end of the ditch. Wearing a rough straw hat, a white homespun tunic and blue shorts, he advanced cheerfully towards Old Pu on bare feet.

"Ah, ah . . . from Little Mou's field. We had a meeting. *Hai*! They said we need guns. . . ."

"Guns? You're not bandits; what do you want guns for?" the young man asked breezily.

"Wu De, don't pretend you don't know. You're wandering around town all day, there isn't anything you haven't heard. . . . I'm worried. What are we going to do? The ward chief says the county magistrate came to town the day before yesterday and ordered that every one join the Agricultural Association; whoever owns five *mu* of land or more has to buy a rifle. They'll be made locally. . . ." His brow furrowed unhappily, Old Pu halted beneath a tree.

The young man pulled a fan of woven rushes from his belt and plied it vigorously. His screwed up ruddy face relaxed, and he laughed mockingly. "Of course. The Agricultural Association is a watchdog for its members' property. It's no use without a lot of weapons. A splendid organization! . . . And unless they put the pressure on, who would be willing to spend money for rifles? . . ."

"Tell me, Wu De, are our local guns any good?"

"Why not? A few villages chip in and build a forge. We have excellent craftsmen. . . . I've fired some of our locally made rifles. They shoot quite straight.

"I hear they're fifty yuan each. Is that right?"

"Yes. A forge has already been set up in the courtyard of the temple in town. They've got three blacksmiths working there now. For fifty yuan you get a rifle and a few dozen rounds of bullets.... It's not a bad idea, Wu De, but where can families like ours raise the money?..."

"Leave me out of this, dear Old Pu. I'm not in your class. You've land of your own and you're doing nicely. Fifty yuan for a gun shouldn't mean a thing to you. Naturally the ward chief couldn't ask me to attend that meeting." His laugh sounded tinged with both satisfaction and envy. Wu De knocked some ants off a poplar leaf with his fan. He seemed entirely unconcerned with Old Pu's worries.

"It's not fair. We've got less than four and a half *mu*, including the land we've rented. Only two *mu* are our own. What are they worth? Where will I get fifty yuan? This spring we had a big hailstorm; I may not even harvest enough to cover the rent this autumn. I don't know who the ward chief's been listening to. He's put me down for a gun and given me ten days to pay! I've nothing to say. How can we refuse to obey the order of the county magistrate?..." Old Pu was extremely agitated. He was hoping Wu De would at least give him a little sympathy.

"Dear Master Pu, really... we're all old neighbours. No one can conceal his wealth," the young man teased. "If I went for a gun, they wouldn't give it to me. But you've been doing quite well on your land. All those years you've been earning money as a servant too — everybody knows. And nobody in your family spends any money. Of course the ward chief must have got wind of it."

He knocked a leaf down with his fan and ground it

to a pulp in the hot soil with the rough sole of his bare foot.

Only now did Old Pu take his towel and wipe the sweat from his face. His eyes staring dully, he said nothing.

"Respectful words aren't enough; official edicts must be obeyed!" Wu De cried sarcastically. "They're pushing very hard to get people into the Agricultural Association. Three or four are being held down at the district. I hear if they don't pay up soon they'll be paraded through the streets in disgrace. It's much better to buy a gun to guard your property. If I had fifty yuan, I'd certainly buy one of those playthings. The trouble is I don't have any property to guard. Take a broad view, Master Pu. Surely you want to be ready in case the bandits call! . . ."

"If they broke into my home, what could they find of any value?" Old Pu's sweat, running from his cheeks and neck, dripped faster.

"Of any value? Let's look at it this way. . . . If I were a bandit, I'd definitely put you on my list. Who cares whether a family is rich or poor? Anything you can get your hands on is sure to be worth a little money. You think we're still back a few years ago when the bandits only raided families rich enough to pay ransom?"

These words from the irreverent young drifter made Old Pu most unhappy, but he was unable to refute them. He didn't know where he was going to raise the fifty yuan, and if the bandits thought the same way as this young fellow and really put him on their list, what was he to do? Another smouldering grenade was added to his heart.

"Why worry? Just live from day to day. What are

you trying to do — make rich men out of those two sons of yours? . . ."

Wu De tucked his fan back in his belt and airily strolled off along the ditch.

The old man looked after him, unable to summon the courage to call him back. His feet seemed rooted to the spot; he breathed with difficulty. He could see the harsh visage of the ward chief before his eyes. Old Pu had known him for years. Originally he came from a rundown family that wasn't even as well off as Old Pu's; he had been a worthless idler who floated about the teahouses, carrying a pretty thrush in a cage, learnedly examining and discussing the merits of various imported bicycles. As soon as he became ward chief he began to put on airs; he was even more pompous than the county magistrate on a tour of the villages.

At the meeting in the field just now the ward chief had been ruthlessly inflexible. "Fifty yuan, ten days to pay. If you don't produce the money you'd better not count on our being old neighbours. Official business must be done in an official manner. I can't be responsible for the consequences. . . ." His voice had been loud and he made a chopping motion with his hand — like an executioner's axe.

Recalling the ward chief's behaviour, Old Pu momentarily forgot about his worries over raising the money and the danger of the bandits putting him on their list. The ward chief's high and mighty airs, his overbearing manner, truly had exceeded the old man's expectations.

He raised his head and glanced towards the west. The sun was nearly set. It was covered by blood-red clouds. Their grisly colour startled the old man.

On the road back to his home, which was half a mile

from the town, he kept looking at those blood-red clouds. A bad omen! The smouldering grenades in his heart knocked against each other uneasily.

Old Pu's home in the outskirts of town was not in a village but beside a grove of pines which enclosed a cemetery. Pu's father had settled there as a squatter and was permitted to remain by the owner on condition that he and his descendants take care of the cemetery for ever.

But the original owner's family had gone down financially, and now the cemetery was shared by others. Except for a few old cedars with hollow centres, most of the trees had been cut down and replaced by white poplars. Several of the grave mounds had long since been levelled and their gravestones demolished. Weeds and wild grass grew everywhere. Although Old Pu lived there technically as a caretaker, little remained of either the graves or the trees that he could care for.

His house consisted of a few rooms in a thatched shack with mud walls, surrounded by a bramble fence. Inside the few slats that formed his compound gate was a hamper of grain. Because the courtyard was so small, the brushwood they used for fuel had to be piled outside the gate. In summer and autumn evenings he and his family would sit on large stones and chat, soothed by the rustle of the cedars and poplars.

Townsfolk claimed the cemetery was haunted, and some people urged him to move. But Old Pu hated to give up land he used rent free, and he certainly couldn't take the house with him. So he remained. As to the ghosts, not only didn't Old Pu believe in them, even the children frequently passed the cemetery after dark without the slightest fear.

That night at supper, Old Pu ate very little, and he said nothing. His elder son knew he had been to a meeting in town and, observing his distressed manner, was able to guess pretty well what was wrong. There was no need to ask. He would wait patiently till the old man was ready to talk. Something troublesome had surely occurred. But the younger son, after having finished off two bowls of millet, couldn't restrain his curiosity.

"What's wrong, *die*,* tell us. What happened? They're squeezing us farmers again, aren't they?"

Old Pu knocked the ashes out of his long black pipe against the stool he was sitting on and shook his head. "It's strange. What have people like us got to protect? And there are no marauding soldiers passing through this part of the country," he muttered. He looked at his two sons, sitting bare-torsoed in the pale moonlight, and sighed.

"Young Zhu," he said, "you're still immature. Your brother knows much more than you. You're always so rash. It won't do nowadays. It's too easy to get into trouble.... Your grandfather and I worked as servants all our lives.... Two generations.... By humbly serving others our family reached its present status. But we can lose it through one little blunder. We'd have to leave here...."

The old man's mind had wandered far from the problem of having to raise money to buy a gun. He was taking this opportunity to give his younger son a lecture on social proprieties.

"How am I rash, *die*? I've been sticking to the fields,

---

* *Die* – father.

planting, pulling weeds. I haven't provoked anyone." Twenty years old, tall and strong, Young Zhu was quick to resent injustice. He wasn't at all docile like his father and elder brother.

"Don't think just because you're sticking to the fields that nothing can go wrong. The way the world is today, anything can happen! At my age I can pretty well guarantee that I won't make any slips. But you, Young Zhu . . . I'm always worried about you! . . ."

The brothers had rarely heard their father speak so gloomily. It made them feel uneasy.

Young Zhu's brother was called Pu Gui. Although past forty, he knew little except tilling the soil. He seldom even went into town. Old Pu was the servant of a prominent family in town and he gave the running of his farm over to this obedient elder son.

Young Zhu was a primary school graduate. Of course he was much better informed than Pu Gui. But the family had been unable to afford any further schooling and at the age of sixteen he had joined his elder brother in the fields. Always a boy of spirit, Young Zhu had some idea of the concept of country and citizenship. Although he toiled honestly as a farmer, he was not timid like his *die* and Big Brother.

This boldness disturbed Old Pu. He was sorry he had ever let the boy go to school. Old Pu placed a strict control on Young Zhu and forbade him to have dealings with anyone outside the family. The boy spoke too freely — that was the easiest way to get into trouble. Old Pu had learned this while serving two generations of masters. Conditions in the countryside had become especially unsettled in the last few years. There was a lot of seizing of conscripts and executing of suspected bandits. If you were the least bit implicated, you and your entire family could be wiped out in a flash.

The gentry in town were proudly overweening; it was even more dangerous to cross the touchy young squires in the countryside. Young Zhu's rash manner and bold way of speaking at a time like this was therefore a source of considerable concern to his honest old father. Today it had started a long train of thought in Old Pu, and he had felt constrained to speak to the boy about it.

Young Zhu sat in the tree shadow cast by the pale moonlight, one leg resting on a protruding root.

"I can't help it if you're worried about me! Three years ago when I wanted to go beyond the Great Wall to the northeast, you wouldn't let me. . . ."

"Young Zhu," Big Brother, afraid their *die* would get angry, interrupted. But after calling him by name, he said nothing further.

"Big Brother, you, of course, are a paragon! Even if *Die* doesn't say it, the neighbours will. . . . As for me, though I'm not a thief and I don't run with the bandits, everyone's worried about me. It seems I say disagreeable things. How shall I be agreeable — by speaking softly and always remembering to address the gentry as Elder Master this or Younger Master that? I haven't got that kind of mouth. I just won't do it! Is that a crime?"

The young man's voice kept rising, and with it his easily excited temper.

Ordinarily Old Pu would have brought his hands down sharply on his knees and scolded Young Zhu.

But today he only puffed hard on his pipe, the embers glowing and fading in the darkness.

The female members of the family were sitting in the doorway of the house. One was Big Brother's wife, another was the brothers' nineteen-year-old sister, the third was Big Brother's little daughter. Pu Gui also had a three-year-old infant son, who had long since gone to sleep on the bed.

"Young Zhu! . . ." began his sister-in-law. She was an intelligent alert country woman who had been the mistress of the household ever since Old Pu's wife died several years before. She addressed the younger brother in a conciliatory tone.

"*Die* is only trying to do his best for you," she said. "A clod like your Big Brother — *Die* never bothers to say anything to him. But you're educated. Some day you'll prosper and support the whole family. *Die* has worked hard all his life and he's learned a thing or two. You're still young. What's wrong with knowing how to get along with people? These are difficult times. *Die*'s got a lot of experience. You ought to listen to him."

"Daughter-in-law, I've always said you're a very bright woman. She's right, Young Zhu. Do you think I'm scolding you just for amusement? . . . The troubled times are starting all over again; don't you think I can see it? After all, I've lived a few dozen more years than you. I'm not so useless as you think! About the northeast, just think what would happen if you left. I'm old, and have to work in town every day. Your brother and sister-in-law are here at home. For generations we've relied on the land for our food. Do you think in two or three years you could come back from the northeast laden with gold? It's not that easy! You shouldn't take such a simple view of things. Labour is expensive. At harvest time we'd have to pay a hired hand about a yuan a day if you weren't here. Where would I get the money? But you're so impetuous. All you can think of is action . . . action! *Hai*! . . ."

Old Pu rapped his pipe out against a rock while Young Zhu looked sulkily up at the moon, saying nothing. His elder brother said even less.

A breeze blew through the branches of the old cedars. It was pleasantly cool out in the country.

"I'm not looking for an argument, Young Zhu, you must understand that. I'm so upset, I couldn't even eat supper tonight. You're young. You don't let me say two words before you jam them back down my throat. And you won't talk sense; you just argue for the sake of arguing. Is it any wonder I'm upset?"

Daughter-in-law ladled out three bowls of cool millet gruel. She handed the first one to Old Pu.

"*Die,* don't be like younger brother; talk about something important. Tell us what you learned in town today."

"*Hai*," the old man sighed, "they want us to pay out fifty yuan!" He sounded completely dispirited.

"Fifty yuan? What for? We don't have to contribute to a ransom; the bandits haven't kidnapped anybody. . . ." Daughter-in-law stood beside a small date tree.

"It's a new rule. The ward chief gave us only ten days to pay. That's even less time than we get from the magistrate's office to pay the grain tax."

Starting with the meeting in the field, Old Pu slowly related everything that had occurred that day. Finally, he filled his pipe and lit it, as if seeking consolation in the smoke.

"What a world! No one will listen to reason!" Young Zhu cried. "It's bad enough we don't have enough land, to say nothing of money . . . but suppose we take that gun, *die* — you say I'm not practical — suppose our family has such a gun, with us living alone out here in the country, if the bandits come, do you think one rifle can stop them? Actually all we'd be doing was getting it ready to make them a present of it!"

"Keep your voice down. You never know who's listening outside the fence." Big Brother was always cautious.

Old Pu could think of nothing to say in refutation of his younger son; he was too dizzy with the prospect of being paraded through the streets in disgrace for not being able to raise the fifty yuan within the ten-day limit. His family had lived beside this cemetery undisturbed for years. Even though, a few years before, the bandits were much more active than now, they had never bothered him. What was the use of arming? Every one knew that his family owned only two *mu* and that the other few *mu* were rented. Under the circumstances, wouldn't buying a gun stir up trouble? He had no money, but the bandits might very well come for the rifle. A new weapon was worth more to them than ten men. Spending those fifty yuan would be the equivalent of hanging a placard on his bramble fence inviting disaster to descend from the heavens! He recalled the ward chief's parting words:

"Every gun will be stamped with the seal of the town government. The weapons may not be transferred. When a man is sent out on military service, he must bring his rifle with him. If you lose it . . . beware of the law against dealing with the bandits! Even if you're not convicted, you'll certainly be under suspicion!"

At the time every one had been so worried about having to raise fifty yuan, that few paid any attention to the rule on care of the gun after you got it. But now Old Pu remembered.

Beset with this additional headache, the old man smoked pipe after pipe. He had nothing to say to his rash young offspring.

"*Die,* you know the town well after being a servant there so many years. Isn't there anyone you can speak to? How about the head of the Agricultural Association? Why not say we're willing to pay ten yuan or so if we don't have to take the gun?" This was clever Daughter-in-law's proposition.

"Mmm . . . not a bad idea! Every one says I'm honest, and an old man always gets some respect. But I've already had one refusal. . . ."

"You spoke to the association head?" asked Big Brother.

"Yes. He's a whole generation younger than my present master, and a very nicely-spoken young man. I've known him since he was a babe in arms. Of course I went to see him. He was very reasonable."

Young Zhu, who took quite a different view of the matter, brusquely demanded, "What do you mean, reasonable? What did he say?"

"He said the question of who has to buy a rifle and who doesn't is decided by the various ward chiefs. He's head of the Agricultural Association; he can't interfere. . . . The county magistrate is going to enforce the rule strictly. No one dares to do any private favours. . . . That's what he said."

"Humph, so he can't interfere! And what about the fact that we have less than five *mu*? Why aren't they strict about that part of the rule?"

"I asked the ward chief about that at the meeting. It didn't do any good. The ward chief said he had made a careful investigation. Everybody told him we had enjoyed several good years. We need protection, he says, our money won't be spent in vain. Even though we've less than five *mu*, we still have to buy the gun."

Old Pu's torn black tobacco pouch was empty, but he mechanically dipped his pipe bowl into it.

"An old neighbour . . . how could he be so unreasonable!" Daughter-in-law sighed.

Her husband, seated on a stone, also sighed deeply. The old man continued:

"It's the same for every family — not just for ours alone. Whoever violates the law will be punished according to law. Several have been arrested in town already. I never dreamed anyone would be so cruel as to put us on such a list. I've been careful all my life, never saying a cross word, and this is my retribution! Naturally, if I had been a rash blundering youngster like you, Young Zhu, we'd have met with worse disaster long ago."

"Well, since there's no way out, we'd better start thinking of how to raise the money," said Daughter-in-law. "You shouldn't keep criticizing Younger Brother. I'm sure he feels just as badly as you do."

Young Zhu jumped to his feet. "We can't harvest enough to eat, but we've got to buy a gun, do we? Good! It's no damn use running around begging for favours.

Anybody can fire a gun. When we get ours, I'll be responsible. Military service, killing — great fun! We'll go broke this year whether we buy the gun or not. What do you say, *die*?"

"And the money?" Big Brother asked dejectedly.

Young Zhu only laughed scornfully, but made no reply. Dark clouds concealed the moon and the wind began to blow. A storm was brewing.

It was pitch dark. Dully, Old Pu sat tapping his bronze pipe bowl against a stone.

No one said a word.

Old Pu borrowed some money and bought the rifle. A month passed.

It was the night of the second day after the Autumn Festival.

With the build-up of the Agricultural Association and the issuance of many guns, it was possible to set up a regular rotation system of guard watches. The heads of the association were commended by the county magistrate; there had been no disturbances during the past month and they were very happy. In the light of the Autumn Festival moon, they threw a big outdoor banquet where they drank large quantities of potent sorghum whisky. Then they repaired to a club in town for an all-night session of gambling and carousing. Their guards were also treated to food and drink, and everyone was extremely pleased.

Now, two nights later, a small local personage invited the head of the Agricultural Association and the chief of his ward to a drinking party, continuing the holiday atmosphere of the Autumn Festival. The place where the party was held was a hundred odd paces from the house in which Old Pu worked as a servant. Only a low wall separated the two residences.

Even before darkness fell, a dozen or more armed guards patrolled the lane. Their masters had already joined the host; they were inside playing boisterous drinking games. All this was a rare and exciting event for the quiet little lane. The housewives came out and stood in their doorways, discussing the fine clothes of the officials; children raced to and fro; several large dogs frolicked among the crowd. Old Pu, who was spending the night in town, saw all that occurred very clearly.

Not far beyond, two turns down the lane, was the town wall, topped here by a cannon tower in which a few soldiers always kept a vigil through the night. The bodyguards of the celebrating officials, having no place else to go, congregated in the stone tower, some thirty feet above the ground. They played cards and drank tea to while away the time.

The party evidently was going to last all night. From the wide-open doors came sounds of music and wild laughter. The revelry was clearly audible to the men in the cannon tower.

It must have been some time after ten that Old Pu blew out the lamp in his small servant's room and prepared to retire. Ever since the previous month, he had begun suffering from insomnia, an ailment he had never known before. Conscious of the increasing debility of old age, he was filled with gloomy forebodings. Although he had borrowed the fifty yuan interest free on the strength of being an old and respectable servant of the community, the debt had to be repaid by the end of the month.

But the autumn harvest had been poor. After deducting a portion to pay the hired hand and something for the coming winter, there might not be enough grain left for the rent. Although Big Brother and his wife worked hard day and night, what was the use? Where would Old Pu get the money to clear the debt and pay the rent? That Young Zhu had learned to fire the rifle merely added to the old man's disquiet. All sorts of reasons now kept him from sleeping peacefully. In a few score days he acquired many new white hairs.

Moonlight shining through the lattice-work paper window illuminated the old man's woven grass sleeping mat, increasing his irritation. The merry-making of the gentry a few walls away grated on his ears. Opening his shirt, Old Pu massaged his protruding ribs and gazed at the centre of the earthen floor. A dizzy spell nearly sent him rolling from the bed. About to lie down and rest, suddenly from the south he heard a succession of shots. Dogs in the lane began to bark and people ran. Old Pu leaped from the bed and rushed outside.

"To the cannon tower! To the cannon tower! The shots were from the south!" Several bodyguards raced down the lane towards the town wall.

Most people were still awake. They hurried out to see what was wrong.

Dozens of men peered from the battlements of the tower. More timid individuals gathered at the foot of the wall to listen for news. The firing, due south, could be heard clearly. It was not very heavy, only a shot or two every few minutes. Those high in the tower could even hear shouts and curses.

The residents of the lane knew the trouble was outside the town wall. No one had been caught napping.

The town had armed guards and the bandits didn't dare to attack the town directly. So people were not particularly frightened.

Only Old Pu was upset. The two grenades in his heart seemed to explode! He had no time to think. An unexpected surge of strength brought him to the cannon tower on the town wall. Young guardsmen were squatting behind the battlements, aiming their rifles. Old Pu stood and watched a few paces to their rear.

The moon emerged, bathing the fields and scattered trees in light. Then a white layer of clouds covered the silvery orb and dimmed its radiance. Dogs barked, and to the southwest a flame glowed and bullets cut red streaks in the night. No question about it — the firing was near his home beside the old cemetery! The bullets flew from more than one direction. There was a lot of shouting, though he couldn't distinguish the words, as if many attackers had encircled the place.

Stupefied, Old Pu leaned half-way out of the battlement. Luckily one of the guardsmen pulled him back. "It's you, old uncle! Pretty risky. Squat down, quickly, quickly! Bullets have no eyes. What's the use of looking? It's your family that's in trouble, isn't it? I knew it the moment I heard the first shot. . . ."

Old Pu seemed not to have heard him. He shouted: "Save them. . . . Save them! Brothers, masters, I'm ruined! . . . Two small children at home . . . save them! . . ."

"Quit yelling. They're liable to shoot in this direction."

The well-meaning guard insisted on dragging Old Pu down to a lower platform.

"Are you only here to watch the show? Your guns,

why don't you fire your guns? Send a few dozen rounds into the bandits . . . scare them off!" Old Pu cried in a strange voice.

"How can we do that, Uncle Pu? Hurry and find the head of the Agricultural Association. We can't act without his orders. What's actually happening out there? Who knows how many men they've got?"

"Quick. . . . Bring the officials up here for a look. They'll surely know what to do. The party isn't over yet. They must be still there."

This forceful suggestion sobered the old man, wounded and dazed by the exploded grenades in his heart. Without a word, he turned and hurried down the ramp. There was surprising vigour in his legs. Ordinarily he would have had to stop and rest several times to mount and descend the wall. Now, even if he tumbled he probably would be unaware of it.

It proved unnecessary for Old Pu to seek out the officials. A number of them, plus the chief of the local ward, came running towards Old Pu, cocked pistols in their hands.

Their whisky-induced bravado had long since been dispelled by the sound of the shooting. Followed by several armed guards, they hastened to the cannon tower, Old Pu panting in their wake.

They agreed it was Old Pu's house that was under fire. Streaks of flame and flashlight beams gleamed among the surrounding old cedars and white poplars.

Someone suggested that a dozen or so guards rush out and give battle and save Old Pu's family. But one of the officials said:

"It's nearly midnight. Do you know how many men

they've got? Maybe it's just a trick to lure us out and leave the town undefended."

"Would they dare act so boldly," said another hesitant voice, "if they didn't have all the roads blocked?"

Hearing this colloquy by the officials, the guards looked at one another, bewildered.

Old Pu dropped to his knees.

"Masters . . . brothers . . . save them! . . . Think of my two little grandchildren! I'm just an old bag of bones. What use is letting them die and keeping me alive?" He sounded as if he wanted to cry but couldn't.

"This is no time for personal sympathies. Can you guarantee that if we open the town gate the bandits won't come swarming in? Don't you realize how many lives, how many weapons, we can lose here? Save them, sure, you're frightened witless. But who will dare to take the responsibility? All right . . . go see the head of the association. He's still in the parlour. See what he has to say."

A thirty-year-old town official gave Old Pu this advice. He was the chief of Old Pu's ward. "Come on," he said. "We'll go together. This is no joking matter!"

"Chief, when we formed the Agricultural Association, didn't you say that whenever any of us gets in trouble . . . everyone will turn out to help? My family's sole protection is that one locally made rifle! . . ." Only because Old Pu was hopping with anxiety did he dare speak so boldly.

"Hurry. Take him down to see the association head. Who can argue with you about the rules at a time like this!" Someone pushed Old Pu from the rear, then quickly squatted down again behind the battlements.

Just then several torches appeared at the edge of the grove and the firing became very heavy, bullets whistling madly from all directions.

The flames grew larger as the brush and firewood stacked outside Old Pu's gate burst into blaze.

"How awful! They're finished! The bandits have set the place on fire! That's the end of Old Pu's family!" Some of the guards were very agitated. But without orders they dared not sally forth, nor even fire from the wall.

The shooting continued. Flames were now leaping on Old Pu's thatched roof, their glow reflecting redly on the faces of the men in the tower.

By the time Old Pu and the ward chief brought the order of the association head up to the tower, the fire diagonally opposite was erupting like a small volcano, accompanied by the crash of collapsing beams and the crackle of rifle shots.

The ward chief relayed the order of the head of the Agricultural Association, "Fire a few dozen rounds from here, but the town gate is to remain closed. . . ."

At this, the impatient guards opened fire with a will, pouring rifle and pistol shots into the perimeter of the volcano.

It was already nearly one o'clock in the morning.

While the men in the tower were firing so excitedly, and so blindly, Old Pu suddenly collapsed at their feet. This was his third trip up the wall; he was exhausted. Now, seeing his home go up in smoke, he fainted.

After two intense volleys, one of the guards blew the bugle call to assemble. The mournful notes aroused the entire town. Immediately, the shooting around the grove stopped. The bandits, perhaps afraid that the guards and the armed members of the Agricultural Association would all turn out, abandoned the attack and fled.

Fortunately, the flames of the volcano did not spread. Before long, the blaze gradually died.

It was still dark when Old Pu revived. He pleaded that the town gate be opened so that he could go and see the charred remains of his home. At last his request was granted. The first to go with him was the town's famed drifter, Wu De.

They were followed, of course, by armed officials, leading their troops.

Except for what had been destroyed in the fire, Old Pu had lost no property. His bramble fence and wooden gate had been reduced to ashes; the roof and the ox pen were gone; the mud wall of the house had collapsed in two places. Inside, Old Pu found his elder son lying dead on the earthen floor with a bullet hole in his left temple. Young Zhu sat leaning at an angle on the brick platform bed. A bullet had gone through his left leg and he was unable to move. Luckily neither bone nor ligament had been hit. The locally made rifle rested across his thighs, its bullets completely expended.

The women were in another room, dazed with fear. They had not been hurt, but Old Pu's grandson, who was lying on the bed, had been hit by a bullet in the buttocks. His face yellow, the child was so terrified he was unable to cry.

In addition, a small hamper of grain and a haystack had also been consumed by the flames.

The incident provoked considerable discussion in town. Some said that Old Pu, although he pretended to be poor, had hidden wealth which attracted the bandits. Others said it had nothing to do with wealth; it was definitely an act of vengeance. Most people felt the bandits had come to capture the rifle! As to the members of the family itself, none of them was able to say why they should be made to suffer such grievous losses, with dead and wounded.

The head of the Agricultural Association and the young men who strutted around town with their guns all day had nothing but admiration for Young Zhu. With less than a hundred bullets, and aided only slightly by Big Brother and his crude home-made fowling piece, he had held the bandits at bay; they had set fire because they were unable to enter the house. Who said the Agricultural Association was no use? Old Pu had been unwilling to buy the rifle at first, but hadn't it saved his family from complete annihilation? . . . What if the bandits had captured one of the family and demanded ransom? Wouldn't Old Pu's loss have been much greater?

To the town officials the incident afforded conclusive proof of the excellence of the locally manufactured rifles. Young Zhu's weapon had fired dozens of rounds without going bad. The products of the local gunsmiths were plainly in no way inferior to those of the army arsenal. The officials called a meeting the same day and framed a report to the county, then discussed what steps to take against the bandits and how to intensify self-defence measures. Finally, they passed a resolution to give Old Pu a few score yuan as a condolence award.

Everything proceeded smoothly. Two days later, people seemed to have forgotten the tragedy. It was hardly ever mentioned.

The house which Old Pu's family had occupied for three generations was no longer livable. They couldn't afford to erect a new one, nor did they have the courage to face another possible raid by the bandits. His heart shattered by the grenades which had burst in his chest, after much seeking and pleading, the old man was finally permitted to use a shack in town as a temporary dwelling.

A month later, Young Zhu's leg had healed. But the wound in the child's backside became infected. Only after three probings in the foreign-style drug store was the bullet recovered. The child was very young, and he lost a lot of blood. Exactly thirty-five days after the bandit attack, the innocent child followed his simple honest father into the earth.

Medical expenses came to several score yuan.

Old Pu had acquired a new debt before the original one had been paid. By selling his two *mu* of land, he managed to pull through the disaster. Although his clever daughter-in-law was so ill she couldn't rise from her bed, the doctor assured him he needn't worry — there would be no third death in the family.

Nothing further was heard of the condolence award promised by the Agricultural Association. People urged Old Pu to go to the officials and make an earnest plea that they carry out their resolution. But the old man was never one to question the conduct of his superiors.

"Never mind," he said. "I can afford it. The two of them . . . they're dead already. To take the money . . . would go against my conscience! . . ."

His anger was directed against the gun. He became furious whenever he saw it standing behind the door.

One day he ordered Young Zhu to take the accursed weapon and go with him to the ward chief. Old Pu told the ward chief he didn't care about the money, but he couldn't keep the rifle any longer. Now that he was living in town, he had less use for it than ever.

But the ward chief wouldn't hear of it.

"We can't let you set such an example. Everybody would be turning their guns in, the next thing you know! That would be the end of our association. Even though you're living in town, someone in your family will still have to shoulder that rifle in military service when the time comes. You're all muddled, old man. If it weren't for that gun, Young Zhu wouldn't be alive today. . . ."

In the end, Young Zhu had to carry the root of their troubles back to the dilapidated old shack.

Autumn.

Old Pu could no longer work as a servant. His appetite was poor. All day he stared up at the sky with blurry eyes, mumbling incomprehensibly to himself. He was also much deafer.

Young Zhu had not much to do after his leg healed. They had sold their two *mu* of land to pay off their debts. Although they still cultivated some rented land, there was little work in the fields this season of the year anyway. Young Zhu was seldom at home. The townspeople had praised him for his marksmanship, his courage. But what was the use of fine words? The family was in difficult straits. Some days they had only one meal, in the morning. A healthy young fellow like Young Zhu — how could he stand going around half starved?

He spent a lot of time wandering about with Wu De. The old man didn't seem to have the energy to interfere.

Ever since Wu De had carried him out of the burning building on his back, Young Zhu realized that he was not just a propertyless unemployed drifter. Although many people said Wu De talked too much, Young Zhu got along with him very well. Besides, Young Zhu found his home unbearable. Here was only idleness and an atmosphere of hardship and tragedy.

One dark frosty night, while the town was still asleep, there was a low whistle outside the shack. Young Zhu immediately bounded through the door.

"Wu De, did you arrange everything?" he asked excitedly.

"Idiot, of course! There isn't one of those birds who I don't know well enough to punch on the arm or slap his backside. How could I fail? Take a look at this!" From his tattered jacket he drew out a gleaming metal object with a barrel a foot long.

"I've got bullets, too," he added. "Go get your gun. We've a place to go. I made all the contacts. . . ."

Young Zhu went inside and brought out the ill-fated rifle.

"It's just that . . . the old man. . . ." He looked through the window with tear-dimmed eyes.

"Can you support him? No, you can't. . . . It's better to leave. . . . Maybe some day you'll come back and they'll make you chief of the guards!" Wu De was always joking.

"Hurry," he said. "I've tied the rope in place. If we wait too long, we're liable to run into someone and not be able to get off the town wall."

Young Zhu said nothing, but followed his guide to a new life into the dense mist.

The following morning it was discovered that the guards in the cannon tower had lost an automatic pistol and a bandoleer of bullets. Also gone were the disaster-inducing rifle for which Old Pu had paid fifty yuan and his son Young Zhu.

1933

Translated by Sidney Shapiro

Rou Shi

ROU Shi (1902-1931) was born in Ninghai in Zhejiang Province. He was a participant in the New Literature Movement during his middle school days and later became a teacher. He went to Shanghai in 1928 where he became acquainted with Lu Xun and worked with him on the monthly magazine *Tatler* and at the Dawn Blossom Press. As well as publishing his own writing he was active in introducing foreign literature and graphic art to China. In 1930 he was elected as an executive member of the China League of Left-wing Writers and later became a member of its standing committee. He was executed by the Kuomintang in 1931.

Rou Shi wrote not only about intellectuals, but about peasants as well, and about much-oppressed peasant women in particular. The post-Liberation film *Early Spring in February* was adapted from his important novel *Threshold of Spring*. His best-known short story, "A Slave Mother", which takes as its theme the suffering of ordinary people in the old society, was written in 1930.

A Slave Mother

HE was a dealer in animal skins which he bought from hunters in the countryside and sold in town. Sometimes he also worked in the fields; early each summer he turned farm-hand, transplanting rice for other people. As he had learned to transplant the seedlings in wonderfully straight rows, the peasants always asked him to help them. But he never made enough money to support his family and his debts mounted with each passing year. The wretchedness of his life and the hopeless situation he was in caused him to take to drinking and gambling, and he became vicious and bad-tempered. As he grew poorer and poorer, people stopped lending him money, even in small sums.

With poverty came sickness. He grew sallow: his face took on the sickly colour of a brass drum and even the whites of his eyes became yellow. People said that he had jaundice and urchins nicknamed him "Yellow Fellow". One day, he said to his wife,

"There's no way out of it. It looks as if we'll even have to sell our cooking pot. I'm afraid we have to part. It's no use both of us going hungry together."

"We have to part? . . ." muttered his wife, who was sitting behind the stove with their three-year-old boy on her lap.

"Yes, we have to part," he answered feebly. "There's somebody willing to hire you as a temporary wife. . ."

"What?" she almost lost her senses.

There followed a brief silence. Then the husband continued, falteringly,

"Three days ago, Wang Lang came here and spent a long time pressing me to pay my debt to him. After he had left, I went out. I sat under a tree on the shore of Jiumu Lake and thought of committing suicide. I wanted to climb the tree and dive into the water and drown myself, but after thinking about it, I lost courage. The hooting of an owl frightened me and I walked away. On my way home, I came across Mrs Shen, the matchmaker, who asked me why I was out at night. I told her what had happened and asked her if she could borrow some money for me, or some lady's dresses and ornaments that I could pawn to pay Wang Lang so that he'd no longer be prowling after me like a wolf. But Mrs Shen only smiled and said,

" 'What do you keep your wife at home for? And you're so sick and yellow!'

"I hung my head and said nothing. She continued,

" 'Since you've got only one son, you might find it hard to part with him. But as for your wife. . . .'

"I thought she meant that I should sell you, but she added,

" 'Of course she is your lawful wife, but you're poor and you can't do anything about it. What do you keep her at home for? To starve her to death?'

"Then she said straight out, 'There's a fifty-year-old scholar who wants a concubine to bear him a son since his wife is barren. But his wife objects and will only allow him to hire somebody else's wife for a few years. I've been asked to find them a woman. She has to be about thirty years old and the mother of two or three children. She must be honest and hard-working, and obey the scholar's wife. The scholar's wife has told me that they are willing to pay from eighty to a hundred dollars for the right sort of woman. I've looked around for one for several days, but without any luck. But your wife is just the woman I've been looking for.'

"She asked me what I thought about it. It made me cry to think of it, but she comforted me and convinced me that it was all for the best."

At this point, his voice trailed off, he hung his head and stopped. His wife looked dazed and remained speechless. There was another moment of silence before he continued,

"Yesterday, Mrs Shen went to see the scholar again. She came back and told me that both the scholar and his wife were very happy about the idea of having you and had promised to pay me a hundred dollars. If you bear them a child they will keep you for three years, if not — for five. Mrs Shen has fixed the date for you to go — the eighteenth of this month, that is five days from now. She is going to have the contract drawn up today."

Trembling all over, the wife faltered,

"Why didn't you tell me this earlier?"

"Yesterday I went up to you three times, but each time I was afraid to begin. But after thinking it over I've come to realize that there's really nothing to be done but hire you out."

"Has it all been decided?" asked the wife, her teeth clattering.

"There's just the contract to be signed."

"Oh, what a poor wretch I am! Can't we really do anything else?"

"It's terrible, I know. But we're poor and we don't want to die. What else can we do? I'm afraid this year I won't even be asked to do any transplanting."

"Have you thought about Chunbao? He's only three. What will become of him without me?"

"I'll take care of him. You're not nursing him any longer, you know."

He became more and more angry with himself and went out.

"Oh what a miserable life!" she sighed faintly yet tearlessly. Chunbao stared at her, whimpering, "Mummy, mummy!"

On the eve of her departure, she was sitting in the darkest corner of the house. In front of the stove stood an oil lamp, its light flickering like that of a fire-fly. Holding Chunbao close to her bosom, she pressed her head against his hair. Lost in deep thought, she seemed absolutely dead to the reality surrounding her. Later, she gradually came to, and found herself face to face with the present and her child. Softly she called him,

"Chunbao, Chunbao!"

"Yes, mummy!" the child replied.

"I'm going to leave you tomorrow. . . ."

"What?" the child did not quite understand what she meant and instinctively cuddled closer to her.

"I'm not coming back, not for three years!"

She wiped away her tears. The little boy became inquisitive,

"Mummy, where are you going? To the temple?"

"No. I'm going to live with the Li family, about thirty *li* away."

"I want to go with you."

"No, you can't, darling!"

"Why?" he countered.

"You'll stay home with daddy, he'll take good care of you. He'll sleep with you and play with you. You just listen to daddy. In three years. . . ."

Before she had finished talking the child sadly interrupted her,

"Daddy will beat me!"

"Daddy will never beat you again." Her left hand was stroking the scar on the right side of the boy's forehead — a reminder of the blow dealt by her husband with the handle of a hoe.

She was about to speak to the boy again when her husband came in. He walked up to her, and fumbling in his pocket, he said,

"I've got seventy dollars from them. They'll give me the other thirty dollars ten days after you get there."

After a short pause, he added, "They've promised to take you there in a sedan-chair."

After another short pause, he continued, "The chair carriers will come to take you early in the morning as soon as they've had breakfast."

With this he walked out again.

That evening, neither he nor she felt like having supper.

The next day there was a spring drizzle.

The chair carriers arrived at the crack of dawn. The young woman had not slept a wink during the night. She had spent the time mending Chunbao's tattered clothes. Although it was late spring and summer was near, she took out the boy's shabby cotton-padded winter jacket and wanted to give it to her husband, but he was fast asleep. Then she sat down beside her husband, wishing to have a chat with him. But he slept on and she sat there silently, waiting for the night to pass. She plucked up enough courage to mutter a few words into his ear, but even this failed to wake him up. So she lay down too.

As she was about to doze off, Chunbao woke up. He wanted to get up and pushed his mother. Dressing the child, she said,

"Darling, you mustn't cry while I'm away or daddy will beat you. I'll buy sweets for you to eat. But you mustn't cry any more, darling."

The boy was too young to know what sorrow was, so in a minute he began to sing. She kissed his cheek and said,

"Stop singing now, you'll wake up daddy."

The chair carriers were sitting on the benches in front of the gate, smoking their pipes and chatting. Soon afterwards, Mrs Shen arrived from the nearby village where she was living. She was an old and experienced matchmaker. As soon as she crossed the threshold, she brushed the raindrops off her clothes, saying to the husband and wife,

"It's raining, it's raining. That's a good omen, it means you will thrive from now on."

The matchmaker bustled about the house and whispered and hinted to the husband that she should be rewarded for having so successfully brought about the deal.

"To tell you the truth, for another fifty dollars, the old man could have bought himself a concubine," she said.

Then Mrs Shen turned to the young woman who was

sitting still with the child in her arms, and said loudly,

"The chair carriers have to get there in time for lunch, so you'd better hurry up and get ready to go."

The young woman glanced at her and her look seemed to say, "I don't want to leave! I'd rather starve here!"

The matchmaker understood and, walking up to her, said smilingly,

"You're just a silly girl. What can the 'Yellow Fellow' give you? But over there, the scholar has plenty of everything. He has more than two hundred *mu* of land, his own houses and cattle. His wife is good-tempered and she's very kind. She never turns anybody from her door without giving him something to eat. And the scholar is not really old. He has a white face and no beard. He stoops a little as well-educated men generally do, and he is quite gentlemanly. There's no need for me to tell you more about him. You'll see him with your own eyes as soon as you get out of the sedan-chair. You know, as a matchmaker, I've never told a lie."

The young woman wiped away her tears and said softly,

"Chunbao. . . . How can I part from him?"

"Chunbao will be all right," said the matchmaker, patting the young woman on the shoulder and bending over her and the child. "He is already three. There's a saying, 'A child of three can move about free.' So he can be left alone. It all depends on you. If you can have one or two children over there, everything will be quite all right."

The chair bearers outside the gate now started urging the young woman to set out, murmuring,

"You are really not a bride, why should you cry?"*

The matchmaker snatched away Chunbao from his mother's arms, saying,

"Let me take care of Chunbao!"

The little boy began to scream and kick. The matchmaker took him outside. When the young woman was in the sedan-chair, she said,

"You'd better take the boy in, it's raining outside."

Inside the house, resting his head on the palm of his hand, sat the little boy's father, motionless and wordless.

The two villages were thirty *li* apart, but the chair carriers reached their destination without making a single stop on the way. The young woman's clothes were wet from the spring raindrops which had been blown in through the sedan-chair screens. An elderly woman, of about fifty-five, with a plump face and shrewd eyes came out to greet her. Realizing immediately that this was the scholar's wife, the young woman looked at her bashfully and remained silent. As the scholar's wife was amiably helping the young woman to the door, there came out from the house a tall and thin elderly man with a round, smooth face. Measuring the young woman from head to foot, he smiled and said,

"You have come early. Did you get wet in the rain?"

His wife, completely ignoring what he was saying, asked the young woman,

"Have you left anything in the sedan-chair?"

"No, nothing," answered the young woman.

Soon they were inside the house. Outside the gate, a

---

* In old China, a bride usually cried before leaving her family.

number of women from the neighbourhood had gathered and were peeping in to see what was happening.

Somehow or other, the young woman could not help thinking about her old home and Chunbao. As a matter of fact, she might have congratulated herself on the prospects of spending the next three years here, since both her new home and her temporary husband seemed pleasant. The scholar was really kind and soft-spoken. His wife appeared hospitable and talkative. She talked about her thirty years of happy married life with the scholar. She had given birth to a boy some fifteen years before — a really handsome and lively child, she said — but he died of smallpox less than ten months after his birth. Since then, she had never had another child. The elderly woman hinted she had long been urging her husband to get a concubine but he had always put it off — either because he was too much in love with his wedded wife or because he couldn't find a suitable woman for a concubine. This chatter made the young woman feel sad, delighted and depressed by turns. Finally, the young woman was told what was expected of her. She blushed when the scholar's wife said,

"You've had three or four children. Of course you know what to do. You know much more than I do."

After this, the elderly woman went away.

That evening, the scholar told the young woman a great many things about his family in an effort to ingratiate himself with her. She was sitting beside a red-lacquered wooden wardrobe — something she had never had in her old home. Her dull eyes were focussed upon it when the scholar came over and sat in front of it, asking,

"What's your name?"

She remained silent and did not smile. Then, rising to her feet, she went towards the bed. He followed her, his face beaming.

"Don't be shy. Still thinking about your husband? Ha, ha, I'm your husband now!" he said softly, touching her arm. "Don't worry! You're thinking about your child, aren't you? Well. . ."

He burst out laughing and took off his long gown.

The young woman then heard the scholar's wife scolding somebody outside the room. Though she couldn't make out just who was being scolded, it seemed to be either the kitchen-maid or herself. In her sorrow, the young woman began to suspect that it must be herself, but the scholar, now lying in bed, said loudly,

"Don't bother. She always grumbles like that. She likes our farmhand very much, and often scolds the kitchen-maid for chatting with him too much."

Time passed quickly. The young woman's thoughts of her old home gradually faded as she became better and better acquainted with what went on in her new one. Sometimes it seemed to her she heard Chunbao's muffled cries, and she dreamed of him several times. But these dreams became more and more blurred as she became occupied with her new life. Outwardly, the scholar's wife was kind to her, but she felt that, deep inside, the elderly woman was jealous and suspicious and that, like a detective, she was always spying to see what was going on between the scholar and her. Sometimes, if the wife caught her husband talking to the young woman on his return home, she would suspect that he had bought her something special. She would call him to her bedroom at night to give him a good scolding. "So you've been seduced by the witch!" she would cry. "You should take good care of your old carcass." These abusive remarks the young woman overheard time and again. After that, whenever she saw the scholar return home, she always tried to avoid him if his wife was not present. But even in the presence of his wife, the young woman considered it necessary to keep herself in the background. She had to do all this naturally so that it would not be noticed by outsiders, for otherwise the wife would get angry and blame her for purposely discrediting her in public. As time went on, the scholar's wife even made the young woman do the work of a maidservant. Once the young woman decided to wash the elderly woman's clothes.

"You're not supposed to wash my clothes," the scholar's wife said. "In fact you can have the kitchen-maid wash your own laundry." Yet the next moment she said,

"Sister dear, you'd better go to the pigsty and have a look at the two pigs which have been grunting all the time. They're probably hungry because the kitchen-maid never gives them enough to eat."

Eight months had passed and winter came. The young woman became fussy about her food. She had little appetite for regular meals and always felt like eating something different — noodles, potatoes and so on. But she soon got tired of noodles and potatoes, and asked for meat dumplings. When she ate a little too much she got sick. Then she felt a desire for pumpkins and plums — things that could only be had in summer. The scholar knew what all this meant. He kept smiling all day and gave her whatever was available. He went to town himself to get her tangerines and asked someone to buy her some oranges. He often paced up and down the veranda, muttering to himself. One day, he saw the young woman and the kitchen-maid grinding rice for the New Year festival. They had hardly started grinding when he said to the young woman, "You'd better have a rest now. We can let the farmhand do it, since everybody is going to eat the cakes."

Sometimes in the evening, when the rest of the household were chatting, he would sit alone near an oil lamp, reading the *Book of Songs*:

> "Fair, fair," cry the ospreys
> On the island in the river.
> Lovely is this noble lady,
> Fit bride for our lord.
> . . . . . .

The farmhand once asked him,

"Please, sir, what are you reading this book for? You're not going to sit for a higher civil service examination, are you?"

The scholar stroked his beardless chin and said in a gay tone,

"Well, you know the joys of life, don't you? There's a saying that the greatest joy of life is either to spend the first night in the nuptial chamber or to pass a civil service examination. As for me, I've already experienced both. But now there's a still greater blessing in store for me."

His remark set the whole household laughing — except for his wife and the young woman.

To the scholar's wife all this was very annoying. When she first heard of the young woman's pregnancy, she was pleased. Later, when she saw her husband lavishing attention on the young woman she began to blame herself for being barren. Once, the following spring it happened that the young woman fell ill and was laid up for three days with a headache. The scholar was anxious that she take a rest and frequently asked what she needed. This made his wife angry. She grumbled for three whole days and said that the young woman was malingering.

"She has been spoiled here and become stuck-up like a real concubine," she said, sneering maliciously, "always complaining about headaches or backaches. She must have been quite different before — like a bitch that has to go searching for food even when she is going to bear a litter of puppies! Now, with the old man fawning on her, she puts on airs!"

"Why so much fuss about having a baby?" said the scholar's wife one night to the kitchen-maid. "I myself was once with child for ten months, I just can't believe she's really feeling so bad. Who knows what she's going to have? It may be just a little toad! She'd better not try to bluff me, throwing her weight around before the little thing is born. It's still nothing but a clot of blood! It's really a bit too early for her to make such a fuss!"

The young woman who had gone to bed without supper was awakened by this torrent of malicious abuse and burst into convulsive sobs. The scholar was also shocked by what he heard — so much so that he broke into a cold sweat and shook with anger. He wanted to go to his wife's room, grab her by the hair and give her a good beating so as to work off his feelings. But, somehow or other, he felt powerless to do so; his fingers trembled and his arms ached with weariness. Sighing deeply, he said softly, "I've been too good to her. In thirty years of married life, I've never slapped her face or given her a scratch. That's why she is so cocky."

Then, crawling across the bed, he whispered to the young woman beside him,

"Now, stop crying, stop crying, let her cackle! A barren hen is always jealous! If you manage to have a baby boy this time, I'll give you two precious gifts — a blue jade ring and a white jade. . . ." Leaving the last sentence unfinished, he turned to listen to his wife's jeering voice outside the room. He hastily took off his clothes, and, covering his head with the quilt and nestling closer to the young woman, he said,

"I've a white jade. . . ."

The young woman grew bigger and bigger around the waist. The scholar's wife made arrangements with a midwife, and, when other people were around, she would busy herself making baby's clothes out of floral prints.

The hot summer had ended and the cool autumn breeze was blowing over the village. The day finally came when the expectations of the whole household reached their climax and everybody was agog. His heart beating faster than ever, the scholar was pacing the courtyard, reading about horoscopes from an almanac in his hand as intently as if he wanted to commit the whole book to memory. One moment he would look anxiously at the room with its windows closely shut whence came the muffled groans of the expectant mother. The next, he would look at the cloudy sky, and walk up to the kitchen-maid at the door to ask,

"How is everything now?"

Nodding, the maid would reply after a moment's pause,

"It won't be long now, it won't be long now."

He would resume pacing the courtyard and reading the almanac.

The suspense lasted until sunset. Then when wisps of kitchen smoke were curling up from the roofs and lamps were gleaming in the country houses like so many wild flowers in spring, a baby boy was born. The new-born baby cried at the top of his voice while the scholar sat in a corner of the house, with tears of joy in his eyes. The household was so excited that no one cared about supper.

A month later, the bright and tender-faced baby made his debut in the open. While the young woman was breast-feeding him, womenfolk from the neighbourhood gathered around to feast their eyes upon the boy. Some liked his nose; others, his mouth; still others, his ears. Some praised his mother, saying that she had become whiter and healthier. The scholar's wife, now acting like a granny, said,

"That's enough! You'll make the baby cry!"

As to the baby's name, the scholar racked his brains, but just could not hit upon a suitable one. His wife suggested that the Chinese character *shou,* meaning longevity, or one of its synonyms, should be included in his name. But the scholar did not like it — it was too commonplace. He spent several weeks looking through Chinese classics like the *Book of Changes* and the *Book of History* in search of suitable characters to be used as the baby's name. But all his efforts proved fruitless. It was a difficult problem to solve because he wanted a name which should be auspicious for the baby and would imply at the same time that he was born to him in old age. One evening, while holding the three-month-old baby in his arms, the scholar, with spectacles on, sat down near a lamp and again looked into some books in an effort to find a name for the boy. The baby's mother, sitting quietly in a corner of the room, appeared to be musing. Suddenly she said,

"I suppose you could call him 'Qiubao'." Those in the room turned to look at the young woman and listened intently as she continued, "*Qiu* means autumn and *bao* means treasure. So since he was born in autumn, you'd better call him 'Qiubao'."

The scholar was silent for a brief moment and then exclaimed,

"A wonderful idea! I've wasted a lot of time looking for a name for the baby! As a man of over fifty, I've reached the *autumn* of my life. The boy too was born in *autumn.* Besides, *autumn* is the time when everything is ripe and the time for harvesting, as the *Book of History* says. 'Qiubao' is really a good name for the child."

Then he began to praise the young woman, saying that she was born clever and that it was quite useless to be a bookworm like himself. His remarks made the young woman feel ill at ease. Lowering her head and forcing a smile, she said to herself with tears in her eyes,

"I suggested 'Qiubao' simply because I was thinking of my elder son Chunbao."*

Qiubao daily grew handsomer and more attached to his mother. His unusually big eyes which stared tirelessly at strangers would light up joyfully when

---

* Meaning "Spring Treasure".

he saw his mother, even when she was a long distance away. He always clung to her. Although the scholar loved him even more than his mother did, Qiubao did not take to him. As to the scholar's wife, although outwardly she showed as much affection for Qiubao as if he were her own baby, he would stare at her with the same indefatigable curiosity as he did at strangers. But the more the child grew attached to his mother, the closer drew the time for their separation. Once more it was summer. To everybody in the house, the advent of this season was a reminder of the coming end of the young woman's three-year stay.

The scholar, out of his love for Qiubao, suggested to his wife one day that he was willing to offer another hundred dollars to buy the young woman so that she could stay with them permanently. The wife, however, replied curtly,

"No, you'll have to poison me before you do that!"

This made the scholar angry. He remained silent for quite a while. Then, forcing himself to smile, he said,

"It's a pity that our child will be motherless. . . ."

His wife smiled wryly and said in an icy and cutting tone,

"Don't you think that I might be a mother to him?"

As to the young woman, there were two conflicting ideas in her mind. On the one hand, she always remembered that she would have to leave after the three years were up. Three years seemed a short time and she had become more of a servant than a temporary wife. Besides, in her mind her elder son Chunbao had become as sweet and lovely a child as Qiubao. She could not bear to remain away from either Qiubao or Chunbao. On the other hand, she was willing to stay on permanently in the scholar's house because she thought her own husband would not live long and might even die in four or five years. So she longed to have the scholar bring Chunbao into his home so that she could also live with her elder son.

One day, as she was sitting wearily on the veranda with Qiubao sleeping at her breast, the hypnotic rays of the early summer sun sent her into a daydream and she thought she saw Chunbao standing beside her; but when she stretched out her hand to him and was about to speak to her two sons, she saw that her elder boy was not there.

At the door at the other end of the veranda the scholar's wife, with her seemingly kind face but fierce eyes, stood staring at the young woman. The latter came to and said to herself,

"I'd better leave here as soon as I can. She's always spying on me."

Later, the scholar changed his plan a little; he decided he would send Mrs Shen on another mission: to find out whether the young woman's husband was willing to take another thirty dollars — or fifty dollars at most — to let him keep the young woman for another three years. He said to his wife,

"I suppose Qiubao's mother could stay on until he is five."

Chanting "Buddha preserve me" with a rosary in her hand, the scholar's wife replied,

"She has got her elder son at home. Besides, you ought to let her go back to her lawful husband."

The scholar hung his head and said brokenly,

"Just imagine, Qiubao will be motherless at two. . ."

Putting away the rosary, his wife snapped,

"I can take care of him, I can manage him. Are you afraid I'm going to murder him?"

Upon hearing the last sentence, the scholar walked away hurriedly. His wife went on grumbling,

"The child has been born for me. Qiubao is mine. If the male line of your family came to an end, it would affect me too. You've been bewitched by her. You're old and pigheaded. You don't know what's what. Just think how many more years you may live, and yet you're trying to do everything to keep her with you. I certainly don't want another woman's tablet put side by side with mine in the family shrine!"

It seemed as if she would never stop pouring out the stream of venomous and biting words, but the scholar was too far away to hear them.

Every time Qiubao had a pimple on his head or a slight fever, the scholar's wife would go around praying to Buddha and bring back Buddha's medicine in the form of incense ash which she applied to the baby's pimple or dissolved in water for him to drink. He would cry and perspire profusely. The young woman did not like the idea of the scholar's wife making so much fuss when the baby fell slightly ill, and always threw the ash away when she was not there. Sighing deeply the scholar's wife once said to her husband,

"You see, she really doesn't care a bit about our baby and says that he's not getting thinner. Real love needs no flourishes; she is only pretending that she loves our baby."

The young woman wept when alone, and the scholar kept silent.

On Qiubao's first birthday, the celebration lasted the

whole day. About forty guests attended the party. The birthday presents they brought included baby clothes, noodles, a silver pendant in the shape of a lion's head to be worn on the baby's chest and a gold-plated image of the God of Longevity to be sewn to the baby's bonnet. The guests wished the baby good luck and a long life. The host's face flushed with joy as if reflecting the reddening glow of the setting sun.

Late in the afternoon, just before the banquet, there came into the courtyard from the deepening twilight outside an uninvited guest, who attracted the attention of all the others. He was an emaciated-looking peasant, dressed in patched clothes and with unkempt hair, carrying under his arm a paper-parcel. Greatly astonished and puzzled, the host went up to inquire where he hailed from. While the newcomer was stammering, it suddenly occurred to the host that this was none other than the skin dealer — the young woman's husband. Thereupon, the host said in a low voice,

"Why do you bring a gift? You really shouldn't have done this!"

The newcomer looked timidly about, saying,

"I . . . I had to come . . . I've come to wish the baby a long life. . . ."

Before he had finished speaking, he began to open the package he had brought. Tearing off three paper wrappings with his quivering fingers, he took out four bronze-cast and silver-plated Chinese characters, about one square inch in size, which said that the baby would live as long as the South Mountain.

The scholar's wife appeared on the scene, and looked displeased when she saw the skin dealer. The scholar, however, invited the skin dealer to the table, where the guests sat whispering about him.

The guests wined and dined for two hours and everybody was feeling happy and excited. They indulged in noisy drinking games and plied one another with big bowls of wine. The deafening uproar rocked the house. Nobody paid any attention to the skin dealer who sat silently after drinking two cups of wine. Having enjoyed their wine, the guests each hurriedly took a bowl of rice; and, bidding one another farewell, they dispersed in twos and threes, carrying lighted lanterns in their hands.

The skin dealer sat there eating until the servants came to clear the table. Then he walked to a dark corner of the veranda where he found his wife.

"What did you come for?" asked the young woman with an extremely sad note in her voice.

"I didn't want to come, but I just couldn't help it."

"Then why did you come so late?"

"I couldn't get any money to buy a birthday gift. I spent the whole morning begging for a loan and then I had to go to town to buy the gift. I was tired and hungry. That's why I came late."

The young woman asked, "How's Chunbao?"

Her husband reflected for a moment and then answered,

"It's for Chunbao's sake that I've come. . . ."

"For Chunbao's sake!" she echoed in surprise. He went on slowly,

"Since this summer Chunbao has grown very skinny. In the autumn, he fell sick. I haven't been able to do anything for him because I haven't had any money. So his illness is getting more serious. I'm afraid he won't live unless we try to save him!" He continued after a short pause, "I've come to borrow some money from you. . . ."

Deep inside her, the young woman had the feeling that wild cats were scratching and biting her, gnawing at her very heart. She was on the verge of bursting into tears, but on such an occasion when everybody was celebrating Qiubao's birthday she knew she had to keep her emotions under control. She made a brave effort to keep back her tears and said to her husband,

"How can I get hold of any money? They give me twenty cents a month as pocket money here, but I spend every cent of it on my baby. What can we do now?"

Both were speechless for a while, then the young woman asked again,

"Who is taking care of Chunbao while you're here?"

"One of the neighbours. I've got to go back home tonight. In fact I ought to be going now," he answered, wiping away his tears.

"Wait a moment," she told him tearfully, "let me go and try to borrow some money from him."

And with this she left him.

Three days later, in the evening, the scholar suddenly asked the young woman,

"Where's the blue jade ring I gave you?"

"I gave it to him the other night. He pawned it."

"Didn't I lend you five dollars?" countered the scholar irritably.

The young woman, hanging her head, answered after a moment's pause,

"Five dollars wasn't enough!"

The scholar sighed deeply at this and said, "No matter how good I try to be to you, you still love your husband and your elder son more. I wanted to keep you for another couple of years, but now I think you'd better leave here next spring!"

The young woman stood there silent and tearless.

Several days later, the scholar again reproached her, "That blue jade ring is a treasure. I gave it to you because I wanted Qiubao to inherit it from you. I didn't think you would have it pawned! It's lucky my wife doesn't know about it, otherwise she would make scenes for another three months."

After this the young woman became thinner and paler. Her eyes lost their lustre; she was often subjected to sneers and curses. She was for ever worrying about Chunbao's illness. She was always on the lookout for some acquaintance from her home village or some traveller going there. She hoped she could hear about Chunbao's recovery, but there was no news. She wished she could borrow a couple of dollars or buy sweets for some traveller to take to Chunbao, but she could find no one going to her home village. She would often walk outside the gate with Qiubao in her arms, and there, standing by the roadside, she would gaze with melancholy eyes at the country paths. This greatly annoyed the scholar's wife who said to her husband,

"She really doesn't want to stay here any longer. She's anxious to get back home as soon as she can."

Sometimes at night, sleeping with Qiubao at her bosom, she would suddenly wake up from her dreams and scream until the child too would awake and start crying. Once, the scholar asked her,

"What's happened? What's happened?"

She patted the child without answering. The scholar continued,

"Did you dream your elder son had died? How you screamed! You woke me up!"

She hurriedly answered, "No, no . . . I thought I saw a new grave in front of me!"

He said nothing, but the morbid hallucination continued to loom before her — she saw herself approaching the grave.

Winter was drawing to a close and the birds began twittering at her window, as if urging her to leave quickly. The child was weaned, and her separation from her son — permanent separation — was already a foregone conclusion.

On the day of her departure, the kitchen-maid quietly asked the scholar's wife,

"Shall we hire a sedan-chair to take her home?"

Fingering the rosary in her hand, the scholar's wife said, "Better let her walk. Otherwise she will have to pay the fare herself. And where will she get the money? I understand her husband can't even afford to have three meals a day. She shouldn't try to be showy. It's not very far from here, and I myself have walked some forty *li* a day. She's more used to walking than I am, so she ought to be able to get there in half a day."

In the morning, as the young woman was dressing Qiubao, tears kept streaming down her cheeks. The child called, "Auntie, auntie" (the scholar's wife had made him call her "mummy", and his real mother, "auntie"). The young woman could not answer for weeping. She wanted so much to say to the child,

"Goodbye, darling! Your 'mummy' has been good

to you, so you should be good to her in the future. Forget about me for ever!" But these words she never uttered. The child was only one and a half years old, and she knew that he would never understand what she wanted to say.

The scholar walked up quietly behind her, and put ten twenty-cent silver coins into her palm, saying softly,

"Here are two dollars for you."

Buttoning up the child's clothes, she put the ten silver coins into her pocket.

The scholar's wife also came in, and, staring hard at the back of the retreating scholar, she turned to the young woman, saying,

"Give me Qiubao, so that he won't cry when you leave."

The young woman remained silent, but the child was unwilling to leave his mother and kept striking the scholar's wife's face with his little hands. The scholar's wife was piqued and said,

"You can keep him with you until you've had breakfast."

The kitchen-maid urged the young woman to eat as much as possible, saying,

"You've been eating very little for a fortnight. You are thinner than when you first came here. Have you looked at yourself in the mirror? You have to walk thirty *li* today, so finish this bowl of rice!"

The young woman said listlessly, "You're really kind to me!"

It was a fine day and the sun was high in the sky. Qiubao continued to cling to his mother. When the scholar's wife angrily snatched him away from her, he yelled at the top of his voice, kicking the elderly woman in the belly and pulling at her hair. The young woman, standing behind, pleaded,

"Let me stay here until after lunch."

The scholar's wife replied fiercely over her shoulder,

"Hurry up with your packing. You've got to leave sooner or later!"

From then on, Qiubao's cries gradually receded from the young woman's hearing.

While she was packing, she kept listening to his crying. The kitchen-maid stood beside her, comforting her and watching what she was putting into her parcel. When the young woman left she did so with the same old parcel she had brought.

She heard Qiubao crying as she walked out of the gate, and his cries rang in her ears even after she had plodded a distance of three *li*.

Stretching before her lay the sun-bathed country road which seemed to be as long as the sky was boundless. As she was walking along the bank of a river, whose clear water reflected her like a mirror, she thought of stopping there and putting an end to her life by drowning herself. But, after sitting for a while on the bank, she resumed her journey.

It was already afternoon, and an elderly villager told her that she still had fifteen *li* to go before she would reach her own village. She said to him,

"Grandpa, please hire a litter for me. I'm too tired to walk."

"Are you sick?" asked the old man.

"Yes, I am." She was sitting in a pavilion outside a village.

"Where have you walked from?"

She answered after a moment's hesitation,

"I'm on my way home; this morning I thought I would be able to walk the whole way."

The elder lapsed into sympathetic silence and finally hired a litter for her.

It was about four o'clock in the afternoon when the litter carriers entered a narrow and filthy village street. The young woman, her pale face shrunken and yellowed like an old vegetable leaf, lay with her eyes closed. She was breathing weakly. The villagers eyed her with astonishment and compassion. A group of village urchins noisily followed the litter, the appearance of which stirred the quiet village.

One of the children chasing after the litter was Chunbao. The children were shouting and squealing like little pigs when the litter carriers suddenly turned into the lane leading to Chunbao's home. Chunbao stopped in surprise. As the litter stopped in front of his home, he leaned dazed against a post and looked at it from a distance. The other children gathered around and craned their necks timidly. When the young woman descended from the litter, she felt giddy and at first did not realize that the shabbily dressed child with dishevelled hair standing before her was Chunbao. He was hardly any taller than when she had left three years before and just as skinny. Then, she blurted out in tears,

"Chunbao!"

Startled, the children dispersed. Chunbao, also frightened, ran inside the house to look for his father.

Inside the dingy room, the young woman sat for a long, long while. Both she and her husband were speechless. As night fell, he raised his head and said,

"You'd better prepare supper!"

She rose reluctantly and, after searching around the house, said in a weak voice,

"There's no rice left in the big jar. . . ."

Her husband looked at her with a sickly smile.

"You've got used to living in a rich man's house all right. We keep our rice in a cardboard box."

That night, the skin dealer said to his son,

"Chunbao, you go to bed with your mother!"

Chunbao, standing beside the stove, started crying. His mother walked up to him and called,

"Chunbao, Chunbao!" But when she tried to caress him, the boy shunned her. His father hissed,

"You've forgotten your own mother. You ought to get a good beating for that!"

The young woman lay awake on the narrow, dirty plank-bed with Chunbao lying, like a stranger, beside her. Her mind in a daze, she seemed to see her younger son Qiubao — plump, white and lovely — curled up beside her, but as she stretched out her arms to embrace him, she saw it was Chunbao, who had just fallen asleep. The boy was breathing faintly, his face pressed against his mother's breast. She hugged him tightly.

The still and chilly night seemed to drag on endlessly. . . .

1930

Translated by Zhang Peiji

Yang Zhensheng

YANG Zhensheng (1890-1956) was born in the coastal city of Penglai in Shandong Province. He became familiar with the miserable conditions of the local fishermen and developed an increasing opposition to the abuses of the old society. He was active in the New Culture Movement while a student at Beijing University, and his first short story was published in the progressive periodical *New Tide*.

After graduation, he travelled to the United States where he studied at Columbia University. On his return he devoted himself to educational work for many years and taught at several universities including Qinghua and Beijing Universities.

The majority of his literary works are short stories and novelettes which in their themes reflect opposition to the old order. He is noted for an elegant, expressive style with an economic use of language and lively, tightly knit plots.

Yang Zhensheng

YANG Zhensheng (1890-1956) was born in the coastal city of Penglai in Shandong Province. He became familiar with the miserable conditions of the poor at first hand and developed an intense aversion to the abuses of the old society. He was active in the New Culture Movement while a student at Beijing University, and his first short stories were published in the progressive periodical *New Tide*.

After graduation, he went to the United States where he studied at Columbia University. On his return he devoted himself to educational work for many years and taught at several universities including Qingdao and Beijing Universities.

The majority of his literary works are short stories and novelettes which in their themes reflect opposition to the old order. He is noted for his elegant, expressive style with its economic use of language and lively, tightly-knit plots.

One-Sided Wedding

SHORTLY before noon in late autumn a few wispy clouds scudded across the sky and sunlight glared whitely on streets that had been swept clean by the wind. Women and children stood in front of their doorways, animatedly conversing. The wind brought the call of trumpets, clear and mournful.

"See, there they come," said one of the women, craning her neck.

A ragged line of marchers approached, holding banners, followed by a sedan-chair covered with blue felt. A wooden memorial tablet reposed inside. Behind this came another blue felt sedan-chair occupied by a girl of eighteen or nineteen. She was dressed in mourning garments. The ends of a piece of black silk draped over her head dangled to her shoulders. She was very pale. Only her lips had a bit of colour. She sat motionless, staring straight ahead, like a plaster image.

"That's the Zhang family's daughter," a woman announced to an old granny, pointing at the second sedan-chair.

"They say the man died only a few months after they got engaged. She never saw him."

"*Ai*, a nice-looking girl like that. How can her parents let her —" The old granny's remarks were cut short by a spasm of coughing.

"Is it a funeral, ma?" a little boy raised his head and asked his mother.

"Hush your mouth," she chided. "They're bringing home the bride."*

"Then where's the groom?" the child demanded.

"There, in that first sedan-chair," his mother retorted impatiently. The little boy peered, then gaped. He was about to reply, but his mother had already turned and was talking to a neighbour. Pouting, he dropped his head.

"It's only a wooden tablet," he muttered.

When the procession reached the gate of a large compound, two men wearing long gowns and short jackets came forward and carried the wooden tablet from the first sedan-chair. Two women, dressed in white mourning clothes, helped down the bride. They slowly advanced, the wooden tablet in the lead, the bride in the rear, tied together by a swath of black silk about ten feet long. While the band played dreary music, they stood side by side on a blue carpet — the wooden slab on the left, the girl on the right — and bowed to Heaven and Earth, then to the ancestral shrine, then entered the hall and bowed to the father and mother of the groom. Again with the tablet leading, the bride following, still connected by a length of black silk, they were escorted into the marriage chamber.

Confronting them immediately as they entered was an altar table. On this the groom's memorial tablet was stood upright. A flickering oil lamp, emitting

---

* In some parts of old China when a couple became engaged and the man died before marriage, the girl nevertheless went through with the wedding ceremony and moved in with his family, where she lived out her life as his widow.

feeble blue flames, was placed before the tablet. A plain white coverlet draped the bronze bedstead by the window. The pillow slips were embroidered with the traditional mandarin duck and drake,* but in neutral colours.

Late that night when all was still, the bride sat in a chair beside the memorial tablet and stared at the bed. A gust of west wind blew in through the window, causing the lamp flame to dance and emit a cloud of black smoke that rose like a dark shadow. Outside, the leaves of the bamboo trees rustled noisily.

One afternoon towards the end of the following spring, the bride awakened from her nap and strolled into a rear garden. The air was laden with the fragrance of flowers. Her limbs felt deliciously soft and relaxed. Willow fluff rolled itself into balls on the ground. Startled butterflies rose in pairs from amid the blossoms and flitted by her face. Idly, she picked a few willow tendrils and sat down beside a stone in the rock garden to weave something. But she couldn't think of what.

She gazed at the peonies. They had shed half their petals. Those that remained clung precariously to their calyxes, a prey to any passing breeze. A couple of sparrows nested in the fallen petals, preening their feathers and billing and cooing in the light of the setting sun. Two squirrels jumped down from a branch, and the birds took off with a whir of wings that sent several of the petals flying. Chirruping, the squirrels also dashed away.

Coming back to reality, the girl discovered that she had broken the willow tendrils into bits. They lay

---

* They symbolize love as they never separate from each other.

scattered on the ground. She rose and straightened her clothes. Listlessly, she wandered back to her room. Her face felt as if it were burning. She looked at herself in the mirror. Her face was splotched with pink and white. Her cheekbones were like crimson flowers. She stepped back a few paces and sat down on a chair. Dully, she gazed at the wooden memorial tablet.

The next morning she did not emerge from her room, even at the hour sunlight filled the windows. A maidservant several times brought water for her morning ablutions, but the girl's door remained locked. Inside, there was no sound. The maid became suspicious and peeked in through the window. What she saw frightened her speechless. Wide-eyed, she ran to the chamber of Madame Li, mother of the groom. Only after some time was she able to blurt: "The young mistress has hanged herself."

1920

Translated by Sidney Shapiro

Wang the Miller

IT was a hot summer afternoon, shortly after the midday meal. The shadows of the trees lay upon the ground. Not a breath of air stirred. In the oppressively close atmosphere the earth appeared to have stopped breathing. A burning awesome sun, slowly creeping across the sky, seemed to have melted the entire world. It was frightfully quiet. There was no movement, no sound, anywhere. Grass and flowers drooped. The usually noisy birds were quiet. Only the ants had no fear of the heat; they scurried back and forth across the scorching earth. And bees buzzed diligently around the flowers. In the northeast corner of the garden stood a tumble-down thatched shack. Through the rotted frame of its window the heavy rumbling of a mill roller could be heard, breaking the death-like silence.

A man in his thirties was grinding wheat. Rivulets of sweat ran down his sallow cheeks, flour powdered his matted hair like frosty grass in autumn. Sweat-drenched blue denim trousers, worn through at the knees, clung to his legs. He had been milling ever since his early teens, when he lost both his parents. At first the work had made him dizzy. The day seemed too long. His legs were so stiff he couldn't walk. Later, he got used to it. He became as mechanical as those two mute insensible millstones.

The stones were ground down several inches. Wang's dropping sweat wore pits in the earthen floor, his steps tramped out a groove, whiskers sprouted on his cheeks and around his mouth like weeds. But except for a neighbour's spotted dog which trotted over occasionally, wagging its tail for a bit of left-over food, Wang's only companions were those cold hard millstones.

The shadows at the foot of the yard wall gradually lengthened. A cow, lying beneath a tree, lowed for her calf. Baby rooks in a nest stretched their necks and opened their mouths wide, calling their mother home. The sun, pressing on the western mountain tops, reddened half the sky. Wang emerged from the dim mill shed, patted the flour from his hair and walked to the stream on the left for a wash. Then he sat on the bank and watched the spotted dog romping with a black one. The Zhangs' little boy, Prosperity, his hands black with mud, popped out from behind a tree and ran up to Wang.

"Mama wants you to grind some wheat for her, will you have time tomorrow?"

"Yes, I'll do it first thing in the morning," Wang replied. The child smiled.

"Mama's going to make me some fritters. The day after tomorrow is Double Seventh."* The little boy ran over to where the dogs were sporting, flung his arms around the black one's neck, and wrestled with them gaily. Then he got up and dashed north towards a vegetable garden, the two dogs racing behind him. "I've got to call Papa home for dinner," he shouted over his

* The seventh day of the seventh month in the lunar calendar when the heavenly lovers the Cowherd and the Weaving Maid are reunited in the sky.

shoulder. Soon Zhang appeared, his hoe on his shoulder, Prosperity trotting before him. The boy stopped and waited for his father, raising his small face to ask some questions while tugging Zhang by the hand towards the western end of the village.

Wang watched, entranced. The child's smiling face was adorable, his liveliness seemed to bring everything to life. The scene made a deep impression on Wang, it stirred his imagination. After he sat musing a while, Wang wandered back to his shack. Something evidently was on his mind, for he couldn't eat. He lay motionless on his bed, his eyes open. Now the heavy earth was mantled in darkness. Except for the hum of the insects outside the window and the far-off barking of dogs, all the world was still.

It seemed to Wang that he was in the mill shed. But he wasn't pushing the roller — a big donkey was doing that. All Wang did was feed in the wheat and sweep up the flour. The long-faced donkey, its big ears erect, practically flew around the millstones. Flour poured out very quickly. Wang observed this happily. A voice behind him asked:

"Papa, aren't you going to eat? Mama has everything ready." Wang turned around. There stood a five-year-old boy. It was his son, a somewhat better-looking boy than the child named Prosperity whom he had seen during the day. Wang picked him up and kissed him. He was so happy his lips trembled.

"Are you milling flour for my fritters?" the child queried, wrapping his arms around Wang's neck.

"Yes, yes, a whole string of them, and on the end we'll hang a small crab-apple. How will that be?"

Wang replied. The child laughed delightedly, revealing a mouthful of even white teeth.

With the little boy in his arms, Wang came out of the mill shed. His wife, a young woman in her early twenties, was busily setting a table. The eldest daughter of the Huang family on the west side of the village, Wang thought to himself. His wife pointed to the table. "Hurry up and eat," she urged. "The food's getting cold." The sight of the steaming platters of stewed beef and cucumbers and freshly made bread made Wang terribly hungry. The meal was delicious, but the more he ate the hungrier he felt. Seated at the end of the table, the little boy stretched forth his hands for bread, and opened his small mouth for vegetables. Wang was happy beyond words. He gazed lovingly at his son through the tears that misted his eyes.

There was a flurry of advancing footsteps and his neighbour Zhang burst into the room. "Prosperity," Zhang shouted, "I've been looking for you all over. So this is where you are." He picked up the child and rushed out. Struggling, the little boy extended his arms towards Wang and cried: "Papa, stop him. I don't want to go."

For a moment, Wang was paralysed with fright. Just as he was hurrying after Zhang to snatch the child back, he awakened, his heart beating wildly. The room was pitch dark and deathly still. He could hear only a cock crowing in the distance and the hungry rumbling of his own stomach.

Staring, he lay motionless. Only when the paper window-pane had turned white and the sparrows twittered in the trees did he rise listlessly and resume his pacing around the millstones. But today he was different. His mind was troubled. He walked slowly. At times, without realizing it, he stopped. At times, he suddenly quickened his steps. Instead of its usual even drone, his milling sounded sporadic — now fast, now slow. Perhaps he was thinking of the child of his dreams, or of his donkey. In any event, he grew thinner by the day.

Late one autumn afternoon, when the dying sun was turning the piles of leaves in the yard a golden yellow, and the crickets in the thatched shack were chirping intermittently to their companions, Wang lay on his bed. He hadn't eaten for several days. When he first caught the flu he went on with his work, though he burned with fever. Later, his legs and back ached so painfully he had no choice but to part company with his cold, hard millstones. Though he lay on his bed, no one brought him anything to eat or drink. The dog of the neighbour across the way thought of him sometimes and ambled over once or twice. When he saw that Wang was lying down, he put his paws up on the bed, wagged his tail, barked a greeting, then trotted out again.

Wang had frequent bouts of dizziness. Finally, the room seemed to light up. He saw his donkey pulling the mill roller, and there was his wife, cooking. His little boy was playing in the yard, a smile on his darling face, holding out his hands and calling him. Wang also smiled, and hurried out to where his child was.

1921

Translated by Sidney Shapiro

Li Song's Crime

THE night of the sacrifice to the Kitchen God, the wind buffeted the paper window-panes with snow. There wasn't a soul on the streets. The icy blue-white sheen of the snow reflected only the images of a few bare willows by the roadside, trembling in the frigid wind.

Head down, Li Song plodded home from town. For more than half a month now he had been unable to find work. As he walked, he thought of his widowed sister-in-law, his niece and his two nephews. They all were completely dependent upon him. It didn't matter that he would go hungry if he couldn't get a job. But when the children cried for food and his sister-in-law wiped her tears behind his back, *hai*! The year was soon coming to a close, and everyone was busily preparing for the New Year Festival. But what joy would his departed brother's poor children have?

Li Song's eyes went dark a moment. Was it hunger again? If he hadn't leaned against a tree, he might have fallen into the snow. He took a grip on himself and continued walking.

His sister-in-law and the children were waiting for him impatiently when he got home. As soon as he entered the door, the kids flocked around him joyously, like fledglings around a swallow returning with food. They vied with each other to brush the snow from his clothes. His sister-in-law was about to query whether he had found any work, but when she saw the expression on his face, she didn't have the courage.

Instead she asked if he had eaten. Noticing how closely the children were watching him as they waited for his answer, he said that he had. The kids ran to the stove and took down the bowl of rice gruel they had been keeping for him. There before the stove, each taking a sip in turn like kittens, they finished it off. Li Song sighed. He went to his own room, lay down on his bed and slept.

When he rose the next morning, the sky had cleared. A red sun was shining on the snow-covered peaks in the west. At the foot of the mountains, trains of donkeys were carrying brushwood into the town. He could hear the faint tinkle of their bells. When he observed how little firewood was left by their stove and saw that only half a bowl of rice flour remained on their table, Li Song became a bit panicky. He paced the floor a moment, then left.

He didn't return till after the noonday meal. His expression was grim. He strode about the room like a madman. None of the family dared ask any questions. Finally he lay down on his bed, facing the wall, and seemed to sleep. He rose suddenly at lamp-lighting time. Going without a word to the corner of the southern wall of their yard, he pulled free a big stick from a collapsed gourd trellis, and went out.

Before he had gone very far, he stopped. Lowering his head, he pondered. Then he turned and dejectedly trudged home. At the compound gate, he saw the shadows of the family on the paper window-panes. His sister-in-law was stroking her children's heads with one hand and wiping her eyes with the other. Li Song just couldn't face them. Again he turned. Carrying his big stick, he hurried to the highway and hid himself beneath a bridge.

By the following night, Li Song was in jail. A bright red light in the corridor cast thick shadows of the bars upon the wall. Other prisoners sprawled in grotesque positions on the floor of the big cell, sleeping with their mouths open, yellow teeth fiendishly bared. Li Song's experiences of the previous day and night seemed but a dream. It wasn't until this moment, lying like the dead in this tomb of a jail, that he could review the events with any clarity.

The first one to come by the bridge had been an old man. Li Song had sighed and let him pass. The second one was a fellow in his prime. Li Song had sprung forth and snatched for his purse. But several days of hunger had weakened him. While they were struggling, Li Song fainted. When he came to, he was in the county courtroom. The magistrate questioned him sternly and sentenced him to five years in prison.

Five years. In that time what would happen to his sister-in-law, his nephews, his niece? Li Song remembered as if it were yesterday the scene three years ago, when his elder brother was dying. Lying on his bed, his brother had gazed tearfully at the wife and children he was leaving behind. He clasped Li Song's hand in an icy grip, trying vainly to speak. Li Song understood. His brother was pointing at his wife and kids when he breathed his last.

As he recalled this, Li Song wept, his tears trickling to the cold stone floor beneath his head. Gradually, he fell into a stupor. He seemed to see a hole in the corner of the cell, and he wriggled through it. Sure enough, he was outside the jail. He ran all the way home. Outside the door, he stopped and listened, but he couldn't hear a sound. Entering, he found his sister-in-law stretched out on the floor, as if she were dead. The children were lying upon their mother's body, apparently faint from weeping. He knelt down on one knee and raised up the children. When they recognized him, they threw their arms around his neck and cried. Also crying, he held them to his chest and stroked their hair.

Suddenly, he felt a punch on the head. Vaguely, he heard someone swear and growl: "He grabs people even in his sleep." Li Song opened his eyes and saw a dark face surmounted by a mop of hair half a foot long. Eyes as big as the sightless sockets of a skeleton were glaring at him venomously. Li Song realized that he was still in jail.

1925

Translated by Sidney Shapiro

Hu Yepin

HU Yepin (1905-1931) was born in Fuzhou, Fujian Province. He first began his studies at a traditional school, however, poverty forced him to discontinue and he became an apprentice in a pawn shop. He subsequently moved to Shanghai where he attended Pudong Middle School and then transferred to a navy school in Tianjin. Two years later he moved to Beijing where he became involved in the New Literature Movement and in 1924 he started writing poetry and stories and editing the weekly *Popular Literature.* "The Brightness is Ahead of Us" is his representative work.

He was an executive member of the China League of Left-wing Writers and also chairman of the Workers-Peasants-Soldiers Communication Committee which was actively engaged in promoting the new literature. In 1931, at the age of 26, he was executed by the Kuomintang in Longhua, Shanghai.

A Poor Man

FOR two days now Botao had not tasted food. Pangs of hunger roused him from his sleep early on the third morning as sunlight began to peep from behind pearl grey clouds. Quietly he lay on the cold hard bed, his round sunken eyes staring with a strange glint at the bare date tree outside. His mind, however, was busy picturing the delicious products of his home village, the pomelo, sugar-cane, potato and figs; the fresh carp, frogs and shrimp from the river, the lotus-seed dumplings at Dragon-boat Festival and the cassia moon-cakes at mid-autumn. . . . His thoughts dwelt on everything that was edible. Although mere thinking could not fill his rumbling insides, he let his mind dwell in detail on every delicacy, placing them in fancy on the table by his bed until it was overloaded and another table and then yet another had to be added. It was only when the room was full of tables all groaning with delicacies that he mentally picked up the choicest morsel — his favourite of course — put it slowly into his mouth and chewed it daintily before letting it slip down his throat. . . .

"Disgraceful!" He could not help feeling angry with himself.

Even as he raged, he noticed once more the old torn ceiling, with dangling pieces of paper which looked ready to fall any minute. The wall-paper was even more dingy and yellow, besmeared with dead flies and mosquito blood. Someone had written on the wall in fancy characters, "A monk takes a wife," and "So and so is a bastard." Some child or maybe even an adult must have written this to mark his presence.

"Really, this is no place for human beings," he thought again.

Slowly the kindly sunlight began to stream down on him through the tree, the eaves and the latticed window. Wafted in by a gentle breeze came the clear crisp song of a child: "Little sister, it's time to rise!" As Botao listened, a ghost of a smile appeared on his face. Quickly he jumped out of bed, picked out a picture of "Spring Morning on the West Lake" from the pile of tattered books and papers in one corner of his room and dashed out of the door.

The singer was a little girl. School-bag slung across one shoulder, she was on her way to class. Botao had grown attached to this child two months ago; sometimes he gave her postcards and pictures. Feeling the gap between them, and for another reason as well, he wavered, an expression of shame and indecision on his face. "This can't be the kind of thing I do! Shameless and vile!" Still, the fiery burning sensation was working havoc in his empty stomach, tempting and urging him. He went up to the child.

"Look, Little Lai," he said, showing her the picture in his hands. "Like it?"

"Give it to me," she demanded, quite delighted.

"What's that bulging in there?" Botao pointed at her school-bag.

"Cakes."

"Will you give me them in exchange?" he asked timidly.

"All right." She went away very pleased.

Holding the cakes, Botao felt wretched. As he avidly gulped them down, he told himself, "Too low and vile for words! Cheating a child of her breakfast!" The little cakes barely filled the spaces between his teeth and were all too quickly digested, leaving his empty stomach emptier than ever. The fiery hunger seemed to burst into a stronger flame. This was quite unexpected. You'd think it would be better having a little to eat than nothing at all, yet hunger was torturing him worse than ever. A weary pallor made his haggard face paler. His lips quivered and his body shook as if with cold. . . .

"I might as well starve," he told himself silently in white fury.

The little girl's voice had died away in the distance. Sunlight carpeted the ground with infinite warmth as more people appeared in the little lane.

"I've done something shameful. But what kind of misfortune is this? I have become such a person, so. . . ." In a dreadful, hushed voice, he added, "There is no doubt that I will do something desperate today, just one bold deed . . . something . . . I must. . . ." Vaguely, and still trembling all over, he headed for the street.

As he turned into another lane, a fat, black pug-dog jumped out from behind a threshold. The little bell round its fat neck tinkling, it began to growl at Botao. Again he felt the wrath of one insulted and humiliated.

"Men are so snobbish that even their dogs are snobbish. This is indeed a snobbish world."

The little dog followed close at his heels, barking annoyingly until he at last lost patience. Picking up a piece of broken brick, he hurled it at the pug with all his might. The brick landed with a thud on a bright crimson gate. This unexpected result gave Botao some sense of satisfaction anyway because within the gate lived rich people and through the gateway a cook, in a long black gown, often carried heavy hampers of food — big chunks of pork and mutton, juicy white plucked chicken and duck and other delicacies. This evidence was enough to convince a man who had not eaten for two days that those within were his absolute enemies.

"Grrr. . . . " The little dog, its tail between its legs, growled at him from a distance, but Botao had already forgotten all about the pug. His thoughts lingered on the hampers of pork, mutton, poultry and other food and he remembered their delicious f'avour. Once again he was only too painfully aware of his empty stomach and the feebleness of his legs.

"What shall I do? This hunger!" He walked down the road, his head bent in thought.

The cool autumn wind hit him in the chest, he trembled a little. "Cold and hungry!"

Just at that juncture, something hard bumped into him and a voice cried loudly, "Watch where you're going!"

He looked up to discover a young restaurant lad of about fourteen standing close by, a look of disgust and anger in his eyes.

"What's the matter with you?" asked the lad. "Look!" and he pointed at the muffins and fried bread on the ground.

"What the devil. . . ." Botao wondered.

"Pay me," shouted the lad.

"But it was you who bumped into me."

"You must pay me for the muffins I lost."

"When a man's poor, he's out of luck in everything." Slowly, Botao walked away. The lad rushed up and grabbed him by his long cotton gown which had not seen water for some time. "Running away eh?" he shouted. "Come on, give me back my five muffins and fried bread."

"Go away!" Botao was at last roused to fury. He gave the lad a vigorous push and slowly continued on his way.

The lad scrambled up, sobbing loudly, picked up the soiled muffins and fried bread and cursed under his breath, "Damm you . . . you bandit."

For some time the word "bandit" rang in Botao's ears. "Bandit," he muttered to himself savouring the multiple meaning of the word. It brought to his mind a very different meaning of life. Slowly, before his tired eyes there appeared a vast uninhabited forest where a score of gallants sat merrily drinking and smoking. Piles of gold and silver lay beside them, to say nothing of the pigs, sheep, chickens and ducks which they could kill and cook as their fancy desired. On a misty moonlight night, Botao hid with these bold fellows in an ambush deep in some long weeds. He aimed at one of those so-called dignified officials or rich men and opened fire at him . . . bang! . . . and then . . . then . . . .

The idea so ticked him that he couldn't help chuckling. But he didn't have strength to carry the thought a step further to an even more pleasant situation.

"Bandit!" He thought with pride and satisfaction as he strode ahead, his footsteps stronger and surer now.

A small grey cart wheeled past, sending a strong

aroma of baked sweet potatoes to his nostrils. Instantly the mental picture disintegrated.

"Mm. . . . Delicious!" He again felt the emptiness of his stomach.

"I must do something daring today," he thought. "Only one thing, one. . . ." Then he was somewhat angry and disgusted.

"Let it be just this one thing! Just this one thing!" he made up his mind. Again a sense of satisfaction and pride filled his heart, his legs strode bravely down the road but this time in the direction he had come.

Soon, he was back in his own room. Lying on the bed, he contemplated on how mighty, magnanimous and happy he would be, and this made him laugh aloud.

"Are you in?" suddenly a voice coming from the doorway broke through his laughter.

He knew it was that miserable landlady of his, that lonely and grey-haired old woman, come to ask for her rent. "Come in," he called.

"Have you any money for me today, Mr Chen?" she asked at the door.

"Plenty," he sounded extremely confident and self-satisfied.

Suspicion and surprise were in the old woman's face but she said with the hint of a smile, "That's good. Please give me some, I must buy some flour. I'm very hungry."

"I'll go and get the money." He still had that gloating look on his face.

"Must you? . . ." The old woman hesitated a moment. "Hurry and go, then. Lord of heaven, I certainly need some food to fill my stomach."

"All right, all right," said Botao firmly and with some arrogance. Brushing past the old woman, he quickly sailed out of the room.

"That wretched swindler and rogue, he still owes me three months' rent," cursed the old woman every time she looked at the pile of tattered books left behind by Botao.

Translated by Tang Sheng

Wang Luyan

WANG Luyan (1901-1943) was born in Zhenhai, Zhejiang Province. In his youth, he joined a Mutual-assistance Part-study Part-work Group and studied Esperanto. He started his literary career under the influence of the New Culture Movement. After 1923 he was engaged in editing educational and cultural works in Wuhan and Shanghai. He died of illness in 1943.

During his twenty-year career, he translated more than thirty books and wrote numerous short stories. His forte was in writing about the lower middle class and about farmers in the countryside. *Wild Fire* reflects his talent for meticulous characterization and description of context.

The Sorrows of Childhood

HOW fearful this is, the speed with which time is flying!

Like a shooting star early in the morning, like a flash of lightning on a summer night, it has slipped past in a twinkling, unwittingly bearing away with it the dearest page in my life.

I feel the same infinite dread as when the sun has set behind the hills and little by little night spreads its veil of darkness. I know the same boundless horror as when a raging wind sweeps up wild clouds and a waterspout draws up the whirling waves. My heart is filled with the same indescribable terror and despair as when wailing, disconsolate ghosts flit among stark corpses.

Who says youth is life's most precious, golden age? Not in my eyes, not to my knowledge. I have seen nothing but darkness and loneliness, I have known nothing but distress and sorrow. I would willingly make over this age to whomsoever says this, whomsoever desires it.

Ah, how willingly I would return to the dear years of my childhood, return to those insubstantial years of dreams!

Grant me great strength, God, so that if it may not be granted me to return to that age, at least my memory may take wing and fly to that most desolate nook, and for a short space I may steep myself in that sorrowful dream. This is my wish, for even the sorrows of childhood are more dreamlike and sweeter than the joys of youth.

I forget the exact date, but fancy I was eleven or twelve at the time.

It was just after the Lunar New Year, when gongs sounded all over the village where I was born, while processions of dragon and horse lanterns came and went.

This is the season of good cheer, when country folk who have toiled the whole year through set down their weary load for a while to wash away fatigue in merriment. Shops are closed, card-players gather in groups in the temple and on the bridge. At this time the most tight-fisted wander around eating handfuls of melon seeds, while even the gravest and most respectable citizens go out with banners on their backs or beat copper gongs in the lantern processions. All is song and laughter, not one face is clouded. The children rush helter-skelter as if just released from a cage. They light firecrackers or take possession of street corners where they squat in circles, trace a square on the ground with some sharp stone and play shovelboard.

Mother was very strict with me. To her mind no decent child would play games like shovelboard with coins. She seldom allowed me to join the other children's games, and kept her money under lock and key. If I found a few coins in the corner of some drawer and slipped out to join other youngsters at shovelboard, she would find me almost at once and drive me home. A scolding would follow, sometimes a spanking as well, and I would go hungry to bed.

But over the Lunar New Year Mother let me have my fling. No hunting in drawers for odd coins now — under my pillow was her liberal gift of New Year money. And we could play shovelboard under her very eye, if we kept off the main street.

Shovelboard is a fascinating game and needs no elaborate equipment. Two children have only to meet for one to say:

"Take you on!"

"Who's afraid of you?" retorts the other.

They choose a stone slab neither too slippery nor too rough, find a flint to scratch a square intersected from opposite corners, and start. One by one, other children join them, putting down their coins and crowding round the board.

Though I was so seldom able to play and never acquired a really lethal shove, I was pretty good at dislodging tactics. In other words, instead of flipping my coin forward, I dropped it behind my opponent. And although this did not always succeed in pushing the other fellow off the board or across a line, my own coin generally stayed inside the square, whereas when I shoved it it shot dangerously out of bounds.

My companions were mostly boys of my own age, who played a fairly steady game. Younger children stayed away from our group, and we turned away most older boys or those who played roughly.

The first few days after the Lunar New Year we played all over the village. The ancestral temples, streets, bridge and paving stones under the eaves were covered with shovelboard squares. Excited as a wild colt, I forgot to go home for meals.

But one day just as the fun was at its height, a young bully came along.

He was older than the rest of us, fourteen or fifteen. His name was Shengfu and he was an orphan who made a living by helping the boatmen. Able to do as he pleased with his earnings, he spent his spare time in the gambling booth or playing shovelboard with his own gang. He didn't much like using small cash, thinking it no fun to play for such insignificant stakes. But still he was a terror at the game. By gripping his coin tightly sidewise and hurling it down, he often knocked out coins lying snugly on the board which no one else could dislodge. He was quick as lightning too, and before a smash often flicked the coin he was aiming at, so that without anyone seeing what had happened a coin which had been steady started to wobble. With his way of playing, none of us dared take him on.

Probably because he had quarrelled with one of us the day before, Shengfu strode over and plonked down a copper in our square. In general newcomers are allowed to join in with a copper even though the others are playing for smaller stakes. But as this bully played such a rough game and was obviously out to make trouble we waved him away.

Shengfu became angry. He planted a foot in our square and cried:

"Does this stone belong to you?"

We raised our eyebrows. But nobody wanted to quarrel just after the Lunar New Year. Besides we were a little afraid of Shengfu. We pocketed our money and moved off.

"Come and play by our house," suggested one boy.

We went straight there and drew another square.

That house faced the river and was next to ours. The boy's family had had a rice shop in one room on the ground floor, but after losing money on it the previous year when New Year came round they decided to close down. Now the door of what had been the shop was half open. The outer room was used as a sitting-room, while some of the old shop equipment was stacked inside. As this building belonged to our friend's family, of course so did the stone paving under the eaves.

But just as we were going to resume our game, Shengfu came up again and put another copper on the board.

"I'll join you," he growled.

"This belongs to my family!" protested our friend.

"Can it answer you? Can your family slab talk?"

We stood up, clenching our fists indignantly. Anger blazed up in our hearts. We treated Shengfu to a flood of abuse.

He contracted his shaggy black brows like a furious tiger, glared at us with bloodshot eyes and charged with raised fists.

But before he could hit the boy whose house this was, someone caught him by the ear, and a man's voice challenged him:

"Can't you pick someone your own size to fight?"

Taken agreeably by surprise, we cheered.

It was Acheng, a favourite with us all.

"Give him a good box on the ears, Acheng! The great bully!"

Shengfu was taken aback. He was obviously afraid. Acheng was much the taller of the two and considerably stronger. He was a man of twenty. He could carry heavy loads and walk great distances. The year before this he had hulled grain in the now closed rice shop. We were sure he would give Shengfu a good thrashing.

But that was not Acheng's way. He let go of Shengfu's ear.

"What's all this?" he asked.

We told him the whole story.

He laughed and turned to Shengfu.

"Come on!" He took some coppers from his pocket. "How many coppers do you have?"

This attitude enraged Shengfu again. He promptly put a copper in the square.

"You can't beat me at shovelboard!"

Acheng smiled as he put down a copper too.

We gathered round to watch, worried for Acheng's sake. We had never seen him play shovelboard and were afraid Shengfu would beat him.

Indeed Shengfu was in such a rage that he played like a man possessed. He won half a dozen of Acheng's coppers in a row. As soon as Acheng put down a copper, it was knocked off the board. And he had no chance to get his own back.

Still he only smiled, watching his opponent win.

Presently Shengfu's copper landed out of bounds.

Then Acheng, from steady fingers, flipped down a copper with no effort at all.

His coin and Shengfu's rolled off the board together.

"That's the way to throw," he said with a smile. "You need a steady hand." One after another he shoved the coppers out.

"Shall I knock it over here?" he asked, and proceeded to knock Shengfu's copper where he wanted.

"Knock it over there!"

Shengfu's copper rolled over there.

"Put it where you like — I'll shove it over this line!"

And sure enough Shengfu's copper rolled over the line.

Shengfu was staggered. Each time Acheng's coin

knocked his out, it rolled off the board behind it. This went on and on — Shengfu hadn't got a look-in.

The rest of us watched raptly.

"Smashing tactics aren't fair. People aren't impressed unless you play steadily." With this, Acheng knocked a few more coppers off.

"You have a go now! I've won five of yours."

He stopped and put a copper on the board.

But Shengfu had lost his nerve. He missed Acheng's copper and his own rolled off the board.

We kept a close watch on Shengfu's pocket. As the minutes went by it grew noticeably lighter.

"How much more do you want to lose?" Acheng asked with a grin. "Keep a little to buy sauce and vinegar!"

Shengfu was completely demoralized. He picked up his copper and stood up.

"You're older than I am," he mumbled, as if in excuse.

"And you're older than the boys you bully — more shame to you! I haven't boxed your ears because it's New Year. Take your coppers. I don't want money from a poor worm like you!"

With a laugh, Acheng threw the coppers on the ground and went into the rice shop.

We set up a roar of laughter, pleased beyond words.

His face crimson, Shengfu hesitated for a moment before picking up the coppers and slouching off.

We stuck out our tongues as we watched him round the corner. Then we burst into the rice shop after Acheng.

Acheng had fetched his two-stringed fiddle from the inner room, and now sat on a bench to tune it.

Though he did rough work, he was quick with his head and hands and a first-rate fiddler. After work he liked to sit and fiddle by the river, singing a tune while the villagers crowded round to listen in silence. As I loved the sound of the fiddle, I was often one of his audience.

Music was rather rare in my native place. The grown-ups were such a serious lot that to hum tunes was considered frivolous. As for fiddling, that was left to scamps. Almost the only music we heard each year was the discordant tunes the blind fortune-teller played on his three-string fiddle when he visited the village, the small gong and bamboo drum of the blind news-retailer who came round on summer nights, and perhaps a dulcimer ballad in the ancestral temple after the harvest. During the lantern festival soon after New Year there were plenty of fiddles, and there were quite a few different instruments in the drum-stand during the processions in the second and third months. But as most of the musicians had no regular jobs or worked at humble trades, self-respecting citizens looked down on them. Still, such is the power of music that as soon as the country folk heard the first strains, men and women, old and young, they flocked to listen though they had no wish to play themselves.

Acheng was known in our village for his playing. That was why the grown-ups liked him. We children often begged him to play, and during the first month of the Lunar New Year he generally roamed the countryside with his fiddle, wherever the dragon and horse lanterns went. But these last few days, for one reason or another, he had stayed at home.

Perhaps routing Shengfu had put him in a good mood for he had brought out his fiddle again.

This fiddle was simply and even crudely made. Instead of snake skin on the end of the body, it had thin wood which seemed on the verge of cracking. The neck, the pegs and the body were painted a light red. It can hardly have cost much to start with, and now that it was old there were streaks of grease on the varnish, while in some places the colour had worn away. White pine resin had scattered all over the top of the body, the wood and the lower end of the neck. The bow was fearfully bent, and the last of its horsehairs seemed about to fall out. It had no beauty in my eyes. I asked Acheng several times to let me play it, but could only draw the ugliest screeches from it.

The curious thing was that in Acheng's hands this fiddle had the sweetest, most golden tone. Sometimes the music seemed to laugh and leap, at other times to weep. I would watch round-eyed, quite carried away by the music he produced.

"Which of you will sing?" he asked with a smile that day when he had played one tune. "Let's pick a song everyone knows — *The Railings by the West Lake.*"

We all flushed, and protested:

"Don't know it!"

"I don't believe it. Everyone knows *The Railings by the West Lake.* Well, I'll sing it first — there's nothing to be shy about!"

"Yes! You sing! You sing!" we shouted.

"Will you sing after me?"

"You can pick anyone you like."

Acheng tuned his fiddle again, and started to sing to his own accompaniment:

Cold the railings by the West Lake
When first the maiden sighed:
"Now you are leaving home, dear,
Be careful on the road.
Don't pluck the flowers
That blossom by the way. . . ."

Acheng sang in a falsetto as clear and pure as a woman's voice, in perfect tune with the fiddle. We listened in absolute silence.

When the song was over he played an interlude, and then stopped to ask with a grin:

"Now it's your turn — who's going to sing?"

Faces turned red again. Everyone wanted to slip away. Some boys edged up to the door.

"I can't! I can't!"

"Let's hear Xiqin!" He jumped up and seized my hand.

My heart started thumping and my whole body burned. Unable to speak, I tried to wriggle out of his grasp, shaking my head.

"No . . . no. . . ."

"Yes! Xiqin can sing! Xiqin can sing!" The other boys jumped and shouted.

"Don't be afraid. We'll shut the door. Nobody else will hear."

Acheng let go of my hand and closed the door.

I was completely hemmed in. The boys had crowded round, shouting. I had to sing. But how could I? Though I knew the first verse of *The Railings of the West Lake*, I had only sung it to myself when there was no one about, or in my sister's presence at the most. I had never sung in public.

"Go on! Sing! The door's shut!" Acheng urged me.

"I can't. . . . I don't know how."

"Go on, sing, Xiqin! Don't be shy!" The boys raised another shout.

As they would not let me off, I flushed and said:

"Well, you mustn't laugh."

"He's agreed! Listen quietly," Acheng told the others. "I'll play it through once, and then you come in. Just keep in tune with the fiddle."

He began to play. As I listened to his playing, the rhythm of my heartbeats changed and my whole body seemed to be swaying.

Light and lilting to begin with, the music grew grave and sad. It quavered and wailed, as if sobbing: "When first the maiden sighed. . . .

"Cold the railings by the West Lake. . . ."

After his opening bars I started singing, while his fiddle played on without a second's hesitation, in perfect tune with my voice.

". . . ."

"Bravo! Well sung!" shouted the boys.

When I finished the part I knew, the fiddle stopped. I did not know what I had sung or how. All I knew was that my heart was beating wildly. I must have been in a trance.

"You're a first-rate singer!" Acheng sounded delighted. "The best grown-up singer couldn't do better! That's the first time I've heard you, Xiqin!"

The rhythm of my heartbeats suddenly changed again, as an almost unbearable happiness flooded over me. I sat down quietly. I felt as if my head were burning, my soul soaring off on a mad, headlong flight.

From that day on my soul flew in search of music.

It became a necessity to me. I snatched at music as Acheng had snatched at my hand.

That is how I came to love Acheng more than anyone else in the world.

Sometimes Mother said to me: "Go and see if Uncle Asi, Grandfather Lianpin or Brother Acheng has time tomorrow or the day after to hull rice for us."

I always went first to Acheng. If anyone else came to hull the rice, I lazed in bed till it was late and grumbled about helping, however much Mother scolded. But when Acheng was coming I got up first thing to open the storeroom and carry out all the lighter tackle. Then I helped Mother get breakfast while waiting, and if it was still early I ran to the bridge to watch for him.

He was always very pleasant, with a smile for everyone. But I fancied he had a special, warm smile for me as if we were brothers. I wished I could be with him always. While he hulled rice I took a bamboo and sat opposite him to keep the hens away. When he sieved, I picked out the unhusked grains.

There are ten verses to *The Railings of the West Lake,* and while hulling he taught me the other nine.

When he was free, he often brought his fiddle to our house and would play while I sang.

He told me that fiddles with snake skin at one end of the body were called *pihu* or skin-fiddles, while his with a piece of thin wood was a *banhu* or wood-fiddle. He preferred wood-fiddles, as their sound was clearer and crisper. Fiddles were better than pipes or flutes because you could transpose easily from one scale to another and you could accompany yourself. So though he could pipe and flute, he had just bought a fiddle.

It was he, too, who told me that the outer string was

called the minor string, and the middle one the second. Some players used only the second and the major string, but the result was disappointing, because the thicker the string the less crisp the sound.

He also taught me how to hold a fiddle, and which notes were produced by different fingers.

He told me all there was to know about fiddling.

Then I longed more passionately than ever to have a fiddle of my own.

But this was too much to hope for. Mother would never hear of such a thing.

The main reason was that singing and fiddling were low-class amusements.

My father was a respectable citizen, manager of a foreign firm, who made a great deal of money. One year he would buy land, the next a house. He and my mother commanded tremendous respect in the village. And as I was their only son, they had high hopes for me. They wanted me to become a compradore, build western-style houses, buy land, and be generally respected — in fact they hoped to make me a cut above my fellows.

It would never do if word got round that a manager's son or a compradore played the fiddle.

"Do you mean to make a living by fiddling?" Mother demanded, whenever I showed the least sign of wanting to buy a fiddle.

It was true. You could not make a living by fiddling, or even if you could I did not want to. How humiliating it must be to play to give pleasure to your hearers and then get your food that way — like a beggar!

But I loved fiddles. My ears delighted in their strains, my fingers itched to touch their strings, and I longed to produce that music with my own hands. This longing goaded me on — come what might — to possess one.

At last I hit on a way.

It was the summer of that same year when our house was being remodelled. Carpenters and masons were working every day in our courtyard, which was stacked with planks, bricks and tiles.

While the carpenters were at a meal, I found a long thin piece of wood. I determined to use this for the neck of my fiddle by chopping it to the right size with a carpenter's axe. But these axes were so heavy that I found them unwieldy, and I worked for a long time without success. Afraid I would be forbidden the use of such a heavy tool, I handled it only when no one was about, putting it down and hiding the wood before the carpenters' return. This went on for several days, until one of them discovered me. When he asked what I was making I would not tell him, for fear he would laugh at me or tell my mother.

"It's just something I need," I muttered.

He asked what shape I wanted. I told him flat and square. He smiled and puzzled over this, but could not guess my secret. Seeing how hard I found it to use the axe, however, and afraid I might cut my hand, the good man chopped the wood for me.

"Is this the right size?"

"A bit smaller."

"How about this?"

"A bit flatter."

"All right now? I'll plane it for you."

No sooner said than done.

When the wood had become a long, smooth, flat

neck, I put it away. The bottom part of the neck had to be rounded, but for safety's sake I kept this job for myself and carried it out in secret. As the plane was much lighter than the axe, I found this quite easy.

Next with a plane and a file I made two round pegs for the strings, larger at one end than the other.

Then in a pile of old tins, I found one that had held condensed milk. I cut off the thick base, leaving the thinner end, and made two holes with scissors in the back for the base of the neck.

Still a difficult problem remained.

How was I to make two holes for the pegs in the head?

I tried with a chisel, but it was too big and threatened to crack the neck.

After thinking hard, I remembered the marks of scorching round the holes in the head of Acheng's fiddle. But could you burn holes without burning the whole neck?

I decided a hot drill must have been used.

So in the oven I heated the flat-iron used at home for dressmaking, and tried using its tip.

It simply scorched the wood slightly.

I had to think again.

I recalled the bellows-furnace with which Uncle Dingfa the coppersmith heated a drill till it was red-hot. When he drove this in, the metal would sputter and smoke. That would be the way to make holes in the neck of my fiddle.

I scouted round his house several times to see if he was using his furnace or not, and a few days later he lit it.

Then, taking my fiddle neck and a long, thick nail,

I asked him to let me use the furnace when he had finished.

Uncle Dingfa agreed at once. Of all the grown-ups he treated me the best. He always did what I asked. If I wanted to make a fish hook out of a needle, he would lend me small pliers and a file. When Mother wanted something from Daqietou, about three *li* away, he usually told me not to go but ran the errand for me. Working in one and the same room as a coppersmith and the proprietor of a small store which sold wine, paraffin and cigarettes, he was very busy; yet he found time to act as carter for one family or run errands for another, and refused all offers of tips. Mother did not like to impose on his good nature too often, but he frequently came to ask if there was anything she wanted done. No one could have been more honest and obliging.

So that day as usual when he saw that I was going to find it hard to bore holes with my nail, busy as he was he produced a slightly larger awl, heated it red-hot in his furnace, rubbed a little resin on my fiddle and in no time at all had bored two holes for me.

Strings cost next to nothing. I bought two in a small shop in Daqietou.

From our pile of firewood I picked out a slender bamboo which I stripped of its leaves. Then I cut a length of pure hemp from a skein in my mother's work-basket, and made a bow of these.

The resin had been a present from Uncle Dingfa.

At last my fiddle was finished.

In raptures, I tried it where Mother could not hear me.

But not a sound could I get from it, try as I would —

the bow simply slipped noiselessly over the strings.

This was a terrible blow. I could not think where the trouble lay. I puzzled hard to find out just what difference there was between my fiddle and others; but all I could see was that where I used hemp they had horsehair. At first I did not believe that this made any difference, because unspun hemp looks so like horsehair. But assuming that the fault lay with the bow, I decided to buy another in Daqietou.

Here three difficulties occurred to me. First, all the bows in the shops were attached to fiddles, so I might not be able to buy one separately. Secondly, if everything depended on the bow, it must be expensive. Thirdly, if I was seen taking such a long bow home from Daqietou, all the people I met on the road were sure to laugh.

But my first two fears were unfounded. The shopkeeper agreed to let me buy a bow alone, and it was extremely cheap, less than ten cents.

There was a solution for the third problem too.

I wore a long cotton gown to town, put the bow under my gown and slipped my right hand inside to hold it as if my hand were in my pocket. So I hurried home. Whenever I met anyone I knew, I turned red and brushed quickly past; for though hidden, the bow could easily be detected.

That day I had a genuine fiddle.

It had the most resonant tone.

My mother and sister came running out in surprise.

"Wherever did you get that?" There was nothing reproachful in Mother's tone, in fact she was smiling in pleased surprise.

I made a clean breast of everything, and told her I

would like to ask Acheng to teach me to play. She consented on condition that this remained a hobby and I did not play outside, for to play in public would mean a loss of face. This was my opinion too.

That evening I invited Acheng over. He was equally amazed, declaring he had never seen anyone so clever. He tried my fiddle and found it most resonant, but the antithesis of his with its sobbing note — due, no doubt, to the milk tin.

It was this sobbing I liked particularly. I found it so appealing. It sounded like a man with a hoarse voice sobbing and complaining. Acheng agreed that this tone was extremely rare, as most fiddles could only produce a shrill, womanish note — even the lowest note of the major string of a skin-fiddle was not much like a man's voice. And the sobbing effect was even more unusual. On other fiddles you could produce it only by making a tremolo with your left fingers, but then it was less natural.

"This fiddle has one fault, though," remarked Acheng. "It can't play anything gay the way it's made."

I did not mind this at all, quite the reverse. Let others play cheerful music — I would play sad.

Very soon Acheng had taught me several tunes. He could not write a musical score, only read it. He often came to our house and read off the score as he fiddled, while I wrote it down. Once I had the notation I did not need him by me all the time, but could gradually learn the tunes myself.

In the spring of the next year I transferred from our village school to the primary school in town. At our weekly singing class I jotted down quite a few song tunes, which I took home and played on my fiddle. As I was a boarder, I longed to take my fiddle to school, but was afraid of a lecture from our teacher. So I simply fiddled when I went home on Sundays, and practised the organ at school.

Acheng was then working in a rice shop at Daqietou and did not go home too often. Neither did I, so we seldom met. When we did, he would bring his fiddle to our house and we would play together. If he had left his fiddle at the rice shop, one of us would play while the other sang.

Acheng's family had a boat, and as a boy he had helped his father with it. He had an elder and a younger brother, but because he was the most capable of the three he was the one sent out to work in the rice shop. And he was still an excellent swimmer, though seldom on the river now.

One summer afternoon, while sitting on the bridge chatting with some friends, he happened to make a bet with one of them. He said he could swim across the river with a rice bin on his back. No one believed him, for a rice bin was so big and heavy that it took a strong peasant just to carry one down the street. It might be possible to push or pull the floating bin across; but with that on his shoulders a man would be unable to move, the weight would push him under. Still Acheng insisted he could do this, and bet a water-melon on it.

A rice bin is square, larger above than below, like a huge peck measure. As a child I had crept inside to play with my friends, for four or five children could hide in one of them. Now Acheng hoisted one of these on his back, chose the widest part of the river, and started to swim across. I stood on the bank watching, in a cold sweat for fear his head would go under. For then not only would he lose the melon but have to swallow some water.

I need not have worried — he swam across that river as if he were walking in the water. You could just see one arm moving, as he carried the bin over on his back; but his head was above water all the time. The crowd on the bank clapped and cheered.

Encouraged by this applause, Acheng swam back empty-handed with his whole chest out of the water as if standing erect — at moments even his stomach was visible. This made all the spectators cheer still more wildly. None of us youngsters had ever seen swimming like this, nor had many of the old folk for that matter.

Acheng climbed ashore amid shouts of applause and after changing his clothes in a boat by the wharf came back grinning to the bridge, where a huge melon was cut and waiting. Seeing me there, he promptly handed me a slice.

"When we've finished this melon, let's go to your house," he suggested cheerfully.

His eyes were shining with happiness, his face was beaming. And I was too happy for words. I admired him more than anyone else in the world.

That afternoon, staying with us for nearly two hours, he drew quite a new music from my fiddle — blissfully happy music reflecting his mood.

But that was the last happy summer Acheng enjoyed. From the next spring to the next summer he went through a bad time indoors.

The blow fell one afternoon in the third month, when the fie'ds were filled with golden rape flowers.

He was too happy. For the next day his family was going to hold his second or final betrothal ceremony, and in the tenth month he would marry. The whole household was busy preparing betrothal gifts, and he was on the move from morning till night.

He was striding home followed at some distance by his elder brother, who was carrying a basket of gifts. They were more than half way there — passing a pavilion and skirting a row of houses would bring them in sight of home — when Acheng saw a dog.

It was lying in the middle of the path, and did not move away when he came up.

Acheng stepped round the dog, but something about it annoyed him. He turned back, glanced at it and gave it a kick.

"Get out of the way, can't you!"

The dog leapt up with blazing eyes, and quick as thought, without so much as a bark, bit Acheng in the leg. Then it slunk off as if nothing had happened into the rape field.

Acheng fell to the ground with a cry. The dog had bitten through his trousers and blood was streaming from his leg. In his haste that day he had forged ahead. By the time his brother came up, he was too dizzy to stand.

His brother carried him home, where he lay in a fever for several days, while his family was plunged from happiness into despair. When rape blossoms turn golden, snakes creep out of their holes; and if a dog eats a poisonous snake its eyes turn bloodshot and it becomes rabid. Its bite causes death within a hundred and twenty days. In all the centuries since the time of Shen Nong,* no herb has been found to cure hydrophobia.

Why had this happened on that day of all days? Everyone brooded in despair. It was a most sinister omen. No one thought for a moment that Acheng could recover.

Still, in an attempt at self-deception, his father searched frantically for a herb doctor, who prepared a potion and put a poultice on the wound. This physician stipulated that Acheng should stay in an absolutely quiet room with the windows tightly closed. His one chance was to shut himself up for a hundred and twenty days, first away from contact with women, secondly away from tobacco, wine and meat, and thirdly away from noise.

Before long, though, Acheng recovered. His wound healed and stopped aching, and all his energy returned. Not believing the physician or his family, he refused to lie low for a hundred and twenty days. He insisted on going out. But there were so many in the house to advise and soothe him that he always calmed down again after making a scene.

As I was at school at the time, I did not hear the news from Mother till my return home. I wanted to visit him, but Mother would not hear of it, on the grounds that this would disturb him and make him worse. What Mother told me appalled me. She said there was no hope for anyone bitten by a mad dog, for the poison which seeped in through the wound grew into a small dog in the victim's stomach. Though the wound

* A legendary Chinese ruler, reputed to have invented the first agricultural implements and to have taught his subjects husbandry and the use of medicinal herbs.

might heal, dog's fur would grow on it, and in a hundred and twenty days — unless the man recovered — his eyes would turn flecked and red like a mad dog's, he would not recognize anyone, and would start to bark and bite. And whoever was bitten would die like a mad dog. She forbade me to see him and indeed I dared not, though I missed him intensely and asked after him each Saturday when I got home. His calamity plunged me into dreadful despair. I had no hope that he could be saved. Not once in all those weeks did I touch my fiddle. As Mother knew how I felt, she kept asking for news of Acheng, which she told me as soon as I reached home.

When I went back for the summer holidays she said it looked as if Acheng would be all right. The incubation period for rabies was sometimes a hundred days; now that time had passed, yet he seemed as healthy and cheerful as ever. He slipped out sometimes to the street, and on the one occasion when she had met him he had asked the date of my holidays. Still, Mother would not let me visit him. She had heard that Acheng had several girl friends, and if he should carry on a love affair his life was still in danger, for the hundred and twenty days were not yet up.

One evening, at last, I met him.

He seemed unchanged, perhaps just a trifle thinner. But he looked as strong as ever, and his ruddy face was merely a shade paler — no doubt owing to his long confinement. He was walking along the bank with a fishing rod, looking for the bubbles which betrayed the presence of a carp. Forgetting that he had ever been ill, I rushed joyfully up to him.

He had obviously missed me, for his eyes lit up and he put away his rod to go straight home with me. At the sound of his voice, Mother made a cup of tea and asked with much concern about his health. He replied that there was nothing wrong with him, no one need worry. He didn't think a mad dog's bite was all that dangerous. He stretched out his right leg and removed the poultice to show us that there was no blood or pus and the wound had healed completely. In fact he thought the poultice unnecessary, and applied it only because the others insisted; but he blamed his family for making such a mountain out of a mole-hill. What harm could one little bite do to a strapping great fellow like him? His manner was absolutely natural. In his pleasure at being with me again he made light of his danger.

When I brought out my fiddle and handed it to him, he looked at it and said:

"It's thick with dust. You can't have played for some time."

I nodded.

Then Mother told him how much I had missed him and longed to see him, explaining that I had stayed away for fear of disturbing him.

Acheng replied warmly that he had missed me too, but his family would never let him out. He had not fiddled either for a long time, because playing and singing alone were not much fun.

Then he started playing with evident enjoyment, and I watched wide-eyed, very touched. I soon discovered that his style had changed. It was one of our usual tunes, but it sounded heart-rending as he played it that day, and the sobbing notes were unusually deep and protracted. My heart felt curiously heavy, in spite of my joy at seeing him again and sitting beside him as he fiddled. My happiness was shot through with a strange, sad foreboding. Hard as I listened I could not concentrate, for in fancy I saw a fearful picture: A mad dog with red eyes slunk up to Acheng and bit him on the ankle. Acheng fell down and his bright blood stained the ground. When he stood up his eyes too were red and staring. He bared his sharp fangs and chased after anyone near him, snapping at stones and bushes till his jaws were streaming with blood. Then from his stomach he threw up some small mad dogs, which leapt up and down and ran after everyone. . . . At last he collapsed and died in a welter of blood, to the sound of weeping and wailing. . . .

"Xiqin!" Mother's voice recalled me to my senses. "Why are you sitting there in a brown study? Aren't you glad to have Brother Acheng back? Why don't you sing while he plays?"

My cheeks burned. How could I sing?

This was the last time that Acheng and I were able to see each other. His lot was cast: he was fated to leave me, to leave the whole world of men. And soon, very soon, only three afternoons later.

No one could account for the curious change in the weather, which suddenly turned as chill as my heart. A high wind sprang up and clouds covered the sky, sombre and menacing as my mood.

When I saw a few people talking fearfully in low voices on the street, I knew that something untoward had happened. I went over and found they were discussing Acheng.

". . . Nearly broke the rope, he did. . . . Turned the whole room upside-down. . . . Ground his teeth and snapped at his father and brother . . . swore his father had been his enemy in his last life. . . . He half batterd down the door when he tried to burst out, but after a fight they managed to tie him up. He bit a teacup to pieces, spat out mouthfuls of blood.... Just a hundred and twenty days, of course nothing could save him...."

As if soused in icy water I shuddered in terror. I ran in confusion through the streets till I found myself staggering across the field outside Acheng's house.

A woman was crying in one room. All else was still. I saw no movement inside or outside the house, over which a bitter, desolate wind was howling.

My eye fell on a patch of bloodstained ashes in the paddy field at my feet.

I jumped up fearfully, and pelted home....

My heart was hammering, my head was burning. As soon as I fell on my bed I lost consciousness.

Acheng, living, was the man I loved most in the world. Dead, he was the ghost I feared most.

I had known quite a number of our neighbours die, but had never been so terrified before.

That night the wind carried over bitter sobs, and the desolate tattoo of nails driven into a coffin. . . .

I had lost Acheng, lost everything. . . .

Why should fate inflict such a deep wound upon my tender heart? I have no means of knowing. It has meted out joys to me, sorrows as well. And these sorrows are fathomless, boundless.

Now all has slipped away with the flight of time, leaving only these sorrows still in the depths of my heart. Whenever music reaches my ears, grief floods my heart, reminding me of Acheng.

Acheng's fate was too cruel, and I cannot bring myself to tell what indignities he suffered after his death. . . .

As for me, from that time on happiness has shunned me.

Two years after he died I left my old home, and since then I have been drifting about outside.

When I went home a couple of years ago, my mother brought out the fiddle I had made and told me:

"Look! The fiddle you made as a boy has been kept safely for you."

But I could have no further traffic with that fiddle. Fled and gone were my earlier enchanting dreams of music. Even this was out of the question: To fiddle for a living and, as my mother had said, spend my life in this despicable way.

Lately, happiness has fled me further and further. My fiddle and my old home, rebuilt when I made the fiddle, have both been turned to ashes. This seems to augur a yet more fearful future.

Perhaps for others youth is a golden age. In my case, at least, there is nothing to warrant such a statement. I have known too many days of hardship and distress, have never seen a glimmer of happiness.

To live on in this way is too painful. . . .

I would rather. . . .

1931

Translated by Gladys Yang

On the Bridge

CHUG, chug, chug. . . .

The rowing boat equipped with up-to-date rice-hulling machines could be heard in the distance again.

Uncle Yixin's grasp on the rope of his balance slackened. Countless black circles formed before his eyes, rolling nearer and nearer across the hills and valleys.

Swallowing back a groan, he breathed out deeply and pulled himself together.

"Forty-nine!" he shouted.

"That's not right!" cried a woodcutter from the hills with a grin, as he lifted the firewood higher. "The wood's still touching the ground."

"Get along with you! It's fuel we're weighing, not gold! Fifty-one . . . fifty-five . . . fifty-four . . . sixty! There's too much hard wood in this lot. How do you expect a housewife to burn that? How many mouths do you think she has to feed? Forty-eight!"

"You can open it up and look at it! See how big that pile at the bottom is?"

"I haven't got all day. If you don't agree, that's all right with me. Fifty-two. A bundle of soft wood is always less than thirty catties. How can two bundles weigh more than sixty? Fifty-three! Fifty!"

"Some bundles may be bigger?"

"Isn't that your job? You're used to tying bundles.

I've followed this trade for pretty well twenty years. Fifty-one! Who are you trying to fool? Fifty!"

Chug, chug, chug. . . .

Yixin felt his legs tremble. The rice-hulling boat had come back to South Bridge, at the end of Xue Family Village. Though he was standing on North Bridge, half a *li* away, he could already see the revolving black circles, smell the stifling paraffin fumes, and make out the large boat through the jumble of black rings. It was vibrating and slapping the water. The jetty swarmed with men and women, who were feeding crate after crate of paddy into the mouth-like peck measure among the black circles. It champed and chewed greedily before swallowing the grain. . . .

Uncle Yixin sat down woodenly on the bridge, the balance propped against his chest.

He was in the rice business himself. . . . No, he was the owner of Changxiang Store at the foot of this bridge, the first building in the street. He had kept this shop for twenty-three years. At fifteen he was an apprentice in Beiqie, at twenty he married, early in his twenty-fourth year his first daughter was born, and towards the end of that year he opened shop here. A year later his elder son was born — first a girl and then a boy, that was good luck — and his business had prospered steadily. At first he sold only groceries, with stationery as a sideline. Then he branched out to sell soya sauce, paraffin and wine. Later he went in for cigarettes and money-changing too, and finally he hired a couple of full-time assistants to hull grain, and went into the rice trade. As if that were not enough, he became a middleman too. First he weighed goods for the pedlars in front of his shop on the village market-days

— the days of the month which ended with five or nought. Later he acted as middleman for the hill people's cabbage, turnips, bamboo shoots, plums, apricots, peaches, melons, pumpkins, white gourds. . . . They rowed up boatload after boatload for him to weigh and sell to pedlars or other customers. Eventually they asked him to weigh and sell their firewood too.

He was seldom idle for a moment. Though business was good, he did everything single-handed, having no manager, accountant, assistant or apprentice. His only help was his wife. But she could neither read nor keep accounts, and her memory was poor. She simply wrapped up a few coppers' worth of white or brown sugar, and watched the shop for him. She could not sit too long in the shop either, as she had to cook, wash and mind the children. As for him, far from having any help, he helped others. He never refused a request from anyone. If there was a wedding or funeral in the village, or someone wanted to buy in vegetables, he was invariably asked to lend a hand because he made the best buys. Most letters that came to the village were addressed to his shop, and he always made time to deliver them, sometimes reading them to the recipient, or writing an answer and taking it back to his shop to give to whoever was next going to Beiqie to post.

He ate home-salted vegetables and wore cotton. And he neither smoked, gambled, nor drank to any extent — half a catty of wine would make him red in the face. As a young man he practised economy for the sake of his ancestors, in order to be pointed out as a filial son. He kept this up as he grew older so that his children might live in greater comfort. He set great store indeed by his good name, and would not lay himself open to any criticism. Just after the birth of his second son he won general respect by rebuilding his parents' tombs in style. "If I use up all my money, I can save some more," he thought. And sure enough in a few more years he had prepared his own final resting place and repaired his elder brother's grave. Next he married off his sixteen-year-old daughter with even more of a flourish. By the time his elder son had served three years' apprenticeship in Shanghai and was making three dollars a month, he had built himself a fine new house in the village.

Still he did not retire to take his ease. He went on working as hard as ever, harder if anything. There were the village fairs, of course, on the days ending with a five or a nought. And on those ending with two, four, seven and nine — the market days in Hengshiqiao — he would stand on North Bridge and intercept a couple of boats of firewood.

"Can you find customers?" the woodcutters would ask.

"Sure! Hand your fuel over. I guarantee to get rid of the lot!"

Uncle Yixin had his own sales methods, though there was no fair and very few passers-by. He knew just how much firewood each village household had left, and found time to settle the transaction with them.

"Take a boatload, Sister Agen!" He stood up, smiling, when she came up the bridge.

"Half!"

"Such good fuel isn't easy to come by, sister. You'd better take a whole load! It's going specially cheap today, for five dollars twenty cents. You'll need it all in the long run, so why not buy a little more? Hey!

Bring us that firewood, Changsheng!" By now he had picked up his balance.

"Fifty-one! Forty-nine! Fifty-three. . . ."

Chug, chug, chug. . . .

The rice-hulling boat could be heard in the village bay.

Something seemed to be blocking Uncle Yixin's ears so that he could not hear clearly the figures he was shouting. Black circles blotted out the small numerals on the balance close at hand, swallowed up the firewood and the woodcutters, and even blurred Sister Agen standing by his side.

"Business is good today!" Someone spoke loudly into his ear and then was gone. Uncle Yixin pulled himself together. That had been Grandad Xinsheng.

"Please sit down!" He called out as if he were in his shop.

But Xinsheng passed on without a look behind.

Xinsheng's manner, like everyone else's, seemed to have changed. He was a good sort, who always made tactful remarks. But today he had sounded sarcastic and contemptuous.

Chug, chug, chug. . . .

The rice-hulling boat again.

It had arrived just as Uncle Yixin was building his house. Before the builders set to work he had heard that Lin Jikang, owner of Yongtai Rice Shop in Beiqie, was going to start running a rice-hulling boat. He knew that this would affect his rice business and mean a drop in his income. But as the news about his house had spread, he could not go back on his word. If he did he would lose face completely, and that might be bad for his credit.

"Is this machine-polished rice all right?" several customers sounded him out.

"There's something to be said for both sorts," he answered with an air of great confidence. And he moved the building date forward.

Though a huller would affect his trade, he did not believe it would put him out of business. Many of the villagers believed that machine-hulled rice gave you beriberi. Besides, he was on good terms with most of them, and if his rice business were hard hit he had other sources of income. There was his grocery store. If one line failed, there was always the other. No, he was not afraid.

But it seemed that Lin Jikang knew he had put the date forward, for he sent out his boat at once. On the auspicious day chosen for erecting the framework of the new house, the boat came to Xue Family Village.

Chug, chug, chug. . . .

Every soul in the village was agog at the sound. They flocked to the water's edge to stare at this strange monster. Despite all the fire-crackers Uncle Yixin let off, very few villagers gathered round. The boat moored at the jetty near his new house, as if to intimidate him. As this was its first appearance, no one took grain to be husked. The boat polished what it had on board.

Chug, chug, chug. . . .

This clatter went on till noon, when suddenly word was sent out that the boat would husk a hundred catties of rice for each household — free and gratis — if it was brought before six that evening. This news spread like the wind, and caused a tremendous sensation. Load after load of paddy was carried to the boat. In less than an hour the road between the jetty and the bridge was blocked by sacks and crates.

Chug, chug, chug. . . .

Not for one second did the racket stop. Black circles chuffed round and round, reaching right out to Uncle Yixin's house. The boat's arrival meant that this day, which should have been such a triumphant occasion, the day on which he achieved his final ambition, had turned to dust and ashes. All was black before his eyes as the motor chug-chug-chugged like the stroke of an axe. He was nearly fifty and had seen a good deal in his time. A piddling rice-hulling boat was nothing to him, especially as rice was not his sole means of livelihood. But how ominous that it should come on this day of all days, when he was setting up his pillars and beams! He nearly panicked and lost all hope, seeing himself a ruined man. That was a sleepless night for him. The boat kept up its clatter till dusk, and moored there during the night. At the crack of dawn it started chugging again. This went on for two and a half days before it finished polishing all the grain carried there before half past three on the first day. Some villagers took paddy, carried it home, and took it back again the next day, till finally it was hulled.

Uncle Yixin kept hearing remarks which boded no good. One commented on the speed of this huller, another on its convenience. The boat was the talk of the village.

"Time will show," he said to himself.

He would watch developments calmly. Some things made a great stir to begin with, owing to their novelty, but as time went on folk saw them at their true value. He had known this to happen quite often.

After that the boat kept coming. It charged thirty-five cents for polishing a hundred catties of paddy, which Uncle Yixin calculated was no cheaper than what he charged for hulling rice by hand. A workman, paid fifty cents a day, could hull two hundred catties. You had to offer him a catty of wine at thirteen cents, which brought costs up to sixty-three cents; but you could give him coarse food, not like the meal a tailor demanded when he worked in someone's house. And as every household had plenty of vegetables, jelly fish or preserved sea-food, there was no need to buy these, while the rice did not add up to much. Sometimes the workman did not drink, in which case thirteen cents could be saved. There was no denying that machine-polished rice was whiter than that hulled by hand with a pestle. But country folk were not too particular, and if you wanted white rice you got less than one bushel for two hundred catties of paddy. Beside which, there was a good deal of breakage. The only advantages of the boat were that it saved time and trouble. But was that so important? Households used to hiring a man did not find it a nuisance, and speed did not matter either. No family waited till its rice was finished before hulling another lot.

Uncle Yixin's view proved correct. The rice boat did very little business. The other villagers made the same calculation, and realized the relative advantages and disadvantages, while many of them continued to shake their heads over the man who had eaten machine rice while in Shanghai and Hankou on business, who had suffered from beriberi for many years, not recovering till he came home and ate unpolished rice.

When Uncle Yixin made up his accounts at the end

of the month he found that his business had fallen off very little. Only five of his former customers had stopped coming, and that meant little loss, as they ate only a few pecks every month. Most of the villagers hired men to hull their rice at home. Those who bought small quantities of polished rice from him either had no hulling implements of their own, or could not afford to buy a hundred or two hundred catties of paddy at a time. And besides, he allowed them credit. The five households won over by the boat were not too poor but could not afford the hulling gear. The boat's best customers were those who had both grain and implements. But these had never dealt with him anyway.

Within two months, two of the five families started buying rice from Uncle Yixin again, and the rice boat's visits became less frequent as it was doing less business than in the first month.

"It can't win away my customers!" thought Uncle Yixin with secret satisfaction. He was not afraid of anything now. He simply found the boat an infernal nuisance, with its foul smell and its clatter. Particularly maddening was the way it had moored at the jetty on the day that the foundations of his house were laid, and tried to frighten him. But much as he disliked it, he said nothing against it. That would have seemed too petty-minded.

"Others will do the complaining," he thought. It was not his job the boat had taken, but that of the men who went from house to house hulling grain. Each two hundred catties of rice hulled by the boat meant one day's less work for them, one day's less food, and fifty cents less earnings.

"We shan't starve because of it!" He heard them growl angrily.

That was true, as he knew. Men who were strong enough to turn mills and wield heavy pestles could do other work. Besides, very few of them lived entirely by hulling rice.

These men figured it out, and said: "They'll never make it pay — that large boat with the huller and one workman, one accountant and one apprentice."

But the owner, Lin Jikang, had given thought to this. He had plenty of capital. In Beiqie he owned Yongtai Rice Shop, Wanyu Wood Shop, Xingchang Silk Shop, Longmao Soya Shop, and Tianshengxiang Grocery, to say nothing of the money-changer's business he ran with a friend in the county town. He could afford initial losses for the sake of future profits. At the beginning of the third month, his boat suddenly lowered its price. Instead of thirty-five cents for a hundred catties, it now asked thirty cents.

This considerable reduction threw Xue Family Village into a ferment again. Households which generally hired men to do their hulling jumped at this chance, and took their grain to the jetty.

"I shan't be the loser," declared Uncle Yixin calmly.

His rice accounts at the end of that month showed that only six customers had left him. He watched impassively as the boat's trade picked up and then slowly fell off again. There were already many complaints that the machine-hulled husks were too bitty to use as fuel, while the bran was too coarse to feed to hens and could only be sold as duck-feed for less than five coppers. It fetched merely three coppers per catty, in fact, and they had to sieve it first again and again. As the villagers liked big hulls and fine chaff, they would have liked to hire men to remove the husks and then get the boat to polish the rice. But for that they would not pay thirty cents a hundred catties. All they offered was fifteen.

This the boat would not accept, however. The accountant explained that unhusked and husked rice meant the same amount of work. A hundred catties of paddy produced only five pecks of machine-polished rice, but the same amount of husked rice produced nearly a hundred catties of polished rice. That was already to their advantage, and they could not ask the boat to halve its price. At the most it would come down to twenty-five cents. But to this the villagers did not agree. They chose to go on hulling rice at home.

So Uncle Yixin saw the boat's trade fall off again.

"It's not a paying proposition," he remarked with secret satisfaction.

But if one method won't work, you can always try another. Lin hit on a new solution. As he owned Yongtai Rice Shop in Beiqie, rather than admit defeat he made the boat sell rice.

That was when the boat became a serious rival. It undercut Uncle Yixin. As he had a fund of goodwill, went out of his way to help others, and could keep his own accounts, it had not crossed his mind that anyone could steal his customers; but now they were rushing to the boat to buy at the cheaper rate. The first and second grades were not important, as few of the villagers ate white rice. But the third grade was another matter — and here the boat had made the biggest cut.

"Is it going to damage me too, after all those others?" he wondered.

He manipulated his abacus, and found he still had a margin of profit.

"I'll come down to your price, and see if you can still steal my customers!"

Uncle Yixin brought down his prices to the boat's: Six twenty for the first grade, five sixty for the second, and four eighty instead of five dollars for the third.

Once again the boat's business fell off. After all, the villagers were Uncle Yixin's friends. They came back to his shop. Not one bought from the boat.

"Machine-polished rice — poor stuff! Gives you beriberi. Who wants that?"

When Lin Jikang knew that his plan had failed because Uncle Yixin had lowered his prices too, he made another cut. He reduced the two top grades by five cents, the lower by ten.

Uncle Yixin flicked the beads of his abacus again, and reduced accordingly.

The trade remained his.

Then Lin slashed his prices again, selling the third grade for four dollars sixty cents.

Uncle Yixin made another calculation. Fresh paddy cost a dollar ten every hundred catties and a tenth of it disappeared during the drying. A bushel of rice cost four dollars, a day's labour thirty-five cents. With food this came to over four forty a day. If you added rent, taxes, transport, incidental expenses and interest, he could only sell at a loss.

Make another cut or not? Unless he reduced, he wou'd lose his customers. New rice would soon be on the market, and keeping old stocks would make his losses greater. Gritting his teeth, he brought the prices down.

Apparently Lin was tired of losing money, for now the boat stopped coming. It moored idly in Beiqie.

Uncle Yixin sighed with relief. He had not yet lost too much, and should be able to recoup during the next two quarters.

"The scoundrel must have hurt himself as much as anyone else," he reflected angrily. "If not, why should his boat have stopped coming?"

Little did he know that Lin had decided to destroy him.

Chug, chug, chug. . . .

The harvest was no sooner in than the boat re-appeared in the village.

It was still hulling and selling rice. But the price in both cases was lower than ever. It charged fifteen cents only to hull rice, the price the villagers had asked. And the price of rice went down from day to day, till the third grade had fallen to four dollars.

Uncle Yixin, who had just bought in new supplies, cut his prices in desperation. But his rice would not sell. The whole village knew that Lin was playing with him and did not mind losing money. Each time Uncle Yixin cut his price, Lin would cut his again. So though Uncle Yixin made reductions, nobody bought from him — next day they could buy at a cheaper price from the boat.

Uncle Yixin dared not go on losing like this. He announced that he had stopped selling rice, closed down half his shop, paid off his assistant, and prepared to sell the rice he had bought in.

"This is the end!" he sighed. "The man has capital — what can I do?"

But Lin had not finished with him yet. Knowing

that Uncle Yixin wanted to sell, he played another trick. When the new rice came on the market he had bought in large quantities, and now he started dumping this on the market. Uncle Yixin did not want to sell, but his hand was forced. If he hung on to the grain, there was no knowing how good next year's harvest would be. Besides, to keep all that rice instead of changing it for money would tie his hands in his grocery business. He had to sell out at a loss again.

Chug, chug, chug. . . .

The boat's business picked up once more. It captured not only the rice trade, but the hulling as well. It came every few days — sometimes every day — to the village.

"The devil!" Uncle Yixin ground his teeth and swore under his breath each time he saw the boat. He was in a cold sweat at the thought of his debts. In all his years of trading, he had never suffered such a setback before.

He saw business boom for the boat, and rice go up again. When he had sold all his paddy, the price of that rose too.

"Well, I can take it!" he thought, and this was his answer to questions about his affairs. "Rice was a sideline for me in any case. I shall concentrate on my main business now. I've got some good lines there."

It was true. His one hope now lay in his grocery. If not for this, he could never have hoped to raise his head again after such a crash.

His Changxiang Store was an old establishment, his credit was good, and so was the location. The shop was the first building after North Bridge at the top of the street, so that anyone passing that way by land or water could be seen from behind the counter. On market days pedlars and customers crowded round his entrance, making it easy for him to do other business and for them to buy from him. The rent was forty dollars a year, which was not exorbitant for a double frontage, with store-rooms and a kitchen at the back. Now that he had stopped dealing in rice, he had much more space; but he did up the premises and turned one room into a public parlour, to give the place a more prosperous appearance. Quite a number of folk liked to drop in for a chat, and once there was this parlour they did not have to squeeze behind the counter but could sit longer. As they all had the surname Xue and Uncle Yixin was such a good-natured fellow, they could sit there as long as they pleased whether he was in or not, chatting, listening to the news, and watching the road or the river. Though the shop had no manager, accountant, assistant or apprentice, all this coming and going made it a lively place.

Among these habitués were some who felt concerned for Uncle Yixin, as well as some who just came to have some fun. One day one of them said:

"They say the rice boat's business is so good that Lin Jikang wants to rent a shop front from you."

Uncle Yixin glared.

"Never!" he growled from between clenched teeth. "The man must be dreaming! I wouldn't take him as a tenant for a hundred dollars a month! Not unless I were bankrupt!"

"Quite right too," agreed the others.

It was the village head who had spoken first. As he was fond of a joke, Uncle Yixin thought this was just a bit of his fun. That was why he revealed his true feelings. The fact was, however, that the village head had been asked by Lin to see how the land lay. If Uncle Yixin were to refuse, that would mean a loss of face for Lin, which explains why he asked the village head to sound him out casually. As he had expected, without caring whether the proposal was serious or not, Uncle Yixin flew into a rage.

"We'll wait till he's bankrupt then!" Lin reacted with a laugh.

He started planning how to get his way.

He was in no hurry to drive Uncle Yixin out of business, but preferred to bankrupt him slowly. First he took a copper or two off the price of soya sauce in Longmao Soya Shop.

It was only two and a half *li* from Beiqie to the village — no distance at all. Some of the villagers went there every day, and although the price reduction was so small they heard of it at once. As two and a half *li* was nothing to them, they took their soya sauce bottles to Beiqie.

"Times are certainly bad!" Uncle Yixin shook his head, not realizing that this was aimed at him. As he did not sell much soya sauce in any case, he decided not to lower the price but wait to see how things went.

Before long wine went up, and it was quite commonly said that the wine tax would be increased from five dollars a keg to seven. And glutinous rice would go up like other grain, because of the general unrest in the district.

"What I lose on one line I can make up on another," thought Yixin.

He made some calculations, and as glutinous rice had

not yet risen much he borrowed money and bought in a stock of wine.

Sure enough, grain went on rising, to Uncle Yixin's delight. Wine was beginning to go up too, and he increased his prices.

But before long the price of wine in Lin's shop was reduced. As Uncle Yixin did not believe it would go down any more, he kept his stock to sell later rather than cut his price. Then all his drinking customers went to Beiqie.

The prices in Longmao Soya Shop fluctuated, till Uncle Yixin believed Lin was unsure of himself, and this made him more determined not to reduce.

But on the first of September the wine-tax collector arrived. There was no increase after all, and times were more settled again, so the price of wine dropped. Then Uncle Yixin knew he had made a mistake, and brought his price down too. But Lin seemed to be the more nervous of the two, for he sold more cheaply than anywhere else, cutting his prices again and again, till wine that had sold for thirty coppers a catty was going for twenty.

By this time Uncle Yixin had to do the same. Other shops could keep their wine for a year or a half., but not he. He had to repay his loans, and the interest was heavy. If he kept his wine, it might depreciate. Just the interest on the interest he owed was a sizable sum.

He was going bankrupt again in the same way as before, and this made his life a nightmare. He dared not keep up the price of soya sauce either.

But Uncle Yixin was an experienced tradesman, who had watched countless shops thrive and close down. He combined caution with boldness. In debt as he was, he did not give up hope.

"I've done business since I was twenty-four," he said. "And for the first few years I did well enough out of groceries alone."

"We shall see," was Lin's laconic comment. "We shall see."

He started lowering the prices in Tianshengxiang Grocery too, and posted up announcements to this effect all the way between the village and Beiqie. It was now approaching the end of the year, when everyone buys more groceries than usual. The practice had always been to give customers a bonus in the shape of one packet of sweetmeats to sacrifice to the Kitchen God, but now Tianshengxiang gave two packets, and its goods were much cheaper. The villagers flocked to Beiqie again. By the middle of the twelfth month there was still no New Year spirit in Uncle Yixin's shop. Though he lowered his prices too, his business was poor. And the men who used to drop in to chat had nearly all stopped coming, for they were busy at the end of the year. The money-market was tight too, and statements of his account started coming in from his wholesalers, while the money-lenders sent to demand payment.

As far as Uncle Yixin could see, he was finished. He had spent all his savings and raised loans to build his house that year, confident that a few months would clear his debts. He had not foreseen the ruin of his rice and wine trade, nor the fact that now he could make nothing on his groceries. If not for his popularity, the fact that his was an old establishment and his credit was good, he would long since have lost room in which to manoeuvre, and had to close down as a bankrupt. Luckily many of the housewives had a high regard for him. They tided him over by depositing with him the New Year's money sent home by their sons and husbands, or their savings, fifty or a hundred dollars at a time.

So he got through New Year. But he hardly dared think of the future, which he knew was even more black. He tried to delude himself by saying:

"Now I'll make a fresh start. Luck changes every year. There's no reason why Lin should have it all his own way; he may break up even faster. And there'll be no way out for that scoundrel once he crashes, while I can still get along as a middleman." Indeed, he could make a living as a middleman. There were goods to be weighed all the year round. Cabbage, turnips, bamboo shoots, plums, apricots, peaches, melons, gourds . . . and firewood pretty well every other day.

The firewood alone was almost enough to keep him busy, running here and there looking for customers.

"I guarantee that fuel isn't damp!" He stood up on the bridge to stop Sister Pinsheng, when he saw her putting one finger into a bundle. "If any were damp I'd have picked it out. And the price couldn't be fairer — five twenty."

"Can't you come down a little?"

"I'll give you a good weight. This is the market price, we can't go below it. Fuel isn't like other goods. I burn the same at home, and only wish I could get it cheaper myself. Do you only want two bundles? Here, let me weigh it. Forty-eight. All this wood makes just forty-eight catties — that shows you how dry it must be. Fifty! Fifty-one! Forty-nine! . . ."

Chug, chug, chug. . . .

The boat started up its huller by the jetty at North Bridge.

Uncle Yixin could see nothing but those hated black circles, going round and round, blotting out everything else. He nearly choked and could hardly keep his eyes open. Horrified to feel the strength ebbing from his limbs, he hastily sat down, clutching the balance.

Chug, chug, chug. . . .

His heart was thumping loudly. He made a tremendous effort. All his energy seemed to have been drained by the boat, leaving him fearfully empty — like his shop. It was still open, there were goods on the shelves, and the signboard was hanging out; but in actual fact he was already bankrupt. The old stock in his store-room was finished, and no new goods had come in. He was heavily in debt.

"I want a catty of dragon-eyes,* Uncle Yixin!" Aunt Jisheng had come in.

He opened a drawer in the counter, and discovered there was only half a catty left.

He hurried into the store-room, but found only mouldy black dates there.

He came quickly back to the counter and opened several drawers, but all were empty. Hastily hiding these from Aunt Jisheng, he closed them again.

"Sold out. Shall I send you some this afternoon?"

She shook her head and left.

There was a quizzical look in her eye, as if to say: "You'll be going bankrupt any minute, I see!"

---

* Nephelium longan.

"A tin of bamboo shoots!" Sister Benquan was at the counter.

"Please have a seat!" He took a quick grip on himself and conjured up a smile. But afraid she would notice something wrong, he turned and went to the cupboard.

He stayed there for a time as if lost in thought, and finally found a tin. He wiped the dust off it.

"Why is it rusty?" Sister Benquan stared in surprise. "Give me a better one."

"The outside doesn't matter. It was brought here in the rain, that's why it's rusty. Take it and try it. I'll change it if it isn't good." He was afraid as he spoke. Sister Benquan was gazing round her searchingly, appraising the goods in the shop. As she took the tin and left, she seemed to be saying: "Changxiang Store is going to close down!"

"He'll have to close down!" He heard her announce outside.

"He's going bankrupt!" others chimed in, coming towards him.

Uncle Yixin hastily opened the back door and walked to the bridge.

"Please settle for the firewood for me," said Sister Pinsheng.

That was not what she meant. She wanted her deposit back.

"Fifty for me."

"A hundred for me."

"Three hundred for me."

"Please pay me back, Uncle Yixin!"

". . . ."

". . . ."

". . . ."

Chug, chug, chug. . . .

"Give me your house to settle your debt."

Chug, chug, chug. . . .

"Make over the shop to me!"

Chug, chug, chug. . . .

Sister Changsheng, Sister Wanfu, Aunt Xiankang, Alin, Uncle Guicai, Uncle Mingfa, Sister Benquan, Grandad Xinsheng, Sister Agen, Hunch-back Meisheng, Lame Ali, Pock-marked Third Brother . . . the wholesalers, the money-lenders . . . all had come. Like the converging black circles, they were surging towards him from all sides.

Uncle Yixin stood up by the parapet, letting go of the balance. He could not even go on as a middleman now. He must get away at once.

"All right. All right. Tomorrow is market day. Come back tomorrow! I'll have your money ready."

As he spoke he walked down from the bridge.

Chug, chug, chug. . . .

His footstep sounded heavily in his ears.

1935

Translated by Gladys Yang

Zhang Tianyi

ZHANG Tianyi (1906-) was born in Nanjing. He entered Beijing University at the age of twenty but was forced to abandon his studies after one year owing to financial difficulties. His first story "A Three and a Half Day Dream" was published in 1928 in the periodical *Rapids* (*Benliu*), edited by the celebrated author Lu Xun. His writing has a realistic, acerbic quality and his vividly expressed criticism is sharp and original.

Zhang Tianyi has also written many outstanding children's stories and in 1953 won the Children's Literature National Award.

New Life

WHEN Mr Li Yimo first came to this middle school to see Principal Pan, many teachers and students gasped in surprise. What? Was this the writer and artist Li Yimo?

The thick overcoat in which he was clad, and the two small but heavy suitcases he was carrying were covered in dust. A rather dark-complexioned face topped his tall and lean frame. It seemed he had not shaved for weeks, for a stubbly beard stood on his chin. Although only around forty, he looked ten years older. Even the myopic lenses of his spectacles were yellow with dust, like window-panes that had not been cleaned for a whole year.

If you had read some of his exquisite short essays, if you had been told that a certain publication once called him "the purest artist", you would certainly have felt that his appearance was completely at odds with his work.

Now Mr Li was saying to Principal Pan, in a voice full of emotion:

"My former self died yesterday and what happened in the past died with it. Old Pan, I was dreaming for a long time, but I am awake now. Really I must thank the Japanese brigands. If it hadn't been for their cannon shots waking me up, I would still be leading the life of a hermit."

He talked about conditions in his native place as it was about to fall into the hands of the Japanese and how he had fled. He was speaking very rapidly. The skin over his prominent cheek-bones glowed slightly. Sometimes he stopped suddenly, as if, for the moment, he had forgotten what had happened next. Then he gave an uneasy jerk and hastily resumed his narration. Old Pan could see that although his friend was full of deep indignation it showed as impatience since he was usually a very calm person and did not easily lose his temper.

Mr Li had fled with his wife and daughter when the Japanese were only about twenty miles from his native place. Usually he collected seven hundred piculs of rice every year from his tenants as rent, but this year he would get nothing. He had left his wife and daughter with his in-laws in a village somewhere in the southern part of Zhejiang Province, and come here alone to look up his old friend.

"It would be meaningless to bury myself in a village with my wife and daughter. My decision is made: I want to do some work in the rear. I want to begin a new life!"

He had heard that the senior section of this middle school needed a teacher for art classes, four periods per week, and he offered to take this job, since he considered it quite proper under the circumstances to accept such a minor position.

"*Aiya*!" Old Pan said, half jokingly and half seriously. "You condescend to teach in our school! I am really overwhelmed by this honour. . . ."

Mr Li stood up and said solemnly:

"What nonsense! . . . The present Yimo is no longer what he was before. The Yimo of the past followed the poet Tao Qian who led the life of a literary recluse; but the Yimo of the present will emulate Mo Di with his philosophy of service to the country and the people. I want to work. I want to suffer. Millions of people are suffering now, while I — I. . . . In fact, even the life of a middle school teacher cannot be considered hard. I would be willing to teach even in a primary school!"

Old Pan assigned a small house in the school garden, formerly used by people who needed quiet and rest, for Mr Li to live in, and Mr Li began his new life. He joined the cultural group at the school as one of its directors. He wrote a few articles for a little weekly magazine issued by this group. He also intended to paint some pictures — pictures to suit propaganda purposes.

"We must propagandize everyone," he said to the students agitatedly, his hands twitching nervously. "We must show the whole world that China is straightforward, tolerant and peace-loving, while our enemy is a cruel beast. We must make everybody understand that we are struggling not only for the continued existence of our country, but also for the maintenance of dignity of mankind."

He walked back and forth uneasily in the classroom, as if he were looking for something. He concentrated all his strength in his right hand, clenching his fist, then stretching the fingers again. His cheeks were burning and he felt a strange tingling in his nose, as if he were going to cry.

Several of the students were watching him intently. He glanced at them, and his eyes met theirs. A mute clash. He walked to the window and stared outside for a few minutes in order to avoid another visual encounter.

The weather here was always bad. Dark clouds hung overhead like a leaden slab. In the school garden bare branches, adorned only with some crows, were trembling in the cold wind. Inside although it was not yet five o'clock, it was already very dark but outside there was still a cold, grey-greenish light in the sky which made one shiver in spite of oneself.

Suddenly Mr Li's thoughts wandered to his native place; he remembered how he used to stand for a while by the window of his study and look out at his charming little garden whenever he felt tired from his work. He remembered how the moss in the gold-fish pond had stayed green even through the winter.

"That Japanese allspice is probably in bloom now," he said to himself.

He shot a glance at the student nearest him as though afraid that they might guess what was on his mind. Then, arms crossed, he tried to put himself into the proper frame of mind, telling himself coolly that in a great era like the present one when there was so much suffering, nobody should long for the comforts he had enjoyed before, and people could no longer lead a leisurely life behind closed doors.

But here, the circumstances were so completely different from those he had been used to before. . . .

Quietly, he heaved a deep sigh. He didn't quite know what it was, but he felt that these new circumstances definitely lacked something. He suffered from a kind of oppression that prevented him from being active, both physically and mentally. Even his righteous indignation seemed somewhat lack-lustre. It had become something very sombre, deeply mixed with melancholy.

In order to divert these unpleasant feelings, intentionally he turned his thoughts to something else.

"Really, why should these four lessons be put all together on Wednesday afternoons?"

A hissing sound issued suddenly from the end of the room. It was not clear whether a student had laughed or just blown his nose. Mr Li was startled and turned around slowly. He wore the sort of embarrassed expression a sensitive child might make in front of strangers after crying. Mr Li asked the students rather too casually:

"Are you . . . eh, do you paint anything outside class?"

Several of the students exchanged glances with a smile.

"Those of you who are in the second and third year take art as an optional course," Mr Li said with some displeasure. "Since you have chosen this course, you must have some interest in art. But I do hope you will do more propaganda pictures for exhibition outside the school, in order to arouse the general public. As long as you can make your meaning clear in your pictures, it doesn't matter if your technique is rather childish. Anyway, this is . . . this is not the time for us to talk about art. Art is useless now."

The students again looked at one another, obviously exchanging meaningful glances. Then a student, with hair cropped closely like that of a Buddhist monk, lifted himself up only a little from his seat instead of standing up and asked:

"And what about propaganda pictures, Mr Li? Aren't they also supposed to be works of art?"

"No, they definitely are not!" Mr Li answered, with some agitation.

"You mean that no propaganda pictures can be considered works of art?"

The teacher felt a kind of pity for the student. What ignorance! Still he explained patiently. A propaganda picture or poster was only an instrument of propaganda. It had nothing whatsoever to do with art. He also repeated over and over again that what was needed was merely something to encourage the people, something to wake them up. He sawed the air with his right hand and spoke more and more rapidly.

"An eye for an eye, a tooth for a tooth! Our enemies are bombarding us with big guns. We must answer them with big guns. The greatest people now are the soldiers on the frontline, and the most useless people are we, the so-called artists. We must drop art for the time being and do what every Chinese should do. . . ."

"Mr Li!" This time the student with the closely cropped hair didn't even bother to lift himself up from his seat. He just sat in front of his easel and said, in a hoarse voice: "Then what about the woodcuts by Käthe Kollwitz and Soviet artists? They are meant for propaganda. Can they be considered works of art?"

"Aha, another follower of Lu Xun!" thought Mr Li.

Teacher and student glared at each other. There was an embarrassed silence. A crow flew over the roof, cawing. Perhaps it had been secretly listening for some time and made the noise because it found the silence too oppressive.

Mr Li guessed that the expression on his face must have been rather strange, for one of the students laughed softly and glanced out of the window. With a great effort, Mr Li put on a smile to show that he was indifferent to what had happened, but he found his voice rather unnatural when he said:

"About this question . . . this . . . this . . . well, it can't be clearly explained in a short time. This . . . this is a question of aesthetics. Why art is art . . . is a complicated subject. . . . If you come to see me after class, I'll gradually help you to clarify this point."

But the student never came to see him. Every Wednesday afternoon thereafter, several cartoons were handed in for his opinion. The question of art was never raised again.

The students did not try to approach him. It might have been that they considered him too great a man to be bothered but they might also have looked down upon him. Sometimes, a few students would come to ask him to write an article for the little weekly, or consult him about its layout and make-up. But they went away again as soon as business was finished.

When he walked through places where students gathered, he would hear someone say behind him: "That's Li Yimo." But from the tone, he could never be sure whether it was said in awe or in ridicule.

However, Mr Chen, the physics and mathematics teacher, seemed to be well liked by the students. Short in stature, with a few pockmarks on his face, Mr Chen had many things to occupy him. He led discussion groups and study groups, and every Saturday evening he lectured in the Public Education Centre for an hour on wartime precautions. The topics he wrote about were many, from dumdum bullets, to Japan's economic crisis. Mr Chen always inclined his head respectfully whenever he met Mr Li.

Old Pan, the school principal, had mentioned Mr Chen several times to Mr Li:

"He has the best spirit of all the teachers here. He is enthusiastic about his work and not at all stuck-up. And he knows his stuff on social problems. . . . Wouldn't you like to talk to him?"

"I think Mr Chen is living a hard life, and a very dull one at that." Mr Li paused for a while. He smiled out of the corners of his mouth. "I suppose you are fond of people like that because your life is exactly the same."

That was true. Old Pan had sat in the principal's chair of this middle school for nineteen years. Recently he had even sent his family away to the countryside and now spent all his time at the school doing the same things day in and day out. Perhaps this was the only kind of life that did go well with the grey school buildings and the grey sky. And the seven or eight teachers who lived in the school dormitory led the same sort of monotonous life. . . .

One Saturday evening, Mr Li simply could not stand the dreariness any longer. He appeared in the principal's room like a man walking in his sleep.

"Old Pan, there is a strange disease about this place already I've caught — it! Monotony or the grey disease, you could call it. . . . I am bored to death. . . . Let's go out and drink some wine!"

"All right," Old Pan nodded gently. "Only with my heart trouble I dare not drink. . . . Shall I ask somebody else to keep you company? How about asking Mr Chen along?"

"Does he drink?"

The principal shook his head with a forced smile and then said, rather apologetically:

"In our school . . . hm, there's perhaps only old Mr Zhang who can drink a few cups. . . ."

"Get him to come with us then, eh? Is he an interesting person?"

"Interesting?" Old Pan gave a laugh. "Eight words will describe him: His sayings are insipid; his appearance is repulsive."

Then Old Pan gave an appraisal of old Mr Zhang from a school principal's viewpoint. The old man might be quite a scholar. He wrote beautiful enough calligraphy. But he definitely was not a good teacher of Chinese. He strictly forbade the students to write in the modern vernacular. When once a student used the modern term "purpose" in an essay, Mr Zhang furiously struck out those two written characters.

Old Pan struck his knees with his palms.

"Just think! There's a teacher for you! And he has been teaching here for sixteen years now! But I can't cancel his contract . . . an influential member of the local gentry supports him. Such is our sacred educational field! Even so, to tell the truth, conditions here in this school are still considered better than elsewhere. What can one do? Unless you have no intention whatever of doing any work for the public, you have to compromise, bow your head and keep your temper! . . ."

The other yawned, lit a cigarette and cast a pitying glance at Old Pan.

"That old man is rotten all the way through, one

hundred per cent," Old Pan added. "When you talk to him about current events, about the war of resistance against the Japanese, he . . . the ideas he expresses are really those of a traitor!"

That evening, the two friends sat in a restaurant for over two hours. Mr Li consumed one catty of yellow rice wine by himself, sipping at his cup continually and refilling it from the pewter wine pot as soon as it was empty. His thin face turned more and more pale as he drank.

When Old Pan warned him that he might be drinking too much, he clutched at the wine pot and said:

"Old Pan, let me tell you a story. A hard drinker once said, 'Hot wine hurts my lungs. Cold wine hurts my liver. But not to drink would hurt my heart. I'd rather have my lungs and liver hurt than my heart.' That man really knew how to live. . . . I am sorry for you people who never drink."

He sipped some of the wine, smacking his lips loudly and leaning back in his chair with an air of great ease. He half-closed his eyes with an expression of bliss, but their bloodshot sockets made one suspect that he had wept not long ago.

"At first, I did not intend to drink the wine produced on this soil." He pointed to the ground. "I thought it would be bad. But, really, it's quite all right. . . . Old Pan, do have a drop! You must savour it. . . ."

Old Pan obligingly took a tiny sip. Then he said, ashamedly:

"I used to drink a little. But I could never tell whether a wine was good or bad."

"This wine certainly does not compare with that of my native place. I had nine jars of old Shaoxing wine at home, said to have aged sixty years. Perhaps its vintage was only thirty or forty years ago, but definitely not less than that. I often invited friends to stay for a few days in our little town. We would talk and drink. . . . I can't drink much, but I like the feeling one has when one is drinking. . . . Oh, you've been to Hangzhou, did you go to a wine shop there?"

"No."

"Oh, but you should have gone!" Mr Li raised his hand excitedly. "The people who go to drink there . . . that kind of . . . that kind of. . . . Oh, they really know how to drink. One dish of dried beancurd prepared in mushroom juice and two bowls of old wine can last for over two hours. . . . You should not have missed the chance to experience that pleasure!"

He closed his eyes and sighed wearily. He remembered the fine porcelain set of wine jug and cups he had at home. He also recalled the finely carved seals, books, the masterpieces of old calligraphy and paintings he owned. Then suddenly he thought how interesting the painters and engravers had been in his little town. Where were they now?

He sighed again. He felt the need to talk, so he told his friend of his family life and how his thirteen-year-old daughter had always stood by his table, bent over and taken a sip from his cup when he was drinking, while his wife would scold her smilingly, "Look at that imp!"

Old Pan listened to him patiently, like a diligent student attending lessons in the classroom. Mr Li realized that his remarks could not be of any interest to his friend, but he had to say these things. He felt there were a great many things pressing on his mind that he had to get rid of.

He was dizzy. He rested his elbows on the edge of the table, and cupped his head in his hands.

"Drunk?" his companion asked him. "Shall we go back to the school?"

He shook his head.

All the other customers had gone. The place had become very quiet, not like a restaurant at all. And there were not many people in the street either. Occasionally a swishing sound came from outside, difficult to tell whether it was the wind blowing or a car passing by.

Mr Li suddenly raised his head and asked:

"Eh, Old Pan, where is your wife staying now? Is she with her family or with yours?"

"With mine. Why?"

"That's good. That's good," he muttered. "The most unpleasant people in the world are one's in-laws. I have nothing against marriage, but parents-in-law. . . . I'm really afraid of them!" At this point, he opened his eyes quite wide and continued: "If our town had not fallen into the hands of the Japanese, I would not have sent my wife to her family, even if I'd had to beg for food! My wife's family, her family . . . from her father down to her little nephew . . . all of them are despicable, nasty, mean and selfish! And how vulgar they are! None of them are at all human! . . . And then she . . . she . . . in a letter . . . grumbles . . . complains. . . . She cannot get used to living with them again. . . . She wants to come here. . . . What am I to do! If my wife and daughter come, what will they live on? What work can they do? If they don't work, why should they come here? . . . If I hadn't thought I'd find some work, I would not have come here either. Let the devil come, instead! What . . . what a dead place this is! Absolutely without any life! And so grey! . . ."

The two of them got back to the school after nine o'clock in the evening. All the shops had closed their doors. The street lamps shed such a feeble, dim light that it made one feel gloomier than if there had been no light at all.

Mr Li thought of the house he was living in, and his heart sank.

The little house stood all alone. It seemed to Mr Li that, apart from himself, there were no other creatures in the world. The walls of the place were painted a lemon colour. They were clean but their cleanliness only increased the monotony of the room. There were no decorations of any kind, just a few simple pieces of furniture, the necessary utensils for writing and his two small suitcases. When the bright electric light was on, it made one feel only colder and more lonely.

And in such surroundings, he had to begin his "new life".

He suddenly felt sick at heart, all alone, without any relatives or friends. Nobody was concerned about him. Nobody looked after him. This was really the first time he was in such a strange situation. When he was small, there had been his mother and elder sister, and later, his wife, who had always known his wishes and desires simply by looking at him. And his friends had gathered around him, making him the centre of attention. But now. . . .

"Perhaps it's all just a dream. . . ." he muttered unhappily to himself.

He hoped he was only dreaming and would wake up to find himself still at home, lying on his own soft, warm bed; and on the table beside his bed, there would be a pot of strong black tea which his wife had prepared for him, a tin of the "Three Castles" cigarettes he liked and a volume of Wu Meicun, his favourite poet. His daughter would place a cigarette between his lips, light it for him and then say, with her childish smile:

"What a long time you've slept, daddy!"

Everything would be exactly the same as it used to be every morning. The curtain on the window would be half-drawn to let in the sunshine. The bamboo outside the window would be scattering a slanting pattern across the floor, giving the room a hint of fresh greenery. He would, as usual, remain in bed until he finished smoking, reading a few of Wu Meicun's poems. Then he would slowly get up.

The world, just like himself, would be peaceful and undisturbed.

"How unthinkable that war should break out in such a tranquil world!" he thought. "This is indeed a very long dream. . . . But then, Chunyu Fen in the story *Governor of the Southern Tributary State* . . . passed several scores of years in his dream . . . and yet it actually . . . actually . . . was only a short while. . . ."

He belched, drew a handkerchief from his sleeve and wiped his mouth. He was still sitting on the old sofa in the principal's room, for he had refused to go to his own. The school servants were all asleep. Old Pan had gone to the kitchen to boil some water for Mr Li to drink.

Mr Li tried desperately to steady his confused mind, to remember when this dream of his had started.

The Marco Polo Bridge Incident on July 7, 1937, that started the war with the Japanese, it must be a dream. . . . The Battle of Shanghai in the following month just couldn't have happened. . . .

What about the September 18th Incident of 1931 by which the Japanese had occupied China's northeast? He had to think that over carefully. And there was also the January 28th Incident in 1932 when the Japanese attacked Shanghai. . . . How could China lose four of her provinces without hitting back at the aggressor at all? At this point in his reflections, he stood up resolutely, wiped his lips hard with his handkerchief, and told himself firmly:

"No, no, impossible! The September 18th Incident never actually happened. Neither did the January 28th one. It must still be . . . still the time before September 1931 now!"

"Here's a potful of strong tea I've made for you, Yimo," Old Pan came in, looking at him cheerily. "Hadn't you better take a piece of *baguadan* for your headache first?"

Mr Li sighed, took a small piece of the medicine from Old Pan's hand, and put it into his mouth absent-mindedly. Then he sat down again and felt his right temple with his finger. It was throbbing. He said to his old friend, with some remorse:

"I really don't know what I have been thinking about just now. I am too sensitive, too full of fantasies. My nerves haven't been too good lately."

"Go to bed early. I think you're a bit tipsy."

"That's got nothing to do with it," he said rather

impatiently. "You don't understand me. . . . My. . . ."

Looking at the principal's face, he checked himself. They had become friends in Beijing at the time of the May 4th Movement in 1919. Since then, they had followed different courses in life and developed in different ways. Now, Mr Li thought that he could see through Old Pan at a glance, while Old Pan never understood him at all.

But in the whole school, in the whole town, there was only Old Pan who sometimes talked to him. When he wanted company, he had to put up with Old Pan's longish, honest face before his eyes and Old Pan's high-pitched voice in his ears. It was like having the same dish at every meal every day, with no variation allowed. He hoped some other colleague might join him. Little Mr Chen would be all right. Even old Mr Zhang would be welcome. Otherwise. . . .

"Otherwise my stomach will really be upset."

After that Mr Li drank wine every day. Sometimes he went to a restaurant; sometimes he asked the servant to go out and buy some for him, but still Old Pan remained his sole companion. One day he nearly lost his temper and asked Old Pan in a loud voice:

"Isn't there anyone else in this school besides that old Mr Zhang who can drink? Isn't there someone among the students, or even among the servants?"

Eventually he did get to know the short Mr Chen. But he was a thoroughly uninteresting fellow. All he cared about was keeping himself busy. All he talked to Mr Li about was how to improve that little weekly magazine, or to ask for more articles for it. And as soon as business was finished, he nodded respectfully and went away, as if he had been in mortal fear that

Mr Li might seize him and force him to drink wine!

"After all, this magazine also represents work," Mr Li told himself.

Though he was not entirely happy with this kind of work, he did once draw a cartoon after he had had his wine, showing a soldier walking hand in hand with a civilian. For a caption, he wrote: "The military forces and the people." But suddenly he felt rather ashamed of it. So, after some hesitation, he decided to give it to the periodical without signing his name.

"How rotten of them!" When he saw his cartoon in the periodical with his name printed under it, he felt as if someone had slapped his face. "They've dared to put my real name under it . . . those scoundrels! From now on, the name 'Yimo' will be a disgrace. How could Yimo draw such a picture! . . . Oh, what scoundrels! . . . Scoundrels! . . ."

He suspected that Mr Chen and some others were maliciously trying to undermine his reputation. The student with closely cropped hair was certainly one of the gang, for last Wednesday afternoon he had dared to ask Mr Li in class for more pictures for the periodical.

"No!" Mr Li had answered coldly. "I am in a bad mood and I can't produce anything!"

As soon as the class was over, he returned to his quarters, greatly annoyed by the injustice done him. He took out a less expensive "Golden Dragon" cigarette from the tin that had once contained the fancier "Three Castles" brand and lit it. He lay down on the bed. A copy of the day's newspaper fell to the ground. He did not pick it up. This was the paper he subscribed to with money out of his own pocket. The school took in seven or eight newspapers, but they were all put in the reading-room and there were always groups of people around them. He simply could not get accustomed to reading newspapers in a crowd.

None of the ways in which things were done in the school suited him, as if they were trying on purpose to outrage him. The cooks should have been sentenced to several years' imprisonment for always preparing the same, tasteless food. Mr Li disliked eating in the dining hall with so many people around, so he had his meals brought to his own room. And because of that, they played more tricks on him so that he would become angry as soon as he saw the food sent. Every morning, when he wanted his tea, he had great trouble getting the servant to brew it! The tea leaves which he had brought himself tasted bitter and had not the slightest fragrance although they were supposed to be the best, from Qimen in Anhui Province.

"How very strange!" He threw away his cigarette. "How can these people be so happy here, so energetic!"

He stretched himself, got up and sipped some of the cold tea. Then he set the cup down on the table with an angry knock. Better to go and have a few cups of wine. He locked his door and went out.

Who could he get to go with him? Old Pan again? Mr Li hesitated. As soon as he thought of the principal, he had a queer, sickly feeling in his throat right down to his stomach, the kind of feeling one has after eating something too sweet.

He slowed down his steps, pretending that he was just taking a walk and had happened to drop in on the principal quite accidentally.

The row of willow trees in the school garden had

put forth buds and, under the dark-red clouds in the sky, they looked like strips of soiled green cloth. The grey school buildings seemed to have been washed with purple water, looking a most incongruous colour.

Happy shouts came from the basketball field. Some students were singing a marching song with great zest. Laughter was also heard from the teachers' quarters. Then he heard someone say: "How can the general public understand these abstract theories you expound? . . ." Probably that little Mr Chen again! Talking over some more business!

Mr Li walked on purpose by the window from which the noise came and looked in. He hoped Mr Chen might see him and ask him in. He walked even more slowly than before, fixing his eyes on the ground as if he were measuring the path. For a moment, he almost wanted to overcome his habitual reserve and walk into Mr Chen's room without being invited.

But he did not stop after all.

"Why can't they come to me? Why must I go to them?"

And so that evening when he was drinking wine, he had nobody but Old Pan for company — the same dish all over again!

"I really can't get used to living here. It's too boring!" He cast a complaining and almost censorious glance at Old Pan, as if the latter were responsible for his misfortunes. "I want to go away. . . . But where can I go? . . . I have no friends elsewhere and it is difficult to make a living. . . . I am tied to this place! . . ."

He neither wrote nor painted anything. He was not in the proper mood for these things. When he finally got acquainted with old Mr Zhang, he borrowed from him a lithographic copy of rubbings of ancient stone inscriptions and, using its ideographs as models, practised his calligraphy every day.

Mr Zhang was an old man with a ruddy complexion, slightly lame and hunchbacked. To Mr Li, this teacher of Chinese did not appear so repulsive as Old Pan had described him to be. He and Mr Li even had some interests in common. Mr Zhang also liked to buy stone-rubbings and collect seals. When they discovered by chance that they both were enthusiastic about the rubbings from the stone engravings of the Buddhist Diamond Sutra on sacred Mt Taishan in Shandong Province, they became quite drawn to each other.

"I'd collected rubbings of one thousand and five ideographs of this sutra. Even museum director Yi Peiji had fewer than mine in his collection. But now. . . ." Mr Li sighed deeply. "Now my collection may have been burnt or stolen by the Japanese."

"That's why," old Mr Zhang responded quickly, narrowing his eyes in disgust, "I am discouraged. I haven't been looking for such things recently. What can one do about it in such chaotic times? This is really a predestined calamity! Some people simply can't stand peace in the world, so they must stir up war. *Ai*!"

Mr Li, smiling politely, ventured to refute him:

"But when others invade our country, if we don't offer any resistance. . . ."

"Hm, resistance!" The corners of old Mr Zhang's mouth were drooping. "Can we resist and win? Or are we just inviting trouble and suffering?"

"Then should we just let them come and occupy China?"

"This is not a question of our 'letting' them or not. . . . In a word . . . in a word . . . well, if you can't win by fighting, why fight and get into trouble? You're bound to suffer more when you fight. . . ."

"No wonder Old Pan says he thinks like a traitor!" thought Mr Li.

Foam appeared at one corner of the old man's mouth. He wiped it off with the scholar's long nail on his little finger and went on indignantly:

"For instance, when the Japanese first came to a place, they didn't really harm the inhabitants. But later guerrillas and anti-Japanese elements showed up, so the Japanese of course had to make searches and arrests. Some people even got killed and the inhabitants could no longer go about their business in peace. . . . What's the use of guerrillas? They can't possibly defeat the Japanese, but they just rush around and make attacks here and there. When the Japanese come in bigger numbers, they always run away. It's only innocent people who get sacrificed when the Japanese search for guerrillas. . . ."

"But there's news from many sources that the people do welcome the guerrillas," said Mr Li, still smiling. He thought this argument very ludicrous and a waste of breath as far as he was concerned. Still he could not help saying something. "In many places, the guerrillas really are self-defence units organized by the people themselves. Naturally they are not willing to stand by and have their own places ravaged in front of their eyes."

"Hm, self-defence! Hm! Do they have big guns? Are they as well armed as the Japanese troops? . . . Self-defence! Self-defence indeed! All they actually do is to create disturbances wherever they are!"

"So your idea is that our people should become obedient slaves of the Japanese and traitors to China!" thought Mr Li, but he did not say these words to old Mr Zhang. He suddenly remembered an article "On a Certain Kind of Traitor" he had seen in that little periodical. Whoever wrote that must have had this old man in mind. Now that Mr Li himself had heard the old man's arguments, he thought that article very powerful and pertinent.

Impatiently Mr Li lit a cigarette. Impatiently he sat down on a chair. His fingers trembled with indignation and his cheeks burned. He considered it his duty to refute this man Zhang from a human standpoint at least. He wanted to teach this man some common sense, tell him the facts, explain to him what blows our guerrillas had dealt the enemy, how they had turned his rear into another frontline, and how useless it was for the Japanese to occupy a few big cities. He felt it didn't matter even if he used harsh words. Perhaps he should lecture this old fool severely with words like: You should know this is a difficult period, and everyone, as long as he is Chinese, as long as he wants to be called a human being and not a beast, should struggle with clenched teeth. . . .

But he did not open his mouth. He was not used to quarrelling with others on such topics. And besides, these were not words he had thought up himself. People might sneer when they heard him and say: "Ha, Mr Li is only parroting others!"

He also remembered Voltaire had said that the first person who compared a woman to a flower was a genius and that the second person who did the same thing was an idiot. The ideas he wanted to express were contained in that article, very lucidly and very adequately.

"That weekly magazine . . . Mr Zhang, do you ever read it?"

"I don't understand things written in the modern vernacular!"

After that retort, both of them fell silent. Mr Li wanted to leave, but he felt it was not quite the polite thing to do. So he kept looking at the door now and then, hoping that someone would come in to end the embarrassing situation. Suddenly he noticed Mr Zhang was staring at the cigarette in his hand. He got the hint, took out his case and offered the other one.

The old man lit it and took one puff. Then, holding it at a distance, he squinted to read the name of the brand. His tense, ruddy face gradually relaxed. But he held on to the cigarette firmly with his stained fingers, as if he were afraid that it would run away unless he retained it by force. With each puff he took, he made a loud noise.

Thinking, perhaps, that he had to make some polite remark to the man who had offered him the thing he was enjoying, old Mr Zhang asked how many cigarettes Mr Li smoked per day. Then he mentioned wine.

"I heard you like to drink a few cups too. . . ."

"Yes," Mr Li hastened to answer. "Only I can't find a drinking companion." He looked at the other with an expectant expression.

"I'll invite you to my house one day for a drink."

Mr Li suggested that they go to a restaurant that evening. Old Mr Zhang said in a frank tone:

"Unfortunately, I haven't any money on me

today. . . . I'd like to invite you to my place, but my family hasn't been told to prepare anything. . . ."

So they went to a Tianjin restaurant and Mr Li paid for the wine and food. Friends who drink wine together do not have to stand on ceremony.

Thus they became bosom friends and thereafter frequented small restaurants together. Old Mr Zhang always happened to have no money on him, and never invited Mr Li to his house for a drink. The first time Mr Li went there was to return the stone-rubbings. They talked from five o'clock in the afternoon until seven-thirty. The women in Mr Zhang's family were whispering uneasily in the next room, sometimes peeping in through the door and window. In the end, the visitor asked the host to go out with him. When they arrived at the restaurant, old Mr Zhang pretended he had to go back because he had forgotten to bring his wallet. "Oh, how stupid of me!" The old man reproached himself as he limped into the restaurant. "I really should be the host this time!"

But his drinking capacity was not impaired. He gulped down one cup after another without batting an eyelid. And all the time he smoked the cigarettes from Mr Li's case on the table. When the case was empty, it was old Mr Zhang who ordered the waiter to go out and buy some more. His words were still coherent and clear, and the more he drank, the more slowly he spoke. Only his nose turned purple.

And with such a man Mr Li had become friends! Old Pan was really surprised.

"How did this happen? Do you find old Mr Zhang congenial to talk to?"

"Just so so," said Mr Li, looking at his friend's

longish face with some annoyance because he thought Old Pan was using his authority as school principal to interfere in other people's private affairs.

Mr Li therefore explained his attitude with great self-confidence: "It doesn't matter if friends have different views. Life is richer when people are unlike one another. If you had many, many friends and they all looked at things in more or less the same way, wouldn't your life be very monotonous? Tell me now, wouldn't it? . . . Besides current events there are a lot of things I can talk about with old Mr Zhang — poetry, seal carving, calligraphy and painting. . . ."

But in the last few days Mr Li had been able to see for himself that there wasn't much left to talk about with his drinking companion. Old Mr Zhang kept boasting about his private collection. He had a seal carved and given him by Wu Changshuo, well-known as a painter and seal-carver. He also had a landscape by Ni Yunlin of the Yuan Dynasty that had calligraphy by Chang Tingji of the Qing Dynasty on it. He always made this sort of remark.

"He is only bragging," thought Mr Li. "I've been to his house several times. Why didn't he show these things to me then?"

Mr Li made no reply. Lowering his head, he sipped some wine. This suddenly reminded him of his young daughter and he heaved a deep sigh.

Old Mr Zhang obviously felt he had to say something to cheer his companion up. Perhaps he wanted to compensate Mr Li for the many entertainments he had had at the other's expense, and at the same time fulfil his duty as a drinking companion. So he began to talk about the school and to impart its secrets with the most confidential air.

The people in the accounting office were experts in making money on the side. They always deducted the income tax from the salary and gave stamps instead of cash for the small change. In this way, they were lining their own pockets.

"Let me tell you, Mr Li." He moved so close that his bad breath nearly suffocated Mr Li. "Next time you go to get your salary, have the amount for income tax ready and give it to them. Then you will get a round sum. That's what I always do. I don't want their stamps."

He paused and thought for a while. Then he drew even closer. Mr Li had to lean back just to be a little farther away from the old man's face.

"Principal Pan used to have great confidence in me. But recently he has surrounded himself with a group of scoundrels. Mr Chen is one of them. Do you know him? Mr Li, let me warn you. You must be careful. He is a reactionary, that Mr Chen."

He closed his mouth tightly and nodded significantly, repeating:

"Re-ac-tion-a-ry."

Mr Li considered all these so-called secrets as other people's personal affairs and never mentioned them to anyone else.

"Oh, how monotonous it all is!" he complained. Why did he have so few friends? Why must he seek this old man's company as he had sought Old Pan's before? Why always the same dish?

His drinking with old Mr Zhang as a companion

grew into an unavoidable obligation which he had to fulfil.

And this obligation added to his financial burden. He was the host every time he went out with Mr Zhang. He had come to the school with some four hundred dollars in his pocket. Now over a hundred were gone. If he went out with Old Pan he could save some money, for Old Pan insisted on paying for both of them.

"Let me pay," Old Pan always said. "You are more hard up than I am."

This Saturday evening, asking nobody to go with him, Mr Li had a catty and a half of wine in a small restaurant all by himself. When he returned to the school, he went straight to his own room and bolted the door.

The light shed by the blue bulb mixed with the lemon colour of the walls to give the room a tint of pale green. Somewhere in the distance a night-watchman was beating his bamboo. Every stroke seemed to fall on Mr Li's heart. He fancied he could hear the watchman's steps echoing from the long, dark lane.

As usual, Mr Li lay down and smoked. Recently a few cups of wine had been making him sensitive and irritable. He no longer reached that stage of elation he used to at home after drinking. Something was now gently irritating him all the way from his heart to his nose. He longed to roll on the ground, clutch something in his arms and cry until he felt better.

Formerly he had made friends with only a few people who shared his interests. He had never helped anybody, and there had never been an occasion that required him to ask others to help him. Loneliness, something that used to be unimaginable, now stabbed at him with excruciating pain.

"Except for Old Pan who is a warm-hearted person and willing to lend a hand, I have no friends at all," he muttered sadly. "I don't get along well with other people."

He became rather remorseful when he remembered how aloof and haughty his own attitude had been when he played the part of a "pure artist". But . . . oh, how could he foresee then that this war would break out? Now, he and his family did not get along well even with their nearest relatives, his in-laws.

He got up, unlocked his small leather suitcase and took out the express letter he had received from his wife that day. Always the same remarks, the same complaints! She even warned him that she might get seriously ill if she had to stay with her family any longer.

Mr Li bit his lower lip. His bloodshot eyes fixed on the window for a while. Then he crumpled the letter into a ball and forcefully threw it on the floor.

"Why complain to me like this? As though I were to blame for all her troubles!"

The cigarette in his hand dropped to the floor. When he bent down to pick it up, he picked up the paper ball at the same time. He had concluded that their not getting along well with relatives and friends was chiefly due to his wife's stinginess. He remembered how severely she had treated the tenants on his land every year when she collected the rent. He also remembered how one of his old classmates had asked him for the loan of ten dollars and how his wife would not allow it. At that time, the reasons she gave him had seemed adequate, though.

"To help friends is the proper thing to do," she said. "But your help often becomes an obligation instead of a favour if you extend it many times. And if once, for some reason, you can't do as the friends ask you to, they will bear you a grudge; therefore it is much better for friends not to lend money to each other. Anyway, we have enough to live on. So it is unlikely we shall ever have to borrow from anybody."

Formerly Mr Li had been very grateful to his wife for being so shrewd. Sometimes he had even helped her in her calculations and offered suggestions. But now he considered his wife alone was to blame for the difficult position in which he found himself.

He sat down and began a reply to her. With the brush Old Pan had given him as a present, he wrote very slowly in the manner of the calligrapher Li Beihai, choosing his words as carefully as when he wrote essays, smoking one cigarette after another meanwhile. He told his wife that he himself was leading a very hard life, but that everyone should be patient at this time when the war of resistance was being fought.

"I have repeatedly asked you to be patient. I'm asking you again to be patient."

He sighed and took another puff. The smoke from the cigarette in his hand made him knit his eyebrows slightly while he continued to write. He said that all the members of his wife's family were vulgar and grasping, and had nothing but their own interests at heart. Since he was afraid that one of his in-laws might open the letter, he wrote on the envelope, "Anyone who opens this letter without permission is a scoundrel" and put an exclamation mark at the end of the sentence. But after a while he thought the mark too evident a sign of bad temper and blotted it out again.

That night he slept worse than usual. Again and again the two questions nagged at him:

"When will this war come to an end? How can victory be brought about more quickly?"

He tossed and turned. The old mattress on his bed was very hard and made him uncomfortable. He turned again. He found it too hot to keep his arms under the cotton quilt, but too cold to put them outside. His head was burning. He felt dizzy. He had thought he could find the correct answers by following a straight line of reasoning, but now this line seemed to be thrown askew by too many chaotic events.

Suddenly he remembered Washington Irving's story about Rip Van Winkle. Oh, if only he, Mr Li, could fall into such a sleep . . . for just a few minutes . . . and then walk out of the cave when he woke up to find a happy China, a China with the hard struggles of fifty years behind her. . . .

Then he reproached himself: "This is too negative a way of thinking!"

Yes, he, too, ought to contribute some of his own strength. He ought to take part in this hard struggle, so that China could be liberated more quickly. Then he thought of Aladdin's lamp. If he had that, all he would have to do was to rub the lamp and an omnipotent genie would be at his disposal. . . . After a while, other beautiful fairy tales came to his mind. An angel might grant him three wishes. He tried to put his confused thoughts in order, to decide what these three wishes should be, wishes for positive things. . . .

It was already ten o'clock in the morning when he woke up. There was a bitter taste in his mouth. He remembered the wild fantasies he had had the previous night and how they had kept him awake for a long time. He was bored by these reflections. He stretched, walked over to the calendar and tore off a sheet.

"Sunday again, alas!"

Little Mr Chen had gone out early that morning, leaving a note asking Mr Li to come to a meeting at one o'clock that afternoon to discuss something about the weekly magazine. A school servant handed the note to Mr Li.

"Hm," he threw the slip of paper on his desk. "Business again, always business!"

Sunshine came through the window on the southern side, and shadows danced in his room. In the school garden, the twittering of the sparrows blended with the students' singing and shouting. How could they be so cheerful!

Mr Li stayed in his room all alone, reading the newspaper and sipping his flavourless tea. He seemed to be angry with someone for something and unwilling to see anybody.

"The people in the occupied areas. . . . How do they live?" he asked himself.

Perhaps some were carrying on their business as usual, while others were cultivating their land as before. And if he had not left his native place, perhaps he could have collected the rent from his tenants as usual, could have painted pictures and carved seals as before. All these things had nothing to do with military actions and politics. So long as he expressed no anti-

Japanese sentiments in his essays, he might not have been molested.

But then he sighed in despair, for he remembered the atrocities committed by the Japanese.

Only Beiping, he thought, seemed to have escaped this kind of fate. Beiping and Tianjin fell into the hands of the Japanese without a battle, and so people could continue to live there peacefully. Some scholars who could not get used to life in the interior had gone back to Beiping.

Mr Li sipped some more tea, frowned and read through the letter he had written the evening before. He decided not to post it, after all, and locked it in his suitcase.

"Why reproach her? She is miserable enough as it is!"

Sitting on the hard chair hurt him. He lay down again on the bed. The ticking of the watch by his pillow seemed to beat against his brain so that he almost suspected the noise came from the throbbing of his own temples. Often he had tried to think of his wife's good points when he was away from her, and now he did the same thing. He recollected how capable she was and how attentive to his comforts. If she could have seen the hard life he was leading. . . . *Aiya*!

"Perhaps so-called enemy atrocities are not committed everywhere," he said to himself.

But then he paused, bewildered. What did he mean by these words? If his wife and daughter had remained in his native place. . . . He shivered.

He was hoping that the reports about enemy atrocities in occupied areas were exaggerated; yet he immediately corrected such a thought. If the enemy troops had behaved in a well-disciplined manner, perhaps the Chinese people would not have risen so resolutely to defend themselves.

"The guerrillas are very active in my native place." He had often said that to Old Pan.

He lit another cigarette and asked the servant to make him another potful of tea. Then he tried to compose his thoughts so they would not run wild. An idea flashed strangely through his mind:

"Perhaps I'd better go home and see? . . ."

It had been said the occupied areas remained peaceful and quiet at first. Atrocities were committed only later when guerrillas had appeared and the Japanese were searching for them. . . . All this seemed to be true, but who set this kind of talk in motion?

When he remembered that old Mr Zhang had spoken of these things, he felt as if someone had suddenly hollowed out his whole inside. He was seized by a sudden emptiness and despair. He felt furious for no apparent reason. Like someone who had been fooled, he lost his temper, and at the same time wanted to explain it away.

"Traitor! Traitor!" He tried very hard to bend the fingers which held the cigarette, as if he wanted to clench them into a fist but could not. "These kinds of ideas must be rooted out! I shall certainly report what he said at the meeting this afternoon and ask everybody to write articles against him! . . ."

He put out his cigarette carefully. Then he folded Mr Chen's note twice over into a tiny square and stroked it with his finger.

White clouds were sailing across the sky. The sunlight now vanished from the room, now reappeared, and Mr Li's face darkened and brightened at intervals too.

He rubbed his hands. He intended to write a short article and deal old Mr Zhang's ideas a telling blow; yet he did not take up his brush, and did not even begin to think out what he wanted to say because he suddenly felt that it was somehow not quite the thing for him to do. Perhaps he felt this way because he had not written anything for a long time and might not put his thoughts as well as he should. Or perhaps it was just because he was in such a bad mood? No, probably it was because he feared people might discover from his article that the ideas he attacked were exactly those he had unconsciously adopted himself.

He took his handkerchief from his sleeve, wiped his lips and sighed gloomily.

"Really, he who has too cool a head and too analytical a mind is often unhappy."

Yes, he had gone too far in analysing himself. He was not writing this article, he tried to convince himself, simply because of the black mood he was in.

"Oh, what a rotten mood I'm in!" he repeated, firmly. "Unless I join the guerrillas, there is no point in my going back to my native place. But I can't join the guerrillas. Artists are useless. I can't help it."

He sighed in relief. And since he could not find a way out of this dilemma, he decided to take a stroll to the principal's office. He had to amuse himself somehow in order to while away the time. He could not stay in this foul mood all day long.

But Old Pan was talking to a visitor, obviously a stranger, for the two of them faced each other very solemnly. Business again! Evidently they were discussing problems of wartime education.

When Mr Li sauntered in, the formality in the air disconcerted him. He felt his whole body stiffen, and he was in despair.

"What am I here for?" And then he scolded himself. "They are discussing important matters. Did you have to break in like this? Do you mean to ask Old Pan again to go to have a drink with you?"

He made a meaningless gesture to Old Pan, turned around and went out. He walked very fast but he didn't know where he was going. His quick steps echoed on the pebbly lane. His shadow quivered and jerked on the ground as if it had great difficulty in catching up with him.

It was no fun, really, to continue with Old Pan as a bosom companion. He did not take a single drop and worried all the time that Mr Li was drinking too much, probably because he was unwilling to spend that much money!

Mr Li walked out of the school gate. He remembered his drinking alone the evening before and drew a deep breath, allowing his feet to move towards the house of his other drinking companion.

Some students walked towards him, in groups of threes and fives. They were probably coming back for lunch. Mr Li lowered his head, pretending that he did not see them. Somehow he felt rather awkward. Something seemed to have a hold on him. What was it? Ah, yes! There was a meeting he should attend that afternoon.

He heard someone whispering and then a loud laugh.

Startled, he turned back and looked. Two students had just entered the school gate.

"Hm, am I not allowed any freedom even on Sundays?" he thought, indignantly. "I just won't go to the meeting! Why should I take orders from that fellow Chen? . . . Let them say whatever they like about me. I am not afraid. Quite frankly, I am not the man for trivial business. Every person has his own way of living. I have mine! After all, is it a crime to go and ask old Mr Zhang to drink a few cups of wine with me? Bah!"

And he quickened his steps.

1938

Translated by Zuo Cheng

A Summer Night's Dream

EVERYWHERE the ground gave off a stifling hot steam that seemed to rise lazily to the stars, enveloping them and making them blink fretfully.

To the east, a meteor streaked across the heavens and dropped, apparently, into the next-door courtyard. A snowy-white arc was sketched upon the dark blue sky, then instantly vanished.

"A star has fallen," Xiao Yunfang said to herself. She sighed.

The two guests still hadn't left. They were all sitting out in the courtyard. Young Master Shi, seated quietly smoking on the bamboo reclining chair, kept staring at her. He seemed to be waiting for something. From time to time with his left hand he smoothed his glossily oiled hair.

Young Master Shi is also a star, thought Yunfang. A college graduate, and his family has money. Why in the world doesn't he find something to do?

He could be found in the teahouse — the Blue Cloud Pavilion — nearly every night, and always in the company of the son of the proprietor of the Lushan Photography Studio. Without fail, when the show was over, they came and sat here in the rear courtyard for an hour or so, talking of all manner of things. Yunfang couldn't understand very much, but she liked to listen.

The lower lip of the proprietor's son stuck out in a very unattractive way, indicating his contempt for anything and everything in heaven or on earth. He tried very hard to speak Beijing dialect, wrenching his words out through tight lips.

"Yunfang," he said, "have you seen yesterday's *Song Lovers' Tabloid*? It had a picture of your older sister, 'Xiao Yunyan'! Ah, beautiful! Yunfang, we'll take an art photo of you and put it in the picture magazine too, what do you say? Your photo . . . much more sensational. Why not, eh?"

"You mean that magazine that has so many pictures of girl students?" She gazed abstracted at the stars, then added softly: "They're all lucky."

Her teacher sat on a low stool, tapping his legs lightly with a plantain fan. Whenever there were guests present, he talked of the past. His back was more and more bent, as if the breath were completely gone from his lungs, but he still struggled to say a few words.

"In the old days, ha, such excitement. All my friends flattered me. I paid for everything — food, drinks, entertainment. I learned opera, sang a few amateur roles. I didn't bother a bit about what was going on in the shop. Later on, when it failed, I didn't even know."

"What kind of shop did your family have?"

"We sold furs. Our family ran that shop for three generations. Everybody knew us." The teacher, his head down, seemed to be talking to himself. "I played it away."

He paused. Everyone quietly listened to the drone of the mosquitoes. He sighed silently and without breath.

"An amateur should never turn professional. They all flatter you when you're an amateur. As soon as you become a pro, you're finished. Those friends of mine — not one of them was dependable. When you're poor and have to sing for a living nobody wants to have anything to do with you."

There was no resentment in his tone. But when, with an effort, he raised his thin face, lamplight shining through the window revealed that his eyes were filled with tears, glittering like crystals.

From childhood, Yunfang had always called him "Elder". She didn't remember whether he liked that name, or whether Mama had instructed her to address him that way. Yunfang sighed and said:

"Don't talk about those things, Elder."

Although his past had nothing to do with her, somehow when she heard him telling about it, she always wanted to cry.

The old man again went into a discourse on the unfairness of her "Sister" Yunyan's fate. Sister's father had been a general under the last emperor before the republic was formed, and had been awarded a high decoration, but now his daughter was singing in a teahouse.

Mosquitoes droned listlessly. Far off, a girl was singing a weepy ballad, going on and on. Yunfang couldn't distinguish which one of the sisters she was. The sound seemed to be squeezed out, then muffled again. It was suffocating to hear it.

Gazing up at the sky, Yunfang let her imagination soar. The Milky Way was being melted by the rising steam. It had faded into a vapid white blur.

"Where are the Cowherd and the Weaving Maid?"* she asked in all earnestness. "Why did they have to be separated?"

"Don't chatter!" Elder quickly interrupted. "That child! . . . *Ai*, your mama still isn't back yet."

He listened to that muffled voice, shook his head, then again lowered it. "None of those girls take care of their throats. She's already going hoarse, and still she sings."

Young Master Shi tossed away his cigarette butt. "What was your name originally?" he suddenly asked Yunfang.

"I don't know. I only remember my father. . . ."

But her recollection was vague. She herself wasn't sure whether it was only a dream or whether she truly had such a father. His hair had been combed back, but the front section, at the hair-line, had been shaved off, like a black-faced general in the opera. She had been sold to a woman. Yunfang could still remember that the woman had a mouth full of blackened teeth. Then she had been turned over to her present Mama. She was only six at the time.

What business was her father in, she wondered. Maybe he was still in this city. Maybe he would come to the Blue Cloud Pavilion to drink tea.

When Elder left for a few minutes, Young Master Shi again asked her his favourite question. "Really,

---

* Two constellations on different sides of the Milky Way. Legend has it that Cowherd was a mortal who married the heavenly Weaving Maid. But their happiness aroused the jealousy of the Queen of Heaven who separated the lovers by cleaving the sky with her hairpin to make a celestial river now called the Milky Way.

Yunfang, don't you want to go to school and study?"

Patting his hair, he turned to the proprietor's son and remarked thoughtfully: "Yunfang is an intelligent child. It's a pity she doesn't study. Sixteen isn't too late to start school. I won't say anything about anything else, but at least on this thing I certainly can do my best to help her along."

"This thing" sounded possible to Yunfang, yet it also seemed very remote, very hazy. Timidly, she asked: "But — Mama?"

Laughter and noisy voices rose in the front courtyard. A man began singing in a high falsetto. They knew at once that it was Big Turnip. Still singing, he entered the rear courtyard followed by the girl performer Liu Xiaokui.

"Hey, Big Turnip, don't sing," called the proprietor's son. "Bring me two bottles of soda water, will you?"

He was on excellent terms with Big Turnip and his cronies. Because of this he could go into the theatre any time he pleased without buying a ticket; the manager of the teahouse feared and respected him.

"Don't look down on them because they're plainclothesmen," the proprietor's son often said. "They're very useful friends."

Xiaokui's arrival livened things up. A noisy merry girl, she loved to talk about other people's affairs. She told the gathering: Yang Meiqin has been entertaining men in her flat again. If not for Big Turnip, the police would have nabbed her long ago. Nü Jiaotian, the moment her "Mama" left for Shanghai, ruined her throat.

"Her mama said: 'I'll be back in three days. You

behave yourself. If you spoil your voice, you'll have to account to me!' Now she's worried stiff."

"How did she do it?" Yunfang asked, very concerned.

Xiaokui whispered in her ear and Yunfang's face reddened.

"*Pei*! You're making it up!"

After the two guests had gone, Elder lit a cigarette butt. Coughing, he said:

"People like Young Master Shi —" He shook his head. "You're young now, so they flatter you. Later on, when you really sing well, they won't have anything to do with you. They're all that way."

Yunfang listened to something a while. "He said he'd send me to school. . . ." she offered furtively.

"You'd better not say that before your mama! It will only mean another beating!"

He brought a torn sleeping mat under his arm into the anteroom and spread it on the earthen floor.

"That fine Mr Ma of yours — doesn't come around any more, does he? You see, they're all the same."

Mr Ma was an officer in some magistrate's yamen. His face was long and so were his teeth. Always frowning as if in pain, he often said incomprehensible things. One minute his voice might suddenly become shrill with anger, the next minute all would be calm and serene.

"I'm just the same as you singers, just the same. I may even suffer more, in fact. I'd really like to go away with you, get away from this place. . . . Tell me, Yunfang, would you be able to stand hardship?"

She had thought his words very strange. But they had rested on her heart like a warm soothing hand. For no reason at all, her tears had begun to fall.

Would he really go away? She wondered.

Sister was already home. Her frequent caller Councillor Wang and his friends were in her room, and Mama was there too, helping Sister look after them. The men talked in boisterous shouts, arguing which of them had drunk the most. Then the conversation turned to a popular opera actor. A phlegmy voice strained to inform everyone that he had seen him perform one role thirty times.

Hearing them wrangle, you got the impression that they had bought the world. Whatever they wanted, they could have. From time to time they would suddenly think of Yunfang, and one of them would ask:

"Where's Yunfang?"

To them Yunfang was just a child. Old Master Xiao patted her on the head when she came in. Stroking his goatee, he asked:

"Can you guess how old I am?"

Everyone laughed. Before Yunfang could answer, he turned and talked to her sister about something else. He was the girls' godfather, but Yunfang could never figure out what sort of person he was. She heard that he wasn't an official; he just wrote poetry. But he had only to show his calling card and a man could be carried off to the magistrate. What was it all about?

The old clock on the table struck two deep chimes. Somewhere, a fiddle was playing, its voice sobbing and trembling.

The objects in the room wavered as if in a dream. Yunfang's eyes ached; they kept wanting to close. Although she only sat by without saying a word and seemed to have no part in this world, if she had tried to leave, everyone would have been displeased. They would have discovered that something was missing. Old Master Xiao's hand would have paused in mid-air as he raised it to stroke his beard, and he would have demanded:

"Didn't we have another one here?"

She wished no guests would ever come again, yet she liked having them. When there were many people around, something seemed to be added to her life.

All the hooks on Sister's high-necked collar had been unfastened. She looked very sleepy. But a cigarette dangled from her blood-red lips, and she talked and laughed with the same vigour she displayed when quarrelling with Mama. It was as if she had a bellyful of repressed resentment and was using this laughing manner to get rid of it.

Councillor Wang kept singing a line from a Beijing opera tune over and over in his thick rough accent.

Yunfang stealthily heaved a sigh. Something seemed to be pressing on her heart. The wrangling of the guests gradually grew muted, as if cut off by several walls. But she could still hear the mosquitoes humming in the corner. The sound turned to fine silk slivers — one after another they stabbed into her heart.

How lucky they are, she said to herself dizzily, meaning the guests. They can be wild when they want to and go home when they want to. After they've slept enough, they can get up and go visiting friends again.

Suddenly, she remembered the stories Elder had told her. When he reached the middle, she was always able to guess the ending. But whether this was because she had heard them before or because these stories had some special connection with her fate, she didn't know.

She thought about them even as she got into bed. She lightly waved a fan to cool her face.

"If only a person is good, she's bound to be reunited with her loved ones." That was often the moral of the old man's stories.

She concentrated on trying to recall what her father looked like. Her impression was that he was big and tall and kindly. Who knows, maybe he's become rich and is searching everywhere for his daughter. Maybe the gods will help him and send a scarlet ray that will lead him to the Blue Cloud Pavilion to drink tea and listen to the singers, and then he'll follow me here to this rear courtyard.

For some reason she imagined him with a ruddy complexion, and dressed in a voluminous black satin gown. He would stroke her face and she would fall on her knees and fling herself upon him, crying:

"Papa! . . ."

Tears ran from the corners of her eyes and rolled down her temples to the mat covering her pillow. They brought a momentary warmth in their wake which quickly cooled.

Hastily, she wiped her eyes and turned her face to the wall so that Mama wouldn't notice.

Mama was clad only in tight fitting vest and panties. Her fat body was as bloated as a fish bladder, and the creases of her several chins had been reddened with briny sweat. Looking in a mirror, she opened the folds carefully and dusted them with talcum powder.

Next door, Elder was talking in his sleep:

"Strange times. . . . Anyone who likes can insult me. . . ."

"Just listen to him," Mama grumbled. "He always says other people are insulting him. And he's always coming to me for money. No wife, no children — what does he need so much money for? If it weren't for me he'd starve to death, or pretty near it!"

Gradually, the night grew quiet. It was as if the city no longer had the strength to struggle, and could only lie there gasping soundlessly.

Yunfang closed her eyes. She seemed to feel the earth breathing, slowly, deeply. She concentrated hard on an imagined meeting with her father, knowing that if she thought only of this, she might dream about it.

Wouldn't it be wonderful if I could just keep having such dreams and never awake?

But her dream that night was annoying and exhausting. She was standing on the small stage of the teahouse. Above hung a large red sign with her name in white letters. Her back against the edge of a table, she faced the backdrop, which was decorated with many pavilions, and prepared to sing. The fiddle emitted high-pitched squeals, as if in pain. But no matter how she tried, she couldn't utter a sound.

The teahouse customers at their tables below laughed and hooted and stamped their feet.

Elder gazed at her tearfully. Mama seized her by the ear and mercilessly rapped her head with those gold-ringed fingers.

"Take that! And that!"

Yunfang awakened, drenched in perspiration.

Mama was snoring loudly. The room was frighteningly dark. Only at the window was there a thread of light. You couldn't exactly see it, but you could feel it was there.

After nine the next morning, Mama pinched her into wakefulness.

"Lazy wench, so young and not a bit of life in you! All you do is sleep!"

Elder was seated on a bench, his back terribly bent, as if shrinking from something fearful. Listlessly, he tuned the fiddle. It was such an effort for him to move the bow, you got the impression that it weighed several catties. When the fiddle was in tune, Elder paused as usual and muttered:

"Of the old actors, only Big Head Wang came to a good end. He became a Taoist priest and retired to a monastery. None of the others ended up nearly so well. Of course to become a Taoist priest you need money. The monastery won't take you otherwise."

Glaring sunlight baked half the courtyard. A steamy stench rose from the ditch. Buzzing flies settled on the electric light cord, forming a darkly coloured band. Things seemed to keep dropping from the ceiling, hot burning objects. When they struck against moist sweaty skin, they adhered to it.

Yunfang shoved her bare feet into embroidered slippers. Green and red stripes marked her legs. It was difficult to tell which were the result of Mama's beatings and which were from scratching insect bites.

The old man played a few bars, then nodded to Yunfang:

"Sing out, child. That same part we did yesterday."

As was her custom, she first uttered a loud high cry to open her larynx. Then she stood straight, facing the mirror on the clothes closet door, and began to sing. Her face, blanched by perspiration, had an undertone of blue. The tightly buttoned sleeveless jacket she wore made her look even smaller and thinner. Her chest was slightly concave.

Mama, who was powdering herself, kept glancing over to inspect her posture.

The fiddle stopped.

" '*Jya*' is sung *gee-ya*. Remember: *gee-ya*."

"*Zee-ya*."

"Not *zee-ya*. That's the way the brothel girls sing. '*Jya*' has a round tone: *gee-ya*."

Smack! Mama slapped her face. Mama's fleshy cheeks trembled, she struck so hard.

"Little wretch! After studying all these years, you sing like a brothel girl! Bitch!"

The teacher looked at Yunfang. The light dusting of powder on her face had been blotched by her tears. With a sigh of self-reproach, Elder pointed at the girl with his chin and started his fiddle again. He listened attentively, his head low and slightly to one side. From time to time he glanced at the mirror to observe the movements of her diaphragm.

They began once more from the beginning.

Her quavering voice was like a fragile thread in the wind. The slightest carelessness and it might snap. Singing squeezed the sweat out of her. It ran itchily down her face. Her whole mouth tasted of salt.

"Not bad, not bad," Elder muttered. He seemed moved. Tears glittered in his eyes.

Mama was gloomily beating time on the floor with her foot, wrapped in some kind of troublesome thought. She had just finished pinning up her bun in the back, and she patted her sleek hair. A sickening stench of hair oil pervaded the room. Mama's face was stern. A few more folds seemed to have been added to her chins.

Suddenly, her foot speeded up the beat. She whirled around and grabbed Yunfang's thin arm.

"What's this, what's this!"

When Elder explained that the girl hadn't lost the beat, she grew even more furious.

"You — you — you're lower than an animal!"

With a great sigh, she sat down and fanned herself vigorously.

"You must understand, I'm doing this for your own good." She gestured at Yunfang with the fan. "Do you want to spend your whole life singing in a teahouse?"

She was off again on her favourite theme: All her hopes rested in Yunfang. If she learned to sing well and became a famous opera singer, then life would really be worthwhile for Mama. But, she sighed, you must practise hard while you're young. Tears came to her eyes and she again spoke of the girl who had died six years before.

"A real good one —but she had to die. How she loved me. Very smart, too. But . . . ah! Get on with it, Yunfang, get on with it!"

From her room, Sister yelled:

"Mama, Mama, come quickly! I've got a toothache!"

"Hm, that sister of yours just isn't human," Mama complained in a low voice. "Now that she's prospering, she has no respect, even for me. Ungrateful hussy!"

Elder saw that the strain of singing had brought the veins out in Yunfang's forehead and turned her face red. He softened his fiddle accompaniment.

"Buy Yunfang a sesame seed bun," he pleaded with Mama. "She has no strength. She's a 'full stomach' singer!"

Mama was on her way to Yunyan's room. "She is, eh?" she ranted. "It's lucky she's not a 'smoky throat' singer. Otherwise, I suppose I'd have to go out and buy her some good opium!"

Though her voice was hoarse, Yunfang doggedly continued practising. But the moment Mama left the room, she sang any old way, not caring how she looked. She allowed a mournful expression to appear on her face. It made her feel better somehow.

Finally she mopped her face with her handkerchief, poured some tea from the pewter pot, lowered her head and drank avidly. She didn't dare to look at her teacher. She didn't have to. His withered body, his air of unspeakable bitterness — she could see them always in her mind. They depressed her dreadfully.

Now, in a low voice, Elder criticized her. He advised her to beware of sloppy singing. He told her that the word "wine" should be projected in a narrow tone. Not many people cared much about round and narrow tones these days, he sighed.

In the next room Sister and Mama were quarrelling. Exasperated, Sister was shouting:

"Who says you love me? All you want is money! If my corpse were worth money, you wouldn't be able to wait for me to die!"

Wide-eyed, Yunfang listened. She thought of something.

"Elder," she asked softly, "why can't people pick their dreams? I keep dreaming things I don't like. What I want to dream about, I never do."

Again a vague recollection possessed her. She saw a small room, very dark. A big vat of some sort was gleaming in the corner. A woman's hand stroked her face. Then someone pressed an icy nose against her forehead, and she burst out crying.

What was that place? How old had she been? She couldn't remember any more.

Wistfully, she stared at the open window. She could almost see the hot air rolling in. She felt there was something she wanted to ask Elder, but it slipped away like a shadow before she could catch hold of it.

The squeal of the fiddle pierced her ear-drums like a needle and drove into her brain.

Elder was really good to her but, like Mama, he only wanted her to practise hard, to become a famous opera singer. He seemed to have been brought into the world for the express purpose of teaching her. Elder had a remarkable sensitivity to her voice. Whenever he saw her slackening, he would tell her stories of the great names of the past. This one practised the same role every day as soon as he got up in the morning: later it brought him fame. That one — a female impersonator — kicked his wife to learn how women walked when they limped.

Then he would gaze at the floor dully, and his eyes would fill with tears as he recalled the past.

Why doesn't he ever let me learn anything else? Yunfang thought.

Once she heard Xiaokui singing *Moonlight Beams* in the teahouse, and she wept in spite of herself. It was a tune from a film Mr Ma had invited her and Mama to see. She had wept bitterly, sobbing aloud in the theatre. Mr Ma had wiped his own eyes with his handkerchief. But Mama, as if having a premonition of bad luck, had snapped at her:

"What are you bawling about, stupid! People will laugh at you. Movies aren't real."

If only Elder would let her sing that tune. Ah, it was beautiful!

But when she had proposed it he retorted contemptuously:

"A vulgar song!"

So she still practised the same old passage from the same old aria, tapping the beat with her foot.

Yunfang felt she wasn't singing but rather that things, tightly bound, were being dragged forcibly from her mouth. Her throat was dry, scratchy. Her thin body contracted with every breath she drew. Again sweat poured down her face, accentuating its paleness.

Mama emerged from the room next-door complaining about Sister:

"Just because she's got a nice godfather and some gentlemen friends she thinks she's wonderful. She tries to sit on my head. Who brought her up? That's the thanks I get for all my kindness. The bitch!"

From the room Sister again yelled for her, and she shouted back:

"I'm steeping the tea, my fine young lady! It's coming, it's coming!"

She grumbled, then raised her voice, probably to let others hear.

"How those girls aggravate me. Always getting sick. The younger one, too. At her age, she still has no curves. What's wrong with her anyway!"

Yunfang became very frightened. Whenever Mama was angry with Sister, she took it out on Yunfang. A couple of hard slaps, a few vicious pinches, and then Mama would sobbingly announce: She and Sister were finished; her only hope was that Yunfang would feel for her and study hard. Then, twisting Yunfang's ear, she would grind her teeth insanely and hiss:

"But you're useless, useless! You make Sister laugh at me!"

And Elder would look at the girl sadly and mumble in a hurt voice: "Ah, Yunfang, Yunfang. . . ." No one ever knew what he meant.

Of all the people living in the big compound, Xiaokui was probably the only happy one. She usually came running over as soon as Yunfang finished her lesson. Her chatter was very amusing. She told Yunfang everything about her men friends, whom she referred to as sugar daddies.

"One sugar daddy asked me how old I was. I told him eighteen. He really believed it." Xiaokui laughed.

Yunfang wanted to tell everything to Xiaokui too, but something inside her prevented her from putting her feelings into words.

Today Xiaokui talked about Sister. She thought Sister was a fool.

"Why does she carry on so? If I were her I wouldn't quarrel with Mama like that."

"You're much better off than us," Yunfang said with a long sigh. "Your mama is your real mama. Your kid brother is your real brother."

Xiaokui picked up a swatter and killed a fly. "Me, better off than you?" she demanded loudly in a dissatisfied voice. She gave a snort of laughter. "Whatever you do, it's up to you. She's not your real mother anyhow. Me — sometimes my ma gets sick. It breaks your heart to hear her cry. Says she's a burden to me. 'If things go on like this, what shall we do!' She cries and moans and never stops. It makes you tired, but it also makes you sad."

She thought a moment, then added: "Do I know what we ought to do? That's a laugh!"

Nevertheless Yunfang felt that Xiaokui lived in a different world. She had seen real mothers, with weepy faces, talking garrulously to their daughters, but this only made her search all the more desperately through her vague recollections: That dark room, that tall ruddy-complexioned man. It was all so distant; she couldn't see it clearly. Yet she seemed to feel that those scenes sooner or later would be re-enacted.

But the moment she saw her fat mama, she abruptly came to her senses. She wouldn't believe she would be so lucky.

Gnawing the edge of a plantain fan, Yunfang kept her eyes cast down. She didn't look at Xiaokui.

"What has she got to worry about?"

Xiaokui was lively again as she chatted about the girls they knew. She didn't like their pretending to be respectable while secretly carrying on with men.

"It's obvious they haven't any other way out, so why pretend? Can you support a family on just what you earn from singing? That's a laugh! I don't care what people say about me. Everybody's the same. We all have to eat and we all have to earn money. Live from day to day and that's that."

In the next room, Mama and Sister were quarrelling again. Sister was stamping and shouting:

"I'm going to ask for a day off, that's what I want, a day off! You're afraid they'll dock me one day's pay. You're driving me to my grave!"

Mama complained that Sister didn't understand her.

As soon as a girl grew up, she wanted to fly away. Sobbing, Sister yelled at the top of her lungs:

"Oh yes, you treat me fine! . . . I'm fed up, just fed up! My dear mama!"

Yunfang trembled from head to foot, as though she had caught a chill. She sighed heavily. There was some invisible evil in the way they lived, something that hung upon her body and weighed her down.

"Is good fortune or bad fortune just a question of fate?" she asked of nobody in particular. "Who decides it? Why is it decided the way it is?"

Shortly before noon a messenger came from a nearby restaurant saying that Mr Ma was waiting for Yunfang there and that she should go immediately.

"Mr Ma?" the girl exclaimed in surprise.

A gleam of light appeared before her eyes. She wanted to cry. It was like those stories that Elder told her: A happy ending after many tribulations. Hastily averting her face, she blinked the tears from her eyes and began to make up.

Mama scornfully curled her lip. "That Mr Ma must be a little crazy. One day he suddenly asked me how much it would cost to buy Yunfang over. Don't think because she's young that she's not worth much, I told him. No one can touch that girl for less than eight thousand dollars. He was stunned."

As she said this, Mama watched Yunfang's face. And she followed her with her eyes as the girl went out the door. Mama felt vaguely uneasy. About five minutes later, she put on her black silk tunic, and followed Yunfang to the restaurant.

Mr Ma was his usual frantically busy self. It was as if he was full of words, full of ideas, but didn't know where to start. He ordered a few dishes in his agitated way then, looking very troubled, sat down in a chair. His lips moved quickly, and his long face was wrinkled in a frown.

"I've been away for a while. I went to — to. . . . But first let's talk about serious matters."

He pulled his chair closer, hesitated, then said excitedly: "You can't go on this way. Neither can I. We simply must do something. Why don't we go, Yunfang, you and I go off together?"

The girl stared at him with large eyes. Her lips moved several times, but no sound emerged.

A fly, struggling against the air current of the droning electric fan, was forced to circle, then was blown against the wall. It seemed to be pondering how to break out.

Oily smoke rolled in through the window, and the sound of a spatula on a skillet reminded them that they were in the pot.

The man talked incessantly. He said they would carve out a new existence. She would be able to go to school. He would be very good to her. At times his voice was low, at times high. He was not so much conversing as pouring out his heart.

He stood up and cupped her face with his hands.

"You can't spend your life like this. I want you to be free. Together. . . ."

Yunfang burst into tears.

She didn't know where Mr Ma wanted to take her or what he intended to do with her, but she was amazed that a man could be so good. Could she really escape from her own world to a life of freedom?

This was something she had never even thought about before.

A fleeting picture flashed through her mind: A small room with a bright sunny window. At night she could sleep as much as she wanted. She could sing what she liked. She wore the blue cotton gown of a girl student. There was no need for her to use cosmetics.

Words crammed into her throat. She wanted to tell Mr Ma: As long as there was no Mama compelling her to lead her present kind of a life, she could put up with any hardship. She would look after him like a daughter. Even if he swore at her or beat her, she wouldn't mind. All she wanted was — as he had said — to carve out a new existence.

But she couldn't utter a word, and she wept again. When the man asked her what was wrong, she raised her tear-stained face and smiled.

"I don't know myself why I am crying."

Mr Ma drank as they talked. Great beads of perspiration broke out on his face. He seemed to be suffering. He said he would take her to his home town. After the summer, he could get a job there as a teacher. Like a man in a dream, he described his old home: Bamboo trees on a hill behind the house rustled when the wind blew. Beside the house was a small pond. You just pulled out a fish any time you felt like eating one.

The girl ate very little. Her heart was pounding. She listened carefully to his words as though savouring their flavour. She breathed a shivery sigh.

"How would Mama let me go?"

"You're really a child!" the man cried. "Your mama buys and sells girls. That's illegal — understand? — illegal! She wouldn't dare do a thing!"

"Don't shout so! People will hear. . . ."

"What are you afraid of!" Perhaps it was anger, perhaps the wine, but his voice rose higher. "Afraid of your mama? Hah, I'll complain about her to the police. I'll put you under police protection first. Then we'll see what she has to say!"

Yunfang thought she heard a sound, and she stared at the partition wall. She didn't dare interrupt Mr Ma for fear of angering him.

Somewhere a cicada was shrilling loudly, as if the cry were being scorched out of it by the blazing sun. The room too seemed to be gasping from the heat; you could feel it trembling. But the electric fan blanketed all other sounds, roaring menacingly, louder and louder.

"You're telling me the truth?" she asked softly in a very timid voice. "You're not just teasing me?"

"Teasing you?" the man countered irritably. "Would I be such a fool?"

The girl smiled contritely. She stared straight ahead for some time.

"What are you thinking?" he asked.

Yunfang didn't like to let others see her tears. Lowering her head, she replied:

"I'm afraid . . . afraid that I'm dreaming."

Then a shadow loomed before her eyes. The room darkened — Mama had entered soundlessly. With an apologetic smile at Mr Ma, tenderly, lovingly, she led the girl away.

As Yunfang left, she turned a face drained of colour for a final look at Mr Ma. Her whole body seemed to have ceased functioning. Her mind was numb, devoid of thought.

When they got home, Mama immediately went out again, grinding her teeth.

"Fine, fine! A sixteen-year-old girl wants to fly! I'm going to the restaurant to get this straight — want to know what you two were up to. Fine, so you're going to complain to the police about me! Fine! . . ."

Xiaokui came running over. "What's wrong? What's happened?"

Yunfang threw herself on the girl, sobbing:

"I don't know, I don't know. . . . She's plainly broken the law. . . ."

"What's it all about?" Elder demanded urgently, his hands trembling. "What stupid thing have you done? . . . Yunfang! Yunfang!"

When Mama came home, she pulled Yunfang into the house and barred the door. This was soon followed by screams, panted curses, and the endless flail of a bamboo stick whacking solidly against flesh.

All the residents of the compound crowded round outside. Xiaokui and her mother were shouting incoherently, probably pleading for people to save the girl.

Elder tottered, and supported himself with his hands against the wall. With tears in his eyes he cried: "*Ai,* Yunfang. *Ai,* Yunfang."

Sister burst from her room. Her left cheek was a bit swollen and her eyes were puffy, as if she had been weeping for a long time. She hadn't made up, and her face looked sallow and pale. She herself didn't know whether it was because the noise was annoying her or because she pitied Yunfang, but she fiercely pounded on the door, yelling to Mama like a maniac:

"Open the door! . . . Open the door! . . ."

The wounds on Yunfang's legs became infected. They still weren't cured after more than a week. But Yunfang sang, as usual, in the Blue Cloud Pavilion.

Xiaokui was very contemptuous of Young Master Shi.

"A fine gentleman! He's nothing but a rascal! Your mama went to see him about you, and she also looked up that proprietor's son. They got Big Turnip and his gang to invite Mr Ma for a chat. Big Turnip warned Mr Ma not to come here any more. He said — he said — 'If Yunfang runs away, you'll be hearing from us again!' You can thank Young Master Shi for that!"

"And Mr Ma?" Yunfang asked softly, as if afraid.

"Mr Ma? Could Mr Ma stand up against those police snoopers?"

Yunfang couldn't believe Young Master Shi could be so mean. Hadn't he offered to send her to school?

"You think he really would put you through school?" Xiaokui scoffed. "He's just stringing you along. If you really wanted to get away from here, do you think he'd help you?" Woodenly, her face devoid of expression, she told Yunfang:

"You're much better off than me. I couldn't leave even if I wanted to. I haven't got the heart to let my whole family starve."

Turning, Xiaokui left, holding her head low to hide her face.

Has Mr Ma already returned to his home town? Yunfang wondered. She felt as though something had withered within her.

Young Master Shi and the proprietor's son called, accompanied by Big Turnip. Mama showered them with courtesies. She served them tea, offered them cigarettes, her fat cheeks trembling like jelly with every step. Inviting them to sit in the courtyard and enjoy the breeze, she lit a coil of incense to drive off the mosquitoes. It glowed like a red eye watching them in the darkness.

The proprietor's son disdainfully brought up the subject of Mr Ma. His voice was joyous, and the higher it rose the more effort he had to put into speaking Beiping dialect.

"Who does he think he is, anyhow? Hasn't got the money to buy the girl over, so he wants to steal her away!"

Big Turnip spat. Gesticulating, he reported his accomplishments, his voice also rising. It was a rambling account, but the substance was this:

"At first that Ma fellow tried to get tough. But when he saw that we were from the police, he shut up. His face turned purple, he was so mad, but he couldn't say a word."

Mama sighed continuously. She poured out her grievances so vehemently, the hot sticky air seemed to quiver. She didn't blame Yunfang. No, it was Mr Ma she hated. Why did he want to lead the girl astray? She was only a child. Mama gasped for breath, nearly suffocated by the injustice. It was as if the rolls of fat beneath her chin were strangling her. Mama's eyes reddened, and she snivelled:

"And Yunfang! I brought her up all these years but she hasn't the slightest gratitude. To pull a trick like that on me — I'm simply heart-broken. Who will I have to rely on in my old age, who? . . . The girl has no conscience!"

An indefinable something was suffocating Yunfang. Seated with her back to the lamp, she kept her eyes fixed on Young Master Shi. He patted his newly barbered hair, but didn't speak.

Why doesn't he say anything? the girl thought. She could feel her icy hands trembling.

She wanted to shake her finger at him and berate him. He was exactly like those sneaky men she had heard about in stories. Though he flattered her to her face, behind her back he had hurt her. Staring, she clamped her jaws tight to keep from weeping, her cheeks twitching with the effort.

Anyone — she didn't care who — anyone who could take her away, set her free. . . . But where was such a man?

Though her face was expressionless, large tears sprang from her eyes.

Elder also wept easily. He mumbled on whether people listened to him or not. His voice, muffled in the smell of the ditch water and Mama's talcum powder, seemed to struggle to the surface.

"You shouldn't blame Yunfang. Nobody likes his own job. It's the same with everyone. Singing's fun when you're an amateur, but when you turn professional, it disgusts you."

Again he talked of the past. His back bent, facing the coil of incense beneath the bamboo bed, he spoke as if he had memorized his words: When he was young he used to learn a few lines from an opera and keep repeating them to himself; at night, he couldn't sleep. When he was learning the fiddle, he would suddenly remember a tune in the middle of the night, and would get up to practise it. He used to take the bridge off the fiddle so that his father wouldn't hear. Elder heaved a long sigh and was silent for some time.

Then, for some reason, he began to tell again about his days on the stage. They had always performed the opera *Quick Victory* on the first of the year because they believed it would bring good luck.

"Ah, the past, the past," Elder cried tragically.

Young Master Shi and his friends departed. They never came again. It was rumoured that he was playing up to another young singer.

"What did I tell you?" Elder privately asked Yunfang. "None of those gentlemen are reliable. Your sister still has faith in her Old Master Xiao. Those gentlemen really are — they certainly know how to — hah! — wait and see!"

The girl gazed at the sky. "I never said he was a good man."

But she still hoped people would come and see her, be her friend. Mr Ma was just an illusion now, just a dream — she didn't know where he had gone. Although she hated Young Master Shi, she wished he would drop around for a chat. Even when she sat like a fool to one side and never put in a word, even though the sound of their voices irritated her, at least she got a little something out of it. Seeing these men reminded her somehow that the world was large, that she and these people from the outside all lived on the same planet.

Are those stories of Elder's true? She secretly asked herself. Are there really spirits who watch over our existence?

Sister generally had nothing to do with her. The older girl was concerned only with her own affairs, with arguing with Mama and throwing tantrums. But when Old Master Xiao and Councillor Wang called they would lead Yunfang into Sister's room and have her sit a while.

"What's wrong?" Old Master Xiao asked, displeased. He looked at her and stroked his goatee. "Why does Yunfang always have such a long face?"

"Oh, her," Mama hastily interjected. "Yunfang, why don't you tell your godfather? She's been having headaches lately. Speak up Yunfang, why don't you? That child! She is the limit!"

Sister gave Yunfang a glance that contained both scorn and pity. Then she immediately changed the subject, as though she were doing her utmost to forget the younger girl's miserable expression, as though she wanted all the others to do the same. Lighting a cigarette, she talked loudly with reckless abandon, pounding the table with her fist. It was plain that for some reason Sister was seething with hatred for everything.

In an earnest manner, Councillor Wang sang a snatch from his favourite aria.

Remembering something, Sister gave a loud forced laugh, probably to cover certain things that were in her heart. The laugh had such a weird sound, it gave people the shivers.

What is she laughing about? Yunfang wondered, very frightened, stealing a look at Sister.

At two in the morning, the guests finally departed. Yunfang sat a while in the courtyard with Xiaokui.

Elder sat there dozing, breathing heavily. Inside, Sister was complaining about something, and there was a loud rattling of crockery.

"Not one of my children has a good heart," Mama

was muttering. "I'm paying for my sins in a previous life!"

Her heavy hands opened the box of talcum powder and began patting the powder on her fat neck. Her shadow on the wall was frighteningly large. Even sitting in the courtyard, the girls could see it looming before them.

A bit of dark blue appeared in the black night sky. The irritating voices they heard on all sides all seemed to be issuing from there. Blue-white stars, blinking uneasily, stirred thoughts of limitless vistas, thoughts of the heavens, thoughts of the earth. A strange idea suddenly came to Yunfang's mind. She felt that she was the only person alive in the world. Everyone else was far, far away.

"Do stars have eyes?" she asked.

Something hissed in the night. She was sure it was a shooting star, although she had never heard one. Elder was talking in his sleep:

"Everyone ignores me, insults me. . . ."

The usually cheerful Xiaokui breathed a sigh. Until then she hadn't spoken. It was as if the hot sticky night had numbed her. Now she whispered in Yunfang's ear:

"You can still fly away. But not me."

Yunfang's nose tingled, and her trembling lips could say nothing. Even her brain seemed paralysed.

The Milky Way looked about to spill over. It touched the corner of the compound wall. Yunfang thought she could hear it dripping, flowing into her heart, turning her heart colder and colder. She tried to make out which constellations were the Weaving Maid and the Cowherd, but the sky was too full of stars. They all seemed very familiar, yet at the same time very strange.

They're looking at me, she thought, and at Mr Ma's home town. Bamboos are rustling on the hill, gleams of light are reflecting in the pond, fish are splashing in the water. The stars can also see the big ruddy-faced man whose hair is shaven on the front part of his head; he's all in a sweat seeking his daughter. . . .

But the stars only blinked and didn't utter a sound.

"What's the answer? Has anyone seen him, after all?" Yunfang asked, to the mystification of Xiaokui.

Then, as though some force was compelling her, she gripped Xiaokui's hand tightly and silently wept.

Translated by Sidney Shapiro

Luo Shu

LUO Shu (1903-1938) was born in Chengdu, Sichuan Province. After finishing middle school, she travelled to France in 1929 where she studied at the Institut Franco-Chinois in Lyons. Returning to China in 1933 she translated works by Romain Rolland and other French writers into Chinese. She started writing herself in 1936 and "Twice-married Woman" was her first work. Its publication brought her immediate critical acclaim. Following this she wrote "The Oranges", "The Salt Worker" and several prose sketches. All of her writing contains a strong element of empathy with those in the lower depths of pre-Liberation society. In 1937, she began a novel depicting the life of salt workers. At the age of thirty-five however, just as she was reaching the prime of her literary career, this gifted writer died in child-birth.

Twice-Married Woman

NEAR the west bank of the upper reaches of the River Tuo, fold upon fold of hills encircled a mountain hamlet like a bowl. And early on fine mornings men and cattle emerged from the small buildings there to move uphill or down. But they were so easily swallowed up by the multitude of trees, that one might suspect the region to be deserted. When dusk fell, the faint hazy mist peculiar to mountains covered the scattered lights hidden in the quiet forests; and these lights, like expiring glow-worms, intensified the sense of loneliness.

Half-way up a hill on the left, a low hut squatting by itself among the mountain bushes and random boulders was the only dwelling place to show no light. Its inmates, a man and a woman, seemed utterly crushed, neither speaking nor moving, sunk in an eerie silence and a solitude like death.

This couple, husband and wife, were grass-cutters who had only taken to this way of life since moving into this one-roomed hut. It had not belonged to them in the first place; but after losing their few *mu* of land and little house, when a neighbour planned to pull down this hut and move away, they had said:

"We've no roof over our heads. Leave that shack of yours to us, and we'll give you our two goats. They're all we have."

So they had exchanged their goats for this hut, no

better than the sheds put up at harvest time to keep an eye on the crops. It was a dank gloomy place, with cracked mud walls on which moss was growing unevenly near the ground. They were pleased to have it, however, for it meant they could stay on in their native place which they could not bear to leave although it had treated them poorly, and were spared the dreaded existence of wanderers in "foreign parts".

They had two strong sharp sickles, curved as crescent moons. Every day with bent backs and lowered heads they scoured the countryside silently for fresh green grass to cut. Sometimes they would straighten up and stop to draw breath, or lie down at the foot of the hill together. The trim wheat fields before them had once been their own, and the young shoots in them were growing green and lusty. They would exchange glances and then turn away, silently bending to their work again. And when two wicker crates were filled, the man would carry them to the nearest village.

Birds twittered and cheeped at evening in the woods. And gold specks of sunlight contrived to filter through the serried branches of pines and cedars as he sauntered home down the winding path through the forest, his crates swinging lightly now with nothing in them but a little rice, a jar of oil or a packet of salt bought at the market.

Little by little their regret for days gone by gave way to fresh hope. "The fisherman suns his net by the stream where he fishes," and they could surely strike root here. They lived on courageously and strenuously, like two famished wild animals well aware of their exhaustion but forced to struggle for the food in sight, even though this might not fall to their share after all.

Then strange faces appeared in the hamlet, so many of them that you met them at every turn. These newcomers appeared to be looking for something. This mountain hamlet which had been so deserted now seemed a small bowl filled to the brim with water, so that one more drop must make it overflow. And those dislodged were countryfolk like themselves. From this time on, the villages themselves began to change. When the man carried his grass to familiar gates, instead of smiles he was met by long faces, sighs of regret and the news:

"We don't need your grass, mate! Try somewhere else."

When he went to another house, he was told:

"The fact is we can't afford to keep cattle any more. The bit of grass we need I've sent my son out and cut it already."

Sadly disappointed, he bit his lips and stared in bewildered silence at his load of fresh green grass. Again and again he made the round of all possible customers, lowering his prices as far as possible; yet still he had to go home with his load intact. Beside their baked mud stove there was already a big pile of withered grass, heaped up there day after day, its fresh green faded.

Ninth Uncle, who took a keen interest in other men's affairs, may have been touched by his troubles. One day, his pipe in his mouth, he swaggered up and after heaving a great sigh advised:

"You must make up your mind, young fellow. Don't think you can get by. A rope of hemp breaks at the weakest place. What if you fall ill? . . . Are the two of you content to watch each other starve? Take my advice and find another home for that wife of yours. You're still young and healthy, so long as you're willing to wear out a few pairs of sandals what have you to fear?"

These words struck a chill in his heart, his face clouded over and he sat down in the shade of a tree, rubbing his calves as he thought matters over. But inexorably life had closed in on him, and think as he might he could find no way out. Sometimes as he mulled things over, he felt he had discovered a thread of hope, a possible solution; but the next instant it vanished, and there was no escape from the grim reality. The hills here were rich in resources. The durable, gleaming granite fetched high prices, and the forests were full of tall, straight trees; yet for him and his wife the place was an arid desert. What they wanted was something that required no outlay and could be had for the taking, like wild grass. Before the outsiders had come here, anyone who wanted to could easily pick large quantities of the *qinggang* seed,* but now several families were collecting this. And there would be no lichen till autumn when the grass withered. Each time he returned to the present, his thoughts came back to his wife.

"Sell her — that's the best way out for both of us!"

Suddenly a woman with a dark, oval face was standing before him, pointing to the basket in her hand.

"Yes! When Third Grandpa was out, his wife lent me six catties of sweet potatoes on the quiet, and I promised to stitch two pairs of shoe-soles for her in exchange." Watching the small black insects on the floor,

* Can be made into a kind of curd but is bitter in taste. The poor sometimes eat them.

she added, "My, what a lot of ants! Are you rooted there? . . . Come home now to your supper."

When he paid no attention, she left listlessly with her basket. Self-reproach was gnawing at his vitals. "Can't say she hasn't worked hard to earn the food she eats," he thought. In more of a quandary than ever, he hung his head.

During this period of uncertainty, his character, once so grave and dependable, changed. Now he glared round with bloodshot eyes, constantly on the look-out for a quarrel. Anyone who crossed his path aroused his fury. He worked off his anger most of all on his wife.

"Oh, dear, how clumsy of me!" she scolded herself after dropping a bowl and spilling the gruel in it. While she was still speaking, a brick came flying at her head. She dodged it nimbly, too taken aback to be angry, crying out in alarm at sight of her husband's expression.

"What's come over you, man? Flaring up over a little thing like that? It won't hurt us much to miss a meal."

"Flaring up! The mere sight of you is enough to make me angry.... A regular blight you are! With you around, I'll never have a good day." He was bellowing more furiously than ever.

"What's that?" His wife sprang to her feet. "You go about all day with a face like thunder, so you're blaming me for all your troubles. I can't go on like this, and that's a fact!... Who do you think you are!" She flung off, sat down on a tree stump that served as a stool, and hugged her knees in silence.

Her last sentence and her look of scorn offended his masculine pride. In a fit of jealous rage, with a black look he thundered:

"I can see through you, woman! 'When the wine pot's empty, the guest will leave.' I suppose you've picked someone else. I'm not good enough for you!" He gave a fierce snort of laughter. "Very well!" Then he turned on his heel and stalked off, not looking back.

He went to find Ninth Uncle.

Ninth Uncle was standing on the path by a field. With a nod and a smile he said:

"That's the idea! I'll see to it for you."

Two days later, he approached and whispered:

"I've fixed it. It's Hu Da of the Hu family by the dike on the other side of the hill. He's a man from these parts, in his forties, with property of his own, and he never touches a drop. There's just him and his brother, so it's a simple household." He thrust out three fingers. "That's his offer."

Hu Da! A skinflint, always cadging drinks at the market. Everyone spat in disgust when his name came up. How dare such a bag of skin and bones ask for his wife! Shame and outrage bowed his head and he made off without a word.

Ninth Uncle watched in surprise, scratching his bewildered head. But as the other drew away, he felt constrained to call:

"Well, what answer shall I give him?"

". . . ."

"It's a thankless task helping you!" He sounded thoroughly disgruntled.

The other stopped abruptly, and after a moment's hesitation answered:

"All right. I agree to it. That's all right with me!" The reply was firm and decided.

Still more amazed, Ninth Uncle stared after him until he was out of sight.

2

As night deepened, a breeze laden with the scent of broad beans in flower and the aroma of pines, cedars and soil blew over the fields, and the grass beside their stove rustled.

The two of them were quiet, their minds a blank.

Suddenly a plaintive, desperate hoot sounded in the woods behind. It was the owl, bird of ill omen, who wails the whole year round. Both raised haggard faces together, to glance involuntarily at each other in the dark. Indefinable panic had seized them.

"Bah!" He spat in disgust. "Get away!"

With half closed eyes, as if in a trance, the woman chanted like a witch:

"Hoot east, hoot west! To-whit-tu-woo! The wood is one great grave for you!"

As if suddenly recollecting something, the man went to the door and poked his head out for a look, then returned to his original place. His lips twitched as if he wanted to speak, but he was unable to do so. After a few vain attempts he finally said to the woman, "This thing has gone so far, how do you expect them to go back with an empty sedan-chair? What can one do, after all?"

"Hoho, don't give me that!" Standing upright, the woman pointed a finger at her husband. "You're a fine one . . . you're a beast . . . you heartless creature. . . ."

Trembling all over and panting for breath she sank down heavily on the tree stump.

The words flung at him so fiercely smote him in the heart. He could neither evade nor retaliate. He stared at her, wide-eyed. Perhaps he was thinking how to explain and defend himself, but his tongue seemed frozen, he simply could not speak. He stamped with annoyance and uttered his usual "Mother's!" Then he turned his back on her and gazed dully through the small window at the hazy countryside.

The woman stared woodenly at his back, which was broad but already slightly bent. Suddenly, nearby, something exploded with a loud roar, taking her by surprise.

"Am I worse than any other mother's son? What law have I broken? Why has this trouble come on me? Well, it's all the same now. Let's settle scores today, once and for all. . . . Come on!"

Afraid of a beating, the woman jumped to her feet and ran out of the hut.

The man followed, lunging forward as he cried:

"Why are you running away? Afraid the King of Hell is after you? If I meant to give you a licking, you'd never escape!"

She stopped when she understood that he meant her no harm, to stand rather apprehensively by the door.

So a minute or two went by. Then the man produced matches and lit an oil lamp. By its murky light his square, swarthy face looked unusually gaunt and pale, his eyes fearfully sunken. No trace could be seen in him now of the strength gained by peasants from toiling in sun, wind and rain. He seemed an old man about to die, all his vital forces spent. As he stooped to rummage under the straw at the foot of the bed, the woman followed his movements with her eyes. Eventually he produced a folded paper and unwrapping this revealed something white and sparkling, about three inches long and pointed at the ends. She knew it at once. This was the silver hairpin she had worn for more than twenty years till all its designs were rubbed smooth. They had recently pawned it.

"There! Take that along!" The big hand holding the hairpin was trembling.

"When did you redeem it?" Her voice was wavering between grief and joy, as if she had recovered a long lost treasure, as she went over to him with outstretched hands. But then she lowered her hands, while two long pent-up tears held back by the resentment born of misunderstanding rolled down her cheeks. Shaking her head, she sobbed:

"I don't want it! Keep it for yourself — I don't want it!"

The silver hairpin served as a sharp sword to cut through the barrier between them, and through the rift surged genuine, honest affection.

With the hem of her tunic the woman dried her eyes, then gazed at her husband, motionless as a statue.

"I must be going," she said.

The man nodded without a word.

She stumbled off, but had not gone far when apparently she remembered something important. Turning back her head, she called out urgently:

"Husband, your shirt's hanging on the mulberry tree to dry. Don't forget to take it in!"

Then she hurried blindly, as arranged, to the tall tree standing by the road down the hill.

3

There was no moon that night, but the path was faintly illumined by pale starlight. A small sedan-chair swayed slowly up to the tree to come to rest at its foot. The black, ghostly figure standing there stiffly waiting took a few uncertain steps forward when the chair stopped; whereupon the foremost chair bearer, short Young Hu, promptly raised the curtain on the chair to let the shadowy figure slip inside. But hard though he strained his eyes, he could not make out her features. He simply smelt the strong scent of a woman's hair.

With a passenger aboard, the chair moved faster. Having made his way rapidly out of the gully, Young Hu called out arrogantly to the man behind:

"Put it down while I light the lantern."

The sedan-chair halted by the roadside. Young Hu struck several matches in succession, but one by one they were blown out by the wind. The man behind looked on impatiently as Young Hu's left hand, crooked to keep off the wind, glowed red for a few brief instants. Then he squatted down and carefully held out both hands to cup the light.

"That's it! It's a hell of a nuisance jogging along in the dark! I'm covered with sweat!"

"If anyone dares try to nab me for carrying a twice-married woman over his land, I'll teach him a lesson! Bah! He'd better look out."

The sedan-chair on their shoulders swayed in time to the rhythm of their steps; and when their shoulders shook, the circle of light cast on the ground by the lantern appeared to quiver with mirth, contracting or expanding impishly as if afraid the man behind might trample it to pieces; but sometimes it gleamed quietly as the eye of a wicked schemer probing into the secret of his opponent.

In fact, encouraged by that circle of light, Young Hu's desires took more definite shape, and the blame for this must be attributed to that seductive scent of hair. Like an invisible thread it coiled round his legs, till he forgot the signals it was the duty of the first bearer to give.

When the second bearer had stepped on a heap of cow dung, though lucky enough not to fall he lost his temper. Mockingly he called out the warning Young Hu should have given:

"A blossom to the right!"

"Don't tread on it!" Young Hu answered instinctively realizing only then his own negligence. Feeling apologetic, he made haste to shift the poles on his shoulders, complaining with a sigh: "We've quite a load!"

They were approaching the bridge over a quarry when the other man called out:

"Confound it! You're wrenching my shoulders till they ache. Even with a light, you make such heavy going of it! Mind the quarry in front. One false step, and over we'll go!"

After exercising caution in crossing the quarry, Young Hu lurched along wildly, his steps matching the confusion in his mind.

Despite his big head and squat body, Young Hu was not the simpleton he looked. The hunger he suffered in the six years as a cowherd in a relative's house had put an end to his boyish innocence. He had squatted with other lads out of sight of the grown-ups to plot various thefts, and hidden in caves to cook beans and rice or "beggar's chicken" over a fire of dried twigs, till he had acquired a devilish cunning. Upon his return home, his brother spied on him furtively all day to see if he were wasting the family property. His brother was satisfied with his own strict supervision and smiled secretly over it; but Young Hu with narrowed eyes swore to himself: "Think you're smart, do you, brother? It's too bad you can't count every single grain. There's another five *sheng* of wheat missing! That girl in red pants and her mother will have enough to eat for several days — did you know that?"

After they had covered four *li* or more, they passed a stretch of wicker fence and arrived at a tiled house built round a compound. In the yard was a crooked locust tree whose branches swept the roof of the main room, where a tablet which bore the inscription Ancestors and Heaven and Earth stood on a table, and where several candles were burning just as at New Year. The barking of dogs brought a crowd of children rushing out, laughing and shouting. Several burly men followed them into the courtyard, but only to stand at a distance looking on.

"Make way there!" A bandy-legged old woman swept the children aside and pushed her way to the sedan-chair. She drew back the curtain, crying: "You're my nephew's bride — you'll have to call me aunty! Hurry up! Hurry up and come with me!"

She took the woman from the sedan to a room on the left and sat her down on a stool. Then wrinkling her small, red-rimmed eyes, by the light of an oil lamp hanging on the wall she surveyed her narrowly from head to foot. A long face, a little on the dark side! Lovely hair, but badly combed, as if she had been in a fight. With her head on one side, the old woman examined the knot of hair on the nape of the bride's neck, and at once a complacent smile dawned on her wizened face. Without a sound she opened the wooden door and went out. Before long she was back, carefully carrying a new silver hairpin, two red ribbons, a box of powder, some rouge and a small paper package.

"Daughter-in-law!" she cried affably. "You can trust old folk like me to know what's what. My nephew didn't want to buy a hairpin for you, but I insisted. I knew that if a woman like you possessed a silver hairpin, you wouldn't be marrying him. . . . Ha! Feel it — isn't it a weight! A good sixth of an ounce at the very least!"

Carefully undoing the paper package, she took out a pair of red gauze flowers with green leaves. Having held them up to the light to make sure they were undamaged, she tried the effect against the other's head.

"In the first month I saw a good many girls in the street wearing these flowers, and took a fancy to them. I had to ask several people before one would buy me a pair. It wasn't easy! I meant to keep them for my daughter's wedding; but when I heard my nephew was getting married, I decided to make you a present of them instead. My daughter wasn't at all pleased, and said I was favouring you. . . ." She broke off suddenly as if recollecting something. "Ah, now I remember. My memory's not what it was. My old wits keep wandering." Out she stumped again.

She came back this time with a bucket of steaming water.

"It's too much for me, this. I made the men carry it here. It was all I could do to lift it over the threshold. I'm getting thoroughly useless in my old age." This effusion left her breathless. She had to pause before drawing a big cloth bundle from under her arm. Pointing to the other door, she announced, "That leads to the pigsty. Take your light in and have a bath. There's a tub in there. That's the rule, you know, to 'wash away bad luck'. It's not simply a question of cleaning up." Shaking open the cloth bundle, she continued: "After your bath, change into these clothes. I can see the sleeves are too big, but never mind. You can alter them yourself later. Your good man bought them for you, the material's as good as new. If you don't like the colour, you can buy some black dye for a few cents at the next fair and dye them black."

After more muttering she reached for the door, but just before pulling it to turned back to say:

"So you're a daughter-in-law of our house now — congratulations!"

A silence like that after a storm followed the old woman's departure. Then at last the grass-cutter raised her head to look round. The room was a very old one, with a wooden bed covered by a blue homespun canopy beside one wall. The rest of it was cluttered up with hoes, wicker crates and the like, and a newly chiselled grinding stone still lacking a handle. Catching sight of the bucket of water steaming on the floor, the new bride carried out the old woman's instructions and opened the door to the pigsty. A pen, surrounded by short wooden posts, took up one corner of the dank, foul-smelling room. In the sty were some half-grown pigs, apparently hungry, for some of them were licking the scum left in the trough while those who could not squeeze in there were standing behind grunting irately at the rest. The sudden light disturbed them and made them scatter. Then, like suppliants, they raised their slits of eyes embedded in fat to look at the newcomer. She recalled a task familiar years ago, and glanced round till in another corner she discovered a bucket of mash. Hanging the lamp on a nail, she picked up the bucket with one hand, supporting it below with the other, and sloshed the swill into the trough.

"Come on! There you are! Tuck in!"

When all the snouts had a place to guzzle, she smiled.

Then her eye fell on the wooden tub on the floor, and she hesitated for a second. Should she wash, or not? She decided that she would. All the wives sold to second husbands she knew had washed away their ill luck in this way. And she certainly needed all the luck she could get!

Fire-crackers exploded in the courtyard, followed by the shouts and laughter of children and men. By the time she went back with the light to the other room, it was crowded with women and children, who chuckled over her reluctance to enter, dragged her roughly in, and set to work together to dress her up.

"Take a look at yourself in the mirror," urged the young woman who had rouged the bride's cheeks and stuck the red flowers in her hair. "It's no joke making up someone else."

She glanced obediently in the mirror before lowering her head again.

"Well, I declare! What are you crying for? With fresh rouge on too!" The young woman sounded indignant.

"Go and take your places! Go on!" The old woman shooed them out. Smiling all over her face, she examined the bride. "That's more like it," she declared. "Those flowers make all the difference. Come with me. You must offer wine to our relatives and friends."

The instant the woman stepped into the main room thronged with visitors, a sudden tumult burst out.

"I can hardly recognize her!"

"She doesn't look like a pauper any more."

"Brother Hu's in luck. Fortune-teller Zhang's predictions were right."

"Ninth Uncle knows how to pick them!"

She felt she had stepped into a maze of spikes where there was no advancing or retreating. The trembling in her legs made her long to sit down, but no one suggested this and there was no seat. She stood fearfully in one corner, like a mouse that a cunning old cat has played with for hours without finally putting it out of its misery.

Hu Da showed his yellowing teeth in a grin, while Young Hu kept darting glances at this sister-in-law he had carried home. To the scent of her hair was added a strong odour of powder.

The old woman passed a wine jug to her, saying, "Go and offer a cup first to Ninth Uncle. He's been to a lot of trouble for the two of you."

Mention of Ninth Uncle filled her with resentment, but she meekly filled the first cup of wine for him.

Wedding toasts changed the sour taste of the cheap wine, and the guests, not forgetting that Hu was standing treat, got well and truly drunk — as did their host.

"The newly-weds ought to drink to each other!" cried a rough voice.

"That's right!" An approving roar went up from the table.

In a daze, the woman felt a cup thrust into her hand, while she was pushed up to someone. She knew who he was, but could not bring herself to look up at this husband. And Hu for his part refused to reach out for the cup.

"Bashful, I declare! Well, go on and give it to him." Two strong hands seized her arm and, as she shrank back instinctively, the dishes and cups in front of Hu and his neighbours, not to mention the candle stuck in half a potato, were all swept off the table by her big sleeves.

Crash!

Hu glared down at his clothes stained with wine and grease, then at the broken crockery on the floor. Was this woman bent on wrecking his whole house? He grabbed her by the hair and bellowed:

"A pretty mess you've made — and on a day like this! You are an ill-fated slut. You've swept away all your grass-cutter husband's luck. Now you've brought your bad luck to me. I don't want you! Get out!"

Then he realized that he had gone too far. Urged by his guests, he let her go and sat down, fuming, to swear under his breath.

"What are you still hanging round for?" The old woman caught hold of the bride. "You can't blame him."

She hurried back into the other room. All was black there. Neither moving nor crying, she stared stupefied at a patch of grey-blue sky outside the window, where a few stars were twinkling.

All the guests had gone, leaving only Hu and his brother in the main room.

Gradually the woman came to herself and thought over all that had happened. She raised her face and sobbed:

"Why was I born so unlucky? What have I done wrong? If he'd known it would be like this, he'd have starved to death sooner than send me here. . . ." The door creaked open and a short figure loomed before her. She heard him call, "Sister-in-law!"

The voice was familiar: it was the man who had carried her to this place.

She recoiled in fright against the door of the pigsty. But Young Hu stepped forward and called out again.

She knew what this meant, and pointing an accusing finger at him cried:

"Shame on you! Get away!"

"Don't be afraid — my brother's drunk, sleeping it off." He sniggered. As he rushed towards her, she smelt the liquor on his breath. She warded him off so that he staggered and fell.

Young Hu's helpless, floundering attempts to get up filled her with a strange dread and loathing, for he looked more like a ghost than a living man. She pulled open the door of the pigsty and ran out.

The courtyard was as silent as an old tomb. Deep

snores came from the main room, where the lights were out. In despair and stupefaction, she sensed that Young Hu was after her. Without stopping to think, she ran as fast as she could out of the gate, to rush wildly off into the darkness. Paying no heed to the dog at her heels and with no idea where she was heading, she stumbled along the faintly glimmering pathway, fearful panic gaining upon her as she ran, though her pace was slackening. Exhausted by the time she reached the stone bridge, she could hold out no longer: her knees buckled and down she rolled.

For a second or so she could still hear men's voices approaching, but then she lost consciousness.

The stars dwindled and faded, all around was dark and still.

She raised her eyelids, then closed them again, her mind a blank. After a while, she became conscious of her aching cheek and the pain racking her. She opened her eyes, wondering how she came to be among these icy, hard, jagged rocks. There were shooting pains on one cheek, and putting her hands to it she felt a great gash from which the blood was still oozing. Ignoring her other injuries, she tried to remember what had happened. Abruptly everything came back to her, and she repented bitterly of leaving Hu's house. She must have been out of her mind, running away! Recalling the voices she had heard, she reflected: "I'll be bound they've gone to have it out with him. . . . I've landed him in trouble!" A fresh access of courage made her struggle desperately to her feet. But the stones kept tripping her up, and after several falls she sprawled out again in despair, her hands pillowing her head, groaning, as blood soaked her sleeve and dishevelled hair.

She longed to close her eyes and lie here without moving, but something forced her to remain alert and to keep her eyes open till dawn.

Cocks crowed one after another, and the eastern sky started to glimmer like the belly of a fish. All around her emerged by degrees from the long night's darkness to be bathed in the sun's caresses. Pulling herself together, she recognized the stone quarry which was only about two *li* from her old home – her husband passed this way every day to sell grass! Her wounds were powerless to stop her now. Biting her lips, she crawled as best she could over the uneven rocks to level ground. After climbing out of the quarry, no more than six feet deep, she lay down panting by the side of a field. When she was a little rested, she summoned up her courage again to stagger slowly forward towards their low hut. After a painful climb, she came in sight of their roof. Then her steps quickened.

"Husband, are you there?" she called faintly, clinging to a tree for support.

There was no answer.

She pressed eagerly forward. The wooden door was wide open, the oil lamp on the rickety table was flickering dismally, but the place was deserted.

"Where are you? Husband.... Where are you?"

She called frantically through the door and through the window, but her words fell like ashes into a derelict well, unable to reach the bottom.

She paused dizzily for some minutes on the threshold, then forced herself to take a couple of steps and fell exhausted on the bed.

It was broad daylight when she heard steps outside, but she was too weak to stir. Straining her ears she heard people shuffling in the doorway as if looking round, while a low voice remarked:

"Just last night it was! The woman was married off last night and ran away again. At midnight the Hu brothers went to fetch the bailiff to demand satisfaction.... Yes.... He wouldn't go, and there was quite a scrap. What a cunning fellow to have planned such a trick. He seems so honest too, yet he knows how to swindle others."

Translated by Gladys Yang

The Oranges

ALL the oranges on Uncle Aquan's trees had ripened. The fresh, glorious red fruit set in dark luxuriant foliage gave the ramshackle three-roomed thatched cottage an unusual air of distinction.

Dingding, not quite six yet, was a proud and happy boy. Now he had oranges to eat, and his was the only family with orange trees. He seemed busier than anyone else in the household.

For some days a high wind had been blowing — it had still not died down. As he watched the wind-battered branches lashing together, and leaves whirling wildly down like yellow butterflies through swirling dust, he could not help worrying over his oranges.

He was squatting by his mother's spinning-wheel to watch her work; but each time he heard the wind howling outside he set up a fresh clamour himself.

"Oh, bother it! Listen, mum!... What a wind! Just hear it!"

He ran outside to have a look. Then, relieved to find the oranges still firmly attached to the branches, he came back to squat down again in the same place.

"Don't you worry, the wind won't blow the oranges down.... My, those cold hands of yours look like beetroots." With one toe his mother pushed the brazier at her feet over to her son. "Take that to toast your hands."

"I don't want it! It's an orange I want."

"What, again?" She pursed her lips. "Grandad's asleep. We mustn't disturb him. Wait till your dad comes back and he'll get you one. I'm too busy with my spinning."

Uncle Aquan, seated on a low bench, had his hands over a brazier between his knees. With his eyes shut, he did look as if he were asleep. Before one sliver of cotton was finished, Genggui came back. Shouting and skipping, Dingding rushed into the courtyard.

"Out of my way! Do you want this load of bamboo to smash your silly head?" With a clatter, Genggui dumped the great bundle of bamboos he had just cut in the woods. He was panting, his head steaming.

"Dad! Mum said you'd pick me some oranges."

"First fetch me the chopper."

"What about the oranges?"

"Go on. Do as you're told."

Their voices finally woke Uncle Aquan. Rubbing his eyes he looked vaguely from one to another, then muttered half to himself, half to the rest:

"Isn't there going to be any snow after all?"

"Snow, eh? Look over there!"

Genggui was pointing to a relatively bright patch of sky from which distant rays of faint sunshine were falling feebly on the chilly deserted fields. The dearth of rain all winter made him hope for snow; on the other hand, this was a critical time and they needed fine weather. In cold like this people weren't likely to pick their way, shivering, down the muddy road to this quiet, out-of-the-way homestead.

Xiaohua started barking suddenly outside the gate, and at once two big brown dogs came bounding out.

The three of them, keeping their distance, circled the man who had come.

Picking up a length of bamboo just cut by Genggui, Uncle Aquan hurried out. As he called off the dogs he narrowed his eyes to examine the newcomer. It was a man with a pipe in his mouth. Over a none-too-new blue-cloth gown he had a black jacket and a faded red girdle — a relic, no doubt, of the dragon lantern procession during the New Year Festival in the first lunar month.

This was Zhang, a merchant who came to the village every year to buy oranges. Uncle Aquan had sent a message asking him over.

"Well, so it's you, my respected friend!... Get away, Xiaohua! Are you blind?"

Dingding's mother drew a bench from under the table, set it to one side and dusted it off with her apron. Having done this in silence with a lowered head, she went back to her spinning, neither trying to overhear their conversation nor worrying lest the whirring of her wheel disturb them.

"I hear you have a bit of business for me. As I happened to be going to Mr Wang's house to see to the picking of fruit today, I looked in on my way back."

"It's not much, a matter of a dozen or so trees. I've never sold the lot before. I used to keep half for the kid and sell half as candied fruit. But you know how hard farmers have been hit these last years, brother. We have to try to think of ways and means. This year the sugar shop in my daughter-in-law's family had to close down, and I can't afford to buy sugar to make candied fruit. Besides, it's getting on for New Year, and I need a little ready money." This said, the old man sent

Dingding to fetch some oranges for the visitor to sample.

Genggui climbed on a high stool, while Dingding stood below with upturned head, holding out the skirt of his gown to catch the fruit. One, five, ten . . . regular beauties all of them, so large and red and round.

"They've not a bad flavour. Try them, Uncle Zhang, and see," called Genggui, standing in the yard. Then he picked up his chopper again.

Zhang the merchant toyed with an orange, weighing it in the palm of his hand and looking at it narrowly before splitting it open. He put one quarter in his mouth as reluctantly as if it were sure to set his teeth on edge. By the look of it, he perhaps wanted to say the fruit was sour or insipid but in the end he didn't say so.

"In what way do you want to sell them?" he inquired slowly of Uncle Aquan. His eyes were fixed on the orange in his hand while he stripped off the pith.

"You mean what price I want? Let's go by the market price. I'll take the same as everyone else."

"I want to know if you're selling by weight or by the lot?" The merchant flipped the rest of the orange down on the table.

Uncle Aquan was somewhat offended by this cavalier treatment. A hulking great fellow and he ate only half an orange! He had no time, though, to press the merchant to finish. He went on eagerly:

"Sell it by the lot? . . . No, selling it by weight is fairer. That way neither side loses out. A pound is a pound."

The merchant made no reply but strode out of the house. Uncle Aquan tagged after him as he sized up every orange tree before and behind the house. There were twenty of them in all, five beside the threshing floor and fifteen in the vegetable plot. The branches were weighted down with fruit, large and perfectly round.

Completing his tour of inspection, the merchant stood under a tree and shook his head.

"You don't understand, Uncle Aquan," he said. "The price of fruit has gone down this year, and that's a fact. If you don't believe me, go to the docks and see. How many loads of oranges have they shipped off? They can't sell them down river, and who in these parts wants to buy them? In my business there's nothing we dislike more than buying odd little lots. It's different with someone like Mr Wang. If he tells us he's got oranges for sale, we rush there helter-skelter like moths to a lamp. Well, just think, he has seven or eight hundred trees. Yes, that's something. There is more to expect from such a piece of business even if his prices are stiffer. You and I can talk frankly. You had enough faith in me to ask me over, and naturally I'm glad to do you a good turn."

"Yes, I know you're above board. . . ."

"Easy on, I haven't finished. Let's not get worked up over nothing, I want to buy the whole lot, you know, and since the smaller oranges sell for two dollars eighty cents, I'll give you three dollars a load, and we'll count your lot as four loads. It's a small matter and I'm making a favour of it, but never mind."

With a flourish, the merchant fished six dollars out of his pocket, jingled them to show that they were genuine, then tossed them on the table. The silver dollars made a metallic clatter.

"There! Take six dollars to be going on with. I'll give you the other six when my men come for the fruit."

"Three dollars a load!... Four loads!" mumbled Uncle Aquan, shaking his head.

The clink of money and the men's conversation had finally caught the attention of Dingding's mother. She looked up now at the two men in the room. Half a sliver of cotton was on her knees, but her left hand, still on the wheel, had stopped turning it. Dingding, his chin on the table, was playing with an orange with two green leaves.

Seeing Uncle Aquan's hesitation, Zhang the merchant quietly picked up the six dollars on the table and put them back in his pocket.

"Not interested in money, Uncle Aquan? Well, it's up to you. If the deal's off, at least we can part friends, eh?"

At this juncture money had a magnetic attraction for Uncle Aquan. He was unable to watch passively while someone who had brought money to his door took it away again. He needed money desperately. Furrowing his brows, he stared with rheumy eyes at the flat, black square table, thick with dust and bare except for the oranges still lying there. What use were oranges?

So he made a decision.

"Sit down, brother! As long as neither side loses out, I want to make a deal. I need money badly just now, and that's the truth. Just raise your price a little and it's a deal."

"Why, Uncle Aquan, you surely don't think I'm trying to make a big profit out of this small transaction with you? We're old acquaintances; of course I'll help you if I can."

"Just raise your price a little!"

"See here, you can't expect me to lose on this! I've got to meet expenses at least! Besides, to be honest with you, the most I shall do is get a few pounds for myself. There's nothing else in it for me."

Dingding's mother, dismayed by this nearly completed deal, slipped out unobtrusively to the courtyard, where she whispered to her husband:

"That fellow Zhang is such a skinflint, he's trying to make us sell for three dollars a load, reckoning the lot as four loads. Go on in and stop your dad. The fruit won't go bad if we keep it a few days longer."

Genggui's arrival relieved Uncle Aquan, who flashed him a glance inviting him to clinch the deal. Zhang the merchant ignored him, however, as if to say, "I'm talking business with your old man. There's no call for you to butt in."

"Is it settled?" asked Genggui.

"Uncle Zhang wants three dollars a load, reckoning four loads in all."

"Whew! That's nothing like enough. We've a good seven loads here at the very least! If Uncle Zhang really wants it, he can settle for six loads, and we won't haggle over the price."

"Oh, very well, if you don't want to sell. You keep your fruit, and I'll stick to my cash." With this the merchant started out.

Uncle Aquan cast his son a furious look. He had gone too far. Instead of clinching the bargain, in no time at all Genggui had spoiled the whole show.

"Wait a bit, Uncle Zhang! Don't go! I want to do business. Come on, reckon it as five loads, won't you?"

"Four!"

"Four and a half?"

"Four. Twelve dollars altogether!"

He enunciated the words "twelve dollars" as distinctly as if silver dollars were clinking in his mouth, and the effect on Uncle Aquan was irresistible. After a moment's hesitation, he said:

"All right, then. Done!"

A triumphant smile appeared on the merchant's face. Uncle Aquan squatted down to ring the dollars. After turning each over again and again, rapping it and examining it narrowly, he put them carefully in his pocket. But now that the money was his, his face looked graver and gloomier than ever.

The merchant enlisted Genggui's help and borrowed several wicker crates from him. First he picked the fruit in front of the house.

Little by little, the fruit was piled high in the crates, leaving the trees a uniform green as one by one they were stripped of oranges.

Not till then did Dingding realize that the man with the red girdle was going to steal away all his oranges. Clinging to his mother's clothes and ignoring the look on her face, he cried:

"Mum! The oranges!"

This gave her a chance to vent her pent-up anger. She slapped the child.

"Little monkey! Little devil! You were born unlucky. Oranges you want, is it? You chose the wrong mother."

Howling, Dingding pulled away to fling himself into the arms of his grandfather who was sitting under the eaves. Tears stained his sleeves and the lapel of his gown.

Genggui knew the reason for his wife's ill temper and glanced dourly at Dingding without a word. Then he reached up for the basket of oranges handed him by the merchant who was up the tree, and emptied it into a crate. Zhang was the one to feel uncomfortable. With a wave to Dingding, he said:

"Come on, Dingding! Come here! Why don't you come? Go and help yourself then." He turned to the child's mother. "What does it matter, sister-in-law? Tell Dingding to take what he wants."

This well-meant invitation only added fuel to the fire. After driving such a hard bargain, he was posing as generous, was he? Well, she for one wasn't impressed. Why, he owed them one or two crates at least, not a few paltry oranges. Stingy old beast! . . . If she'd had her way, she'd not have let him get away with it. But she had no say in the matter. Her face red with rage, she ran into the house to fetch the oranges on the table. "There you are!" she shouted to Dingding. "Eat all you want. Those are yours! Aren't I always telling you not to ask people for things? Today you've gone and lost face for me, you wretch!"

Not daring to take the oranges, Dingding looked from his mother to his grandfather, then suddenly buried his head in his grandfather's shoulder and burst out sobbing.

To comfort the child, Uncle Aquan led him to the vegetable plot to pull up some turnips.

A row of low trees hedged in this plot, but all the leaves had fallen. Outside was a hillside covered with trees and bushes commanding a good view of Uncle Aquan's house. Some women with tousled hair were collecting fuel there, racing each other to pick up the fallen leaves. When nobody was looking, they would give the trees a good shake or break off little branches to stuff in the packs on the backs, covering them with leaves so that no one could see they had broken the rules. Some, who had filled their packs, stood idly chatting.

A magpie, perched on the tip of a supple bough, cried several times in the direction of Uncle Aquan's vegetable plot, then spread her wings and flew towards it.

"Third Aunt!" said a round-faced young bride to a thin, sallow, middle-aged woman with even white teeth. "Why do you suppose that magpie's calling? Does it mean a marriage or a visitor?"*

"Don't ask me. I doubt if it's anything of the sort. I shouldn't think anyone's proposing a match for an old fellow in his sixties. And Dingding's no higher than my waist — no one will be offering him a wife just yet."

"Why, Dingding's six, Third Aunt. Didn't you buy a bride for your Ming when he was no more than three?"

The young woman's tactlessness made Third Aunt turn to another woman nearer her own age who was gathering firewood.

"Elder Sister!" She pointed to the three-roomed cottage below them. "You didn't see the goings-on yesterday! Widow Zhou asked him for her money. She was frantic. Called on heaven and earth, she did, and tore her hair. She'd have jumped into the well if Ming's dad hadn't been drawing water there! Her blood would have been on their heads."

---

* Magpie in Chinese literally means "lucky bird", bringer of good news.

"Ah!" Elder Sister was sorry to have missed such excitement. "How much does Uncle Aquan owe her?"

"Sixty dollars! Quite a tidy sum! The widow and her child have nothing else to live on. Some people have no consideration for others. They don't care if they die.... And it's no good repaying a debt in another life!"

"But Uncle Aquan really is hard up, you know. He's up to his ears in debt. Would anyone with money borrow at such a high interest?"

This unexpected rejoinder made Third Aunt look grave. She pursed her lips and rolled her eyes to the sky, exclaiming:

"Tchk! Don't talk about him being hard up. Nowadays folk stop at nothing. They try to get hold of other people's silver and lead a gay life for a couple of days. It's no use borrowing from those who want to grow rich. If you do, you'll never clear yourself, not if you sell your children, flesh and bone! But does that mean you can borrow from the poor? The poor have got to live too! Happens it's Widow Zhou. If I were her, why, I'd batter my brains out at their door. With no son or daughter to bury me anyway, I might as well make them wear white at my funeral!..."

Just then the young woman saw Uncle Aquan lead Dingding into the vegetable garden. She shot a warning glance at her companions. Then, as if casually, she called:

"Are your oranges good, Dingding? Won't you give me a few?"

Normally Uncle Aquan would have picked a few for them. Today he hadn't the heart to raise his head. He gazed dully at the child on whose eyelashes tears were still glistening. His daughter-in-law's outburst had upset him. Of course he couldn't scold her in front of outsiders; but his son had taken her side! Did they think he liked selling his fruit dirt cheap? . . . But how could he help it? Both young folk were upset and taking it out on Dingding. Pity and indignation filled his kind old heart. With a deep sigh he reached out to ruffle Dingding's short, soft hair.

"Grandad! Give me an orange!"

Dingding's eyes widened as he spoke, and the bright black pupils washed by tears looked brighter than ever. The gleam in them was like the sun in spring, arousing the old man's heart crushed by care and despair, filling him with incomparable comfort, with bitterness too.

"Grandad!" since he made no move, Dingding called out again, laying chubby fingers on the withered hand resting on his head.

"I'll go and get you some!" Forgetting everything else, Uncle Aquan pushed Dingding aside and in two steps reached a big orange tree. Tugging down a bough, he was on the point of picking some fruit when he heard the voice of the merchant. Instinctively he let go, and the bough rebounded, brushing against another so that two oranges fell to roll off into the vegetable patch.

Smiling, Dingding ran after them.

The merchant came up, carrying a high stool, and smiled at Uncle Aquan. The old man burned with shame. His cheeks were flaming. Turning his back on the merchant, he bowed his head and sat down silently on the mud path. But his heart was bursting with rage. He longed to bellow: "Confound it! Do you think I'm stealing your oranges? They're mine! All right, I'll give you back your six dollars! The fruit is mine! I can do what I like with it."

But no one beside himself heard this outburst. Another tree was rapidly being stripped.

Dingding held up the oranges and smiled. Two oranges were enough to satisfy his small heart.

Abruptly Uncle Aquan stood up, strode over to Dingding and said in a voice that trembled:

"Put them down! They're not for you. Put them down, I say!"

Dingding stared, dumbfounded by his grandfather's strange behaviour. The two oranges slipped from his fingers to the ground.

The young woman beyond the fence waved her hand and called: "They're over there, Dingding! There! By the yellow tile. Why don't you pick them up, Dingding?"

But to her utter surprise Dingding let them lie.

Translated by Gladys Yang

The Salt Worker

THE night was still, the moon hanging high in a vast, deep, cloudless sky. There was no wind. Nobody was moving about and no dog barking. The salt works was still, so still that the occasional croaking of frogs by the pond carried loudly through the darkness.

But the works was not asleep. The sources of its life — the ovens and wells — were turning out the salt faster than ever.

Salt wells sprawled all over the hill. Every shed seemed full of moving wheels and pulleys. The men's faces were grim and they worked in sullen silence, as if angry with someone or too tired to speak. Yet all shared the same impatience, the same longing: Let time fly quickly, let the barrels soon be filled with brine so that they could change shifts and fling themselves down on straw pallets to sleep till dawn.

Yet Old Melon's pallet was empty.

After peering out of the shed, Huosheng sat down on the bench and heaved a deep sigh. The moon had just risen and the barrels were far from full, yet his eyes....

"I simply can't keep my eyes open!"

Small Three, not yet sixteen, plodded behind the two oxen with a whip in his hand. Whenever they slowed down he cracked his whip, crying, "Giddup!..."

"Aren't you sleepy, Small Three? I don't know what's come over me tonight."

"Do what I do!"

He stuck two mud pellets on a sliver of bamboo and propped up his eyelids with these.

"If you do that often, you'll go blind."

"That would suit me fine. People give food and money to blind beggars."

"What kind of talk is that!"

"It's true. Old Melon's young brother tried begging and died of hunger, yet his old mother who can hardly move hasn't starved to death!"

So they talked about Old Melon's mother, the blind widow. . . .

Old Melon worked at this salt well with the two of them. But tonight nobody knew where he had gone. Perhaps he was drinking at the village tavern, or out robbing somebody's fields again.

The maize was ripening, pumpkins were mellowing, there were plenty of crabs in the stream to be caught with a light, to say nothing of the bamboo shoots in the woods.

The thought of cooked vegetables woke Small Three up so that his eyelids needed no further support. He asked Huosheng eagerly:

"What d'you suppose is keeping him all this time?"

Huosheng burst out laughing. Small Three had just been running down Old Melon's mother and now he was longing for food from the old woman's son.

Rather sheepishly, Small Three denied any intention.

"I often saw her bathe in the mud pool but I never threw stones at her. Heaven knows," — his whip pointed to the roof of the shed — "when she lost one bowl of rice, Old Melon said I was behind it."

"Oh, yes? Well, when she was catching lice by the hedge, who ran off with all her clothes?"

"You talking about me?"

Huosheng chuckled.

This thrust went home and Small Three had no more to say. The shed fell silent again.

The lamp-wick now was so black with snuff that a few feet away from it all was in darkness.

Opposite the empty pallet lay an old palsied cow whose discharges had dirtied the ground. Her breath came in painful gasps as she gazed first at the men, then at the light, with bloodshot eyes, wistful and yearning, that seemed bulging from their sockets. But the men had no sympathy for her, nothing but disgust at the stink.

In the distance dogs started barking, then humming was heard. At last footsteps approached outside.

Somebody in the next shed swore:

"Turning up at midnight again! Dirty dog. . . ."

The newcomer paid no attention but strolled in humming.

Old Melon was empty-handed. Small Three's heart sank.

"About time for your shift. Do you expect us to do your job while you fool about outside?"

"All right, I know."

His face was pale — evidence that he was not drunk.

There was a streak of dried blood on Old Melon's forehead. He looked quite calm, though very tired, as if he had just finished some strenuous job.

"What's up, Old Melon?" asked Huosheng. "What have you been doing? Where did you hurt yourself?"

"Hurt myself?"

"There's blood on your face."

He rubbed the place with his hand, which he then wiped on his clothes. Not looking at them, he said:

"Digging bamboo shoots, I jabbed my hands. Must have smeared some blood on my face."

He walked away to lie down on his pallet, where his snores soon mingled with the hoarse breathing of the cow.

Little by little Small Three slowed down and flourished his whip less vigorously, while the pulleys rolled more lazily too, as if falling asleep.

Huosheng was nodding as he sat there, drooling on his clothes, almost forgetting the barrel of brine that was about to brim over.

"Hey, dad! . . . The ox! . . ." yelled Old Melon, waking with a start.

He was lifting a bowl of delicious beef soup to his mouth, when suddenly the soup turned into his father's rotting corpse and the bowl into a thin wooden coffin from a big crack in which pink blood and pus were oozing. The next instant the coffin became a big yellow ox, charging fiercely at him.

"What a fool you are! Is your father's ghost dragging you off again?"

Old Melon huddled close to the lamp, his face pale. "Can you smell anything?" he asked after a long time.

"Only that stinking cow! You're dreaming — wake up!"

He strode over abruptly to the cow and kicked her with all his might.

"You! You won't let us eat you even when you're dead."

"Why kick the poor beast when she's dying? What harm has she done you?"

Old Melon gave the cow a few more vicious kicks before lying down again. But he lay with open eyes till the time for his shift.

His old man, his blind mother, his young brother and the cow . . . all were haunting him and he could not drive them away.

"I've got indigestion," he thought. "You can't sleep after eating too much."

He seemed to smell the rank yet not too nauseous odour of raw meat. Something swelled in his breast, suffocating him.

2

It was Old Melon's turn to draw water.

Although he had slept so little, he was not sleepy. He felt something swelling in his breast, suffocating him. He thought again, "Yes, I must have eaten too much."

The ox-driver for this shift was a boy younger than Small Three with short, stumpy legs. Instead of his driving the oxen, they were dragging him along.

Old Melon smiled bitterly, shaking his head. When he first came here, he remembered, he too had short legs and short arms and had run after the oxen.

"How long have you been here, kid?"

"One month."

"Your mam sent you?"

"Yes. How did you know?"

"I know all right."

The boy smiled ingenuously, wanting to say more. But Old Melon paid no attention and walked out.

Day was breaking. The hills in the east could be seen in a haze.

At the bottom of the valley, the large building housing the salt ovens still crouched in darkness. Only the chimney stood erect in proud isolation, the fire in the ovens still hot.

He was looking round nervously, as if menaced by something. You might think he was looking at that hill where his mother lived. Yet his head was turned in another direction. He seemed like a man who has committed a crime and suspects that spies are lurking in the darkness ready to encircle him as soon as day breaks.

In despair, he leaned his head against a willow. A breeze spattered the dewdrops from the tree on his face, wetting his hair and eyebrows.

"Brother Old Melon!"

A young woman carrying two baskets with jars in them suspended from a carrying-pole had slipped into the shed.

"What is it?"

"Give me a drop of brine! Nobody's here yet. I haven't tasted salt for days. . . ."

"Get out of here!"

"We're old neighbours. . . . I've just passed by your mother's cave. She. . . ."

"She what?"

"She seemed to be up. There was a fire outside and I smelt meat!"

With lips that trembled, Old Melon dashed towards her, swearing:

"You whore, you. . . ."

Scared, she backed away, ready to slip out through the door, when to her surprise Old Melon picked up one of her jars and, instead of dashing it against the ground, filled it with brine.

Disconcerted by this extraordinary behaviour, she did not even thank him but started off with her load in astonishment, looking over her shoulder for fear he might drag her back. He let her go, however.

"The devil! What devils they all are!"

Old Melon looked up to find a pair of luminous eyes in the corner of the shed fixed on him. He was taken aback and walked slowly towards the cow. She was gasping harder than ever, her belly heaving, her distended eyes expressive of misery. Regardless of the dirt, he patted her head.

Rays of morning sunlight slid quietly in through the window with the fresh breeze. Shadows were dispersed. The stench that had hung about the place all night was at last dissipating.

Yet Old Melon felt tenser with the coming of daylight, though he knew it was useless to worry.

With a wry smile he looked at his mates, lying almost on top of the cow dung.

"And we call ourselves men!"

The slops on the ground glittered dark green in the sun. Flies hummed ceaselessly. Shaking his head, he went out for a crate of sand which he scattered gently on the ground.

He sat on a heap of straw and sang softly to himself while the other two snored.

The pickled vegetables and hot steamed rice had lost their usual attraction for him that day. The others, not forgetting to eat, kept stealing glances at him. From time to time they came out with strange ejaculations which they immediately tried to suppress.

The cook in his big apron was washing up in the kitchen. His fat cheeks, red from the fire, quivered as he moved. As usual he was complaining that the kitchen was too small, the men got in his way. But for once Old Melon was not in his way.

"Why are you behind all the rest? What were you up to last night?"

Old Melon only swore beneath his breath.

One of the men pretended to sneeze and asked, "What's that stink? Smells like ox."

"Must be beef. Only beef smells so strong."

Old Melon did not want to hear more of this talk. Eating only half his usual amount, he dumped his bowl and chopsticks in the basin. He was not allowed, however, to go away.

The overseer summoned him.

He caught his breath at the sight of the earthenware jar which his mother used every day lying at the overseer's feet. He fixed his eyes on it. So did the other, smiling as he drummed with long fingers on a small teapot of Jingdezhen porcelain.

"Recognize it, eh? Whose jar is this, Old Melon?"

"My mother's."

"Your trouble is you work too hard," sneered the overseer, glancing around, tapping the ground with his toes as he shook his head. "Your mother's blind, you should help her wash her jar. See how filthy it is."

Old Melon threw back his head and his eyes blazed. But when he saw the middle-aged overseer's face, he lowered his head again and said sullenly:

"I'm a bad son. You go and be a son to her."

The overseer sprang up in anger and boxed his ears.

"Crazy dog, you! You ate that dead ox. And you dare answer back...."

"You'd rather bury it than let people eat it."

Still the same sullen tone.

"You must be mad! That old ox dragged the cart faithfully for twenty years. So I treated him as a human being, didn't cut up his carcass. You dug up the grave and stole the carcass as well ... that's a serious crime. Your eating it makes it worse."

Having left the kitchen, Old Melon sat by the field, hugging his knees. He was a little ashamed of what he had done. Probably the ox did deserve to be buried entire. Because he had cut a big lump off its leg, it would chase him in his dreams.

"He worked faithfully...."

His old man had stoked the ovens for more than twenty years, but what of his corpse? — like a soggy piece of beancurd!

Old Melon could not help wondering. That box on the ears had jarred him to the depths.

3

Old Melon's real name was Wu Zu. It was after his brother's death that he was nicknamed Old Melon.

The name signified impotence, cowardice, stupidity. It made him ridiculous, a figure of fun.

One stormy night, the year that he was thirteen, when his father was adding water to the salt cauldron, steam and smoke got into his eyes so that he slipped and fell into the seething white brine.

The same day that his father was buried, his mother took him to a man with horn-rimmed glasses.

"Look, he's strong as a young ox. For his father's sake, take him on!"

Though he protested and was afraid of that place, his mother left him there.

So the lad became a worker. Like so many others living around the salt works, he had no choice but to eat this bowl of "briny rice". There was no other way out.

For the first couple of years he fought against it. Every time he went home, his mother had to beat him to get him to go back.

"You're not a child any more, go on! Where else can you find a job?"

At last he understood and stopped insisting that he wanted to come home.

If you move a plant from the hills to a cold, dark, sunless room, it is bound to wither away. The lad's open, sunny character changed completely. He became afraid of people, and even more afraid of the row of salt cauldrons that kept seething with big white bubbles day and night, the whole year round. He dared not go near these cauldrons.

A ludicrous figure he was, beneath contempt!

He carried no sharp, two-edged dagger, could not shoot birds, dared not gamble or make eyes at other men's wives, and could not lift two hundred catties of coal... he had none of the assets, in fact, of the best salt workers.

Among those of no account, Old Melon was of least account.

Though sympathy costs nothing, it is not something to

be wasted or given freely. Old Melon was like a willow crate which holds neither soup nor water.

Huosheng once said, "If you want to be fed, Old Melon, you've got to be up to the job — this is no place for you. Look at your two shanks, as thin as chicken bones. You'd do better begging like your mother and brother."

He may have taken these taunts to heart but he only sighed, hummed a few bars — and let them pass.

It seemed he had been born to draw salt water for others! Every day he watched the oxen draw brine from the wells, every day he poured the brine into the vats, every day he heard it flowing through the underground pipes to the salt ovens on the slope to be dried out and made into big bags of white salt. And every month he got one dollar from the overseer as his wage, while every day he had three meals of rice with pickled vegetables. Drawing salt water, drinking, eating, sleeping — that was his life.

So Old Melon's face grew paler. His head seemed to grow longer. He walked more and more unsteadily, like a shadow.

The men in the works became colder to him and more on their guard against him.

One winter morning, Old Melon was kicked awake. A peasant family at the foot of the hill insisted that he go there at once. His young brother lay curled up like a homeless dog that had died on the pile of hay outside somebody's house. It had snowed in the night, but not too heavily, so that a thin layer of snow served as his shroud. The mistress of the house, coming out to sweep the snow early in the morning, had discovered the corpse and run screaming in all directions, till the neighbours were aroused and went for Old Melon.

"You heartless brute! I've done you no harm, yet you brought this ill luck on me. I've sons and daughters, I'd have you know! I'm not a young fellow all on my own like you. . . ."

His scrawny hand clawing at the long hair that almost covered his eyes, Old Melon looked from the corpse to the wailing woman and blinked in bewilderment.

"I didn't tell him to lie here."

The woman was not angry but kept on crying. After roaring with laughter, the bystanders consoled her, then asked Old Melon:

"What will you do with him?"

"I'll bury him in the ground."

"I should hope so — you can't bury him in the clouds!" They laughed harder than ever. Old Melon looked at them in bewilderment.

That night Old Melon got drunk in the village tavern, and on his return quarrelled with Small Three, his first quarrel! Someone asserted that the money for drinks had come from the clothes given for laying out his brother. The donor of the clothes sent for Old Melon.

"Shame on you, stripping the dead to buy drinks!"

Old Melon did not deny this but answered evasively: "It was kind of you anyway. . . ."

"See here: I gave it to the dead, not to you for drinks!"

"I couldn't carry the coffin myself . . . had to treat the fellows who helped."

After this, Old Melon became the laughing-stock of the whole salt works. But it seemed to make no difference to him at all. He still received one dollar each month, drew salt water, drank, slept and sang ballads.

Only his name was changed. And he frequented the village tavern more often, and was often found asleep among the graves.

Nobody could understand what drew Old Melon so often to the graveyard. Why should he go there when it was neither a day for sacrifice nor any festival? No one believed for a moment that he was putting himself out to protect the graves from wind and rain or from the wild dogs that dug up bones to gnaw.... He must be short of money for drinks, eager for some small windfall: a piece of cloth, a shirt or anything the dogs might unearth.

Once he was followed. The man following him was smiling.

"What are you doing here?" demanded Old Melon.

"Just killing time. I came to see what you're up to."

Old Melon said not a word but made off at once, never to return to the graveyard again.

4

The rosy sky at the horizon held the deep emerald hills in a gentle embrace. The river at the foot of the mountain glinted strangely as it flowed downstream, wave after wave.

Fields stretched away into the distance on the other side of the river, and like black dots crows congregated there. A man's approach did not frighten them away — they merely flew up into the air to flock back again presently.

Old Melon, a crate for crabs in one hand, emerged from one side of the fields. He was heading upstream. The long hair on his forehead was ruffled, his shirt was unbuttoned. Although it was not hot, he was sweating profusely. Even his eyes seemed a little red.

He paused hesitantly from time to time before striding on again. And more than once he stopped to look around.

No peasants were left in the fields. Before him lay the darkening mountains and water, behind the stretch of fields. The crows were cawing and the river gurgling.

Fading from sight behind was the salt works, whose wheels and pulleys could no longer be heard. Only smoke was still clearly visible in the sky; but it formed a dense black cloud and there was no telling from which household it had come.

He had expected the bank to be deserted, but now he thought he could see a shadowy figure.

He strained his eyes and made out a stumpy fellow heading his way. That made him a little angry and nervous too, till he remembered his crab crate and felt reassured. He squatted down on the bank and began to search among the pebbles.

As he lifted the stones he saw several crabs but felt no strong urge to catch them. He took only one, a very small one.

The shadowy figure drew near. He pretended not to see it. But he had already recognized Small Three.

Small Three was more friendly than the others. Old Melon had not seen him for several days and he looked taller by a head. Old Melon stood up.

"Hey, Old Melon, what are you doing here? Why

do you never come to see us since you chucked up the job?"

"I'm catching crabs."

"Got many?"

"Only one."

"But I saw you come down here quite a while ago. Have you only caught one all this time?" Seeing a crab beside him, Small Three pounced on it. "Here you are. . . . There's another, and another!"

Small Three put all three crabs in the crate.

"Heavens! You call that catching crabs? You don't catch them even when you see them! What are you up to?"

"You catch them then!"

Old Melon threw the crate on the ground. Small Three stared in astonishment. He felt Old Melon had changed.

"Are you crazy? It's the first time I've seen you in such a temper. In the few days since you left us you've changed so much!"

This would make a good story. He started bounding off, only turning to taunt Old Melon:

"You don't dare catch crabs! Afraid your hands will get pinched and bleed or hurt!"

When Small Three had made off, laughing, Old Melon threw a stone at his back. "Young devil! You're no better than the rest."

Old Melon went on, leaving the salt works further and further behind. But the smoke was still there to be seen every time he looked back, as if it would dog him for ever, watching him as if he were a criminal.

"You! . . ."

Old Melon shook his fist and clenched his teeth. A couple of steps further on, he growled again:

"You!"

This time he shook his fist not at the smoke but at a face in the smoke wearing horn-rimmed spectacles, and at all the other faces looming before him. He clenched his fist again and went through the motion of hurling those countless lives in his clutch to the ground, to bury them deep under the earth.

As if he had really done such a glorious deed, he broke out in a fresh sweat, not from exhaustion but from deep satisfaction. Feeling thirsty, he lay down by the river to drink, then splashed his face with water. The sudden chill sobered him. He felt tired, wanted to rest.

He sat on a rock. The reeds were in full bloom. A gust of wind set their long leaves swaying and rustling. The sound of the rapids in the distance held a note of sadness and futility. He felt rather cast down.

"Grin and bear it — no use being angry. . . ."

Usually what followed this was the reflection "But it's tough getting boxed on the ears". Abruptly he remembered the overseer.

He shivered, feeling countless eyes watching him. Rising quickly, he walked off again. The wind blew into his face, his shirt was open, his chest thrown out. He was filled with strength and courage. He even felt taller.

The further he went the denser the reeds became. The banks were covered with them, nothing but reeds.

He stood still and looked round but, to his disappointment, there was nothing else to be seen.

"I can't have heard wrong, surely? It should be here."

He threw the crab crate into the river and plunged into the thick of the reeds. With the whole of Nature, he too was lost in darkness.

Once in there where the reeds were thickest, Old Melon's heart started throbbing as if somebody were trying to murder him.

"Done for!"

Nobody came here except during the season for cutting reeds. Yet his bamboo pole had gone. Who had taken it? His axe and pick placed under the big stone had gone too. Who could have guessed his plan?

On this axe and pick he had spent one and a half months' wages, the last dollar and a half he had earned in all these years. With them he meant to get his own back. More, with them he would go far away to make a living as a woodcutter. He stood there as if dazed in the shallow water, resting his heavy, drooping head on his hands.

A large salt junk at anchor ten feet or more away seemed to be sneering at him, scoffing at his defeat.

"If you're afraid to look for them, you're done for!" So saying, he groped for the anchor, untied the cable and swam to the boat.

He knew this junk, had known it indeed for years and knew everything aboard it just as well as his old work shed and his mother's cave. He would look for his axe and pick in the cabin. The cabin was full of salt, lump salt as well as powdered salt, worth a whole packet of money!

"It would be a pity to sink this lot. I can put it to good use."

With a grin he took down the pole on top of the awning. The iron tip of the pole clashed against the pebbles on the river bed as he pushed off with an effort. But once the junk was in midstream Old Melon laid down the pole and crouched by the rudder, guiding the boat as it sped rapidly down river.

The salt works was left further and further behind. The reeds by the river were soon lost to sight. The same moon shone down upon the rushing water and the ceaselessly smoking salt works. The works was nothing to him now, but. . . .

"Mam will cry over this. What's she going to live on?"

He felt a pang, a moment's uncertainty. To go back was out of the question. The bank would be crowded now with men, lanterns and torches. . . .

"They'll never suspect me. Old Melon would never dare do such a thing!"

He hoped Small Three would say something to give them a clue. Failing that, they might guess the truth from his axe and pick.

It is no small thing, the loss of a boatload of salt. The whole works was in a hubbub. The overseer, nursing his small Jingdezhen teapot, spent all his time thinking it over.

"This was a clever job — the work of a gang or some wily old thief, that's certain!"

This was the end of night shipments for the salt works. No one ventured out on the bank once darkness fell, and the peasants went home early too. Obsessed by the idea of a gang of robbers, people paid no attention to Old Melon's disappearance.

Yet as time went by, the two things were linked together and Old Melon's name was on men's lips again. His mother was summoned by the overseer.

"Where has your son gone?"

"How should I know? Our whole family has had to beg for a living. He must be dead like his brother on a pile of straw."

"Not he!"

"What do you mean?"

"They say he's the one who stole that load of salt."

"How dare he do such a wicked thing? I don't believe it!"

"No use covering up for him. I'm holding you in his place."

"What do you mean?"

"I'm going to lock you up till your son comes back."

"Lock me up?"

She blinked her opalescent, sightless eyes and rapped the ground with her stick, as if pondering a problem of vital importance. Quite abruptly she laughed, a rather malicious laugh.

"Very well. Shall I stay here?"

The overseer, highly offended, kicked her and roared:

"Get out! You aren't even fit to be detained. You and your whole family!"

Tapping the ground with her stick, the blind woman groped her way out step by step, murmuring:

"Our whole family, our whole family. . . ."

Translated by Zhang Su

Aunt Liu

I was awakened that day not by the songs the cowherds sang as they drove their oxen up the slope, nor by one of our household speaking loudly to my mother who was hard of hearing. A strange, rough voice exclaiming: "Why, she's grown up now!" woke me.

Rather annoyed I opened my eyes to see who was in the room. Standing by my bed was a shabbily-dressed middle-aged woman with a somewhat flat, pockmarked face under wispy hair. Her lips parted in a fearful toothless smile.

I felt I had seen this unattractive, ugly face before. But I could not place her.

I gazed at her silently, trying to find some record of her filed in my mind.

"I'm Aunt Liu. . . . I knew you'd have forgotten Aunt Liu," she said as if reading my thoughts. "It's eight years since I saw you last. And how you have grown! I wouldn't have recognized you if I had met you on the street."

"What? You're Aunt Liu? The Aunt Liu who took care of me?"

I jumped down from my bed, my face flushed with excitement.

A child easily remembers trifles but is apt to forget what ought to be remembered. How could I have forgotten this woman who had once been so good to me? What an ungrateful little creature!

She backed away as I went up to her. Behind her was a desk where I did my lessons when I came home at week-ends. Bumping against it, she upset the vase of bright summer daisies on it. Quite put out, she hastily tried to repair the damage while I did my best to stop her.

"You. . . ."

I meant to say something to put her at ease but my mind was in a whirl too. I had no idea whether to say "you used to be" or "you are". Maybe what I meant was, "You are entirely different from before!"

Yes, she had certainly changed. She used to feel uneasy only in the presence of my father and mother. Why should she behave like this now in front of me? Wasn't I the little girl she loved and cared for like a mother? Nevertheless, I knew if she had sat down on a stool and offered to hold me on her knee, so that she could croon the ballads my mother had forbidden, tell blood-curdling stories that might mark a young mind, or ask me to hug her and kiss her red pockmarked face, I would have refused without a moment's hesitation.

She was not to blame. Neither was I. Time and hateful conventions had made a wide gap between us.

It was awkward staring at each other in utter silence. I felt I must find something appropriate to say. Mother's arrival saved the situation.

She was in a good mood that day and chuckled as she walked in.

"What a hostess. . . . Why don't you ask Liu to sit down?"

I didn't realize until then that I was sitting on my bed while Liu stood in the middle of the room.

"Look, she has grown taller than I," said Mother. Pointing at the two plaited knots on the back of my head, she continued, "These seem to be the craze with middle-school students! They look quite nice, don't they?"

Liu had not forgotten that she needed only to nod, whatever Mother said. But perhaps she had not noticed what Mother was saying. Her eyes scrutinized me from head to toe. Was she looking for some trace of the little girl of eight years ago?

"You hardly know each other now!" Liu's scrutiny made Mother smile. "One of you has grown up while the other is getting old. How time flies!" Then she said to me, "You ought to be glad. You never expected Liu to turn up in this valley hidden in the mountains, did you? She must have had a time of it finding us. Do you remember the day I fired her? She had just bought you a lot of water-chestnuts and some lotus roots. I sent her away because she was too fond of drinking."

Mother's bluntness amazed me. Fancy coming out openly like that with the ill turn she had done Aunt Liu!

The mention of water-chestnuts and lotus roots did something to me. I tried to avoid the two pairs of eyes fastened on me.

A gust of wind swept the palm leaves against my window. I pulled one off, tore it to shreds and scattered them over the floor.

Suddenly I thought of a question.

"How did you find out that we had moved to this place?"

"I asked! You hadn't crossed the country — it was easy to find you."

She was still so outspoken and sharp.

I was going to ask more questions when Mother sent for a bottle of wine which she held out to Liu.

"I know this is what you like best," she said. "Go and have a drink in the kitchen. This is good seasoned wine, so don't overdo it. Leave some to take home and share with your husband."

When she was gone Mother told me that Liu had married a man who had seven-tenths of a *mu* of land in the hills and who worked as a sedan-chair carrier. She didn't remember where Liu was living now but she sympathized with this ill-fated woman.

I knew very little of Liu's past. Someone might have told me, but it had left no impression. Now Mother told me the whole story again.

When she was fifteen, Liu was tricked into leaving her home and sold as a maid to a rich family. One night, she had too much to drink and was raped by her master, a man of over forty. When she was found to be pregnant, they drove her out of the black gate flanked on both sides by stone lions. The baby was born in a privy by the street and died three days after birth. A good-hearted scavenger cleared away the grubs around the little corpse, wrapped it up in a tattered mat and buried it for her. Thereafter she had managed by mending and taking in washing or by standing at the outskirts of the town and stretching out her hand for alms. Sometimes she sold porridge in the lanes. In the end she contrived to be taken on by us as a servant. This was a remarkable opportunity for her. How good life must have seemed!

If she had not been so fond of tippling, Mother wouldn't have sent her away.

This fondness for drink was her only fault. And my mother was a kind-hearted woman, I knew.... But I recalled the day before Liu left us eight years ago.

It was a summer day just like this one. Thunder was rumbling in the distance. I was watching the yellow ants fight the black ants under a Judas tree. Behind the bamboo door curtain Mother was talking to some woman and her voice sounded angry.

Just then Liu came through the gate. You could see at a glance that she had been drinking again. In her hands were two thick white lotus roots and a package wrapped in a lotus leaf. The pitcher hanging from her arm obviously contained rice wine.

Giving the package to me she said:

"I have brought you something good. Eat the water-chestnuts first while I wash and slice the lotus roots for you."

Mother told me not to eat the water-chestnuts.

When Liu returned with a plate for me, the woman who had been speaking with my mother rushed up to her, jabbed at her forehead and said fiercely:

"You're fired. Pack your things and look for another job. I've done all I could to help you but you just don't try to make good. You never stop drinking that stinking yellow liquor! You've brought this on your own head."

Liu said nothing, just urged me to eat the lotus roots. I could do nothing but accept the plate which I offered to my mother. She was embroidering a white silk pillow-case. The bright flower made her angry face look much sterner than usual. She slammed the plate down on a table and froze me with a look. Although she didn't lay any blame on me I was already trembling. More for Liu's sake than my own.

That night at dinner Liu didn't wait on us and the strange thing was Mother didn't send for her either.

I sneaked to the kitchen as soon as Mother's back was turned. The kitchen door was closed. I dared not knock. Peeping in through a crack, I called Liu softly.

All the servants were sitting round the table, a winecup in front of each. The pitcher Liu had brought was in the middle. They were eating and drinking merrily, unaware that outside the door a little girl was gazing so lovingly at one among them. Liu's face was red, her sleeves were rolled up high and her tunic was unbuttoned, her throat bare. This was the first time I had seen her in such a state and I was puzzled by her strange behaviour. Later on I realized that since she would be eating our rice no longer she felt she could let herself go. To hell with the rules that had bound her for three whole years! She would do as she pleased on the eve of her departure.

"Ask someone to put in a word for you. The mistress may let you stay," suggested one.

"Working for others, you have to do as they say."

"There's no need. No sense in trying to stay when you're not wanted. Servants have one foot inside the door and the other one out. You can step in if things go well or out if they don't. If one family doesn't want you, go to another. With able hands and feet you can make a living anywhere. I've begged for my food before now, what have I to fear?"

Afraid Mother might be looking for me, I hurried back and tugged at the hem of her coat.

"What do you want?" she asked.

"Mother! . . . Aunt Liu! . . ." I had to repeat myself twice before she understood.

"I have told her to go tomorrow. I don't want to leave you in the care of a woman like that. I'll find someone else to look after you, someone kind." Then she remarked, half to herself: "As a matter of fact, she's a good honest creature. The only trouble is the way she drinks. I'm sorry for her, though. . . . I'll cancel what she owes us, give her an extra month's pay and a suit of clothes."

Next morning I woke up to find Liu gone. And since then eight years had passed.

I had never dreamt that she would come to see us. I was pleasantly surprised and rather touched.

If Mother had not dismissed her, she would not have become so bedraggled and haggard-looking. But I could not lay the blame entirely on Mother.

I hoped that Mother would let her stay with us.

When Liu came back after her meal I asked her, "Did you have enough?"

"A very good meal, thank you. It's two years since I've had white rice."

"Are you doing all right?"

"Well, I manage somehow. Whether you get on well or badly, it's all the same. Even if you don't get on well you must go on living."

I was silent for some time and then explained, "I mean, do you have enough to eat?"

"Of course not! He brings home barely enough to feed himself. I live on that plot we have in the hills. I gather firewood every day to make ends meet. When there's no firewood I sometimes do coolie work. I can manage a load of seventy or eighty catties."

"Is your husband good to you?"

"Not bad. . . . Since I left you I have had three men. Every one of them beat me. When I found I could not hold my own with the last of them I ran away and married this one. . . ."

"Does he beat you?" I asked quickly.

"What do you think? All men beat their wives!" She smiled at me as if to say, "Doesn't your father beat your mother too?" Then she said, "I can always run away when it gets too much for me or I can't hold my own."

It was growing dark and she seemed anxious to go.

"It's getting dark and it looks like rain. I still have more than five *li* to go. I'm going to raise two fat hens when I get back; I want you and the mistress to come for a meal in the autumn when it's cooler." Then she shook her head. "But my place is no better than a pigsty — you won't come."

"Stay a bit longer. I've something else to ask you. Do you mean to go on like this? Why not find a job?"

"What job can I find? Even your family doesn't want a beggar like me. Besides, I'm used to running wild and my hands are too rough for delicate work. It's better this way. . . . Just take life as it comes. After all, I won't starve."

I had nothing more to say.

Unable to make her stay longer, Mother gave her a peck of white rice and what remained of the bottle of wine.

Soon after that I went to study in the provincial

town. Mother never told me whether she visited Liu or ate the fat hens specially raised for us.

When I went home the following year, I was told that Liu had left her husband again. No one knew where she had drifted.

I believe she is living still and with all my heart I wish her well, for she understands life.

Translated by Yu Fanqin